DYER CONSEQUENCES:
THE WRONG MAN

MARK PHILLIPS

Cover design by: Ken Dawson (Creativecovers)
Printed by Amazon UK.

FOR ALL THOSE STILL FIGHTING THE GOOD FIGHT
FOR EVERYONE I STOOD SHOULDER TO SHOULDER
WITH ON THE LANDINGS
AND SPILLED TEA OVER.

IN MEMORY OF OFFICER NICK JONES.
A LARGER-THAN-LIFE CHARACTER WHO IS
SORELY MISSED.

*"REMEMBER, IT'S A VERY DIFFICULT TIME FOR THE
MEN!"*

I always wanted to be a writer but a *misspelt* youth and too many distractions, like running, cycling, fishing, golf, swimming, reading and the prison service … you see what I mean … and I'm getting distracted again.

So, it never happened.

I'm older now, slowing down a little, and I've switched my bloody, single-mindedness from physical pursuits to putting pen to paper.

And if anyone can write about murder it's me! Thirty years in the company of serial killers, psychopaths and disturbed individuals makes me more than qualified.

PART ONE

Chapter 1
What it's all about?

Let me spell it out from the beginning. This is not a *whodunnit* but more of a *what-the-f**k!* Sometimes a crime is so outrageous that it is impossible to understand it all. Great men usually step forward in times of need, but in this case, because the crime was unimaginable the great men went into hiding, and we were left with Detective Inspector Dyer. And being full of his own importance, DI Dyer leapt at the opportunity to make his name – and everyone else waited for him to fall flat on his face.

— The Chief of Police (Note to self)

*

And bear this in mind.

If you add the letter 'S' to the word *laughter* you get a new word – *slaughter*.

I've always had a dark side. I think we all have, but most people don't act upon their thoughts. Have you ever wanted to press the iron against your skin to see what would happen? How about a nail gun to the palm of your hand? When I was young my Nan still had a mangle for wringing the water from her wet washing, I remember sitting mesmerized wanting to place my fingers between the rollers. One morning she said, 'Go on then little child' in a voice not quite her own, and I can still see now in my mind little fingers reaching forward to their destruction and at the last second, she slapped them away, shaking her head, returning from somewhere in a part of her brain she'd managed to escape.

— A scrap of paper (unattributed) in the evidence file.

*

A Good Place to Begin – Remember This

Evebury Journal
Thursday 5th September 1995
'Mystery Man Saves Little Girl from River'

A dramatic rescue took place from the River Avon in Evebury on Wednesday morning. Mother of three, Julie Ford, described how her two-year-old daughter had slipped into the swollen river when feeding swans from the slipway near the new bridge. Screaming with panic she watched the toddler float away, air trapped in her coat, and ran after her with her two other children clasped in her arms. 'It was a miracle, a man jumped into the river from the bridge and managed to get her to the bank. She would have drowned if it had not been for this man. He is a hero!'

By the time Ms Ford had made the short distance to where her daughter was being comforted by a couple of local dogwalkers, the hero had slipped away. 'The man saved my daughter's life, and I don't even know his name!'

The man was last seen jogging off toward the cricket club. He was described as wearing a dark blue tracksuit and going 'a bit thin on the top.' If anyone knows the identity of the 'Mystery Man' please contact the Journal offices...

Chapter 2
SEPTEMBER 2019
West Mercia Police Headquarters
Just Desserts?

Detective Sergeant Quirke sat alone in the canteen at West Mercia Police Headquarters, Hindlip Hall. She moved the remnants of a Spotted Dick around her bowl, smiled at the irony that it was an actual spotted copulatory organ that had got her transferred up the M5 from Gloucester, and though she wasn't looking forward to the smutty innuendoes because nothing was ever kept secret for long in the Police Force, she was determined to brazen it out in pastures new.

She had concerns, she was starting over again, and getting her career back on track, and she had promised to be more *open and responsive to challenge her actions and words,* the Code of Ethics, and to attend counselling sessions suggested in her management plan. She would just have to be more discreet.

One thing at a time. Her first problem was the Detective Inspector she had been assigned to as part of the management plan; her former colleagues at Gloucester had called it a punishment when they had eventually stopped laughing and picked themselves up from the floor, and none of them had helped with a description or a story to back their opinion. Their only words of wisdom had been 'it's best if you see for yourself' before one of them had suggested she ask Gloucester's Chief of Police for the *lowdown* – which started everyone sniggering again and it was pointless trying to get any more information after that.

DS Quirke scanned the canteen a second time. She was due to see her new divisional chief after lunch but was hoping to spot DI Dyer before the formal introduction. She pulled at the sleeve of her dark blue suit top, conscious of the white cuff of the blouse underneath, never knowing the correct length to expose. First impressions were important, but she knew she was hiding behind the trouser suit, matching flat shoes and the neat low knot in her dark hair – the face she was *putting on* mirrored the light and natural tones of her make-up. She wasn't used to this, but she had no choice if she wanted to keep her job. Her fingers found a small rubber ball in right hand pocket, something she always kept with her for luck, and she squeezed it five times to release her anxiety. She pushed the last bit of Spotted Dick to the edge of the bowl.

When she returned her tray for cleaning, she scanned the room one last time – she was normally good at picking out the man she was after.

"Are you all right, ma'am, are you looking for someone?" the elderly canteen lady touched the back of DS Quirke's hand with her yellow marigolds, leaving soap suds – *the touch of rubber.*

"Yes, I am, DI Dyer, for my sins."

The elderly lady tutted, "You are in trouble," and pointed toward the window at the far end of the canteen.

No time like the present. DS Quirke approached the man who had been half-hidden by a concrete pillar at the far end of the canteen. She was confused. The man she was expecting was supposed to be a complete idiot but as she stared at the blobs of sugar, from a half-eaten doughnut on his full lips, she had to take a deep breath. She had to stop herself from greeting this Adonis, as he stood up, with a warm embrace and she slapped an image of them naked together in the back of a squad car out of her mind. She realized her former colleagues had completely fooled her with this wind-up.

"Well, you're not what I expected," she managed to mumble.

"Yes, sorry about that. I'm all right now, always go to pieces when my blood sugar drops… shall we get back… make a start as they say?"

"Lead the way, as they say," DS Quirke almost giggled, her eyes glued to the firm buttocks as he made his way to the exit.

"I think I remember the way," he winked over his shoulder.

He was not an idiot either. What a wind-up, this was not going to be a punishment… should she offer to lick the last piece of sugar from his chin? She ignored the puzzled look from the elderly canteen lady as they passed, cloth in her hand ready to wipe the table. So much for a fresh start. Perhaps it was supposed to be a test and she had to resist. She had to *demonstrate courage in doing the right thing, even in challenging situations.*

*

If DS Quirke had waited for a moment longer, she would have seen the canteen lady pause at the table and wave a marigold in her direction. Through the windowed door that led to a small courtyard, a man sat alone at a picnic table, his legs struggling to find a comfortable position where the blood supply would not be cut by the sharp piece of the bench knifing into the flesh and bone. He was staring at the red brick wall in front of him, recounting the bricks, confirming his sum from previous days, and checking nobody had added or subtracted a brick. His hands played the piano over the five Tupperware containers neatly set out on the table; each lid had been removed, and placed underneath the container, ready for the performance. Like a concert pianist, the fingers flexed, clasped, and hovered over them. The left hand began... a square piece of brown bread (2 cm square) followed by a circular droplet of butter from the second, into the mouth, and then the right hand continued, a cube of cheese (1 cm square), half a cherry tomato and the bulb from a spring onion from the fifth... only when each item was in the mouth did the man chew and eventually swallow.

A young constable brushed past the canteen lady and popped his head into the courtyard. He shook his head at the performance and turned to the canteen lady and shrugged.

"You haven't seen a tall, good-looking, gentleman, have you? I can't see him anywhere. Said he was diabetic... explains the funny turn... better check the toilets though I expect he's already gone back to the room for the line-up."

"You just missed him, lovey, he left through that door," she swept a sugar crumb to the floor.

"Thanks, Mabel," he nodded at the man with the bizarre eating pattern, "who's that?"

"That, lovey, is DI Dyer!"

*

The new team
Ten minutes later DS Quirke discovered her mistake. *Doughnut Boy* was not Dyer. She made her apologies and was shown to the correct office.

"Aaargh, Quirke, is it?" his first words to her, "heard you'd gone missing."

"Yes, sir, Detective Sergeant Elizabeth Quirke at your service," she said, showing an eagerness despite her foreboding. "That was a misunderstanding, and please call me Liz."

"Don't like it!"

"Sir?"

"Quirke. Elizabeth. The name. Quirke E. Quirky! I don't like Quirky... um! Got to be exact, precise, by the book and there is no room for quirkiness... um!" and with this, she was dismissed, no eye contact during the exchange, he simply walked out of the office, ignoring her offered hand, a blur of brown corduroy trousers and a slap of bright green socks.

A snigger from someone behind a desktop computer.

"Don't mind him. He's an oddball, he reads Russian shit, you know, as well as being an arsehole."

He returned twenty minutes later, and DS Quirke jumped up from the chair where she had been festering.

"Aaargh, Quirky, still here?" he wiped his hands with a paper towel, concentrating on every finger and every crevasse of his large fingers, "Good, let's go shall we, Quirky? The chief wants me to crack the county lines drugs traffic coming in from Birmingham."

He stooped from his considerable height, dropped the paper towel into DS Quirke's bin, turned, and marched off. DS Quirke felt like punting the bin at the back of his head but her runup turned into a stumble as she was forced to quicken her pace to try to catch up with him, one hand squeezing the rubber ball in her pocket.

Chapter 3
OCTOBER 2nd 2019, 14:00
HMP Long Stretch
Almost the First One

It had taken Virginia days to unpick the stitches on the anti-ligature blue gown with her last two remaining teeth (the only item of clothing she was allowed to wear) and to produce a strip of material for her next game.

They would be coming any minute; it was their job to check her every half an hour to make sure she was still alive; most of the time she was curled up on the thin mattress and gave them the finger when the flap was opened on the cell door; sometimes she would fuck about and sit against the bottom of the door so they couldn't see her, refusing to respond to their calls, and sometimes she would use wet toilet paper to create a paper-mâché work of art stuck to the inside of the glass reinforced observation panel; when she was pissed off she covered the glass with her shit. It was a game. Virginia against the system.

She listened at the cell door for approaching footsteps. Nobody coming yet. She checked her legal documents were secure in plastic bags and that the polystyrene cup was secreted but easily reachable when she was in the set position. A moment of clarity as Virginia looked at the four dull grey walls, the high ceiling with a reinforced fluorescent light-fitting, and the bare concrete floor. A High Control cell in a Maximum Security Prison, where people who refused to comply or were disruptive were located, often for months. Ten feet by twelve. An unbreakable window that did not open but allowed a hazy cataracted light into the cell. Not that there was anything to look at. Solid metal sink and toilet (no seat or lid) and a blue mattress that sat on a solid plastic plinth built into the floor.

Footsteps. They were coming. Game on.

*

Clicking footsteps. A metal plate in the heel of a shoe. It must be Officer Brown. He always had a cheese sandwich in one hand, wiping ketchup from his white shirt with the other, which was failing to contain an expanding stomach. He opened the flap, closed it, and took two clicking steps toward the next cell before registering she was on the floor. Virginia imagined Officer Brown yawning as he casually returned to the cell door to confirm what he had seen. Officer Brown wouldn't panic. He'd take another bite of the sandwich… he'd seen it all before and he wouldn't get excited or overreact… twenty-five years in the game had taught Officer Brown this.

"Oi, dickhead!"

She didn't move. She braced herself.

The door rattled in its frame as Officer Brown kicked it with his size twelves.

She didn't move. She was good at this.

Officer Brown farted loudly, and she pictured him brushing breadcrumbs from his chest and waving at other colleagues for assistance.

Heavy footsteps. At least three officers this time. She listened to their inane banter.

"Why is it whenever I make a team brew some idiot needs me and I don't get to drink it?"

"Evolution, isn't it?" Officer Brown stated.

Silence as the officers waited for the inevitable words of wisdom.

"Since Victorian times, successive generations of prisoners, and you know crime runs in families causing the gene pool to be strengthened, prisoners have spent decades in the prison and the segregation environment. Their senses have become heightened as yours would if you spent hours confined by four concrete walls. Consequently, most prisoners have a super-evolved olfactory system."

"What the fuck are you talking about?" Virginia recognised young Officer Kelly's voice.

"Noses, gentlemen! Super sensitive, can smell a brew from roughly a thousand yards, so when they want to fuck us about, they wait until a pot has just been made and then start to their stupid games."

When they were still not convinced.

"Look, it has been proven statistically, I once kept a log of incidents and fresh pots of tea… strong correlation. Anyway, the tea can wait, as we have a life to save… again."

The cell door was unlocked, and Officer Brown clicked to one side, Virginia heard him sucking a blob of ketchup from his thumb. He'd leave space for the other officers to enter.

"Winter, on your feet!" it was Officer Hassan taking the lead, "if you're going to sleep on the floor I may as well take your mattress out."

"Funny colour, isn't he? Same colour as the floor," Officer Brown observed.

"Winter!" Officer Hassan again, "I can see your bollocks from here! You are a man after all."

Virginia didn't react.

When his strategy did not work, Officer Hassan edged closer until he could see the makeshift rope tied around her feet and the ligature around her neck.

"Quick boys! Dave, call a Code Blue!"

Virginia felt fingers fumbling at her neck. She sensed Officer Brown stifling another yawn before he unclipped his radio and called for assistance.

"Code Blue seg cell 110."

"Winter, wake up! I know you're alive… we wouldn't be so lucky, so stop fucking about, you're not allowed to die, you've still got ten years to serve and it's against Prison Rules… as you would be the first to let us know…" Officer Hassan was getting annoyed.

"Can you smell shit?" Officer Kelly gagged.

"Mark. Mark Winter! Can you hear me?"

That did it.

"It's fucking Virginia! How many more times?" she squirmed from their grasp, though in truth the staff had been loath to touch her when she had not been moving, preferring to wait for healthcare staff to arrive in response to the Code Blue. Virginia reached behind one of the secure bags and threw the contents of a polystyrene cup over the three staff.

Game on.

She dropped the cup from her outstretched hand and looking passed her nails thinking she could do with an intense manicure she caught Officer Brown's eye as he peeked from behind the door. He must have noticed her legal documents secured in plastic bags in the corner of the cell and realized what was going to happen. He hadn't warned his colleagues; Officer Brown and Virginia both knew the staff needed the experience.

Silence.

Officer Hassan slowly shook his head, wiped a tear of liquid excrement from the tip of his nose, and glanced at the officers' splattered shirts, and as the adrenaline coursed through his body, he tried to take a deep breath without swallowing any of Virginia's bodily waste. Officer Brown sniggered at the door. Virginia stood in her best effeminate defensive stance, arm across her chest and one knee turned slightly inward to protect her modesty. She waited for Officer Hassan to move, and she thought he may have been wrestling with the Governor's guidelines about 'decency' and 'not using unnecessary force on a prisoner if they were not a physical threat'.

"Oops!" Virginia smiled, "*One to me* boys!"

Officer Hassan shoved her and delivered a knee strike to the groin.

She slid open-mouthed to the floor, pain smashing around her head like popcorn in a microwave.

"See, you have got bollocks, you horrible little man!"

She was face down on the floor, her hand's ratchet cuffed behind her back screaming – but no sound was coming out. The pain had stopped her breathing.

Officer Brown burped. "You've earned a night in the box for that, young man."

She winced as she was lifted to her feet and dragged from the cell to *the box,* managing to sigh, "I'm a lady."

Officer Brown was staring at her blue toenails. She knew he would search the cell for the felt pen and confiscate it.

"They're going to kill me!"

"Shut up, Mark!" Officer Hassan twisted the cuffs making the metal dig into her bones.

"It's fucking Virginia, screw boys!"

"And we're not allowed to kill you. Worst luck. Prison rules," Officer Kelly hissed.

A couple of other prisoners shouted *Freak* from behind their cell doors.

"They're going to kill me!" Virginia wailed.

"You've been trying to kill yourself for years, you freaking idiot!"

"They're putting me in *the box*!"

The box. A cell designed to isolate a disruptive prisoner and give them the space to calm down. No toilet and no sink. No mattress and no chair. A hard plastic plinth a foot off the floor on which to lie down. No windows and a light controlled by staff outside the cell. An observation panel in the door and two more in the walls high up out of the prisoner's reach.

She slapped the cell door. The officers walked away. She heard Officer Brown explaining there were exclusive clubs in London where you could pay good money to have shit and piss thrown over you.

Chapter 4
OCTOBER 2nd, 2019, 16:30
HMP Long Stretch
Pause for Thought and Death

They were coming for her again.

"Stand at the back wall, Virginia."

She struggled to her feet. The cold wall made her shiver. She couldn't stand tall, her groin ached, and she rubbed at the soreness in her wrists. "You're lucky it's *nice Officer Hughes,* and you called me *Virginia!* You lot had better watch it tomorrow…"

"Stay there, Virginia, I've got your food, and it's your favourite. Chicken curry. You get yours first seeing you're in the box for the night. I've also got a couple of cups of hot water and a few tea bags. Oh, and an orange, okay?"

Virginia nodded.

Officer Brown poked his head in, "And as a special treat, I'm leaving you with two toilet rolls," he said before closing the door.

Virginia smiled; they'd be fitting an en-suite shower next! This was it for the night, yet another new anti-ligature blanket, a cardboard receptacle for a toilet, two toilet rolls, a cup of tea, and chicken curry. Sometimes they lied. Sometimes it was vegetable curry.

The observation panel snapped shut and she gave it two fingers as an afterthought and smiled at the idea of a dopey officer having to check her every few minutes through the night because she was in the box. Small victories. She tried to get comfortable on the solid plinth, noticing how cold it was, as she prized the lid from the food container. She enjoyed the fights with the staff and all the physical stuff, and oddly, it proved she was still alive and not somebody that had been forgotten by the system.

They would not forget her.

Virginia nearly lost it again when she realized the staff had not given her a spoon for the curry. She made a mental note to add it to the list in the 'claims section' of her legal documents when she got them back in a couple of days. She tore a corner from the polystyrene lid to use as a mini shovel. The curry was good, it had a spicy tang that made the tongue tingle immediately and she promised to send an application to the kitchen in praise of their efforts. She'd worked in the kitchen when she'd first transferred in from up north before the other prisoners started to bully her. Only for a couple of days. Mr Lambert, the head of the prison kitchen, had treated her with respect, one of the few members of staff who had, and when she did *kick off* by throwing boiling water over one of her tormentors, she made sure it was on the wing and not in Mr Lambert's kitchen.

She savoured another mouthful. In this game she drew a line at starving herself to death, her preferred methods were ligatures, plastic bags when she could get hold of them, and cutting - her forearms were covered in a criss-cross mosaic of healing skin. She chewed another piece of chicken, she had to keep her strength up as she intended to be a drain on the system for the rest of her sentence – unless they gave in to her demands.

Virginia did lose it when she sipped the tea from the plastic cup. Someone had put salt in it. After five minutes of banging on the box door, until her hands had gone numb, Officer Brown answered the summons.

"How can I be of assistance, Mr Winter?"

"It's fucking Miss, and there's salt in the water!"

"How dare they? I will complete a full investigation seeing you've been so well-behaved… and while I'm at it, would you like some more hot water?"

"You know I fucking would!"

"I'll get it for you. In the morning!" the observation panel closed on Officer Brown's laughing face.

Virginia stomped back to the plinth, picked up the orange and hurled it at the door, missing and exploding against the wall. It clung desperately before plopping to the floor, its energy spent as quickly as Virginia's anger. Her stomach contracted and she doubled over, making another mental note to sue the Home Office for making her live in conditions that gave her indigestion. She wasn't concerned about the blurred vision – symptomatic of a poor prison diet – but when another wave of pain sent her to the floor, the tears betrayed her anxiety.

"Fuck me!"

"Fuck yourself, freak," from a distant cell.

Virginia pulled her knees to her chest and started to cry. She dug her nails into the skin on her shins and scraped. Anything to take away the pain in her stomach. She pleaded for help as soon as the knives stopped stabbing, but Officer Brown would not come running. He didn't run for anyone. He would come when he was ready. She could see him now writing piffle in her file stating, 'screaming for attention, as usual, and being particularly disruptive'.

She lost track of time. Her legs were bleeding, dripping onto the floor, and she couldn't remember sobbing, but she must have been making a hell of a racket as the other prisoners were shouting abuse through their cell doors, attracted by her weakness.

Only when she was quiet did the observation panel open.

"Mr Brown, please help me! My guts are killing me. And I'm bleeding. I need to see a nurse."

"Oh my God, Mr Winter, can it be true?"

"Mr Brown?"

"I've got it! I know what's wrong and you've been right all along. You *are* changing into a woman! You've got period pains!"

"Fuck you!" another spasm of pain shot through her stomach.

Officer Brown walked away. Virginia knew he wasn't bothered, his shift ended soon, and he'd be happy if she was still alive before he went home.

Chapter 5
OCTOBER 2nd 2019, 19:30
HMP Long Stretch
Nobody's Listening

She was losing control. If it wasn't so serious it would have been funny. They would never take her sense of humour from her. She smiled, rolling over on the floor to avoid the jet of excrement shooting from her bowels and her head mashed into the puddle of vomit she'd previously decorated the floor with. Officer Brown was long gone. Officer Stokes was on duty for the night shift. One *old bastard for another*. The noise in the segregation unit was rising and she pictured Stokesy sitting in the stand-down room turning the volume up on his television. He'd be doing a *roll check* soon, checking at the door of every prisoner, not because he had a duty of care but so he could be seen on the cameras doing his duty. Virginia crawled to the back wall, scooping faeces to write a message for him.

"That's enough, girls!" Officer Stokes was on the landing, trying to ride the storm of insults the prisoners were shouting at him with the same routine he used when things were kicking off, "I know the food's rubbish so stop your moaning. I don't care! Put a written complaint to the kitchen in the morning, those of you that can write, now shut up! I've got a family-size pizza I've got to eat…"

Virginia heard every prisoner bang on their cell door. Something was happening and their anger was directed at Officer Stokes and not at her; for the first time in months, she felt part of something, the segregation unit that was going to start *smashing up*. Poor old Stokesy was probably on the telephone asking for help. She could imagine him pouring a strong black coffee, adding extra sugar… it was going to be a long night. Help wouldn't come for a while; the day staff were going home and wouldn't be interested and not until the small team on night shift was in would anyone come to see how he was getting on.

She saw him sipping his coffee and unwrapping the small yellow earplugs that were kept in the office drawer. She smiled. He was fiddling with the remote control trying to get the subtitles hoping the flames would blow themselves out by the time his cup was empty, and then her stomach was ripped apart by a samurai sword and she slumped to the floor, leaving a flourish on the wall that looked like her words had been underlined.

*

The Custodial Manager Jane West (in charge of the prison until the morning) strode up the long corridor with four officers in tow. Her confidence drained turning the corner, hearing the bedlam ahead. A shiver ran down her neck-cold fingertips…condensation dripping from the roof.

A couple of the newer staff were trying to make light of the situation.

"… make a difference', they said, 'change lives', do you think they were talking about this lot?" pointing ahead to the source of the chaos.

"We don't get paid enough for this."

"Oh, my God!"

CM West had opened a secure metal door and stood at the entrance to the segregation unit.

Officer Stokes, trousers rolled up to his knees, stood in the middle of the segregation unit, a plastic dustpan in each hand, surrounded by blue plastic buckets, and every few seconds he swooped to scoop water from the floor. In the lake that threatened to overwhelm his black ankle boots, were islands of bedding, green sheets, blue blankets, prison clothing, and black pieces of prison mattresses. The prisoners had blocked their sinks and drains, and water was seeping from beneath cell doors. Most of the observation panels had been smashed through and anything small enough was being thrown onto the landing. Officer Stokes, with a sixth sense borne of almost thirty years' service, leaned backwards as an orange flew passed his head. He swore loudly but looked like he was miming from CM West's vantage point.

She was hypnotized by every red emergency cell buzzer flashing in the subdued night lighting of the unit. Not knowing what to do she latched onto the one thing she was confident about and sent the officers to cancel the cell buzzers knowing it was an audit requirement (anything not answered inside ten minutes was a failure). Moments later the plan was aborted as one young female officer was almost grabbed by an outstretched arm through the smashed observation panel, and another received a cup full of urine to the face. She ushered her team to the safety of the stand-down room, scowling at Officer Stokes as he brushed past.

Before she closed the door, she saw a dog handler arrive, followed by two healthcare staff; the Alsatian, over-excited leapt forward pulling the handler off balance, who slipped on a rogue orange and was dragged the length of the unit like a fallen water skier. The nurses quickly entered the stand-down room to save the handler's embarrassment.

"You did not say it was a riot, did you?" CM West was glaring, "What have you done to wind them up like this?" she combed her highlighted hair behind her ears.

"Fun and games, Miss," Officer Stokes paused, sniffed the officer standing next to him, and moved a pace away. "Fun and games. Not a riot."

"It's a bloody riot!"

"I've known it worse. Ninety-three... when you were still in school. They're letting off steam, something has upset them, that's all... it'll be all right."

"I'll have to get more staff in... containment... call the National Response Teams... we'll lose the prison if I don't."

"Miss, we should wait, they're all behind cell doors and nobody has ever smashed their way out onto the landing, they'll get tired, and we'll sort it out in the morning. Don't give them the satisfaction of overreacting. Can someone put the kettle on, I'm parched?"

"Overreacting! The roof's coming off!"

"Hardly, Miss, and it's quietening down already," he opened the door just as the screams were giving way to a wave of low guttural moans.

"Still have to contact the Duty Governor at home, see what she has to say."

"It's your funeral. Ruin her evening and she'll think you can't cope and there goes your next promotion."

"I'll give it ten minutes."

Powerless but conscious of new officers in the room she sought to regain authority,

"Officer Stokes, this paperwork is not up to date, duty of care, Mr Stokes, Mr Winter has not been checked for at least half an hour..."

"With respect, Miss, I've been a little busy, mopping up on my own."

"Not good enough, have you ever been to Coroner's Court? 'Man allowed to die because an officer was mopping the floor!' He's in your care."

"With respect, Miss, more like, 'man died due to chronic shortage of prison staff, one man responsible for twenty-nine run ragged during riot!'"

"You said it wasn't a riot!"

"And you've never been to Coroner's Court!"

She glared at Officer Stokes. Dinosaur and lapdog. Her death stare was ineffective, and he slowly cracked his knuckles – one at a time. The nurses squirmed. The officer that smelled of urine volunteered to check Mr Winter. When he passed the dog handler at the door, they looked at each other and shook their heads, and said simultaneously, "What? For God's sake!"

It wasn't good. At the box, CM West checked first and then invited Officer Stokes, and then each nurse in turn to look through the observation panel. The unit went quiet seeming to hold its breath. Winter was curled in the foetal position. Vomit and faeces were matted to her hair and gown and there were blobs flung randomly like a splatter painting. Her eyes were open, but she was dead. Her lips were red as if painted in a last defiant act against the system, but it was blood that had escaped from her throat.

"Too late…" a nurse said.

"Too late…" the second nurse said.

"A lot of blood… did he rupture something?" CM West asked.

"No, it's a squashed orange, Miss. And it's *she*, I believe, show some respect," Officer Stokes deadpan.

"What's killed her?" CM West again.

"Choked on the curry," Officer Stokes pointed at the empty food carton and vomit.

"Nothing we can do…" first nurse said.

"Nothing we could have done…" the second nurse said.

"Always had a lot to say for himself, I mean *herself*" CM stuttered, pointing at the message written on the wall.

I HAVE THE RIGHT TO CHOOSE

AND I AM A WOMAN!

"The freak's dead!" a prisoner broke the truce and the noise erupted again.

In the stand-down room, CM West and Officer Stokes updated the entry in the official documentation. 'Discovered Miss Winter on the floor. She had taken a sudden and unexpected turn for the worse. She had vomited and lost control of her bowels. Despite the best efforts of staff, we were unable to establish a pulse.'

"Do you know the worst part about a death in custody?" Officer Stokes was passing his words of wisdom to the shaken, new staff members, "It's the paperwork."

"You're not kidding," CM West chirped up, confidant again now she was on paperwork she'd revised recently.

"I thought you handled everything very well, Miss."

"Thank you, Stokesy. Thank you all for your help… Thank goodness everything seems to be dying down now."

The telephone rang and someone reported from one of the main wings of the prison that prisoners were complaining about stomach cramps. CM West had thought it was going to be one death, as it turned out it wasn't even the first, and hundreds more would follow.

Chapter 6
OCTOBER 2nd, 21:45
Cometh the Hour… Cometh the Dyer

Miss Courtney Careless licked her fingers one more time. She examined them when she'd finished and was pleased to see some of the barbeque chicken coating had made its way beneath her nails. She used the nail on her right index finger to scrape anything from beneath the fingernails on her left hand before using her tongue to put the remnants into her mouth. The telephone on the desk interrupted the task. She tutted and answered, "Hello, *couldn't nee care less* speaking, how can I help you?"

Courtney flashed her defiant eyes in DI Dyer's direction, daring him to challenge her unprofessionalism, but he ignored her. He was eating peanuts most annoyingly. On the left side of the desk, he had lined up the *half-nuts* that still had the radicle attached, she'd referred to it as the *clitoris* after he'd bored her with this performance for the hundredth time, he'd gone a funny red colour and said it *wasn't humorous*. On the right side of the desk, he'd lined up the *half-nuts* without the radicle. He'd already eaten the whole nuts and was now in the process of testing if any of the *half-nuts* belonged together, a delicate operation for his large fingers, and when he was successful, he would announce loudly, *AHA,* before the whole nut disappeared through his moustache. The leftovers were swiped into the bin.

"Yes, I said Courtney Careless… possibly nineteen deaths? Trouble at the prison? Is that you, Trevor, are you winding me up… because if you are?" She examined the nails on her right hand and was disappointed at not finding any more residual chicken but perked up when she noticed Dyer had raised an eyebrow and was rubbing his hands together.

"Not nineteen? Did you say ninety? Dead? Are you sure? If you're pulling my leg again?"

Dyer took the handset, "DI Dyer here, what's going on? I am the most senior here... well I'll just have to do, won't I? Tell me what you know... when? Yes. I'm sure I'm the only one here... How many more times? Yes, I have never been more certain in my life!"

Dyer hung up.

"Why is this phone sticky?"

Courtney licked her fingers, eyed the discarded spicy wings carton in her bin, and slowly reached forward to press an errant crumb on the desk and popped it in her mouth and shrugged.

"This is not good enough," eyeing the keyboard, "I hate to think how many millions of bacteria are currently infesting your desk."

"Good job you've got better things to think about, eh?"

"Do you know how I got to where I am, Miss Careless?"

Courtney pursed her lips, she knew better than to answer, and she took her smartphone from her bag beneath the desk, sighed, and waited for the words of wisdom.

"I am a DI at forty-five, been promoted more quickly than most of my contemporaries, and do you know why?"

Courtney waited.

"Talented, hardworking, quick-witted' I hear you say? This accounts for nothing, my dear, without being the luckiest bugger in the West Midlands! And now, my dear, *luck* has given me an incident of biblical proportions right on my doorstep! Sort this out and I will be running West Midlands' police by the time I'm fifty. Ninety men dead..." Dyer rubbed his large hands together again, "This is it, my dear, 'this' is <u>it!</u>

I can sense commendations already... maybe an MBE," and he slammed his hands on the desk.

Courtney swiped.

"And call Quirky, get her to meet me there... Don't care what she's doing, this is the biggest thing since..."

"I don't think there is a *since*, sir."

"Quite right. Yes, you are right. Told you I was lucky!"

Dyer left the office moments later. Courtney approached his desk and dislodged any remaining chicken debris from her top before lifting her skirt and rubbing her bottom on the back of his chair.

"Quirky? I think you mean DS Quirke, you *arsehole*." she gave a two-fingered salute at the back of the door Dyer had exited.

By the time Dyer got to HMP Long Stretch over three hundred men were no longer serving sentences at Her Majesty's pleasure.

Chapter 7
OCTOBER 2nd, 22:45
HMP Long Stretch
Forget Normal all who enter here

"You can't park there, sir, that's the Number One Governing Governors' parking bay," an OSG (officer support grade) confronted Dyer with a wheeze as he closed his car door in front of HMP Long Stretch.

Dyer flashed his ID, "Detective Inspector Dyer, West Mercia Police, I think we've got more important issues right now, don't you?"

"She won't like it, sir, have you clamped she will. I'll have to ask you to move it, sir."

"So, ask me, you buffoon!" Dyer surveyed the scene at the front of the prison, five ambulances were queueing at the vehicle gate, their crews were milling by their vehicles deep in conversation, and an orderly line of prison officers stretched past Dyer into the main car park their eyes on the confrontation and a mobile fast-food van that was just setting up. There'd been a tip-off.

"Sir, will you move your vehicle?"

"No, I'm glad that's sorted," Dyer sashayed around the jobsworth as DS Quirke approached from the prison entrance.

"Evening, sir."

"What have we got, Quirky?"

"You won't believe this but close to three hundred dead so far… I had to park up there… took me five minutes to walk to the entrance… called all the staff in…"

"More specifically, damn it."

"It's still a bit patchy, sir, three hundred dead… male prisoners between, I don't know, twenty-one years of age and eighty-something, at a guess, started dying sometime after eighteen hundred hours…"

"And?"

Dyer tried to confuse DS Quirke with his huge hands, gesticulating, he was so excited spittle escaped from his moustache and was caught in one of the prison spotlights in the cold air. It was all DS Quirke could do not to physically jump backwards out of range.

"And sir?" she made a mental note to add this to the list of why she didn't like him.

"Dead, how, damn it? How did they die? Mass suicide was it?" flippantly.

She added this too, "It appears to be poison, sir, first ambulance crews suggest that's what it is but it's too early for definite."

Dyer looked deflated. An outrageous case of food poisoning would not be good enough. No matter how negligent, bad cooking would not work to his advantage, DS Quirke saw the MBE receding. 'Fast-tracking' the line of prison officers they entered the lobby and DS Quirke indicated the person behind the reinforced glass as the person Dyer needed to speak to, and Dyer flashed his ID waiting for her to put the phone down. When this didn't work, he tapped the glass with his knuckle, the twenty or so prison officers who were waiting to pass through what appeared to be a search procedure fell silent, prompting Dyer to state matter-of-factly, "I used to box a bit; you know?"

The OSG on the phone continued to stare into space ignoring Dyer's summons, but it looked like she was staring at Dyer. Quirke was well aware of the effect he had on people, with his large head and with the light at a certain angle, and because of the amount of hair on his upper lip and above his eyebrows, when he turned, his image jumped forward like an exaggerated computer graphic. Numerous people had physically *started* at the phenomenon! Eventually, the OSG stood up, her eyes even wider, and picking up a piece of cloth, she wet it with her tongue and rubbed out the digits 255 on the 'roll board' and replaced it with 254. Underneath someone had written 'extras – 302'. Quirke agreed it would have been in bad taste to write *death toll*.

"Madam, DI Dyer and DS," he paused before eventually adding, "Quirke. West Mercia Police, we need access to the crime scene… scenes. Could you do the necessary?"

"I've been expecting you, can you put your IDs through the slot at the bottom, please?"

"If you're expecting me, why do you need my ID?" Dyer was attempting a joke, but after his run-in with the OSG outside, and his complete lack of humour as a rule, nobody was smiling.

"I need it to log you in the gate-book. Procedure. You can have it back in a minute." She scribbled names and returned them without a smile.

Dyer mimed, 'Good to go', with his large thumbs up and the OSG seemed transfixed again by his hands until the phone rang. She listened and changed the roll – 253.

An officer murmured, "Bloody hell, 304 dead, or is it 303?"

Someone else quipped, "There'll be nobody left by the time we get in!"

"Well?" Dyer's eyebrows peered over his knuckles as he tapped the glass a second time.

"One moment, sir," the OSG turned to a keyboard and started to type.

"Quirky, this is unbelievable!"

"I know, sir, 303 people dead."

"304," a voice from the back.

"I mean, Quirky, trying to get into this place!"

"Oh… Yes… But it is a Maximum Security Prison. They can't take any chances."

"Any chances? Who is going to escape? Most of them are dead!" Dyer with exasperation.

A device to the OSG's left printed a couple of passes to which clips were added to be worn for the duration of their stay.

"Is that it, are we clear to enter?" DS Quirke asked politely before Dyer could say anything inflammatory. She nodded and pointed at the head of the queue before answering yet another phone call.

"Come on, Quirky, follow me… Police, coming through, it is of vital importance we come through immediately…"

The line of officers parted begrudgingly. A head poked through the main lobby door.

"Are you going to move your car?"

A voice from the back, "Yeah, queue-jumper!"

DS Quirke flushed but Dyer never flinched, he picked up a tray, following the example of those around him, ready for the entrance search to the prison.

"Right! You've asked for it!"

It looked like Dyer was about to whack the OSG round the head with the tray, but he was merely holding it up to the light and DS Quirke suspected he was thinking, 'How were they supposed to keep prisoners incarcerated if they can't keep the trays clean?' DS Quirke nudged Dyer through a sliding door before he could change his mind.

At last, they were through the first line of defence.

They left the search area and were greeted by a short, young man, in his twenties wearing a dark blue suit who had such a boyish face, it occurred to DS Quirke, he could be part of a *bring your child to work for the day* and had been lost in the mayhem.

"Hi, I'm Hugh Young, Governor Four…"

Dyer declined to shake the small red hand. "Governor for what, exactly?" He sounded slightly puzzled.

"No, Governor Four, the digit, a lesser-ranked Governor… hardly any responsibility… not very important at all… don't know if I can help really… I just happen to be the first one in… Governor, I mean, can't seem to get hold of the others just yet, always the same when something 'big' happens."

"Tell me what you know," Dyer was insistent.

DS Quirke was thinking, 'bit young, nice bum in those trousers, easy to corrupt if I was given the chance. But not with a disciplinary still hanging over her'.

"Lots of prisoners dying… dead. In the hundreds…"

"Yes, obviously, but what do you think, you must have a theory?"

"I'm not paid to think, DI Dyer, I do what I'm told to do… and isn't that your job? Shall we go to my office?" Governor Young steered them toward the stairwell. "There's a good view of the prison from there. I've got a cracking new coffee machine."

"Like to get to the crime scene straight away." Dyer blocked the stairs.

"But it's chaotic over there, crazy… so busy… panic has set in, DI Dyer… and the dead bodies… everywhere. Probably better if we wait until it's all sorted… We'll only get in the way."

DS Quirke thought he was going to sit on the step.

"Pull yourself together!"

"And we haven't got enough protective gear. We were waiting for a delivery, I assure you, not that I'm the one who does the ordering…"

"What are you trying to say?"

Dyer would not be shepherded.

"Only had eighty of those flimsy white paper suits and the officers tend to rip fifty per cent when they push their big boots through the leg holes. We could have waited for the proper equipment but needs must, DI Dyer, the staff are used to just getting on with it."

If Governor Young had not moved at that precise moment to press an intercom box to let them through into the vehicle compound, DS Quirke firmly believed Dyer would have grabbed him by the shirt collar and pulled him along like an errant schoolboy. They entered a compound roughly the size of five netball courts, a tarmacked area where three ambulances and four prison vans were parked or jumbled together, it was pointless trying to talk as the scene was accompanied by Alsatians barking incessantly – their routines upset. They walked toward the house blocks where the prisoners were located through another secure gate with an intercom. They heard desperate shouts from the nearest block.

"Help me! I'm sick."

"Let us out, you fuckers!"

"Article 4 of the Human Rights Act! The Right to Healthcare…"

The dogs started to bark louder. An intercom gave access to the inside of the prison and as they left the open air, another voice called, "Oy! Young! Get me out of here, you wanker! It's Carter on the threes – I know you can hear me!"

Governor Young scurried through the solid metal door, blocking Carter by informing Dyer that *this* wing was new, one of seven blocks in total, not including the segregation unit, the largest of its kind in Europe.

Dyer simply nodded, DS Quirke could tell he was more interested in the poor state of the paint on the door and the dirt that was embedded in the floor mat.

The dead bodies were arranged neatly. Various states of dress – some in only boxer shorts – most in clothes that 'normal' members of the public would wear. All had either a red or white piece of card Sellotaped to their chest – the cell card giving an identification, their prison number and a surname prefixed with 'Mr'. Two discipline staff entered from the right and placed another body in the line. The overweight one took a cell card from his back pocket, wiped his forehead with it, placed it on the body's chest and watched as his colleague patted his own pockets for the Sellotape. Finding it he stuck the cell card down and declared matter-of-factly, "We're going to need a bigger boat!"

"Eh?"

Governor Young, who had been completely ignored during this process, asked, "Barnes, isn't it? This one's got 'Mr' missing! Who told you to put?" he gesticulated at the bodies.

"It's Perkins, sir. It was *her*," he pointed to the adjoining office and promptly turned, leaving the area before Governor Young could say anything else of importance. The Youngster could be heard muttering, "A boat? Really? And why did you say your name was Perkins?"

"As I said, you youngsters have a lot to learn."

Two women sat at a desk in the office, both in their early thirties, both extremely pale but being revived by steaming mugs of tea and a packet of Jaffa cakes stumbled to their feet as Governor Young addressed them.

"What on earth?" he gestured toward the line of bodies.

The women hesitated in their presence.

"I'm CM West and this is SO Robertson."

"CM and SO?" Dyer asked.

Governor Young interjected, DS Quirke got the impression he was *good* when he knew the answers, "Custodial Manager and Senior Officer, they were effectively in charge of the prison tonight, yes, they were in charge of the prison tonight... until I arrived... after everything had already happened..."

"Good, now we're getting somewhere," Dyer looked at CM West who visibly shrank, "what do you think is going 'on'?"

"It's not my fault. I'd only just come on duty," she dropped a Jaffa cake in the tea, and they all knew it could not be saved.

Governor Young interjected again, much to Dyer's annoyance, "I must insist... The line of bodies... it looks bad as you come through the entrance."

"Running out of space," CM West explained, "paramedics treated the ones that were still alive, stretchered to healthcare, but they wouldn't stop dying."

"And it seemed pointless to return them to their cells..." said SO Robertson.

"And I, *we*, also thought it would be a good idea to remove bodies from the wings as we didn't want to upset *the men* more than we had to... put some in the sports hall as well as the corridors..."

CM West recapped her version of the evening's events. Attending the segregation unit to assist the officer on duty there, being *shocked* at the scale of the *unrest*, discovering the first dead prisoner and not being able to understand what was going on because suddenly the whole prison seemed to be affected by mass hysteria. Out of their depth. Officers ran everywhere in a panic.

"What do you think is going on?" Dyer asked when she paused.

The CM and SO shook their heads reaching mechanically for another Jaffa cake.

"Terrorism?" the CM.

"Extremism?" the SO.

"A mass cult death thing..." the CM.

"A protest gone wrong..." the SO.

Governor Young said, "Do not be absurd."

The SO replied, "Well they have tightened the regime recently... stricter rules."

A voice at the rear of the office, a person hidden from view in a reclining chair, his shoes now visible, piped up, "Food poisoning, if you ask me."

"And you are?" Dyer again – DS Quirke rarely got the chance to speak.

"Steve Gently. Nurse."

Governor Young said, "If it's food poisoning, there could be a realistic chance it's down to the supplier... you may be onto something there, Mr Gently... their accident and not ours... By the way, why aren't you *out there*, if you get my meaning..."

"I'd be of no use, Governor, I'm a CPN – clinical psychiatric nurse – I'll get involved when it's all died down, excuse the pun, and I didn't mean it like that... Poison, yes, a whole lot of poison. The segregation unit always gets its food first, hence 'the first dead person' and I wouldn't call it an accident, a whole lot of poison in the food."

"It could still be down to an outside supplier don't you think?"

Dyer was rubbing his hands, and everyone stopped talking like they were expecting a magic trick, and with the size of those hands, he could have produced a couple of rabbits out of mid-air and not just a dove. The friction warmed the room.

"Now you're talking. A mass poisoning. Not an accident. Deliberate. We are involved in potentially one of the most heinous crimes of our time. Would someone care to take me to the crime scene?"

CM West and SO Robertson led the way, DS Quirke paused long enough to catch Gently's eye, he winked before taking possession of the Jaffa cakes, and heard Governor Young berating Officer Perkins.

"Look, Perkins, I'm telling you what to do… I know you've moved them twice already… I want all the bodies… Yes, I know how many there are… I want all the bodies moved to the vehicle compound… go the back way so the surviving prisoners do not see what is happening… do not argue… How many Governors are there? What's that got to do with anything? And place Carter on report, will you, he abused me from his window…"

On the way to the nearest wing, Dyer asked two pertinent questions: "What percentage of the prison population at Long Stretch was *in* for poison-related offences?" And, "What percentage of the prison population that was currently *using* illegal drugs?"

Nobody had the figures to hand though Governor Young was particularly interested in the second point and could see the blame being placed readily on those smuggling drugs into prisons. A sudden influx of bad heroin could have done the trick.

Dyer listened and commented only once,

"Clean corridors, don't you think?"

Prison officers appeared like soldier ants as they passed by carrying bodies. The Governor seemed pleased everyone adhered to the rule of sticking to the left-hand side of the corridors. On the wing DS Quirke smelled it first – it took a while to permeate through Dyer's moustache – the vomit, the diarrhoea and perhaps death itself. A few prisoners were still screaming through their doors, Governor Young escaped to the wing office when someone indicated he had an urgent phone call, and CM West pointed at a harassed officer.

"Overhill, escort these two, will you, they're detectives… bring them back to the centre when you're done," CM West and SO Robertson left us, DS Quirke had the feeling they would have run if nobody had been watching.

"In all my time, sir, I've never seen anything like this. Where would you like to start?"

"Officer Overhill," Dyer sensed an opening; this man could tell more than any Governor ever could, "at this moment, Overhill, you are the most important man in this case, your evidence and insight may hold the key… In confidence… between you and me… How do you see it?"

"Off the record?"

"In complete confidence… You have my word."

"Grim reaper, sir, it's like he's decided to have a party, settling a few scores he is, in one stroke he's taken murderers, drug dealers, child abusers – you name it – in one judicial stroke… death."

"Yes, but really… taking biblical reckoning apart… How?"

"What's killing them you mean?"

"Precisely."

"The food, sir, in my opinion. Over thirty years I've had to put up with prisoners' complaints on the 'hotplate' when I'm serving the food, and tonight the complaints are valid."

"The curry? I can smell it."

"Yes, sir," Overhill led us to an open cell door, "every prisoner had curry tonight, five choices, veg curry, chicken curry (halal), beef curry, normal chicken curry and halal beef curry. Served at 18:00 hours. Most men take it from the hotplate and eat it once they're locked up for the night."

Inside the cell, they saw the following: a vomit trail on the floor leading toward the sink and toilet, an empty plastic plate stained red with the turmeric from the curry in the middle of the floor, bed clothes discarded in a very Emin fashion, paper strewn everywhere, and a stereo and television smashed to pieces...

Dyer asked Officer Overhill, "What does this say to you?"

"This was Moakes' cell. Late fifties – normally as good as gold – never a problem to anyone. He's dead now. Kiddie fiddler. Always polite..." he paused as someone screamed in a cell above them breaking his concentration.

"By the way, Overhill, about the ones that are still alive?"

"Dangerous men, sir, can't be trusted, can't have unpredictable, dangerous men on the landing, running about, sir, they're prisoners for a reason, you know, can't be trusted, even if they're dying. Can't be sure they've eaten the curry, you see, known to lie, may have flushed the curry down the toilet or thrown it through the window... Anyway, as I was saying, poor Moakes smashed up for a few minutes, couldn't calm him, he was one of the first, by the time he was on the floor and we opened the cell door, not a lot of life left in him... medics pronounced him dead before he was carried off the wing.

Same in every cell... There's not so much screaming now, sir... You should have heard it an hour ago."

"How did you manage to cope, Overhill?"

"What do you mean, sir?"

"With the horror of it all. The screams... it must have resembled hell."

"Someone got some packets of foam earplugs from the canteen... we've all had them in..."

"No, I mean... death... on such a large scale... it looks like over three-hundred dead."

"I see what you mean... I've done this job a long time, nothing surprises you after a while..."

"Aren't you concerned about the effects on the staff... the next day... the next week... or somewhere down the line?"

Officer Overhill took a deep breath, "You're right, sir, some of the men are worried about their jobs... you can't keep all the staff on with a prison that's nearly empty."

Dyer raised his eyebrows, DS Quirke felt the draft, but stepped in to suggest a visit to the prison kitchen, he agreed, but muttered something about 'post-traumatic stress'. Every cell was a crime scene, but the prison kitchen would surely be the hub of this investigation. On route, they learnt from Officer Overhill that a couple of prison catering officers, aided by a civilian catering assistant, with a workforce of the more trusted prisoners, prepared meals for the whole prison. On a normal day the kitchen produced over five hundred meals at dinner and teatime; prisoners usually returned to their wings at 16:00 hours and the staff left by 18:00 hours. It was now close to midnight.

"Do not touch anything in this kitchen," Dyer instructed as Officer Overhill inserted the key in the metal gate, "our forensic guys are on the way... just want to take a

41

preliminary look." S.O Robertson caught up with us at this point to inform Governor Young had returned to his office to check for the information requested earlier, and DS Quirke wondered if they would find him again.

A metal gate, followed by an inner wooden door, led to a wash-up area, stacks of dirty trays, clean metal trays on shelving and food trolleys left haphazardly, so much so they had to slalom our way past before we reached the main part of the kitchen. Officer Overhill noticed Dyer tutting at the mess and assured him it was always spotless by nine in the morning. In the main kitchen area, Dyer approached a bain-marie in which the congealed remains of some of last night's meal remained. Officer Overhill explained food was often left there in case the wings ran short of food and needed a few extra portions.

"Foul play or gross negligence, Quirky?" Dyer pushed his forefinger into the curry and held it under his nose, his attention on a traditional brass handbell on a shelf by itself.

S.O Robertson screamed, Dyer's finger jerked upward, smearing the underside of his nose with the potential murder weapon… Against her better judgement, DS Quirke said, "Don't move, sir, one false lick…"

Officer Overhill offered a paper towel and Dyer wiped the curry away with a flourish.

"Was that supposed to be humorous?"

"No. Sorry."

Officer Overhill saved the day, "Perhaps she was trying to curry favour."

S.O Robertson had fainted, fortunately, her head had landed on a bread crate of pre-prepared baguettes and not the ceramic floor… they were thankful for one less casualty… Officer Overhill going to her aid, stopped, and pointed into a side office. There was a body on the floor.

"Bit difficult to say, with the curry over his face the way it is, but by the look of the suit, and him always wearing the same shoes, I'd say it was the Deputy Governor," Officer Overhill suggested.

"Just for the record, Overhill, how many Governors do you have? I mean Young is a Governor 4, the fact he has a designated number suggests there are others… What number does it go up to?" Dyer asked.

"I'm not sure, sir, I've sort of lost track over the years."

"So, there may be others simply scattered about in unusual locations? Young said he couldn't get hold of some of the others earlier."

"I'm not rightly sure, sir."

"I'm going to need a full manifest of everyone who worked in the kitchen today… everyone… And a list of every member of staff who had access to this kitchen. As soon as possible."

Officer Overhill pulled the smallest of notebooks from his pocket, gulped, and looked rather flustered.

"It's all right, Officer Overhill, I think he's talking to me," DS Quirke interjected.

"What I would say, Miss, for what it's worth, the Deputy Governor would have eaten this before any of the prisoners. He was probably the first to die."

"Thank you, Officer Overhill."

"Perversely it's more important to be the first to die than the last in this sort of incident, don't you think?" Dyer added pedantically.

That was the first crime scene. A Maximum Security Prison. By 06:00 the next morning the final body count sat at one Deputy Governor and 315 serving prisoners. By extraordinary chance, not one prison officer had eaten the curry, this immediately put them in the frame for coordinating the atrocity until DS Quirke read a Notice to Staff (ironically from the Deputy Governor) stating 'the budget for making meals in the establishment was limited and the next officer caught eating prison food would be sacked'.

They found Governor Young in the toilet in the administration block, escorted him back to his coffee machine, and watched from his window as prison officers continued to line up the dead in the vehicle compound. The first media helicopters arrived whilst they were there, their lights pinpointing the bodies, scattering the cards that identified them, they filmed the officers moving the bodies again, back to the sports hall as it started to rain heavily.

Unfortunately, as they left the prison to attend the second crime scene, the first journalists who were lined up on the main road managed to witness the 'detective in charge of Britain's greatest mass murder' assaulting the OSG who refused to remove a clamp from Dyer's car.

*

When You've Got to Go…
WPC Bennett got the first call just after 19:30 – 'Disturbance, nuisance neighbour'. It was an address she recognised – 'Nuisance neighbour, noisy dog'. She completed her order at the drive-thru, said she'd be there as soon as possible, collected one milkshake and a cheeseburger and found the nearest quiet side street. This time the call was from number 15, the loud owner of the deceased *noisy* dog, and not from Mr Lambert, the kind but stressed, middle-aged man, who had made numerous complaints about his neighbour over several years. It sounded like a *tit-for-tat*.

At the second call, she'd just placed an order for coffee with extra cream, at another drive-thru on the bypass, and said she was delayed but was en route. She sat in the car park and watched as numerous response vehicles flashed down the bypass heading toward the prison.

Only after the third call and cussing the absence of any available Community Support Officer, and after she had attempted to stuff the plastic packaging from the fast-food under the passenger seat, where it compressed, resisted, and sprang back onto the footwell, did she eventually make her way to number 15.

WPC Bennett parked in front of number 17. She checked her smile in the dropdown mirror and opened the car door, the light allowed her to spy a mouthful of an uneaten cheeseburger in one of the cartons in the footwell, and though she could not be certain which evening it had been purchased, she reached for it and popped it in her mouth. The diet would have to start tomorrow. There was a moped running at the side of number 17, its engine loud and misfiring, the light from its headlight pointing toward the back garden; it was propped on its stand, and it was secure behind a set of metal gates. WPC Bennett rattled them to make sure and noticed a heavy padlock. The noise she made was the cue for a dog to start barking loudly from number 15 and a woman to scream from her back door, "Tyson! Stop barking! And you, turn that fucking thing off! I've called the police! Tyson!"

WPC Bennett scanned the street. Nobody else stirred in the dark, it wasn't their business, or perhaps it was simply *normal* and nothing to bat an eyelid over. She knocked on number 15 and a little girl peered around the door, a mop of wild red hair threatening to escape onto the street.

"Can I speak to your mommy?"

The girl screwed her eyes, looked WPC Bennett up and down, and closed the door.

"Mammy! It's the fucking pigs!"

"What have I told you about opening the fucking door in the dark?"

"Mrs Tyler, it's WPC Bennett, I was here last time… the incident with your dog?"

The door opened slightly, "Where's your fucking warrant?"

"You called us, Mrs Tyler."

"… so, I did, sort that prick out next door before I lose my temper… so help me God, I'll kill the little shit… for hours that bike's been firing like that… he's done it on purpose… and he has the nerve to complain about the dog barking… and where've you been, you're quick enough to get here when I'm being a problem…"

"Mrs Tyler, I thought your dog was dead?"

"Maybe it is, maybe it isn't? What's it got to do with you?"

"I was here, Mrs Tyler when the unfortunate incident happened… with your dog… I thought he was buried at the bottom of the garden."

"Does he sound dead to you? Tell him to turn the bike off before I ram the exhaust pipe up his…"

The front door slammed.

It was probably a different dog. WPC Bennett turned her attention to number 17. She pressed the doorbell on the porch frame, she couldn't tell if the bell rang out or not due to the noise, but no one answered – she pressed several times. The house was different in the dark. When she'd met Mr Lambert, she could not help but like him, he was friendly, offered her biscuits, and engaged her in conversation about her job, she could tell he was lonely, the house needed a woman's touch, and she also sympathised with his plight – living next door to a noisy dog.

She tried the handle – it opened into the porch – and she could now see a note attached to the front door. Banging on the door she called, "Mr Lambert" through the letterbox and getting no response she fumbled for her pencil torch to read the note.

'Come round the back. I will *deaf*-initely not hear the doorbell! (Gate key is under 'Herbie')'.

WPC Bennett recognised the humour straightaway – but who was 'Herbie'? It was obvious – 'Herbie the Hedgehog' sat on the windowsill. The padlock turned easily, freshly oiled, Mr. Lambert was meticulous with such things, WPC. Bennett killed the moped and put the keys in her pocket for safekeeping. The barking seemed to stop mid-yap.

Mrs Tyler had the last word, "Thank fuck for that, you shit bag!" and she slammed her backdoor, "and I mean him, not you Officer before you get your mates round to kick my door in." She slammed the back door again.

Silence. WPC. Bennett edged along the side of the house. Windowless. Dark and creepy. She thought about calling for back-up as the pencil torch decided to conspire against her by flickering, but her colleagues still called her *probie* even though she'd been operational for four years – so it wasn't an option. She turned the corner to the back of the house, glancing through the net curtain of a large window she could make out strange shapes, odd shadows, cast by bits of furniture in the darkness: 'the only hobby of the lonely man' she had come across before.

On the back door was another note. 'Open. Please come in. Don't break anything!'

WPC. Bennett continued to call his name but there was no answer. This was odd but she wasn't scared, well not exactly, she'd say later she had been more worried about Mr Lambert's wellbeing than for her safety. She found the light switch, just inside the backdoor, and looked at the kitchen with new confidence. A single man's kitchen, a large microwave pride of place, and she smiled with the irony because she knew Mr Lambert was a catering officer by profession. A smell of varnish or glue, she didn't know which, was ever-present. There was a pink laptop computer on the kitchen table with a third note Sellotaped to it.

> 'To the first on the scene,
> I suppose the contents on the laptop will explain a few things. The *whys and hows*. It's a confession and a suicide note. There is nobody else involved and nobody else knew what I was planning to do. Sorry to have been an inconvenience. Please be careful with the furniture, I appreciate your 'forensic chaps' have their bit to do – but the ex-wife will appreciate the windfall. She always said I never did anything, always sitting on my lazy backside, well I bet there are a few people sick at the prison tonight! Nearly forgot... I'm in the outside loo.'
> Fred.'

Several thoughts went through WPC Bennett's head at this point. She wanted to call for assistance but could already hear 'Big John's' laughter at the station – 'is that when you wet yourself?' She was confused by Mr Lambert's *confession* – did he mean he had killed the dog? What was he confessing to? She later confided to a colleague, she had considered walking at this point, driving away, and calling the station asking if somebody else was available, because 'she'd had a mechanical'. Only when she'd stood there for several minutes did her training kick in and she managed to focus on the word 'suicide'.

She followed the narrow beam of light from the kitchen down the garden path to the outside toilet calling Mr Lambert's name. What had she stumbled into? The toilet door would not budge (bolted on the inside?) and when she placed her ear on the wood, she could not hear anything.

"Mr Lambert! Fred! Open the door!" she pushed at the door, kicked it several times with her size fives, and as the panic set in, not wanting to overreact, but needing to know if an ambulance was needed, she hurled her eight-stone with a short run-up. She hadn't expected to have any effect but... the door gave... the top right hinge and the bolt in the middle... she was falling, sprawling, off-balance diagonally through the space in the doorframe... trying to right herself... her hand slipping down the wall... confusedly on one knee, trying to make sense of a body perched on the toilet... fumbling for the torch on the floor... the torch feeling slimy and wet, the light flickering... red everywhere... blood everywhere... most of the head missing... and the ridiculous thought she had managed to decapitate Mr Lambert with the edge of the toilet door... small steps backwards expecting a hand on her shoulder... retching... realising she was holding a shotgun in her left hand which she dropped on the path... vomiting on the lawn... seeing her reflection in one of the glass greenhouses... thinking what beautiful flowers had grown there and the incongruity of the ugliness of a dead body in the loo.

"Shit!" she'd made a right mess of this.

Local Radio Report
Hereford & Worcester Local Radio, 22:20
Graham Torrington

Reports are reaching us of a 'serious and ongoing incident' in a Maximum Security Prison in the West Midlands. Initial sources speak of 'several deaths' having occurred in a short space of time. Emergency services are attending as are all prison service staff. Live pictures from our news helicopter appear to show bodies being lined up on the ground...

Local Radio Report
Hereford & Worcester Local Radio, 00:45
Graham Torrington

'Back to the rapidly developing story at HMP Long Stretch, a Maximum Security Prison in Worcestershire… It is believed more than two hundred prisoners are dead… Our reporter at the scene has more…

"Thank you, John, this story is rapidly becoming the biggest single event in British penal history. We are talking two hundred and twenty-three deaths. It is simply astounding. A Prison Service spokesman has confirmed a high death toll but would not go into more detail. If the numbers quoted are true, this will go down in history…"

Chapter 8
OCTOBER 3rd, 01:00
HMP Long Stretch
Anyone Talking?

"Gentlemen... Boys... Fellas? Kath Mackie, Midlands Today reporter, any comments, off the record of course, about what's happening in there? I know there are several hundred dead. It must be gruesome... Any comments... Anything at all, come on fellas... Off the record... Please... Any quotes?"

"One death is a tragedy, over three hundred is a statistic."

"Shut up, muppet! The POA said, 'Say nothing'."

Another voice, "It won't look good in the league tables, will it? What is the KPI, that's the 'key performance indicator' for you, love, for the number of deaths in a single year?"

"Yeah, not even Group 4 lost this many in one night!"

Chapter 9
OCTOBER 3rd, 01:15

Out of the Fire

"You shouldn't have pushed him, sir."

"He clamped my bloody car and refused to unclamp it!"

"Still… It didn't look good when he fell over, backwards…"

"He tripped, Quirky, over the kerb…"

"If he hadn't landed on the reporter's camera bag, he could have banged his head…"

"Bloody reporter!"

"… And he may have become another to be added to the final count."

"Good riddance."

"You'll have to apologise, I mean, if you want your car back… eventually."

"We'll see about that!"

They were dawdling toward the second crime scene in DS Quirke's Fiat, Dyer's knees at a peculiar angle making a gear change difficult if not impossible, DS Quirke decided third was good enough in the circumstances, as she didn't want to risk physical contact again by slipping it into fourth. Dyer's head was pressed against the roof cocked away from DS Quirke and she was thinking, *that bit of my car will never be the same, invisible bits of him, would forever be embedded in the roof, particles, molecules of Dyer forced into the fabric.* She made a mental note to get the car valeted at the first opportunity. Dyer was hitting buttons on the car radio with his ridiculous fingers, growing increasingly frustrated at his inability to find a local radio station… he stopped, DS Quirke guessed, when he recognised a voice, though it was well past midnight.

'Folks, this could be the crime of the century. Put quite simply, if this is foul play this makes Shipman look like an amateur, I'd be interested to know what you think out there. Over three hundred dead. I'm guessing it must have been a horrible death by all accounts. Prisoners, yes, but human beings… Some of them serving time for truly horrific crimes… murder, rape, you get the picture, but human beings, nonetheless. Caller on line three… Hello, Michael, what do you want to say? Hello, Michael…'

'Yo, yeah, can't speak too loud, you get me, yeah?'

'Michael, what would you like to add to our discussion tonight?'

'Yeah, right, the ting is, you listenin' yeah? I'm inside The Stretch on D wing…'

'What do you mean, Michael?'

'I'm a prisoner, yeah, I'm using me mobile… can't speak too loud, man, know what I mean?'

'A serving prisoner, Michael, actually inside Long Stretch?'

'That's it, man, you listenin'?'

'What happened tonight, Michael? Are you alright? Can you explain to the listener what you've seen or heard… What's it been like, Michael?'

'Bad, man, real bad, man. The screamin', man, they don't shut up… They woke me up, you listenin' man, just screamin' the same ting all the time… They won't shut up, man, screamin' they're dying…'

'Must be awful.'

'No self-control, man, wouldn't shut up even when I freatened 'em… just carried on shoutin'… Screws ignored me

54

cell buzzer, man, for ages… I was gonna smash-up, man, can't ignore me, man… you listenin', yeah?'

'Are any of your friends dead, Michael?'

'No friends in 'ere, man. They wouldn't stop screamin'… And they wouldn't move me somewhere quiet… When they did come to me door, they ask me to 'show some understandin'… I got rights, man, I know I got the right to peace and quiet – a right to be left alone… you listenin', yeah? None of that screamin'.'

'Michael, did you know there are many dead in there?'

'Not my problem, man, life is for the livin', and all I know there'll be a lockdown now for a few days, you get me, yeah, stuck in this cell for at least forty-eight hours, no exercise, no gym… Just me, my TV and nofink.'

'Are you all right, Michael? How comes you're not dead, if you don't mind me asking?"

'I don't eat their shit, I got my homie to cook for us in the wing kitchen, you get me… Got to tink of my six-pack… That's anuvver ting, no proper food for a while… It just ain't fair, bruv!''

'So, you're saying people are dying because of the food… Is it mass poisoning?'

"Quirky, you know his problem?"

"What?"

"Lacks empathy."

DS Quirke made sure she hit the kerb as she parked causing Dyer to bump his head on the roof. He didn't say anything.

"Crime scene two, sir, number 17, a two-bed semi-detached. The home of the main cook at The Stretch."

"Do you realise Quirke, up to this point in time, the only controversy to have struck the quiet town of Evebury was how the town was supposed to be pronounced? Two entrenched camps exist, one firmly believes it should be pronounced as in 'Adam and Evebury', notice the two syllables, whilst the other insists the second 'e' really wants to be an 'a', as in dad, and sounded like a three-syllable word 'Eve-A-bury'. Check the history books and you'll find the English Civil War fought a battle there to try to sort it out or at least that's what local historians will tell you."

*

OCTOBER 3rd, 01:30
Inside the Lair

"Come on, Quirky, let's see the lair of Britain's potentially most prolific mass murderer... and by the way, your parking leaves a lot to be desired."

"I'll put myself on the appropriate course, sir."

Dyer rubbed himself down and though it was dark, Quirke could see the remains of cheese and onion crisps on the seat of his trousers and smiled, though nothing usually got past his nose. Her satisfaction was interrupted when a woman slapped the roof of the car.

"You can't park there! This is my drive..."

"Madam... enough... please refrain from hitting our car... we are the police..." Dyer was at his pompous best.

"It's not a police car and it wouldn't matter if it was! It's my driveway!"

"Madam... It is after two o'clock in the morning, we are on very serious police business... a matter of murder... of mass murder!"

The woman gave the open-handed gesture to ask what possible relevance *mass murder* could have to a car blocking *her* driveway.

"Madam, are you going anywhere tonight?"

"Not the point…" she turned, made a point of waving to the house, "This is my property, and you can't park there."

A dog started to bark.

"Look, madam, it can't be helped, we have important business next door," Dyer walked away, and DS Quirke felt duty-bound to follow, and she caught the woman's eye and mouthed *sorry about him,* but she wasn't having it.

"You will be."

She marched away and shortly afterwards the noise of the dog seemed to increase in volume.

It did not go well from the start. The constable at the front door was slow in challenging Dyer as they approached the crime scene. The constable explained the lack of police tape as all the rolls had been *nicked* for the crime scene at the prison, and his offer to use toilet rolls instead simply made Dyer more uptight. To make matters worse the constable removed earplugs explaining the dog next door had been a right pain in the arse every time someone arrived. When Dyer flashed his ID the constable repeated, 'Yes, a right pain in the arse,' and seemed to count to three before he gestured toward the noisy dog. Dyer had a way of starting on the wrong foot and he quickly placed the other one up to the knee…

WPC Bennett was sitting on the sofa holding a large mug of tea with a blanket placed around her shoulders. Before DS Quirke could say a word, Dyer immediately berated the fact that though resources 'were stretched thinly tonight, on a night that will go down in the history books, when hundreds were put in their graves, let it be mentioned that a local bobby had the good sense to make herself a cup of tea when everything else was sinking into chaos!' Dyer stopped when she started to cry as he wasn't good with the old waterworks, and his attention flitted to a S.O.C.O operative standing in the kitchen.

"Ah, Snotty, you got the short straw then?"

"Dyer, just when I thought it couldn't get any worse. We really are in dire straits now, aren't we?" Snotty muttered to the nearest constable.

If Dyer heard it; he didn't let on. "Quirky, this is 'Snott of the Antarctic', as cold as his namesake and probably just as dead when it comes to ideas or wit."

"Steve Knott at your service, young lady, I'd shake your hand at the very least, but I've just prepped and I'm ready for action… anyway. One. Do not touch any surface in the kitchen. Two. Do not touch the back door. Three. If you must go into the garden, I must insist on the white suits and shoe covers…"

"We have done this before, you know…" Dyer grumbled.

"Four. Do not enter the greenhouse or touch the glass. Five. Do not touch anything in the outside toilet…"

"As I was saying, Snotty, we have …"

"And you have a habit of NOT doing what I ask! Six. For you, young lady, do not vomit on the floor – use the bags provided…"

DS Quirke liked him already. Anyone that disliked Dyer was by default a part of 'team Quirke.'

"I get the point, Snotty, you bore me with this every time…"

"And you never listen."

"I just want to get a feel of the place… get the feel of the man who may be responsible for hundreds of deaths."

"Sorry to thwart your knighthood, Dyer, but seems clear cut to me... No *may* about it."

"I'll be the judge of that."

"No, you won't. I will. Dyer, the only reason you're on this case is nobody else wants to jeopardise a promising career by fucking up a case that will be high-profile for weeks. Television. Radio. Questions asked in Parliament. It's funny you've been lumbered with it. Young lady, no offence..."

"All right, Snotty, what's your excuse for being here?"

"... Well, actually, yes... colleagues already at the prison... I was in the bath... last one to pick up..."

*

DS Quirke left them to it she made a point of talking with WPC Bennett who immediately perked up when confided the man who'd torn her off a strip was an *arsehole* before she recounted her story. When she'd finished, DS Quirke politely excused herself to have a look upstairs.

Every other step creaked. Odd that. DS Quirke started with the first room on the left, she always did it that way, and in this case, it was the bathroom. Old vinyl flooring – not clean, a yellowish colour – on purpose to hide the urine stains of an old single man? It had the stickiness to confirm her first thought. Small – too small to swing a mop around by the tail. She was, of course, drawn to the toilet – you can usually tell a lot about a stranger from their toilet. Brown stains on the enamel and worse on the toilet brush and holder. If anyone was ever brave enough to live with DS Quirke, there would be rules... number one would be a requirement to sit on the toilet even for a wee. The bath had a tide mark no woman would put up with and the showerhead, in the bath itself, was heavily scaled. As were the taps. Cold tap dripping – every seven seconds.

A member of the SOCO team crinkled passed her, as she was surveying the bathroom, unzipped the front of his white paper suit and started to urinate.

"Don't mind me, luv, outside toilets engaged for a bit."

"Heathen!"

She nudged him as she left the bathroom causing him to add to the stains on the floor, "And that's detective sergeant to you."

Working clockwise, the first of the two upstairs rooms contained small pieces of furniture, bedside cabinets, coffee tables and the like, all-in various states of repair. Again, it was a small room with pieces placed on top of each other and each exposed flat surface had a container of varnish, wood stain or resin that made navigation of the room awkward without brushing against something. Carelessly discarded lids accounted for the odours prevalent throughout the house. It was a muddled room, a room of a man that meddled but rarely finished anything. She was thinking it was a fire trap as she eventually got to the one window looking onto the back garden. The SOCO lighting showed a single path leading to a red brick outside toilet. To the right was an area of lawn, not quite overgrown, but it would be a test in the spring for the first cut, and on the left two large greenhouses cordoned off with a highly visible notice which read 'do not enter'. The wooden fence on the left had been repaired in several places and resembled a patchwork of defence but the fence on the right was immaculate. The bottom of the garden was enclosed by a privet with no visible entry point.

Below DS Quirke could see Dyer and Snotty gesticulating at each other.

The last bedroom showed signs of similar neglect. A double bed with a duvet not changed for many weeks; one pillowcase, used and looking sad next to another one that was clean white. She didn't get too close as she was certain samples of Mr Lambert still lived in the bed and forensics might need them. Dust on the headboard. A large double wardrobe towering over the room – old-fashioned. Not sure what period. She also knew Dyer would know and made a point not to ask him. She opened the wardrobe from the centre; on the right, a cursory inspection showed male clothes, not many of them, a couple of pairs of jeans, shirts, jumpers – mostly the uniform used in a prison. Oddly, on the left, were two floral dresses, extra-large, and the kind her nan would have worn to the summer fete, one pastel pink and the second Bailey's whiskey cream. DS Quirke's wardrobe matched the colours of the rainbow for an order – she didn't think there was a better way. A drawer underneath contained socks and pants – pants like her grandad used to wear, pants for going 'over-the-top' in the First World War.

Next to the bed and evidently on *his* side was a single bedside cabinet. A notebook was on the top with an underlined piece of wisdom in, she presumed, Mr Lambert's handwriting – 'The enemy is at their strongest when you think they are strong'. There was an iPad, an alarm clock, and a small stack of reading material. *A Guide to the Poison Garden (and other exciting days' out)*, *The Foothills of Northern India and its Exotic Flowers*, and *The Poisoner's Handbook: Part One*. A couple of bookmarks, from what DS Quirke could see without touching them, were folded appointment letters for an urgent endoscopy – she could never remember if that was throat or bottom – she hoped the consultant could remember. She checked under the bed, noticing slippers and the fact a vacuum had not ventured there for months.

On the back of the bedroom door were two news clippings, each framed behind glass, the first reported on a man jumping into the river Avon to save a little girl from drowning, and as DS Quirke read the second, the colour drained from her face. Her fingers found the rubber ball in her pocket and squeezed.

Evebury Journal
12th September 1995
'Hero Still Unknown'

The 'Mystery Man' who saved a two-year-old from the river Avon has still not come forward. The Town's Mayor has referred to the man as a 'hero' and a man of action but stated it was just what he expected from a member of the local population. 'It shows the country and the whole world what Evebury people are all about.' He closed with a reminder it is against the law to jump into the river from any of the town's bridges.

"Quirky? There you are... Put these on," Dyer tossed a packet containing white paper overalls and a packet of shoe covers on the bed, "Damned imbecile requires we wear these I'm afraid."

"It is the procedure, sir," wiping a tear that was about to stain her cheek.

"That's not the point."

It probably was.

"Sir, what's that on your shirt?"

"Aaargh, yes, mmm, a bit of a scuffle with the idiot downstairs, maybe microscopic cellular matter from the vomit the WPC left behind... I think they're ready to remove the blasted door off the toilet if we hurry. If you could help me with these things…"

Dyer had got the material over his shoes, no problem, and pulled the paper suit up to his waist, but there was no way his hands were going to push through the cuffs at the end… both arms were in the sleeves with nowhere to go… DS Quirke could see a couple of fingers protruding… she collected some nail scissors seen on the bathroom windowsill and managed to free them.

"Thank you, Quirky."

DS Quirke's suit was no better. Only extra-large left. By the time she'd rolled up the legs and the sleeves… giant marshmallow… must have made Dyer feel better but he didn't say anything. At the kitchen door, Snotty gave them the once over and couldn't help grinning, inanely, at Dyer and winked at DS Quirke when no one was looking. Masks and goggles were thrust at them, Dyer remained close-lipped, and that was unusual. It occurred to DS Quirke they were not talking. Never a good sign in a murder investigation.

Dyer stepped into the back garden.

"Has anyone told the neighbour to quieten her dog?"

"What? I can't hear you because of the dog!" Steve Knott pulled a face.

"The dog! Send someone around!"

"We did!" Steve Knott was enjoying this.

"And?!"

"Said she doesn't have a dog!"

"What?!"

"No dog! Said if some arsehole moves their car…" Steve Knott showed the palms of his hands to indicate he who didn't know who the arsehole could be.

DS Quirke had not stepped into the garden, and she volunteered to move the car and speak to the neighbour. Only when she politely informed the woman there was a possibility her neighbour was dead, did she shout inside to her daughter, 'The old bugger's dead!' and the barking stop immediately. The front door was duly slammed in her face.

"So, Quirky, what do we have?" Dyer was halfway down the garden path.

"WPC responds to a call at, eventually, at 21:00... others have been directed to the prison... she finds a note on the front door, accesses the back... turns moped off... enters backdoor... which is unlocked... reads note... does not call for back up... finds a body in the outside toilet... calls for back up... nothing doing as the incident at the prison takes precedence... the link is made between the two... she makes a cup of tea because she's been scared shitless... SOCO get here just after midnight... and we get here not long after them."

"Right. What do you smell?"

"... Dog poo... and I've still got the taste at the back of my throat from the house... varnish... turps or something... and concerned about the stuff lying about the kitchen and in the cupboards... something he's cultivated in the greenhouses... got a particular fragrance... hope it's not harmful."

"Probably a bit late for that."

"I meant to us... and... outside... fireworks... suggesting the discharge of a firearm..."

"Precisely. What have you seen? First impressions."

"In the house... single, middle-aged man... everything's... tired, disrepair... photos of a daughter, I think... none of a wife or girlfriend... furniture in various states of repair... books about poison... poison gardens... stuff in the kitchen I don't want to eat... notes left for evidence... PC and mobile phone bagged for evidence...

suggestion there are video messages pre-recorded for us… a medical appointment slip…"

"I don't like it, Quirky. This is my career he's messing with. Give me something to go on. It's all a bit convenient… this was my chance…"

Steve Knott overheard and couldn't help himself, "No appointment with the Queen for this, Dyer. Told you so, hundreds of dead bodies at the prison and one fat motherfucker, dead in the toilet."

"Have some respect."

"Mr Motherfucker, dead in the toilet. It doesn't take a genius to figure this one out."

A downcast Dyer moved away from Steve Knott further up the path. A rumble of thunder and a streak of lightning were the precursors to a few heavy splats of rain; more sheeting was required if evidence was not going to be lost but supplies were threadbare – the bodies at the prison had taken everything. At the outside toilet, SOCO was ready to remove the door, the door that had partially collapsed under WPC Bennett, not bolted from the inside as she had presumed, but wedged on uneven paving stones, and the rain was already attacking the handprints she had left in her panic. Dyer nudged the SOCO cameraman to one side and asked for a minute before the door was removed, and leaning forward without touching anything he said, "Quirky, note the hairpiece and the spectacles on the shelf. Nothing else."

DS Quirke could see he was disappointed. She almost felt sad for him. They stepped back to let SOCO get to the door, they righted it before releasing the remaining hinge, Steve Knotty made a point of confirming the door had not been locked from the inside with an exaggerated mime characteristic of a magician. At this point, they turned away from the toilet, unconsciously to compose themselves before the body was revealed.

"Quirky, you *have* missed something."

"I have?"

Steve Knott waited. Pretending not to listen. Afraid Dyer had something of ground-shaking importance.

"How many hand-written notes from the suspect do we have?"

"Three, sir, front door, back door and one on the PC screen."

Steve Knott pretended to examine the door as it was placed on the lawn.

"Correct. Now, the notepad, leaves a perforated strip when you tear a note from it… how many perforated strips do you think there are, Quirky?"

"I didn't look, sir."

Steve Knott pretended to blow his brains out with his fingers.

"There are four perforations. We are missing a note!"

"In the bin, sir? He made a mistake in his haste?"

"Do you seriously believe a man of my calibre, who has waited all his life for a career-defining case such as this, would not have checked the bin? The note is not in the house – I got WPC what's-her-name to check, and I do not believe it's in the toilet either… We'll get our best men on the job, not *him*, they can decipher what was written on it by examining the sheets underneath. It could be of vital importance. The *slip* that every killer makes."

"It's in my pocket," Steve Knott edged closer unable to hide the smirk.

DS Quirke thought Dyer was going to implode. She knew there was electricity in the air, by now the rain was falling hard, but she thought she could see every hair in

Dyer's eyebrows and moustache standing on end. His eyes, usually deadpan, seemed to vibrate in their sockets. He clenched his hands as a boom of thunder simultaneously made them jump.

"Only joking, arsehole! Bit of a leap though from a straightforward suicide to 'Dyer's Greatest Case' solely on the evidence of a discarded piece of notepaper"

"Get on with your job, Snotty!" Dyer tried to regain his composure.

They all turned to examine the toilet.

DS Quirke vomited on the lawn. She couldn't help it and she knew Dyer was disappointed in her and was glad when he seemed more interested in what she'd eaten earlier that evening than offering consolation. Most of the head was gone, removed by the sawn-off shotgun, the stocky implement still lay on the path where WPC Bennett had dropped it. Mr Lambert was still in prison uniform; the black fleece jacket was unzipped to the waist showing a white prison shirt and a dark blue prison tie still fastened rather oddly to the shirt collar – only a few flecks of blood and a few traces of brain jelly splattered like a Hockney painting. The rest of the head was stuck to the white wall and ceiling above the body.

Dyer was berating Steve Knott again and DS Quirke managed to transfer her thoughts from Mr Lambert's body, and her rapidly diluting puddle of vomit, to what they were saying.

"I repeat, nobody kills themselves like this, Snotty! In all my years I have never seen a body set like this…"

Steve Knott was wavering, "Well… I can see your point… perhaps he simply had to go…"

"Look, Snotty, I know you're an idiot, but I'll spell it out for you. 'I'm going to blow my head off, but first I need to use the toilet'! No! It doesn't bloody matter. Does it? 'I'm going to be dead in point zero, zero three of a second', you do not pull your trousers down to defecate! He's expecting the boys in blue to be hot on his tail but 'wait a minute I think I need a shit first'! I don't think so! He's just killed God knows how many... he just kills himself..."

"I think you're smelling a rat because you want to. Who knows what the chap's thinking when he gets back here... you're looking for something that's not there... I know you want to dress it up a bit... well a lot... make yourself look like the hero... be the only one who could have solved it... but it is simple? No promotion to Scotland Yard. No knighthood."

"You are wrong, Snotty, and when this blows up in your face, I'll make sure everybody knows how incompetent you are."

"Sounds like a threat."

"You wouldn't know a threat if you fell over it."

At this point, they were nose to nose. DS Quirke wasn't sure if a punch was thrown, Dyer later said he slipped in her vomit, but two SOCO members managed to manhandle him back into the house. He kept muttering 'doesn't smell right' and 'not seeing it' but he was so angry nobody was taking any notice.

Ten minutes later when things had calmed down, Steve Knott entered the house and DS Quirke jumped between them, but in a very serious manner, he said, "You'd better see this before I bag the body... unless you want to have another swing at me now..."

Dyer was transformed. It had to be something to confirm his view of things. DS Quirke couldn't keep up with him though she never could. The body was face down on the tarpaulin... it would have been if there'd been a head, the trousers were down by the ankles, but the fleece was covering Mr Lambert's bottom.

"Well, Snotty, what is it?"

Steve Knott paused for dramatic effect and made sure the cameraman was ready.

"Come on, Snotty, fresh evidence? Something doesn't fit?"

Steve Knott lifted the fleece jacket. Sellotaped firmly to the buttocks was a piece of notepaper.

"The fourth piece and you can stop calling me Snotty!" Steve Knott declared calmly, "It says, 'The last laugh's on you, my bum was the first part of me into the world and now it's the last part of me out of it!'"

Dyer turned away. Dejected. Deflated. He brushed passed DS Quirke on the path, one of the few occasions they touched, but he still managed to state defiantly –

"Have a formal identification with me as soon as you can."

"I accept your formal apology, and I will in my own time, *arsehole*!"

Houses of Parliament
OCTOBER 4th 2019, 13:00
LIVE BBC BROADCAST

The Speaker of the House.
'The Minister of State for Prisons would like to make a statement.'
'Thank you, thank you … If I could have a few minutes without interruption to brief you on the ongoing events at HMP Long Stretch in Warwickshire. The latest figures I have are 315 confirmed dead …'
(There's a pause as a colleague pulls at his trousers and they confer before the Minister resumes, mildly put out.)
'… 316 confirmed dead … in Worcestershire, of course … 132 seriously ill … but I can assure you now, everything possible is being done in such grave circumstances to … ahem … ahem … find the person or persons responsible for such an outrageous act … crime. No matter what the nature of their crimes, all convicted prisoners should have the right to feel safe in Her Majesty's prisons. It is a sorry state of affairs when they cannot.
I have, of course, made arrangements for the survivors of this tragedy to be transferred immediately to establishments of their choice, as I am only too aware of the trauma and psychological damage events like these are likely to have on a prisoner … on an individual. Each person has access to counselling and mobile phones, provided by Government expense, to keep in contact with loved ones at this time of need …'
'Hear, hear …'

Chief of Police

'I want to put the public at ease. Yes, we have many deaths, quite a high number of deaths, it is true, but they are contained within the walls of a Maximum Security Prison. We do not have a cause of death – but there is no reason to be alarmed – preliminary investigations do not indicate anything communicable or contagious. I must stress, there is no reason to panic, I have my best team working on this case day and night... I assure you they are the best of the best. Now, I have reports of people evacuating Evebury – this is ridiculous. The reports on local radio are grossly exaggerated... we are not at the centre of some industrial-scale poisoning that is going to wipe out half of the Vale of Evebury, though some may see this as a good thing (at this point there was total silence before a couple of people sniggered at the back of the room) – I meant in terms of the traffic congestion... Yes, sorry, it was a poor attempt at humour, given the circumstances...'

Houses of Parliament

OCTOBER 5th, 13:05

Address to the House: The Speaker of the House

'The Minister of State for Prisons would like to make a statement.'

'Thank you … I have it on good authority the identity of the perpetrator of the mass poisoning … ahem … if indeed it is established this is the cause of death …'

(The Minister cups his hands to hear advice from a colleague.)

'Strike my last remark … forget I mentioned poisoning. I can say the name of the perpetrator has been determined to be Frederick Lambert, a catering officer of thirty years' experience … a disgruntled and bitter employee … ahem … ahem.'

(The Minister takes more advice.)

'Strike that too. Forget I named the perpetrator, his identity shall be confirmed in due course after a full investigation. Not terrorism. Not human error. And not, as I read in one of the tabloids yesterday, *a government that will stop at nothing to alleviate the overcrowding in our prisons* … Absurd! It is simply an outrageous act of an individual, who for whatever reason, took it upon themselves to poison the inmates of one of Her Majesty's prisons with …'

(The Minister checks his notes.)

'With curry sauce. Sorry! Who may or may not have poisoned prisoners with a curry sauce. It is also true, as some members of the house are already aware, the individual identified, who may or may not have poisoned inmates, has taken their own life though I have not been briefed on those particular circumstances. I must reiterate … the Government cannot be held responsible for someone losing their head in this way …

'Yes … Yes … I have given the order to remove the mobile phones I authorised yesterday … Yes … Yes … Due to unforeseen circumstances … All right … due to the number of takeaways arriving at establishments across the country … Yes … And to stop the alarming number of calls presently being made to the victims of those still incarcerated …'

Chief of Police
OCTOBER 5th, 15:30
STATEMENT TO THE PRESS

'There are over three hundred deaths. I can, however, put your minds at rest. They were poisoned… Curry sauce. No, I do not know the specific type of curry sauce… Is that relevant? You're missing the point… We think poison was added to the specific sauce inside the prison and given to the prison population. It is an isolated case… Yes, I just said, the poison was added inside the prison… Yes! All other curry sauce is safe to eat. And rest assured the people of Evebury can return to their homes… (or at least sit in a traffic jam in the High Street for a couple of hours).'

Chapter 10
OCTOBER 2019
Pressure and stress

DS Quirke knew the chief was under intense pressure from the powers above to get a quick result. He wanted resolution, especially as everything seemed so clear cut, and though hardly anyone slept in the forty-eight hours after the massacre, DS Quirke found she had a lightness of step, but she always did when Dyer had bad days. She'd dropped him off at the corner from where he lived after his run-in with Steve Knott, he'd been unusually quiet in the car, muttering something about recharging his battery and sorting a taxi for the morning. It had been a disaster. Such high expectations when the call had first come in and the anticipation when the death toll snowballed served to increase his excitement. Things were looking up for DS Quirke – tomorrow promised more disappointments, more setbacks for Dyer – but on the downside she knew she would be the one collating the final report, sifting through the evidence to present everything to Head Office.

Sat in her Fiat, the rain bouncing off the roof, DS Quirke swiped the screen of her smartphone. This was not in her Management Plan, but it was a hard habit to break, and things were certainly *looking* up. She'd checked *my profile* on 'Professionals Only' and noticed she had three expressions of interest. Her last date had been two weeks ago. It hadn't gone well. She never mentioned being a detective on a first date, it made things awkward, they always became guarded, clammed up, and began to act like they were *under questioning* – and she was bored of the handcuff jokes. This time she was an undertaker. She thought it would be fun, help to get through some of the time wasters, but unfortunately, as she had entered the Bistro, he was not what she'd expected, most were *not* in the flesh. He was enthusiastic, asking peculiar questions about ambient body temperature and the strangest things she'd seen attached to a corpse – he was *weirder* than she was. When he asked the usual cliché, 'Do undertakers always do it lying down?' she'd made her excuses, reached across the table, grabbed his necktie, looked coolly into his eyes, and stated, 'I only ever have sex with the dead'. Nevertheless, she had still added the tiepin she'd pulled from him to her bottom drawer of trophies.

'Three expressions of interest'. The first was a definite 'no'. A police officer wants to 'take somebody into custody'... The second... a maybe... a chef in a two-star Michelin restaurant... though she knew they tended to be perfectionists with little time for relationships... always in a rush or was that just in MasterChef: The Professionals'... always stop at dessert... and in the light of the present case at the Stretch... The third was a better possibility... a tree surgeon... now that was different... rugged outdoor type... probably fit... healthy... knew a thing about a tidy garden... she tapped a quick reply to see if things might grow or get lopped off immediately...

DS Quirke was in extra early the morning after having her hedge trimmed. Dyer was already there – he was always in before her. She'd checked her car for a tracker once, convinced Dyer knew her every move. He was on the telephone, and she listened to his end of the conversation, he didn't acknowledge her.

"So, when can I get the car back? It's a police car, you know?

"He can't be badly hurt... he fell onto the reporter's bag... No, I categorically state I did not push him...

"Clamped… I know that… Keys? At the hospital with him… and you don't know where the spare set is? Well, I suggest you get someone to the hospital… I am not taking a *tone* with anybody… other priorities? Yes, I know what's happened there… I was there. You'll get back to me?"

They'd hung up.

"Aaargh, Quirky, the laptop's over there. See what you make of his confession… do the usual stuff… I've got a meeting with the chief at eleven… pushing to get the whole thing wrapped up… but we'll see about that… if they ring about the car… can you possibly?"

She nodded. He walked out. She considered offering him the bus fare but knew better than to open a dialogue on the potential historical significance of the omnibus for the working classes of this country during the industrial revolution.

The PC was pink. It didn't fit the profile of a mass murderer, of a five-foot-ten, overweight, prison officer turned prison catering officer of close to thirty years' service. It had belonged to his daughter and the main suspect had conveniently stuck a label on the bottom with the password neatly printed: 'Princess4Ever'. It was an old PC used by his daughter in her sixth form and discarded when she'd upgraded. Mr Lambert had inherited the computer and had used it for his interests.

DS Quirke avoided the file on the desktop, the one in the middle of the screen with the caption *Please read me* until she had examined all the other folders and locations. Nobody was telling her what to do.

Two folders stood out. The first was an extensive photo library – most of his daughter from her childhood and showed a happy, smiling child, a child that wasn't afraid of anything; a face that shouted, 'Push me higher', 'Can we do that again' and 'faster daddy!' In her teens, the face began to taunt but it still said, 'I love you, really', but you could also see it was saying 'Come on, dad, don't be boring' and 'Is that all there is?' By the late teens, the photos had changed and there were far fewer of them. The eyes said, 'Can I go now?' and 'You're disappointed, so what!' DS Quirke could see the tell-tale signs, the weight loss, a common story, a slide into recreational drug use until the drugs had become everything.

The second folder showed photographs of a beautiful flower. Indian Aconite. There was a link to the Poison Garden in Northumberland and a file detailing a holiday to the fabled Darjeeling Hills in West Bengal, India. Monkshood. Aconitum Ferox... Mr Lambert had noted this was seven times more poisonous than average Monkshood. Tea leaves were not the only thing Darjeeling was famous for.

The email account also gave a few more clues. Mr Lambert had methodically contacted numerous companies with his *expiry date* in mind. House insurance, moped insurance and even life insurance policies had been stopped. DS Quirke couldn't help noticing if Mr Lambert had been knocked off his moped on the day of the deaths he would not have been covered! He'd even arranged for a company to complete a house clearance making sure his projects went somewhere useful. His bank account was closed. She would later discover a will in an Evebury High Street law firm giving the proceeds of his estate to his ex-wife.

*

DS Quirke checked over her shoulder, when she was sure no one was within earshot, she whispered, "Now, Mr Frederick James Lambert, are you the man that saved my life when you pulled me from the river when I was two years old?" Her fingers squeezed the rubber ball in the palm of her hand.

The video image of Mr Lambert filled the whole screen. The screen went blank for a couple of seconds… Mr Lambert was now positioned more suitably… further from the camera. He didn't look like your typical villain if there is such a thing. His eyes were tired, and heavily wrinkled, though this was reduced when he put black-rimmed spectacles on. He referred to a checklist, as he went along, simple reminders to keep his train of thought. His hair was a shade darker than his stubble and eyebrows and she assumed he was wearing a hairpiece. She kept focussing on a couple of grey nasal hairs. His flesh was saggy and ruddy… he looked older than his mid-fifties… and he wheezed when he breathed in between the sentences he narrated matter-of-factly, 'Sorry for the inconvenience. I'll try to keep to the point. I tried to carry on… after my daughter died… but it gnawed away at me all those years… too many reminders I suppose… everyone that happens to look like her… everyone that said or did something the way she did… makes you catch your breath every time… no matter how time has passed. Nothing is ever the same… nothing to live for… wife gone too, you know, I suddenly turned into a sad and lonely old man… thought I could make a difference once… Suppose I may have now.

'Drugs did it. Change a person completely. Saw it all the time at the prison – I tried to be a positive influence, tried to change a few lives… but the sense of despair… tried to make up for my failings with her… if I could turn a few young lives around, maybe I thought… I don't know… I was fooling myself. And then *they* tell me… *you're dying*… not straight away… but *your heart's on the way out*… and I thought my bowel problem was the thing that was going to get me… *going to need lifesaving surgery*… well let me tell you something, there's nothing *they* can do for my heart… *she* wrecked it years ago… and it was the drugs that done it.

'And then it came to me. A final hoorah! Some real justice and some real publicity. Not a misadventure and sweep it under the carpet. A life for a life. Her life in exchange for some of them – the drug dealers, the users, or the thugs preying on each other as a way of life in prison. And I had the means to do it. Monkshood. Easy to get it into the kitchen and add it to the curry. I'd toured the poison garden a few years earlier, the Mrs had been an Agatha Christie fan, and Monkshood had been at the back of my brain ever since. Just needed someone to knock it to the front... if you get my meaning. Did my research. Three weeks in India. Smuggled some back and grew the stuff in my greenhouses... I can do anything when I put my mind to it... needed an extra greenhouse... Anyway, I hope the curry went down well... it doesn't touch the sides most of the time... should have caused a few casualties and a whole lot of sickness. The *shits* are on me, boys! Sorry – prison humour.

'So... I'm not sorry for what I've done... they deserved it.'

At this point, he removed his spectacles and cleaned them methodically on his lap, DS Quirke thought he'd forgotten he was being filmed, but then he put them back on. He measured the size of his head, using his hands as a reference before slowly smiling.

'It occurs to me you won't have seen my head before...'

He leant out of the shot before holding up a sawn-off to the camera.

'I am sorry for the inconvenience... the mess in the outside loo... I apologise to the poor sod that has to clean it up... One last request... I've asked to be buried next to my daughter... can you make sure this is placed in the grave...'

Mr Lambert chuckled at the camera before reaching forward… almost toppling as he cut the filming. The last thing in the frame was his hairpiece – the subject of his request.

*

Mr Lambert had a mobile phone. That was pink too – also a *hand-me-down* – an old Samsung recovered from the storage box on his moped. What it told DS Quirke was sadder than she expected… two social numbers only, his ex-wife and Maddie a co-worker at the prison kitchen. The call records gave them little. His wife had no prior knowledge of what he was going to do, their conversations were few and far between and Mr Lambert was frequently exasperated at the lack of his wife's coherence. The calls to Maddie showed he mainly contacted her late at night after too many single malts, offering her financial help, sometimes suggesting he was a better choice than her present boyfriend. He made garbled apologies for the clumsy advances he had made during supper at his house and begged her not to tell anyone. When he was sober it was fatherly advice, though his tone had changed after an assault at work, Mr Lambert becoming prone to furious outbursts aimed at her bad judgement. She had stopped going to Mr Lambert's house a few months after he had returned from India exasperated with his mood changes and his criticism of her love life.

The notepad from the bedroom gave more clues. It detailed the growing cycle and dangers of Monkshood; it included anecdotes of what could happen if you carelessly touched the leaves. It showed plans for the cultivation and preparation of the roots he intended to use in a curry menu. It detailed the amount required for each portion of food, to camouflage with sliced mushrooms, and the trips he would have to make to have enough inside the kitchen to *make a difference*. Further back in the notebook were scribblings detailing a war against the neighbours' dog, it showed a siege mentality and madness DS Quirke assumed had helped to tip him over the edge.

"So, Fred Lambert, who are you? My hero or a deranged psychopath?"

She reasoned no rational man sets out to poison a whole prison population. Long Stretch held over five hundred men, and she assumed many of them were diagnosed with personality disorders, but it seems the one person they should have been watching was *mild-mannered* Fred Lambert.

Houses of Parliament
OCTOBER 7th, 13:00
Address To the House: The Speaker of the House

'The Minister of State for Prisons would like to make another statement. Order! Order!'

'Due to the disturbances …'

'Order! Order!'

'Due to the disturbances in a number of Her Majesty's prisons … I have determined on robust action … I have invited various fast-food outlets to tender for the provision of three meals a day for every serving prisoner in the United Kingdom. This will I hope allay their fears … there can be no repeat occurrence. I believe this will put an end to the chaos and disruption in our prisons.

I can also add that the Long Service Medal awarded for 25 years' service … has been redacted in Mr Lambert's case …'

Chief of Police
OCTOBER 7th
STATEMENT TO THE PRESS

'The perpetrator of the mass poisoning at the local prison is a fifty-seven-year-old catering officer… No, the poisoning was not accidental… Yes. It was a deliberate action. I do not have a motive at present. He'd lived in Evebury for close to thirty years… No, he was not born there, and I suppose he was, therefore, not a 'local man'. The investigation is ongoing, but I believe he has taken his own life. I can't speculate further… I'd be putting my neck on the line… '

Evebury Journal
THURSDAY OCTOBER 10th, 2019
'Noisy Dog Neighbour, not from Evebury, Kills over 300 people.'

Houses of Parliament
OCTOBER 14th 2019
Address to The House: The Speaker of the House

'Order … Order … The Minister of State …Order … for prisons … would like to make a statement … Yes, he does …'

'Thank you …'

'Order! I really must have order! The honourable gentleman will be heard …'

'Thank you, Mr Speaker … I can confirm prisoners are being transferred back to HMP Long Stretch … contrary to an earlier decision … But I must insist … I must point out that each prisoner … ahem … each victim … each of the individuals are being asked if they wouldn't mind … are not averse to returning to the prison. It is not simply a matter of overcrowding … No! No … well I… ahem …I did say we did not have a problem with … ahem … overcrowding … Nobody could have foreseen it! Yes, I hear you … ahem …' (He checks his notes.)

'It is correct. The prison does have a new name, but I can assure you this was planned well before this tragedy. It is now HMP Middle Lartin … Purely procedure. Pressure on the estate … pressure on the prison population has left me with no alternative … I had no choice … The officers? What about the officers?

Houses of Parliament
OCTOBER 17th 2019, 13:00
Address to The House: The Speaker of the House

'The Minister … He wants to make a statement … Order!'
'Due to the shambolic state of the prison service over which I preside … It is with a heavy heart that I tender my resignation …

Chapter 11
OCTOBER 14th 2019, 10:00
Chief's Office
Open and shut

DS Quirke hovered by the door, outside the chief's office, listening to the conversation between the chief and Dyer.

"So, correct me if I'm wrong, DI Dyer, we do not have a maniac on the loose. We are not *looking for, interested in, would like to speak to* – dress it up any way you like, but we are not after *anybody* else in connection with the three hundred and sixteen deaths at Long Stretch. Answer me, man."

The Chief of Police wanted the noose tighter, and DS Quirke imagined his hands fiddling with an imaginary knot in his lap.

"It would appear so. I'm not happy about it though, it doesn't feel right, sir."

"Look, procrastinating, blithering fool! The Prime Minister, no less, have you heard of him? The Prime Minister is expected at noon, and I would like to draw a line under the whole sorry tale. There will be no need for a coroner, the old boys' network will see to that, we have to put an end to this as soon as possible. We have a mass poisoning – we have a perpetrator – we have a motive – we have a house crammed with evidence – we have a body... What *are* you saying, Dyer?"

"When you put it like that, sir, but surely the coroner will want to have a say, sir."

"Oh, I do, Dyer and let others worry about the blasted coroner! We have a formal identification of the body – Catering Officer Fred Lambert. Mr Knott does not have a problem. Suicide. Deranged. Him – not you – don't test me,

Dyer. The Prime Minister, you have heard of him, is very concerned about how unsettled the prisons are, some prisoners are refusing to eat, and there are disturbances at some establishments – we must ease their fears and get everything back to normal. Open and shut case. The Prime Minister—"

"I know who he is."

"You really are dire by nature as well as by name, aren't you? The Prime Minister is already working on a whole raft of measures to prevent this from happening again. He's even drafted Jamie *what's his name* to help alleviate the crisis."

"I'd heard he was at a loose end. It must be serious, sir."

"Don't be flippant with me, Dyer, I can see the wider picture. If the whole penal system collapses because of this incident and if convicted men refuse to go to prison due to fears about their safety, and you know what solicitors are like, then what happens to us, eh?"

In the silence, Quirke imagined Dyer frowning, his eyebrows tangling and the room darkening.

"Us, sir?"

"I mean the Police Force! We *nick 'em and we lock 'em up!* What happens if this is no longer the case? It's been like this for hundreds of years. What about our jobs in the future? If criminals are not in prison they'll be supervised in the community and who do you think will be responsible for that? Yes, Dyer, us and more specifically – me! We need to keep the status quo, *nick 'em and lock 'em up, and* then *forget* about them. No longer our problem. If the prison system is allowed to fail our whole job will change… We can't have that! It doesn't bear thinking about."

"If you put it like that, sir."

"Oh, I most certainly do, Dyer! For all our sakes, things need to get back to normal as soon as possible. Talk to whom you must... Interview people... Tie up the loose ends but I need to present a *closed file* to the Prime Minister this afternoon. Tomorrow at the latest. Am I understood? Submit the closed file in a couple of months if you want... with no nasty surprises but as of noon tomorrow, the case is closed. Am I understood?"

"Sir."

Chapter 12
OCTOBER 15th 2019
The Cat's Whiskers... A Loose End

One-hundred-and-twenty-two miles to go. Confined space with Dyer. Dyer's driving... he drives like DS Quirke's grandad... thirty-nine in a forty... sixty-nine in a seventy... hands in the correct position... she expected driving gloves... brown leather... but no gloves... must be the *large hands*... perhaps he can't get the size... or too expensive... price of three fully grown goat skins... or whatever they make driving gloves out of... pedantic signalling... braking in plenty of time... when she was a little girl the whole point of being a copper – fast cars, high-speed chases – but they are driving to Weymouth in Dyer's lease car to speak with Mrs Lambert... slowly... it's immaculate... gleaming on the outside... fully valeted on the inside... *tidy means clean and clear thought.* She wants to clear her nose in a loud wilful snort and spit a long jet of phlegm onto the windscreen.

How do you broach the subject? Can you tell us anything about your ex-husband that can explain if he was always capable of mass murder? Is there anything we should know, Mrs Lambert? Most killers work their way up the scale. Are there more bodies buried somewhere else?

"Yes, when I was a lad, I collected cigarette stubs. A very large collection. Different types of tobacco, you know, you could tell a lot by what people smoked – and in those days everybody smoked. You were odd if you didn't. And lollipop sticks... from the side of the road... had bags full of the things... could tell the type of lolly from the stick the manufacturer used... Not for any forensic stuff... not as useful as cigarette stubs... obviously... But I used to make roads out of them on the carpet for my buses... I had a large collection… Do you know anything about buses? My mother washed them first… the lollipop sticks, not the buses… See… I was always going to be a detective, collecting the stubs was a sign don't you think?"

The moustache didn't move. The monotone did not miss a beat. All DS Quirke could see from the corner of her eye was the bottom lip in continuous movement. *With a nose like that, why would you underline it?* She couldn't remember who said that. Not politically correct and she had to remember to do everything by the police manual these days. *Respect and courtesy.* Good luck with that! A couple of tiny red veins on the side of the left nostril – perhaps he wasn't a droid after all. The thought she could reach across and flick the tip of his enormous proboscis, and he wouldn't even flinch, messed with her mind. His dead-pan grey, blue eyes surveyed the road ahead and responded with mechanical efficiency… steady brake… fifth to fourth to third… match the speed of the car ahead… the two-second rule…

It occurred to DS Quirke she could straighten a hair on his left eyebrow, pull it to its limit and tie it to a rogue hair on his moustache. Was she in delirium? And then she saw it. A crumb, deep in the bristle, just to the left of the nostril… bread or shortbread? What did he have for breakfast anyway? She'd never asked. She didn't know the man. Well, she knew *everything* about him – the inane stories, the anecdotes, his life story – but not what he had for breakfast… did he eat alone… live alone? She didn't want to know. She attempted to live her life with Dyer avoiding all open questions as she did not want to spend the next three hours of her existence being lectured on her apparent lack of knowledge. This didn't stop him from talking. She sensed breakfast was a dangerous topic and said nothing – that was the rule.

His tongue flicked from his mouth. It was ghastly. She almost gagged. It daggered through the bristles, dislodged the crumb, caught it, and snapped back inside the mouth.

"When I was a lad, I virtually lived in the library. Read everything I needed to. Not the boring fiction stuff, I'll tell you about Dostoyevsky one day, but all the non-fiction books. A to Z. Clear mind, you see, from the beginning to the end, and do you know what I learned?"

She wasn't going to be tricked into an answer that easily.

"There was a lot of information, goes without saying, but the lesson I took away with me, apart from reading concisely and methodically, was even in the simple book, be it a hardback or soft – you can often see clues to the behaviour of human beings, be it good or bad, so many books are returned and left on the shelves with a page turned over at the corner!"

Oh, revelation.

"Sacrilege! So many books on the shelves with minor folds, tears, smudged fingerprints or worse – deposits of food and sometimes dead insects. Over fifty per cent in non-fiction and over eighty per cent in fiction – of course once I'd started, I had to check all the books in every section. I set out to smooth the pages, clean the smudges and remove all superfluous matter. If a job worth doing… It makes you wonder what we pay our librarians for, doesn't it? And missing pages? Less than two per cent. One summer when I was fifteen, I did every library in the county… And do you know the absolute truth it tells you about the wider public and their reading habits? No one can be trusted…"

A bit of a leap… DS Quirke had an image… There had been an arch-villain, always one step ahead of Dyer, she'd never been caught, an individual, probably a granny now in her nineties, randomly folding pages, leaving smudged fingerprints from her clotted cream fudge and streaks of jam from a scone in libraries everywhere… Perhaps she'd confess on her deathbed.

DS Quirke came to, she guessed when Dyer closed the driver's door. She'd broken one of her rules – *never fall asleep in the presence of a man* – but did Dyer count? Of course, he did! No one had ever suggested anything to be alarmed about with Dyer, there were no accusations, and there were no stories about alleged debauched behaviour. She was one to talk. She knew he was in love with himself and probably put women in a sub-category somewhere between pets and ice cream, but she was still annoyed. She knew it was in her head, but she smoothed her skirt, checked her blouse buttons, and flicked the sun visor down to look in the mirror. Perhaps she had an irrational fear of being violated, of being kissed by the caterpillar that lurked under Dyer's nose.

The passenger door opened.

"You can tell a lot by a man's fingernails. When I was a lad, I started to collect the stuff that accumulates under them… The premise of a science project… no one wanted to help me… science is a lonely pastime… got the teacher to back me… wore him down actually… anyway, I collected the muck from under the fingernails… all boys school… until I had to move but that's another story… about half didn't bite their nails… and I spent many an hour with a microscope I'd had for Christmas… you can tell a lot from the stuff under fingernails… with today's technology I could have got a distinction… I was ahead of the game… I was already destined to be a detective… Now, toenails are a different matter… You wouldn't think so, would you, but it's the smell… can be quite pungent… And where does it come from? Your typical toe is encased in a sock for sixteen hours a day, maybe more if you wear them in bed too, but where does the dark green stuff come from that you can collect after about a week or so? And why is it so pungent? Some I've collected have been quite attractive in a weird sort of way, you know, the first time you sniff it you pull away quite quickly, but you can't help having repeated sniffs until the odour becomes quite attractive... Other people's samples differ markedly... if it's kept in an airtight container, it becomes less pungent..."

Dyer was walking half a pace in front of her again; it didn't matter how wide the pavement, the office corridor, or a wide-open space like the car park, he was always in front. It was very annoying. It wasn't a sexist thing – he did it with everybody – male or female. It was like he wasn't really with her, or he was putting up with her in sufferance, perhaps he thought he was leading the way and it made her think of a tour guide. It didn't stop the inane, encyclopaedic commentary, she didn't think anything could once it had started. She'd tried to speed up in the beginning, but the distance remained the same, like a repulsed magnet, only she got breathless, and he didn't notice her effort. Perhaps he kept everybody at arms' length. She'd seen many use this habit to their advantage – if you timed it right you could slip through a door, take a left instead of a right with Dyer and break free of his presence. The next time he bumped into someone who'd pulled this trick he didn't acknowledge what had happened or even refer to their rudeness... she simply hadn't had the courage yet.

"You won't know this, but you can tell a lot about a person by the state of their nails." These were Dyer's last words before the front door was opened.

Mrs Lambert's nails were short. Bitten. They had striations and made DS Quirke think of a person at the bottom of a hole unable to gain purchase on smooth walls. The more she tried to avert her eyes the more she concentrated on them. Mrs Lambert tried to keep them clasped on her lap but could not resist the temptation to lift them to her mouth for a quick nibble. DS Quirke followed fingers to discoloured teeth, the teeth of a smoker, an ex-smoker (no ashtrays or any sign of a packet, smell or lighter) as she removed an imperceptible piece of skin, held it between her fingers before letting it drop to the floor.

Dyer had her where he wanted her. Pinned – surrounded on the sofa. She sat almost folding in on herself, making herself smaller, trying to give eye contact but failing, and only succeeding in looking up and down repeatedly. She was in Dyer's power. The large hands at close quarters, one false move and she would be origami: a horse, or, more appropriately for Mrs Lambert, a baby rabbit about to be snaffled by a fox.

"So, Mrs Lambert, think carefully before you answer. It is a simple question. Where are your tea bags? You stated clearly, I have it on record, you wanted my colleague to make a pot of tea, but to our consternation when my colleague entered the kitchen, she duly reported an absence of the tea bags under question... Now is that a clear and precise statement of the matter in hand?"

"I get flummoxed, I do..." Mrs Lambert looked like she was about to cry.

"Do not move, Mrs Lambert... Look me in the eye and tell me where the tea bags are..."

"I'm not trying to be difficult. I'm a bit absent-minded sometimes..." she sniffed.

"PG or Yorkshire? When was the last time you had a cup of tea, Mrs Lambert?"

"Elevenish. PG by the way. Is this important?" she padded a tear that had formed at the side of her eye.

"Getting your measure, Mrs Lambert. Why eleven?"

"My programme finishes. I have a couple of biscuits…" another sniff.

"Something for the cat?"

"A couple of treats is all, she knows I go to the kitchen then…" Mrs Lambert's face brightens at the mention of her cat.

"Which cupboard are the treats in, Mrs Lambert?"

"On the right as always, I don't mix our food up."

DS Quirke found the tea bags. Large sugar for Dyer though he didn't take sugar. He didn't say anything.

Mrs Lambert had left Fred several years ago – a year to the day that their daughter had died – though she struggled to remember how many years ago that was. She stated dully from her point of view she had nothing to live for. The life had been sucked from her by the tragedy – as DS Quirke studied her face, she could easily see what she meant. Imagine a balloon starting to deflate or better still a beach ball partly inflated but concave on one side. She pictured someone poking a finger in her face telling her to *snap out of it*, and each time the face sunk a little further, collapsing inward – concave from the forehead to the chin. If the eyes had the power to focus sharply, they would have been cross-eyed. Without a doubt, the strength of the tranquilisers accounted for the blank expression; the irony of losing a daughter to drugs and seeing the mother like this was not lost on DS Quirke.

"Mrs Lambert… when was the last time you spoke to your husband… or should that be your ex-husband?" Dyer persisted though DS Quirke thought it was a hopeless case, part of her wanted to pin the cat against the wall and play the bad cop until she talked and gave them something worthwhile, but the cat would have been a *gonna*. Mrs Lambert knew nothing.

"Not 'ex', inspector, we never divorced."

"I see."

"No reason to. He's married to his job. And I've got… my cat… Neither of us is likely to…"

"So, when was the last time…?"

"Difficult to remember… Let me think… Days get all mixed up, don't you see… What's the date today? And you say he's dead? My Fred is dead, you say?"

"Yes, Mrs Lambert, somebody from the police will have told you this and you must have seen it on the news. The biggest story for years," Dyer sighed, and part of DS Quirke willed him to slap her but then she remembered she was supposed to do everything by the book. *Use of force* protocol.

"Not one for the news, inspector, you say he died in an accident?"

"Not exactly, Mrs Lambert. A few days ago, can you remember where you were?" Dyer persisted.

"Yes… Well, no… Not exactly… I expect I was here… I don't go many places."

"Please do not cry, Mrs Lambert, do not worry… it's not that important," Dyer stood up abruptly, DS Quirke jumped back against the wall as he stretched and took a casual walk around the room… with his large stride she counted five for a lap… he surveyed the room in his deliberate manner… an untidy room, even by DS Quirke's standards, nothing in its place, nothing put away properly, and even she could see it needed the vacuum cleaner… and the dust… It must have taken all of Dyer's self-control to force himself to sit on the edge of a chair containing ginger cat hair and biscuit crumbs. And then Dyer surprised DS Quirke… he picked up a discarded TV magazine, perused a couple of stories on the page that was folded open, rolled it up and slapped his open palm with it. DS Quirke took a step forward to stop him from whacking Mrs Lambert around the head.

"Do you think he did it, Mrs Lambert?" Dyer surprised them both with the question.

"Who?" Mrs Lambert replied automatically. She stared into space... a solitary tear toppled from a glazed eye.

"It could have been anyone in the car, Mrs Lambert, and now the police have him, and poor Gail on life support unable to say who ran her over... It's a disgrace... What do you think, Mrs Lambert?" Dyer was picking up the pace.

DS Quirke was at a loss. What was Dyer going on about? He seemed possessed but there was a flicker in the corner of Mrs Lambert's eye.

"Mrs Lambert, three to one, it was Mick Jones driving the car and not poor Tom!"

"Yes... he's a bad one, all right, Bob would never do such a thing... would he?"

"He most certainly would not!"

"Poor Gail, do you think she'll pull through, Mr Dyer... Gail, I mean, she's been through such a lot over the years, hasn't she?"

"Too much, Mrs Lambert, too much, she deserves a break... I've always had a soft spot for her."

"Do you remember when she drowned in Majorca?"

"Nearly drowned. And was left unconscious with carbon monoxide poisoning?"

"And almost died giving birth to Simon?"

"Don't forget the stairs in the hotel in Blackpool... Trevor the psycho Porsche dealer."

"You're right, Mr Dyer, she's a survivor..."

Dyer paused. DS Quirke almost looked at him, but she was saved by the look on Mrs Lambert's face, she was becoming animated, almost inflating with every breath Dyer fed her on some pathetic soap story. And then Dyer threw the curve ball.

"And when was the last time you spoke to your husband, Mrs Lambert?"

"It was just before Gail was seen kissing Christopher through the office window... I knew it would lead to something bad..."

"What did Mr Lambert say?" Dyer tapped the notebook in DS Quirke's hands to make sure she got the details down.

"... he said he was sorry... sorry for everything... he was going to make things right... he said it was about time he got off his fat backside... make amends... justice for our... our... I can't say *her* name, our daughter... sorry for any inconvenience... and sorry for calling when my programme was on... simply, sorry for the fuss it was going to create... *don't speak to the reporters,* he said... She shouldn't have kissed him, should she?"

"No, she should not, but she never learns. And the time before that, Mrs Lambert?"

"Gail was still working in the café then... she hadn't even met Christopher... she hadn't even dyed her hair in that awful bob..."

Ten minutes later Dyer was satisfied with the information. Not the most conventional questioning she had ever been a party to, and she knew she'd be the one to cross-reference the soap storyline to confirm when Fred Lambert had been in contact, she was good at that, but she almost allowed herself the smallest, begrudging, amount of respect for Dyer.

They got back in the car in silence. Unusual. DS Quirke didn't want to give him any openings, they had another long drive ahead, perhaps she didn't want to break his chain of thought... she'd been impressed... almost... but putting the seat belt on, the click like a starter's pistol set him off.

"Another victim, don't you think, Quirky?"

DS Quirke raised an eyebrow; it was a moment of weakness in a long day, but it was enough...

"Opium of the people. Used to be religion. Karl Marx. I think you'll find. You have heard of him? But now it's television, or more specifically these days, technology. Mobile phones. It shouldn't be, 'God, where is my phone?' but, 'God is my phone!' Can't live without it. Life is based entirely around them. It brings joy... it brings despair... it brings purpose. *They* pray to it first thing in the morning, succumb to it during the day and kneel to it with a word of thanks last thing at night."

DS Quirke pushed her phone deeper into her pocket.

"But in Mrs Lambert's case, clearly television... and more specifically... the soaps... Notice the TV guides – open to the soap gossip stories, and the magazine rack full of copies of soap-based reports..."

DS Quirke heard a trumpet blowing.

"Doctors, Emmerdale, Coronation Street... a certain generation call it *The Street*... Neighbours, Home and Away..."

She regretted not putting a couple of Mrs Lambert's tranquilisers in her tea... after a few minutes, it felt like she may have done.

She woke up when the car door slammed again. Quick check in the mirror... everything was in its place. Good. Back to the station...

"… There are seven actors… or actresses, to be politically correct, who have been in four or more of the main British soaps… just to prove my point… money for old soap… ha! Money for old rope… get it?"

*

OCTOBER 16th 2019
Number 15
Why Keep a Dog… Another Loose End

DS Quirke quite liked Mrs Tyler. Brash, defended *her territory* against all comers and instantly disliked Dyer. Dyer had let DS Quirke tie this loose end up on her own.

Her knock on the door was answered by a young girl who immediately sized-up DS Quirke's appearance – sensible shoes, black tights, knee-length plain skirt, blouse, and matching jacket.

"Mam, it's *the filth*, again!"

DS Quirke put a finger to her lips, "Tell your mom it's a drug raid."

The door closed abruptly and two minutes later Mrs Tyler's head appeared round the door.

"Aren't you supposed to kick the door down if it's a drug raid?"

"You've got me, it was a fib… as you can see, I have not parked on your drive… and I'm unarmed."

"Unarmed?"

"Without a man at my side! Any chance of a cup of tea?"

"That's almost funny… You've got a nerve… I've told your lot everything about the…"

"Deceased," DS Quirke interjected quickly.

"I was going to say, *mass murderer,*" Mrs Tyler was a straight talker.

"I believe he killed your dog… We have something in common there."

"What ya saying?"

"I ran over a dog once on my way to work. Killed it stone dead."

She paused, "Almost funny, again… I think you're a bit strange if you don't mind me saying."

"Now that'll be the two of us, then."

"Do you have sugar and milk in your coffee?"

Mrs Tyler was from a large travellers' family and knew how to fight dirty. Much of her aggression was bravado, however, and once DS Quirke was inside her whole demeanour softened. The house was immaculate. Tidy. Her daughter offered cakes and biscuits she had baked that morning.

The feud had started years ago, she couldn't remember exactly, something about Fred bad-mouthing her to the dog, calling her an unfit mother, a slag, and a disgrace to dog owners. Mrs Tyler acknowledged it had gotten out of hand. Tyson had been a noisy dog, but he was the only thing preventing a violent ex-husband from sneaking around the house. Tyson had been the hero on a couple of occasions, saving her from a beating. She hadn't meant the feud to get out of hand but without realising it she had fallen into *all men are the enemy* camp and Fred had become the figurehead.

On the evening of Mr Lambert's suicide and the poisonings at the prison, it had been the moped on his drive that had told her he was home. She thought he'd had the moped modified deliberately, it backfired alarmingly when it sat idle. She showed DS Quirke the speakers and the recording of the dog she'd played whenever Mr Lambert was at home… she'd continued to chip away at Fred, messing with his head, taunting him with the barking… she recognised it hadn't been the most grown-up thing she'd ever done… but she had been devastated when Tyson had died in the freak accident… She *may* have tipped Fred over the edge.

DS Quirke got the impression if Mrs Tyler had known Fred had a shotgun there would have been a mini arms race. She would have had the means to get weapons too. As for the fateful shot… when the recording of the dog was played, and the television turned up so her daughter could watch her programmes, it would have been unlikely either of them could have heard anything at all.

The daughter pulled at DS Quirke's sleeve and said, "One man gone bad and then, in one night, all the bad men gone. Just like my daddy."

Chapter 13
OCTOBER 17th 2019
HMP Middle Lartin
Keeping a secret

It was one o'clock in the afternoon. The surviving prisoners at The Stretch were locked up and DS Quirke was being escorted down empty corridors by Officer Underhill.

"In all my days I'd never have believed it. Just goes to show, don't it, Miss, you can't judge a book by the reader… Fred Lambert, a mass murderer! Who'd have believed it?" He unlocked a heavy metal gate and an inner wooden door.

"This isn't the entrance to the kitchen we used on that night," DS Quirke observed.

"No, Miss, I can't get anything passed you, can I? This is the entrance the prisoners use when they come to work in the kitchen. It's easier for me, that's all, the entrance we used before is further down the corridor and round the corner. The officers use that one when they collect the food trolleys." Officer Underhill led her through a small passage pointing at discarded *whites* on the floor in a changing room. "Prisoners haven't worked in here since that night as we don't need that many prepared meals at the moment."

He pushed another door open, and DS Quirke recognised the kitchen where they had found the Deputy Governor dead on the floor.

"The other door must be over there, yes?" she asked.

"You're right, and who said women had no sense of direction? There's another door over there, to the left, that is used when supplies are delivered. I'll leave you here, Miss, Maddie's in the office over there, the truth is she doesn't like us officers coming in the kitchen willy-nilly and says it's a matter of hygiene. Get her to ring the centre and I'll collect you when you've finished."

DS Quirke tapped on the glass panel on the office door. Maddie's attention was fixed on the computer screen, a spreadsheet scrolling, and though she knew DS Quirke was on the way, she still made a show of reluctantly pulling herself away.

"Miss Madeline Butchart, I'm DS Quirke, West Mercia…"

"I hope this won't take long, I've got the evening meal to prepare, as well as an order to submit for next week's supplies… and I've already given a statement to one of your colleagues…"

"I think there are over three hundred fewer meals to prepare, not including the prisoners that have since transferred out of here to other prisons, so how many meals *are* you in such a hurry to make?" DS Quirke took the wind from her sails.

Maddie stopped, took a deep breath, and the angst left her face she tried to smile.

"You're right," she sat down, "There's less than a hundred left. I don't even need help to prepare the food," she covered her face with her hands, "I can do it with my eyes closed. I'm sorry, DS Quirke…"

"Call me, Liz."

"I'm sorry, Liz, I shouldn't even be here. At work I mean, but someone's got to keep things ticking over. Can we start again? I've got chocolate in my bottom drawer and the coffee's fresh."

Maddie made two mugs of coffee and placed a large, opened block of Cadburys on the desk as a peace offering. DS Quirke saw a woman in her mid-thirties, very thin, with no curves at all, her eyes plastered with make-up, made stark by the pallid colour of her face, neck and forearms. She'd been stood next to the steamer or over a bubbling Bain Marie too often and she'd been blanched. Her hair had been bleached blond for too long and looked brittle and frazzled.

"I shouldn't be here. Every day I sit here knowing Robert was poisoned in this kitchen and his body was discovered right there," she pointed at the floor and sniffed back tears as she averted her eyes.

"How long had you been seeing Deputy Governor Whitmore, sorry, Robert?"

"Only a few months, Liz, but I'm not getting any younger and I thought we could have had a future together."

DS Quirke listened for a while about, Robert Whitmore's virtues and the promises he had made before she turned to the purpose of her visit.

"What was Fred Lambert like?"

Maddie snapped a piece of chocolate and popped it in her mouth and added some more coffee from the jug to her mug.

"Fred was lovely. Kind. One of the kindest men I've ever met. He took me under his wing and taught me how to run the kitchen. I wouldn't be sat here if it wasn't for him…"

"What were you doing before you started here?" DS Quirke asked.

"Catering assistant in an institute in South Wales. An old people's home. I moved to get away from an ex. My little boy's father. Knocking me about a bit, you know how it is…"

"And Fred took you under his wing? Any more to it than that?"

"It's hard, Liz, Fred was a father figure to me. I'm sat here all day and his presence still fills the place. I see his scribble and signature everywhere, they're his systems of work, it's his tidiness… I think his mark will always be in this kitchen. I still can't believe what he's done. All those men. Dead."

"And you had no inkling, Maddie, what he was up to?" DS Quirke prodded.

"Nothing at all. He ruled the kitchen We all did what he said. He was a professional and prided himself on running the best kitchen he could. Why now, Liz, why after all the years in the job? Something must have snapped, don't you think?"

"Was he only a *father figure*, Maddie?" DS Quirke poked her again.

Maddie was silent. DS Quirke thought she was about to speak on a couple of occasions, but Maddie closed her mouth and fidgeted with her mug. Eventually, the silence was too much, and she began again.

"I didn't want to say this. It doesn't seem fair to speak about him in a bad way, now he's no longer... with us... and I'm fond of him. Was fond of him. I've been to his house on a few occasions."

"Go on."

"For a drink. And he bought food when I first moved here, and I was short of cash, you understand? He was harmless, Liz, a lonely middle-aged man," Maddie looked at everything in the office except DS Quirke, "He had too much to drink, he liked his whiskey, and he made a fumbling pass at me, he grabbed me round the waist and tried to kiss me. I pushed him off. He was sorry afterwards."

"And he *begged* you not to tell anyone?" DS Quirke referred to one of the lines she'd recovered from Fred's pink mobile phone.

Maddie opened her mouth but stopped. DS Quirke noticed the pause and waited again for Maddie to decide to continue. A couple of minutes later Maddie said, "Fred had a

108

secret. I promised not to tell anyone. He *begged* me not to tell anyone. I found something in his wardrobe. He used to cross-dress once a month. He caught a taxi to Birmingham and walked round the shopping centre dressed as a woman. He called himself Brenda. Are you shocked? I never told anyone before. I suppose I was protecting him. I didn't want it in the papers."

"I'm not shocked, Maddie, I assure you."

"I'll tell you something, Liz, he was a changed person after the assault."

"How did he change?" DS Quirke stifled a giggle when both were struggling with an image of Fred Lambert *changing* into one of the dresses that had been hanging up in his wardrobe.

"He was unconscious. He banged his head against the side of one of the cooking vessels. He was less patient after that, especially when he returned from India, after his sick leave, things were not the same between us. He was more short-tempered, and we argued about my relationship with Robert all the time. But I swear I kept his secret."

"I'm sure you did, Maddie."

Maddie shortly afterwards called the centre for Officer Overhill and as they waited for him to arrive the two of them stood next to the brass bell used by Fred Lambert to call for silence before the trolleys were allowed to leave the kitchen.

"Do you know, Liz, when this has died down, I'm thinking I'll get the bell engraved on the inside, so his name will live on in his kitchen."

Chapter 14
Dotting the Deano…

DS Quirke watched as Dyer tried not to go ballistic.

"And when can I collect the car exactly? You don't know? Why is that, exactly? Because the car is no longer there? What do you mean it's been stolen?"

DS Quirke edged closer to Dyer to get in the ideal fielding position for his eyes if they popped out of his head. He placed the receiver on the desk, licked his index fingers, and then smoothed his eyebrows with exaggerated strokes. Picking up the receiver.

"One moment, please," he put the receiver down again, licked his index fingers again, and clasped his scalp through his hair… it occurred to DS Quirke he was about to have a fit, "Does your car park… which is a prison, I'll point out… have CCTV? It does! Excellent! Broken? Lack of funding? I'll have to report it as *stolen* to the police. I am the bloody!"

Fred Lambert had been the victim of a nasty assault in the kitchen at the Long Stretch a few months before he poisoned most of the prison population. The perpetrator had been transferred *up north* after the incident and to satisfy themselves that the two were not linked Dyer and Ds Quirke made the long journey for an interview. DS Quirke had discovered prisoner Dean Walters had had the good fortune to miss the mass poisoning at Long Stretch, but his luck had been short-lived; a check of his prison record had shown he had been targeted recently by other prisoners and had been scolded, battered with frozen water bottles, and stabbed with a bladed weapon. Walters was in the hospital again as Dyer and DS Quirke travelled by train, the chief having learned of the stolen Police car and had stated he was not prepared to risk another one.

"Chewing gum is another one, Quirky, at one time it was everyone, wasn't it?"

Quirke didn't answer. She had been hopeful that the noise and motion of the train would sedate Dyer, causing him to fall asleep like most mortals… but he wasn't like other people.

"It was British Rail when I was a lad. Nationalised. Some argue it was a better service back then… but… chewing gum was everywhere. I noticed it, most people wouldn't, unless they sat on it, and it occurred to me that if I collected samples of the discarded gum I could become somewhat of an expert. Always carried little plastic pockets with me. Destined to be a detective. In the seventies, there were considerably more makes of chewing gum than there are today. Do you know how many, Quirky?"

Please, God, she vowed to become a nun if only…

"You weren't even born, how would you? Suffice it to say, I had two drawers full of the stuff neatly labelled. Head of the game again, wasn't I? With today's science, any gum left at a crime scene would immediately trap a suspect with their DNA. Pity the craze for gum seems to have waned…"

DS Quirke daydreamed of the missed opportunities. If only the detectives had had the foresight to collect all the chewing gum discarded by the criminals in the act of their crimes, armed robbers sticking gum to the van before demanding with menace, 'Give us all your money!', the heads of the criminal world sticking their gum on the underside of the table, never expecting to be identified years later… one fatal mistake…' it was the gum that did it for us!'

Her eyes had been closed for twenty minutes before he stopped talking. She pretended to sleep, her fear of falling asleep in the presence of men was heightened on public transport, and it was hard to sit there, head resting on the window, a sliver of light giving her a distorted view of the world, without succumbing. She practised random eye movements in case he caught her. She knew if she dared to open one eye for a millisecond it would be over – another monologue would resume like the pause button being deactivated. The light she filtered had another disadvantage, it allowed her to observe a sneaky fat finger dislodge a flake of nasal matter, and with the disguise of stroking his moustache, flick it adroitly onto his tongue.

Walters was in a side room away from other patients, under the guard of prison officers, the youngest of which was cuffed to him by a chain; DS Quirke found the chain disturbingly exciting. Walters himself was also in a set of solid handcuffs keeping his wrists locked together. Though the interview had been arranged through the Governor at Sull Futton and the prison staff must have been aware of their impending arrival, as Dyer pushed open the door, two of the staff visibly started as if they'd been kipping, and DS Quirke saw Walters nudge the officer to whom he was attached to wake him up. Walters was visibly scared at their arrival, he shrank against the pillow, and as they pulled IDs from jacket pockets, DS Quirke thought he was going to grab the officer to use him as a shield.

"DI Dyer and DS, ahem, DS Quirke... West Mercia Serious Crime Unit," Dyer introduced them.

Walters relaxed when he saw no gun and became a surly prisoner again. He would have smiled but a scar which ran from his mouth toward his left ear stopped him.

"I ain't saying nothing,"

"Young man, you just said something," and addressing the prison staff, "Any chance we could have a *private word* with young Walters?"

"Last time I had a *private word* it broke my nose! Boss don't leave me with these 'wrong'uns." Walters said.

"For someone who isn't saying anything…"

"I can't remove the closeting chain, but two of us can go for a coffee… if you don't mind our colleague. It's the procedure, I'm afraid," the officer in charge apologised.

"I suppose it will have to do," DS Quirke could tell Dyer had had enough of arguing against the *procedure*. When they were almost alone with Walters, she pointedly made eye contact with the young prison officer and said, "Anything said in this room comes under rule 323, in that 'anything repeated or reported back without our say so will lead to criminal prosecution with a maximum of ten years custodial prison sentence'… Is that clear?" she bluffed, trying to ignore the line, *respectful of the authority and influence her position gave her,* from the code of ethics.

The young officer blushed and stammered,

"Yes, of course, 323," and managed to move his chair a couple of feet from the bed to show his complete detachment. She tapped his knee, leaving her finger there longer than necessary, making his face turn even redder.

"Good lad."

"I still ain't saying nothing," Walters turned his nose to the wall.

"Mr Walters, you do not know why we're here," Dyer with feigned exasperation.

"Well… it wasn't me," Walters tried to look away, but Dyer's moustache was starting to work.

"Walters, Dean. *Deano*, whatever do you mean? Of course, it was you."

"Eh?"

"Deano, tell us what you didn't do if you like, I'm not particularly interested, but if you feel you must bore me with the details…"

DS Quirke thought that was a bit rich. She took a step backwards and inadvertently nudged the young officer's shoulder with her bottom.

"Well, I… didn't punch that officer… or assault Crisp in the showers… or put spice in the Governor's coffee…"

"Good, that's all out of the way. I want to talk about Fred Lambert."

Walters paused. Cogs working. DS Quirke saw a fleeting look of realisation, then of horror, that he was *well and truly fucked…*

"Oh, fuck! It wasn't me… Oh, fuck… you can't think… I'm out in three years…"

"But it was, wasn't it?"

"You gonna frame me for all of them poisonings? I was the onion peeler! I know I've done some bad things… is it payback… I'm out in three years!"

Dyer stopped talking. Hard to believe. She reached behind the officer for a glass of water, letting her left breast accidentally caress the back of his neck. *Discreditable conduct?*

"… don't do it, man. I know nothing about it… I sell drugs in prison… I don't give nothing away for free… I use a bit too… Why would I kill my customers? No profit in that, man… no way… I ain't never getting out if you frame me for this. I was the onion peeler!"

Dyer let him finish. There was a single tear running down Walters' cheek.

"Deano, you're a villain, a bad man, a thug, a piece of vile excrement… but you do not have the brains or audacity to carry out such a crime."

"Oh, thanks, man… thank you…" a wide smile lit up Walters' face.

"What you did, was to assault Fred Lambert in the kitchen… remember… he bumped his head… knocked him unconscious…"

"I thought I'd killed him! But I didn't! You can't charge me for that! It's been dealt with, I got fourteen extra days on my sentence for that…" Walters railed against the injustice.

"Deano, you are what we call a loose end, and that's all… nothing more. You were there, in the kitchen… you had a couple of run-ins with Lambert. Just tell us what you remember about him… anything out of the ordinary…"

Ten minutes later DS Quirke summarised what he had told them. "You did not like him. He was firm but fair. He had too many rules. He made you work… God forbid… and he had a hairpiece… and everyone knew this…"

That's all they learned. The taxpayer would not have been happy funding the trip, but before they left, DS Quirke managed to breathe *call me* into the young officer's ear as she slipped her number into his shirt pocket when no one was looking.

When they left, Walters was smiling and full of life. He liked being the centre of attention. DS Quirke when she eventually closed the case file had to add the fact that Walters had been found hanged in a cell three weeks after their interview.

Chapter 15
Chief's Office
OCTOBER 23rd, 15:00
Case Closed… No ifs no buts…

'Rule 323?' the text grabbed DS Quirke's attention straight away. Another one dangling on the line. They sat at the Chief of Police's table, and he was informing Dyer the case was officially closed.

"No *buts*, Dyer, do you understand? The PM has been informed – do not go and upset the bloody apple cart – it is finished. There is a modicum of order re-established in our prisons – the 'Oliver Initiative' has been a PR success and there are now checks in place to prevent this sort of thing from happening again!"

DS Quirke had an image of a very obese prisoner sitting at a desk in every prison kitchen sampling the food before it left the kitchen. A well-paid and specialist position.

'If U brk R323 U sffr the cons,' she replied, '+ U av by txt me!' Her fingers squeezed the rubber testicle in her pocket.

"Dyer, do you understand? Please acknowledge," the chief continued, "there is no room for a loose cannon, we must move forward now, and it is an *open and shut case*."

"B…"

"No bloody *buts*, Dyer! Do I make myself clear?"

"Something does not smell right," Dyer was at his most pig-headed.

"Look, Dyer, with all that hair under your nose, I'm surprised you can smell anything at all… except what you had for lunch! It's over… RIGHT!"

"Right, sir."

"As for you, DS Quirke, stop bloody texting… does anyone under thirty ever do anything that does not involve a bloody smartphone?"

"Don't know, Chief, I'd have to Google the answer."

"Don't be a smart arse, DS Quirke, or you'll stay with *him* indefinitely – that reminds me, make sure he gets that bloody car back, will you? It wasn't stolen, after all, as I was duly informed, just misplaced, and the chap at the prison is willing to accept a full face-to-face apology if you park in the bloody correct parking space – this will happen Dyer, or I will make sure I put you on as many disciplinary charges as I can think of! I hear there's a little promotion in the pipeline for the unfortunate sod you have assaulted, threatened, and ignored."

"Sir, if I may interject."

"No, Dyer, you may not! It's gone on long enough. Apologise and get the damned car back!"

"Sir."

In the toilet, DS Quirke called the Rule 323 breaker.

"I could do a lot to you, Prison Officer Andrew Childs. The fact you are young makes you eminently corruptible… if you get my meaning," she heard a gulp at the end of the line.

"I don't think I do… know what you mean… I mean."

"If you should find yourself in my neck of the woods, the next time you have a couple of days off, I will personally see to it – that you are disciplined for your flagrant breach of Rule 323…"

"Will it be painful?"

"Mostly… pleasurable, I can assure you… but you're young enough to make a full recovery… maybe," she pouted at the mirror.

"I don't know what to make of you?" he stammered.

"But, Andrew, *Andy*, I know exactly what I can make of you… Courage, my young man, is all you need… Call me when you visit… And I feel that you *will* visit…" She hung up and hoped she hadn't scared him too much.

And that appeared to be that. DS Quirke placed a hand on the file. A mass poisoning. A confession. A perpetrator. A suicide. The case had been in the headlines for weeks, Lambert had succeeded in writing his name in history, and he would be right up there in the cases of notoriety – Jack the Ripper, the Wests, Harold Shipman, and *Frederick Lambert*. Some said he was simply settling the score with the *bad men*, the murderers, serial killers and rapists, though the reality was a man who had had some kind of breakdown, tipped over the edge by a head injury (not that they had a brain to examine), a man who had suddenly cracked like the wall of a dam, turning the years of anger and resentment caused by the death of his only daughter by drug misuse, to give a man with the opportunity (through his job) to exact the ultimate revenge – the poisoning of three hundred and sixteen prisoners and one Deputy Governor (and the accidental death of a dog). Justice?

DS Quirke knew the headlines would subside, and the prisons would gradually return to normal – sporadic violence, assaults, drug abuse – the usual. She'd read of a couple of likely *lags* attempting to get their sentences quashed stating 'prison was no longer a safe or suitable environment in which to serve a custodial sentence'. There was even talk of reform and laws were being discussed making it mandatory for prisons to allow food parcels from relatives to be sent in from outside (the Victorians had led the way). She was amused to read a prison in London had already trialled the idea but with unforeseen results. Statistics quickly highlighted a sharp increase in cases of food poisoning from the parcels being allowed in.

She wasn't ready for the case to be closed, and though she wasn't *backing* Dyer exactly, there was an odd feeling she couldn't quite put her finger on. Not one for being sentimental she tried to brush it off but when she closed her eyes at night, she saw Fred Lambert risking his own life to pull her from the river. She squeezed the rubber ball, the same ball her mom had found in her coat pocket on the day her life had been saved. He must have put it there and it had been her lucky mascot ever since. There had to be more.

Chapter 16
Chief's Office
OCTOBER 23rd, 16:00
But he's a legend…

DS Quirke was about to put the closed file on the chief's desk; a sheet of paper refused to fall in line with the rest and she slipped it out and re-read an interview with one of Mr Lambert's colleagues, someone who had known him for close to thirty years and probably knew him better than most. It had been an informal chat in a pub not too far from the prison, he'd approached her on the occasion she'd been forced to accompany Dyer to The Stretch to make the apology over the car clamping incident. He hadn't approached them, in truth, he'd intervened to stop *the apology* from becoming a fistfight – Dyer had parked in the wrong place again, deliberately, and the exchanges with the Officer Service Grade had escalated from there.

Officer Davis could not believe what had happened. He described Fred as the following:

'The man that had pushed an old Escort car from The Stretch to Evebury Town Hall on his own for charity – nearly eight miles. The man who had volunteered on several occasions during his service to remain in the prison overnight during snowstorms or severe flooding to make sure everyone, staff, and prisoners, got a hot meal.

The man who had championed and promoted *drug awareness* and the anti-drug agenda – who had run courses in his own time to help young prisoners lead a healthier lifestyle. This was the man who had calmed Blowers down on Charlie Wing when he'd already stabbed three prisoners and knocked two officers out cold, thus getting first aid to all involved and saving lives.

The man who'd helped Officer Davis come to terms with his marriage break-up and resulting depression. He'd carried him then and physically in yet another sponsored event in the gymnasium – and had been the last man standing in the fireman's lift challenge.

The man was one of the most respected men he had ever worked with. The younger staff had no idea. This was the same man who once turned into the prison driveway on his moped, unaware the barrier had been lowered due to heightened security in the aftermath of 9/11, and had been removed from the moped like a knight with a lance in a joust, left dangling,

momentarily, as his moped continued, weaving drunkenly toward the prison entrance, before sliding to the tarmac floor. Two cracked ribs and a damaged moped and he still completed his shift!'

Lambert had been a *legend* and Officer Davis was baffled. DS Quirke wiped a tear from her cheek and replaced the piece of paper in the file. She was confused about the man she owed her life to.

PART TWO

Chapter 17
20 MONTHS EARLIER
The Real Fred Lambert…

The high pitch of the alarm clock did its job and cut through the hair and ear wax. Fred Lambert fumbled for black-rimmed spectacles on the bedside cabinet and reinstated the silence. The *hallowed silence.* The curtains let enough light in to make the use of a bedside lamp a luxury. He pushed himself to a seated position and placed the pillow behind him, the pyjama bottoms had pulled down slightly with the friction and he used the duvet to cover himself before he checked the other side of the bed; his wife had been gone close to twenty years, but he still checked the pillow was in place and the duvet not pulled across too much. He squinted at a wristwatch to confirm the time, twenty-three minutes past five and reached to the bedside table for his hairpiece. Seven minutes to go.

The slight whistle when he breathed irritated him. He sniffed strongly to cure it but only made himself cough; he held his breath for as long as he could to reinstate the silence, the silence, it wasn't very long, he was unfit, overweight, and getting on a bit. The silence was something to treasure – something you didn't know how precious it was until you'd lost it. The throb he could feel on the side of his head interrupted the silence and this irritated him. Five minutes to go.

Fred felt for a pulse on his wrist but couldn't find one. Dead then? He smiled – death held no fear, he didn't have a lot to live for and he wouldn't be missed. His wrists were thick and the pads on his fingers had lost their sensitivity, though he acknowledged with self-effacement they were his best feature, or they at least looked younger than the rest of him. His wife used to say the neck and the hands are the first to go, as she clipped him round the ear when an attractive young woman on one of *her soaps* caught his attention for too long. He'd like to show her his hands now! The varnish and the glue he used in his furniture restoration must be embalming them... perhaps he should try it on his face? The fact he seemed to have lost motivation in this hobby of late and half-finished projects were lying around the two-bed house also irritated him. Two minutes to go.

The bed groaned as Fred shifted his weight, the hairs pulling on his bottom irritated him, his wife would have put him on a diet long ago, and she surely would not have let him get into this state. Well, not before their daughter died at any rate. The peril of the job, his excuse, he had to test every batch of food leaving the prison kitchen before it was consumed by Her Majesty's guests. All five hundred of them. Motivation was key – and he did not have any... retirement was fast approaching and after that... he had no plans.

His wife had got it right after all. 'Why don't you do something? You just sit there on your backside not doing anything. You're all words and no action, Fred, that's right go back to the kitchen, never mind your daughter, and take your mind off her!' It had been an accusation back then and it had been his way of coping. All those years of *just coping* were coming to an end. What a life! Five-thirty exactly.

The dog next door began to bark causing Fred to clench his fists.

"Bloody dog!"

He released his fingers, tried to put into practice the breathing exercises the doctor had suggested and tried to relax. It was the continuous bark, high pitched, four or five in a row… count them… he tapped the rhythm with a finger on the duvet cover… a pause for a dog breath… four or five in a row… a pause… four or five in a row… a pause… God, he was almost hypnotised and put into a trance-like state. Wake up! Retrieving a notebook from the cabinet he wrote, 'Do not give the enemy the satisfaction of knowing they are the enemy.' After all, this was Level 2 barking, nothing to worry about, this was the *fallback* position, the *go-to* average barking… nothing out of the ordinary. Expected and not unexpected – he made a note of that, 'only the unexpected can truly defeat a man, and when you begin to expect the unexpected, you can never truly lose…'

Every morning was the same. Five-thirty. The Alsatian dog was kicked out of the kitchen next door and chained to a post in the back garden where it would bark nonstop until *she* left the house. *She* was unemployed, had probably never had a job, a single mother, with a little girl, a monster of about ten years of age. She was at home most of the time, therefore, the dog barked most of the time. At nine o'clock at night, the dog was put in the kitchen and the barking stopped. Fred had made tentative enquiries.

'He's a lovely dog, just wondered why he's not with you in the house during the day, as he does seem to bark a bit, doesn't he? And he's such a lovely dog and all.'

"He's a guard dog if it's any of your business, and he's a killer!"

"Barks a lot don't you think?"

"That's what dogs do… why keep a dog and bark myself?"

What can you say to that? Level 2 barking was bad, but Death Com 5 was far worse, a frantic, maniacal yap, a bark far higher and faster than normal like the dog was going to choke if it couldn't bark fast enough. This would stop Fred in his tracks no matter what he was doing, scrambling his senses, making the fillings in his mouth tingle, making his jaw ache, causing his eyes to water, and pushing him into the back of his chair or the corner of the room like some sort of top-secret Government noise weapon, the sound waves slapping and pushing him to submission.

And then *the silence*. Silence did not exist during the day… silence only truly existed between nine o'clock at night and five-thirty in the morning. The silence was also a weapon. Silence in the day was merely the length of time until the next period of barking started… *quiet* became just as bad a state as continuous barking. Fred's mind would play tricks… he would start to count as soon as a period of barking stopped, counting until the barking resumed… in this way, the barking was only ever a second away. Bad for the nerves, he knew he behaved irrationally… 'If I boil the kettle, will it set him off', 'Is the radio too loud', 'If I flush the toilet', and 'If I burp or fart too loud?'

Fred was not even at work today and he wrote in the notebook, 'Strategy for beating the dog going successfully – resolve to wake up before the dog barks and not allowing *him* to wake me up.' It was a small moral victory. He flicked back a few pages; he had trouble remembering exactly what he'd written and when. 'Today gave up the notion of using earplugs. Kept waking up during the night to 1) Check if the dog was barking and 2) Check if I'd overslept because I could not hear the alarm clock or the dog. Earplugs causing/adding to the stress in the conflict against the dog.'

Fred felt an overwhelming urge to use the toilet. He hoped he could go… this irritated him. His feet danced on the floor looking for his slippers… he was getting desperate.

*

Time to act

… *eight, nine, ten,* the Alsatian started yapping again, breaking Fred's mental count, the pauses between the yaps were getting shorter as the dog worked itself into a frenzy. The yapping made the bricks vibrate, it made the double-glazing oscillate, and if he concentrated Fred could see the surface of the cup of tea, he'd just poured tremble. It made his head hurt. And still, Fred sat at the kitchen table, the dog had him in a spell, he could not ignore it, he could not shut it out… the jobs he'd planned on his day off were waiting.

A sudden respite, *thirty-six, thirty-seven…* time enough to make a fresh cup of tea? Dare not move… *thirty-eight, thirty-nine…* Why was he quiet? *Forty, forty-one…* Please God… choked to death on his saliva! It was possible… *forty-two, forty-three…* don't stop counting… he'd got to a thousand on numerous occasions before he was able to break the trance he was in… but it was dangerous to stop counting, as soon as you did, that's when it would begin again… it was torture… tenterhooks… it seemed every thought at home these days was centred on the damned dog… was this going to be a good day or a bad day?'

Fred tiptoed to the cupboard, *fifty-three, fifty-four,* carefully opening the door, every hinge meticulously oiled, you could not be too careful, his mind suddenly distracted by a forgotten packet of chocolate biscuits…

"Yap, yap, yap!!!"

Fred slammed the cupboard door shut. A slap to the face and a resolution… time for action… his hand was on the backdoor handle before he realised what he was doing… depressing it slowly, subconsciously preparing for the increase in volume when the door opened… a sneaky glance at the back of the neighbour's house… his hand already holding the hosepipe, the nozzle like a cocked gun at the hip… Plan F… no car on the driveway… the Alsatian was side-on to Fred barking at the back of the house, straining against the chain and collar... oblivious to Fred.

He remembered the dog as a puppy, being presented to him over the fence, 'this is Tyson, ain't he cute?' he'd managed an awkward smile. The puppy had made its first escape attempt within hours, squeezing under the fence into Fred's garden and Fred had done his *good neighbour bit* and returned him to their front door. The puppy had cried and pissed over his second-best shirt. He should have ended it there – 'Sorry, I was reversing... didn't see the poor thing... wasn't expecting him to be there!'

Hindsight's a wonderful thing.

Fred let fly. Tyson dodged as best he could, at fifty-five Fred didn't have the best reflexes but he had anger and frustration from months of pent-up emotion, his bottle had been shaken so often that the cap was sure to fail eventually. The dog thought about charging the sabre of water, changed its mind and darted for the sanctuary of its kennel.

"Hear that, Tyson? Silence!"

A powerful jet of water hit Fred full in the face. Flustered he didn't know whether to grasp at his dislodged glasses or hairpiece first – and like a clumsy juggler, he waved his arms absurdly achieving neither. *The hose must have malfunctioned.*

"If you ever hose my dog again, I'll have you, Fred Lambert!"

Through blurred vision, he saw *her* marching toward him from her back door. She held the biggest pump-action/shoulder-mounted water pistol he had ever seen.

"If you have a problem, you old bugger, then you deal with me. You leave Tyson out of it. You didn't think I knew what you were up to, did you? You are a useless, pathetic, lump of lard!"

"I… I… err… well… I thought you were out… no car on the road… you should control your dog."

"There's nothing wrong with my dog! The car's being serviced by a cousin, of a cousin, of a cousin, if it's any of your business. Dogs bark. So what?"

What sort of reasoning?

"Just a little consideration is all…"

"You mess with my dog, and you mess with me!"

"Please… a little peace… a bit of quiet…"

"Dogs bark and a big dog barks a lot… right!" she lifted the gun and aimed it at Fred's head, "if I ever find out who's been telling tales about my dog there will be consequences…"

Fred gulped.

"Did you call the RSPCA, you bugger?" she accused.

"RSPCA? I don't know how to spell that."

He knew the humour was wasted but old habits… All they cared about was access to water and shelter even if it was chained up all day. *He* had a kennel covered in black bin liners that added to the noise when the wind whacked against it.'

"Or the dog warden, you old bugger?"

"Dog warden?" The warden had asked for a detailed diary of complaints, a list of the times when the dog was a nuisance but when Fred had written *all day every* day on every sheet the warden had dismissed him stating, 'if you're not prepared to take it seriously!'

"Or the police, you old bugger!"

"Police?" They'd raided her house on his tip-off. The dog must be a guard dog for a drugs' den. Nothing had been found.

"Or the environmental fuckers?"

"Environmental agency?" The dog stunk; he had video evidence, for Christ's sake, of the dog eating its poo, and the food attracted birds which targeted the roof of his car with their shit – he'd eventually got a moped – smaller target.

"And how about the Housing Association?"

"Who?" The dog had damaged the fence – his fence – the housing officer sympathised and 'if he was prepared to go to court?' but 'did Fred know *she* was quite well connected to some of the local criminal gangs, and they would be very interested if a feud was in the offing?'

Fred gripped the nozzle a little tighter, he'd like to wipe the smile off her face… instead, he let the water dribble at his feet, and he turned and retreated to his back door.

"That's right… all words and no action. Next time I'll ram my water pistol up your!"

Fred closed the door. The palpitations in his chest were worse this time despite the breathing exercises. He made a mental note to make another appointment. His hands trembled as he poured another cup of tea. He wasn't afraid of a fight, he'd wrestled with some of Britain's toughest criminals over the years in a Maximum Security Prison, and he'd rumbled with Charlie Bronson in his day, but all his hands did these days was to prepare the meals for the prison population twice a day. Fred wasn't good with women, and *she* scared him. Rumour had it she was capable of the rough stuff, village gossip said she had contacts with the local travelling community – and he wasn't getting any younger. He sipped his tea – he only had five years to go, and he couldn't afford to jeopardise the pension by doing something silly, but the war was taking its toll. Perhaps he couldn't win this one. What did he have to look forward to? Five years to retirement – then stuck in this house with *that* dog next door? Nobody would buy this house from him – not with *them* next door. How long does the average Alsatian live? She'd buy another one simply to spite him. Perhaps the Governor would let him stay at work year to year, better to stay at work than be at home? At least he had his *empire* at work, his kitchen where people took notice of his orders and did exactly what he said. It was the one place he was almost happy, the place they fondly called him Chef Lambert.

The dog resumed its barking. It was a good job his wife had left, almost twenty years ago, as she would not have put up with this – she would have walked out again! His daughter had always wanted a dog and had pleaded throughout her childhood, but Fred had stood firm. Perhaps Tyson was some sort of joke sent from her grave and he smiled, all the years he'd refused to have a dog – he certainly felt he had one now.

*

Losing the War...
Fred had trouble sleeping. He was restless. He could not get comfortable. Visits to the toilet every hour – the last time he looked at the clock it had said three thirty. Finally, he must have slept.

He was ashamed. Embarrassed. A coward. Losing the war. The dog was wearing him down. There must be a way to fight back. But what would she do? He was on the defensive now, he had to be careful, and there was no knowing what a *woman like her* would do.

She had ten Alsatians – his house was surrounded and there was no escape – a prisoner. He tried to ring the police for help, but all the dogs started to bark at the same time, they were in a frenzy, and he couldn't hear the voice on the other end of the line. Surely someone from work would notice he was absent, surely someone would visit to investigate… What if it was Maddie, he had a soft spot for her, she wouldn't stand a chance... they'd already eaten the postman. The alarm at twenty-three minutes past five saved him.

Fred forced his heavy head from the pillow checking his hairpiece was still attached. Something else to worry about. Nobody knew his hair had thinned so rapidly – it must be the stress of the dog. He had a fear of being rescued from his burning home and everyone had suddenly noticed his bald spot and a fireman approaching with a look of concern stating they were 'too late to save the poor creature'.

Fumbling for the nightlight he eventually located his glasses and then his slippers, threadbare and potentially dangerous with a loose sole, but a present from his daughter. The dressing gown had fared better, it was only worn half the year, and though his elbows poked through the material it was the last thing his wife had given him, and he would keep it forever too.

The toilet seat was colder than normal, groaning under Fred's weight, a plastic buffer was missing, and a hairline crack threatening to pinch an unwary bum cheek. Fred leaned forward in his discomfort and saw a hole in the bottom of his pants and the transparency of his pyjama bottoms. The dog started to bark. With a steady release of gas, Fred counted the seconds, six, before a sudden splattering, a sloppy stream contaminated the water and enamel beneath him. He grimaced as intermittent wind escaped unpredictably and continued to spray the pan. Stomach cramps. He flexed the anus to expunge every drop. Relaxing for a while, waiting for things to settle, no point in a 'premature wipe' as this only wasted toilet paper – bloody dog! The people who marketed the soft toilet paper with cute puppies had never lived next door to a dog like this... Or had to wipe such a sensitive... He checked the toilet before flushing, hoping for a sign of improvement, but was disappointed at the persistence of a dull redness and he resolved, once again, to see a doctor about it.

Catering Officer Fred Lambert aged fifty-seven, looked very different when he checked himself in one of the full-length mirrors in the living room. Shoes immaculate, buffed like an ex-squaddie, black trousers pressed, the crease sharp, though struggling against his flabby thighs, white shirt, well ironed as were the epaulettes and black tie with his POA badge. The shirt button at the collar was uncomfortably fastened, but he would not unbutton it on a 'principle' until he changed into work clothes in the kitchen at The Stretch. Prison cap on top of his hairpiece, hardly anyone wore a cap these days, but he had standards. Picking up his helmet and jacket, he braced for the 'wall of sound' outside especially so on such a clear and still morning as this one in November.

The intruder light did not activate that morning. Sometimes it didn't – everything seemed to be failing. He turned the corner at the back of the house, using the dimness of a streetlamp two doors down to squeeze past his moped to gain access to his iron-railing gate, and balancing his helmet under his left arm he released the padlock. He allowed just enough room to guide the moped through once he had deposited his cap in the seat-box keeping a watchful eye on his neighbour's fence throughout the manoeuvre. Only when he had the moped next to the road did he smell the fresh dog poo. Not unusual as Fred's nose was expert at discerning the various stages of dog poo decomposition but this was fresh. And there it was… plumb in the middle of the path… his first thought was 'you dirty animal', his second that 'it was deliberate… a trap… *a landmine*… payback for hosing the dog', and his third that she would have to be smarter than that! He looked at each of her windows, expecting to see her face waiting for him to tread in it… and when he was sure she wasn't there, he gave the house a two-fingered salute... He never wore gloves... didn't need to... never felt the cold... varnish and resins...

Fred skirted the poo with the moped, making a note to remember to avoid it when his shift was over, he did not want to be late, and he gloried in this minor victory. On the deserted road, the throttle seemed to stick a little, it would need attention, it was like everything else in his life now... needed fixing.

If he'd managed to look over his shoulder without falling off, he would have seen the curtain move in the bedroom window. Two hands returned Fred's finger gesture.

"Did I do good, ma?"

"You fucking did, Taz! The bugger won't even notice the shit on his throttle 'til he gets off. He'll never get his hands clean!"

Chapter 18
A Normal Morning…

Always early. A couple of minutes to six in the morning at the prison entrance. He looked at his watch for the fifth time. Still. Dark. Damp. He was always early – he had to check his hairpiece in the outside changing facility before anyone else arrived. He also didn't want to queue with everyone else, making inane conversation before being searched; he made a point of beating the dog handlers and they were always early too. They were walking across the carpark now… two of them… he recognised Stedders… gave him a wave… his dog a large white Alsatian… impeccably behaved… not a murmur… the other dog handler… didn't know him… so many new staff… struggling with a smaller dog… a Belgium breed… he couldn't remember the name. Dog's whining… pulling at the lead… the dog couldn't wait to get to work… anxious to get in… Fred had been like that once…

The entrance door clicked. Fred's watch said eight minutes past six. He snatched the handle before the operator changed their mind; once inside he stared at the member of staff behind the bulletproof glass and mimed, *what time do you call this?* by jabbing at his wrist. They shrugged and pointed at the computer console in front of them. It was a familiar ritual.

Exasperated he picked up a green tray, noted the number was five, and thankful it wasn't thirteen, he placed the index finger of his right hand on a *reader* and waited for a glass door to open. His finger failed to register. Again. Exasperated further he looked to the Heavens to mime *nothing works in this place*. They use an override button in the gate to let him through – they had to every morning as Fred's fingerprints were infamous for being *rubbish*.

"Computer is now eight minutes slow!"

This was aimed at two Officer Service Grades. They both shrugged; both in the last minutes of a twelve hour shift. "We can't even reset a computer clock. How can we rehabilitate a prisoner with pre-convictions the length of their arm, to organise courses, the interventions, the programmes needed to challenge and change every one of them if we can't even change a bloody computer clock! Five months it's been wrong..."

He continued to berate as he placed his belongings into a plastic tray, taking care with his cap, he would have died if his hairpiece had fallen off and passed through the x-ray machine.

"Did you get out the wrong side of the bed?"

Fred scowled at one of the dinosaurs, like him one of the longer serving officers. You needed at least twenty years service to be a dinosaur.

The new officer asked, "Do you have anything on you, you shouldn't have? And can I see your ID, please?"

"Like what?" Fred showed his ID, the ID of a man nearly thirty years younger, the smiling face of a man looking forward to a career in the Prison Service. A man setting out to make a difference. He frowned. He'd forgotten how to smile and barely recognised the enthusiastic young man he'd once been.

"Anything metal, anything liquid that is not sealed in the bottle you bring..." Fred detected an Eastern European accent ... he wasn't prejudiced but this was a sign, wasn't it?

"Like money, phones, drugs, guns, knives ...?" he listed pedantically. Back in the day, the salary for an officer was sufficient to support a man's whole family. Ten years later it wasn't and women, a second income for the family, started to join the service, and then it was the young people, still living at home that joined for a few years because the salary wasn't good enough any longer and left to better themselves, and now it was immigrants, as long as they could speak enough English, traditionally doing the jobs nobody else wanted to do… it was a sign… Fred was aware of the silence… the officer hadn't expected this and looked like they might cry.

"You're out of order, Fred," the other dinosaur stated.

"Sorry, uncalled for, Miss? Miss Olga Shudyamov?" he read the ID badge, "Sorry, don't mind me. We go through this every morning. You ask. I say no. I don't bring anything in I shouldn't, and you never find anything. I'm sorry. It's pointless."

"I have to ask though," she spluttered.

"I know you do. Now if I was going to get anything in it would be easy."

"How's that, Fred?" the dinosaur again.

"Well, I don't know, let me see," Fred turned as Stedders entered the gate, "for instance, you could befriend one of those big Alsatians, perhaps slip something in its food in the morning, a package or something, and wait for it to do its business inside the prison… See… easy. For that matter when was the last time a dog was ever searched?"

"What are you saying, Fred?" Stedders was immediately on the defensive.

"Just making a point."

As Fred walked through the portal it beeped.

Miss Shudyamov, "Have you got anything metal on you?"

"Still NO! Must have brushed it with my arm," he returned to the front of the portal, waited for it to reset, and tried again – it beeped again.

"Have you?"

"Stop! Still NO! The bloody machine is faulty."

The other dinosaur said, "Fred, you've still got your shoes on."

"They haven't set it off for the last six months!"

"Machine may have been recalibrated."

"Why didn't they change the bloody clock then?"

Miss Shudyamov, "Mr Lambert, please calm down and remove your shoes…"

Fred removed his shoes and walked through the portal. It did not beep.

Miss Shudyamov, "Ah, Mr Lambert, look at this, a drawing pin in the bottom of your shoe."

The other dinosaur again, "Are you smuggling drawing pins in?"

"Very funny!"

"Mr Lambert, I need to give you a wand and a rub-down search," Miss Shudyamov started to approach Fred.

"But it didn't go off."

"BUT it did before… and the procedure is the procedure."

"For Heaven's sake!"

Miss Shudyamov used a handheld wand to confirm there was no metal on Fred's person. The tray passed through the X-ray machine, and she rubbed him down. Her hands barely touched his outstretched arm or his waistband or the material of his trousers. Too timid or too shy to do the job properly. He despaired. It would be too easy for someone determined to bring something into the Stretch. No wonder the wings were awash with drugs – a member of staff was probably on the take.

"Fred, have a good day and stay safe!"

"Well, I was bloody early, twenty minutes ago," he was heard to retort.

Chapter 19
5 YEARS EARLIER
HMP Long Stretch, Visits Room
Slap in the Face

The visits room was packed; it was a large hall where prisoners could receive visits from their loved ones and friends four times a week; it also doubled as the room in which the Number One Governing Governor could address the staff, pass news and present awards; everyone was there – Governors of all levels, custodial managers, senior officers, prison officers, civilian workers, just about everyone who had worked with or known Fred Lambert at The Stretch over the last twenty-five years. A couple of already retired colleagues had even *come in*, especially for the ceremony. It wasn't just Fred's *day*, two other officers had reached the milestone and they sat with officers from their respective wings, being nudged and made to feel uncomfortable at their impending walk to the stage.

First, there was half an hour of the Number One Governing Governor's news to sit through, the boring bit where the staff quickly became inattentive, their minds wandering, yawns being stifled, clock watching, calculating when lunch would start and finish…

"And finally… It has come to my attention… during my rounds… And I assure you, it will be severely dealt with by disciplinary action if the person responsible is discovered… That… and I apologise if I offend anyone in the room… But someone is drawing penises about the prison… Now, these are in areas only staff have access to… Official documents, workshop staff desks, a notice board in the corridor outside my office… This must stop… I will get a firm grip on the matter I assure you… Any questions?"

To stifled giggles, one officer raised a hand and spoke in a very matter-of-fact tone.

"Governor, could you describe the penises… if that is the correct form of the plural?"

"Be careful, Officer Hardcastle, this is a serious matter…"

"I wholeheartedly agree, Governor, but unless I know what I'm looking out for, how will I recognise…"

"Officer Hardcastle…"

"Governor, all I'm trying to do is help… How do you know if only one person is drawing the penises… If somebody could please explain or better still show me a picture… There could be more than one hand at work here!"

"Right, time is moving on and I have a couple of awards to … err… hand out," the Governor's secretary began to pass certificates, one at a time, "the first is for Charlie Wing for dealing with the disturbance last month in a truly professional manner." She handed a box of biscuits to a sheepish member of staff who was applauded by the room. "The second is for the gym staff for organising the sponsored row across the Atlantic… and the third is for the healthcare staff for dealing with the medical emergency of the over sixties team in the sponsored row…

"And finally, finally… Officer David Wynn… Long Service Medal… Twenty-five years' service…"

Officer Wynn walked with an exaggerated limp to the stage, causing a fellow officer to quip, 'He's been on *the sick* for four years of that!'

The room laughed good-naturedly.

"And Officer Miriam Knowles… Twenty-five years' service…" The room stood and applauded again.

Fred must be next. He made eye contact with those near him, rolling his eyes as if to say, *I suppose I have to* and has started to get to his feet before he realises the meeting is over… everybody else has stood up and they are making their way to the exit… The Deputy Governor taps him on the shoulder.

"I don't know what happened there, Fred, my old mate, her secretary must have left yours in her drawer by mistake… It happens… I'll try to get someone to pop it over to the kitchen later…" He shrugged and moved away, leaving Fred standing in the middle of the visitor's room on his own.

The medal didn't get *brought over* and Fred refused to collect it… He told anyone who asked that it didn't matter… he acted nonchalantly, and the medal remained hidden at the bottom of the secretary's desk.

Fred heard the number of penis drawings, because of the Governor's meeting increased roughly two hundred per cent and in length by roughly two centimetres.'

Chapter 20
20 MONTHS EARLIER
Avonside Surgery
Heart and Bottom …

Fred knew Dr Blidasabat was an odd fellow and he should have changed his doctor years ago. But he liked him. People expect to get the truth from their doctor, no matter how painful it might be, but it can become unsettling when their doctor cannot look them in the eye. The doctor had a habit of taking his black-rimmed spectacles off and talking directly to them, holding them to the light, appearing to look for the slightest smudge or defect in the lens. This performance was strange, as without the spectacles Fred was sure he was almost completely blind – perhaps that was why he took them off – all he saw, Fred was certain, was a blur. Dr Blidasabat gave the impression he was avoiding the issue, skirting around the truth, Fred sometimes concluded he wasn't a doctor at all. This impression was reinforced by what can only be described as his catchphrase, 'Don't forget… I am the doctor, Mr Lambert'.

Sat in the waiting room with the condemned. Was this where the resolve to act came from? Surrounded by others… the only thing in common… a shared rectal examination… a spreading of the cheeks… *take a deep breath…* and *don't fight it, Mr Lambert…* and then the waiting to see what the results would bring. The condemned. All expecting the worse… though some would get *a reprieve… somebody must have put a Dinky-sized toy of a London double-decker bus up your bottom when you were a child and if we remove it, you'll be fine!*

"Frederick Lambert, please."

He was certain she'd smirked when calling his name in the waiting room. He heard *Fred the dead*. Probably an essential part of the interview process to get the job. She made eye contact for too long and tried to disguise it with a fake smile, Fred made a note to cross her off the Christmas card list if he lived that long.

"Take a seat, Mr Lambert," Dr Blidasabat messing with the blinds at the window to the side of his desk though they appeared to be opening and closing with ease, the doctor was intent on rotating the bar between his thumb and finger, fixated on the mechanics; eventually, he was satisfied or rather he'd decided to fixate on something else. Dr Blidasabat lifted his right foot and placed it on the edge of his chair, the left shoe would have been too close to his patient, he untied the lace and then retied it with an elaborate fastidiousness, before replacing the foot on the floor. He then tested the friction coefficient of the carpet with the shoe before exclaiming, "That's better, Mr Lambert!"

Fred raised an eyebrow and waited. He thought *he* had problems!

"Now, as you are aware, I am the doctor, Mr Lambert, and I have years of training in this specialised field…"

"Am I going to die, Doctor Blidasabat?"

"We are all going to die, Mr Lambert, but the question should be, how are we going to live, is it not?"

"All right, have I got time to make up my mind, how I'm going to live before I die?"

"Very droll, Mr Lambert, but not forgetting, I'm the doctor, these things are never exactly precise… I cannot say for sure you will die on a Friday afternoon in November… the human body is a complicated thing… very resilient too." He was going through the *spectacle routine* now, switching attention from Fred's notes on the computer to looking like he was magnifying a coffee stain on the desk. "There are, of course, many more tests to perform, many treatments that can be tried to maintain a semblance of quality of life…"

"You're assuming I have a quality of life."

"Very funny, Mr Lambert, always the comedian, so you are telling me you have nothing to live for, that you are at rock bottom, pardon the pun, you have bottomed out, excuse another pun, and that death is something you are looking forward to?"

"Well not exactly, but should I make a bucket list?"

"What would be on your list?" Dr Blidasabat put his spectacles on and for a split-second, Fred thought there was going to be eye contact. The Doctor looked over his shoulder, sprang to his feet, bounded across the office, and splattered a fly on the door frame, "You never know when your end is nigh Mr Lambert, so what is on your list?"

"Always fancied skydiving… and the rollercoaster on top of the skyscraper in the States… forget where exactly…"

"Oh no, Mr Lambert, not forgetting I'm a doctor… not likely, not with your heart!"

Perhaps he should get a second opinion.

Chapter 21
1996 – AGED 4
Your One Daughter

Fred loved to remember.

She loved the rain; heavy rain was better, but thunderstorms were the best; Mary would shrink and hide under the kitchen table if nobody was looking, but Fred's daughter was different, she loved extremes, and couldn't wait to see what a *good* storm had left behind, what havoc it had wreaked on their little village. When she was four years old Fred remembered one storm in particular, the time the static caravans were picked up like lolly pop sticks and crushed against the bridge in Evebury town centre, the time when the Avon flooded vast areas and even managed to cut off parts of Tewksbury. She had red wellies and her tricycle ready at the front door before the rain had even stopped.

"Come on, Daddy, before the water goes! At its biggest... Come on!"

You couldn't say no. She was out of the door and freewheeling down the street, feet in the air, front pedals spinning crazily... Fred knew exactly where she was heading. There was a row of garages around the corner and the tarmac in the middle had a serious dip – it was where the water settled before it had the chance to drain away or evaporate. The drains were nearly always blocked because of the fallen leaves. She used to splash through it in her wellies last year but now Fred knew his job was to launch the tricycle at top speed and watch and hope she had enough momentum to get all the way through before she came to a stop.

Today it was higher than it had ever been. She giggled and called Fred a chicken.

"We can do it, Daddy, we can do it!"

Fred laughed too but there was no way she was going to make it.

"Are you mad? Can you swim, little girl?"

"The bike is the fastest in the world. And I'm the bravest rider in the world!"

"Do little girls float?"

She paused to consider this. Smiled.

"Daddy will save me if I don't make it. Go! Go! Go!"

There was no way she was going to make it but as *they say* 'you learn from your own mistakes'. It was an extra-long run-up; it was only twenty feet across… the puddle may as well have been the Grand Canyon.

She was dead centre… the muddy water above the saddle… her feet were too buoyant because of the trapped air in the wellies, and she was having trouble staying on the bike let alone trying to pedal… But she was laughing so loudly… Fred was worried the neighbours would come out to investigate… She was laughing hysterically… looking at Fred… He'd made the mistake of leaving the house in his trainers… not that his wellies would have been of any use… Waders required… Trainers and socks off… trousers rolled above the knee, mid-thigh… and she was still laughing… When Fred gets to her, he was panting about how cold the water was and she says, "You took your time, mister!"

"Hyperthermia!"

Fred's rescued her and pushed her to the other side of the puddle and she's saying, "Do you know what the problem is, Daddy?"

"Water's far too deep, I believe…" Fred tried to say it in a serious voice, but it was hard because his feet were hurting too much, and he'd hopped from one to the other…

"Daddy is far too slow. Far too slow. This time… faster, much faster!"

2004 – AGED 12
Fool's Gambit

She discovered chess at twelve. Within a couple of days, she could beat Fred. Badgered him to get DVDs on the 'openings' and had books on the 'importance of the middle game' and the 'subtle art of the endgame'. 'Queen's Pawn Gambit' and 'The French Defence' were her favourites; she played for the Alcester chess club and when they bought their first PC, she spent hours playing against the 'Rebel' chess program. She was hooked. Addicted. She didn't lose many games but when she did was inconsolable, spending hours going over the defeat, annotations meticulously recorded in a special filing case. Revise and improve. She entered chess tournaments and won several trophies – her ranking continued to climb rapidly – but then two things happened.

The Internet took off big time. She could play chess any time of the day against anyone, anywhere in the world. At weekends especially, she stopped being Fred's fun vivacious girl preferring the computer. It was impossible to get her away… If he was at work Fred's wife had even less chance than me of getting anything interactive from her. They kidded themselves. 'It's only chess, thank God it's not something dangerous.'

And then Gary Kasparov lost his rematch with the Deep Blue 2 supercomputer. She mourned for a couple of days and then put all the chess stuff in the loft. It was still there.

"Dad, computers will run the world one day. What chance have I got if the World Champ has got his butt kicked?"

*

2009 – AGED 17
No More Red Wellies…

The day the world ended was a Wednesday. It was always Spaghetti Bolognese on a Wednesday at the prison… Fred would never forget. Spaghetti Bolognese was dropped from the menu and replaced with ravioli. Ra-vi-o-l-i.

It was exactly four o'clock when the phone rang. The bell in Fred's hand was primed to ring for the food trolleys to leave the kitchen for the wings; from that day on the trolleys never left at four o'clock, it would always be five past; five minutes of contemplation became a tradition, at the beginning most prisoners knew the significance, but because the turnover of workers in the kitchen was so high, nobody lasted more than six months due to Fred's demands, and most began to assume it was a five-minute 'self-congratulation' for another meal being completed on time. Eventually, only Fred knew the importance of the five minutes. The day his world ended, the day his wife's voice on the line stated his daughter was dead. The day everything changed… but stayed the same. The food still left the kitchen. The bell tolled for him.

"Fred? Fred? She's dead! Are you there?"

He had held the receiver a little tighter against his ear. "She's dead!"

The kitchen had gone quiet as if everybody had sensed something grave had happened. All eyes were looking at him through the glass partition of the office.

"Police had to break the door in… Tom survived… Taken to hospital. Are you listening to me?"

The receiver made Fred's ear red.

"The Police say we need to identify…" his wife had screamed something incoherent and had started to wail.

"All right," he had gently ended the call, "All trolleys ready? Ring the bell. Let the wings know… Go, go, go…"

For the next hour Fred supervised the whole operation; checking the meal numbers matched with those expected, as discipline staff arrived to collect and move the trolleys to the wings; ensuring there were extras in the Bain Marie's to cover any potential accidents or shortfall; helped to search the last few prisoners as they left the kitchen; checked the menus for the following day; checked the fridges and the freezers; double-checked the tool cabinet – surveyed his whole kingdom before his shift finished, leaving the prison the exact minute he was supposed to finish.

He had muttered to himself, "The boyfriend survived?"

The day his world had ended was a Wednesday.

*

2009 – 17 AND COUNTING
No More Red Wellies…

The evening of the day Fred's world ended began with the same routine. He left work at exactly eighteen hundred hours, acknowledged the prison gate staff as they let him through the sliders after checking his ID; he'd driven home on automatic pilot, realised he was home only when he was sat on his driveway, he had been oblivious to the red light on the Cheltenham Road, other road users had parted by some divine agreement.

His wife had been sitting on a chair in the kitchen, her head on the table, hugging its coldness… sobbing quietly. She hadn't moved or lifted her cheek from the surface when he entered… He noticed dinner wasn't ready… not even prepared; he'd closed the back door placing his back against the frosted glass and looked at his wife. Controlled his breathing. Slowing it down. His eyes were drawn to three separate photographs on the walls and shelf: three photographs of his daughter. One on a tricycle aged about four… one with a shovel and a carrot aged about twelve… one holding a kitten, touching noses, aged about fifteen… all taken before…

He had stood there for five minutes. She sobbed. She accused. The silence. The front door rang. It would not stop. The banging of a flat palm on the front door. He walked through the house in his work shoes… she hadn't pulled him up for it.

"You've left your car running, Fred."

He had stared blankly at his neighbour.

"I said your car's still running."

"Thank you…" and he closed the door.

His wife hadn't moved and was still sobbing. Once he'd opened the fridge door he was back on track. The site of the food was a distraction, and he calculated what he could prepare for tea; he cracked two eggs and added a pinch of salt and whisked them with a fork. He grated a small amount of cheese, each swipe he imagined Tom's face being shredded, and made an omelette in a purpose-bought frying pan. He turned the mixture with a spatula until it began to cook making sure it was light and fluffy. He placed it next to his wife on a plate with a fork.

She asked, "What am I going to do?"

"Cup of tea?"

Fred busied himself with his omelette… it took longer… four eggs for him. He made a pot of tea and poured two cups.

"I know I should have made her stay here, after the last time, but you said…" she sobbed.

"It's nearly seven o'clock…"

"She would still be here if you hadn't…"

149

"I know… come on now…" he cajoled to the living room and deposited her in her favourite chair, "get comfortable, it'll be on in a moment…"

"Fred Lambert, you listen to me now. If she hadn't gone… the last time… she'd still be alive… it was *you*… you're the reason…" The music to Emmerdale had started and she fell silent. Fred escaped to the kitchen.

In the kitchen, he muttered, "And we'd still have more than fifty thousand in the bank, wouldn't we?" He sprayed the kitchen table with surface cleaner and wiped it clean, especially the damp patch where his wife had been sitting, repeatedly, until he heard the music signalling an interval in the soap. He washed the plates and cutlery in the sink, dried everything and took his time to put everything away, he had opened the backdoor and looked at the garden… looking for a further distraction… he decided he would buy a greenhouse. Everything was perfectly still outside. Not a breath of wind. He had seen clouds gathering in the distance, grey and heavy, but for now, everything seemed to be on pause. Eventually, he walked round the corner of the house, sat in the car, and turned the engine off… he sat there for a couple of hours until it was dark.

Chapter 22

Here Comes the Angler…

Fred had been in a local pub for lunch on a day off in the middle of the week. He always sat in a dark corner of the lounge, his back to the wall; he had been studying the gas bubbles rising steadily to the surface from the lager in front of him, pushing the remnants of the pie pastry across the plate, undecided whether to clear the plate, knowing the pastry was unhealthy – but the tastiest part. He also knew how many bar staff were on duty today, how many customers were in the lounge, who were the *dodgy* ones and where all the *exits* were. Every prison officer knew this.

That's when he had seen *Smithy* walk into the pub. At first, it was something about the way he'd skulked toward the bar, looking over his shoulder, furtive, checking out the room, making sure the coast was clear… the way he seemed to change his mind when he had seen Fred hiding behind his pint… the way he had turned abruptly to leave the pub, the bar seemed to physically repel him like the opposing charge of two magnets.

He had put a piece of the pastry in his mouth. Yes, it had been Smithy. Same skulk. Carrying a little more weight, lost his hair… the same Smithy he'd placed on report for brewing *hooch* in ninety-seven… the same Smithy who had explained to Fred that 'every prisoner is up to something … I know that and you know that… we know what we can get away with and so do you… and we both know where the line is… and there's only trouble when somebody thinks they can move the line one way or the other… and so we both want the same thing… to maintain the bloody line!'

Smithy had walked back into the pub, keeping to the left-hand side of the room, he'd dug deep in his pockets for coins, paid for half a lager and idled up to Fred and sat down.

"Boss... Mr. Lambert... Wasn't expecting to see you in here on this fine day... mind if I sit?

"Cut the crap, Smithy... by my quick calculation, you must be at the Grunge by now? Day release for work experience... nearing your release date... end of your sentence or out on licence? Remind me."

"Boss, Mr Lambert... Just over two years left, boss, end of the sentence... twenty-six years. They've got me in a warehouse round the corner... shelf technician I think they call it... I've got to jump through the final hoop before I'm released..."

"I bet it's not on your licence conditions to come in here, is it?"

"Boss, Mr Lambert, you won't say anything, will you... Part of my rehabilitation ain't it? Little drink now and then... very, very rarely come in... You know."

"I thought you knew where *the line* was?"

Smithy's face had cracked, "I suppose it gets a bit blurry at our age, don't it... Especially with my eyesight."

"I suppose it does, Smithy."

"You still doing The Stretch, Mr Lambert, you can't have long left yourself?"

"A few years, Smithy."

"You was always *firm but fair,* Mr Lambert, the lads always respected you for it."

Fred had seen Smithy relax but also noticed a gleam in his eye as if he was up to something. He had put it down to the cynicism of his years in *the job.*

*

Old Times...

Fred had seen the funny side. Two ageing men sat in a quiet corner of a pub at lunchtime, reminiscing how times had changed, how prison wa*sn't what it used to be*, how the youngsters had ruined it; sometimes they had sat in silence, each seemed to appreciate the others' mood, knowing when it was appropriate to share the silence, knowing when it was the right time to poke fun at the other; sometimes they had argued, cantankerous ageing men, both certain their viewpoint was the correct one, putting up with the other's opinion, and respecting their *enemy* from a shared experience.

"Fred, when it comes down to it, you have no idea… when that door bangs shut… and it's just the four walls… you have no idea… when you're left in there for hours… The four walls can do strange things to a man…"

"You've got books… bloody television and a PlayStation these days… Oh, it must be tough…"

"From a mental point of view…"

"Psychological."

"Yeah, psychological point of view… Imagine you're in a box… A sealed box… It's like there's no air to breathe… No space to move…"

"I don't think you suffocated to death, Smithy… you're still here… and as for the space to move… I think you went to the gymnasium once in all the time I knew you… You were always a sloth!"

"That's a lie! It was twice…"

"Going to the gymnasium to watch a snooker exhibition match does not count."

"It does… I had to walk there and back, didn't I? Ronnie O'Houlihan weren't it?"

"Something like that."

"Can you see what I mean, though?"

Fred had paused, "Yes I can... strange things to a man... point in case... look at you."

"The Segregation unit then, not just the four walls, but hardly any ventilation, a low ceiling, and a floor with a small drain circle in the centre, makes you feel like you're the one slowly being emptied... no comforts there... soul destroying... I've known a few that have ended end up in Broadmoor..."

"You're all volunteers, Smithy..."

"I know, *if you can't do the time, don't do the crime*..."

"Precisely."

"You've got no idea, Fred... Simply no idea..."

There had been a few minutes of silence.

"Let me tell you something, Smithy... Mine's been a life sentence just as much as yours..."

"Yeah?"

"Don't you think I've been affected as much as you? Nearly thirty years in that environment. The brutality. The violence. The smell. Thirty years of dealing with psychopaths... no offence meant... men who are dishonest and lie as a default setting?"

"Go on."

"I sometimes think I'm infected. I'm less patient for one..."

"That's true..."

"Have difficulty socialising with *normal* people... I mean prison officers generally... we get desensitised by what we deal with daily..."

"Within the four walls."

"Our humour is crude... our normal is not normal..."

"But you get to go home every day so it's not the same."

"I'd argue it was worse… I've taken the disease home with me… infected those people I loved… it wasn't fair on them… When Mrs Lambert said *you've changed,* she was right… the statistics for marriage breakdown amongst prison staff is disproportionally high, you know…"

"You should have got out then, Fred… You were a volunteer."

"Funny! Sort of creeps up on you… regular income… the banter… the adrenaline when you're young… the mortgage… family… and before you know it, middle age, and the feeling it's too late to get out… and the promise of a decent pension wasn't bad in the beginning…"

"Me heart bleeds… don't forget the divorce bill."

"I didn't get divorced."

*

A Right Laugh…

Fred had learned that being himself was the only way to survive in prison. The old prison series *Porridge* remained the closest adaptation to the truth. 'Be yourself and don't pretend to be something you're not.' There was a time for the rules but also a time for laughter.

"Do you remember Healey? On Berrie wing… Largest bollocks you are ever likely to see…" Fred's turn.

"Yeah, I do, he had a condition, didn't he?" Smithy sipped from his beer.

"I hope so. They were <u>not</u> normal. Every time we had a new male member of staff, we purposely sent them to do the monthly search on Healey, just so we could *shock* them when he dropped his boxers."

"Didn't someone faint?"

"Yes, they did… regularly. If they didn't faint, we knew they were going to make it as an officer."

"Wasn't there a scandal?"

"Not exactly... old Healey got so used to *dropping em* for new members of staff... I think he quite liked the infamy... whether it was old age, you know, but on the last occasion a female member of staff, new, walked in to check his bars, as we do, and he sort of dropped 'em automatically... she screamed... he panicked... alarm bell got pressed and poor Healey was restrained... first and only time in his life... Well, the cells are quite small on that wing and in the kerfuffle, she ended up *on the legs* with her face resting on his hairy..."

"Always wondered why she was called fluffer... she resigned not long after, didn't she?"

"Yes. Anyway, Healey's dead now."

"Oh?"

"Heart attack."

"I hope he left 'em for medical science."

"Mm... Or a bean bag for the lounge!"

Next...

"Do you remember Senior Officer Williams? Alpha wing. Retired in the nineties," Fred again.

"I think so... Tattoos?" Smithy takes another sip.

"No... Overweight... The shirt was never tucked in... Got *wedgied* on the threes, once."

"Oh, yeah, Clarky got half an ounce for that... he pulled the back of his pants right up over his head... clean got away with it too!"

"Well, he couldn't see, could he? Anyway, I still laugh when I think about this... it was just when the Prison Service was starting to get more politically correct... you know... more women in the job..."

"Yeah, and you lot had to call us *mister* instead of 'Smith 268'."

"All right, Smithy… Well, Rick decided he was going to take this to its logical conclusion… we had a young lass start on the wing and Rick got me to explain to her that due to the equalities policy, her line manager was registered as being deaf but not to worry too much during her introductory talk as the Senior Officer was an expert at reading lips. Rick was sitting at the desk facing the door when I let the new lass in… I had to bang the desk to get Rick's attention and he nearly jumped out of his seat…"

"Cruel."

"We were watching through the glass panel… the poor lass… every question Rick asked she shouted at him and every time he listened to the reply, he leant forward staring at her lips… I don't know what she thought… I rang Rick's extension, the phone rang until the new lass pointed at it gingerly… Rick picked it up and kept shouting, 'What's that you say?' It was only when Rick stood up and turned round to open the window, we saw his trousers were round his ankles, and only then did the new lass realise she was being had – things like that used to happen all the time."

"Didn't he get warned for that?"

"Yes, but it was worth it… He died last year."

"Exposure?"

"No. Stroke."

*

Baiting the Hook…

Institutionalised… that's what I am, boss, all of them years inside, I'm not the same am I? Being around all of them other prisoners that's done it."

"Volunteered."

"Yeah, yeah, I know what you're saying, boss… but fundamentally I'm not a bad bloke…"

"You killed someone."

"Yeah, it was him or me… I was just collecting a debt for the *main man*, you know, and the dirtbag pulled a knife on me… I'm telling you; it was him or me… you can see that can't you?"

"Sort of, Smithy, but your pre-convictions sheet was already several pages long… I think you'd already done three custodial sentences… so it was only a matter of time. Don't paint yourself as the victim."

"It was two sentences… but I'd argue it's an accident of birth… If I'd been born with a silver spoon in my mouth instead of on the rough side of town, my life would have been different."

"Maybe."

"Conditioned by my environment… that's what it is… put a decent bloke with hundreds of offenders… murderers, serial killers, kiddie-fiddlers… some of its going to rub off. I've been tainted."

"You've been tainted by the programmes they've made you do… you know all the buzzwords! *Institutionalised, conditioned…*"

"Fair comment, but on a simpler level… I always walk on the left side of the pavement… I keep my tobacco in my pants… I have a habit of looking over my shoulder… when my top's dirty, I turn it inside out to get an extra couple of days out of it… At the warehouse, I still find myself standing by a closed door waiting for an officer to unlock it for me… and I call everyone, *boss…*"

"For God's sake, why don't you look on the bright side?"

"Go on."

"Free board and lodging, including three meals a day… if you behave yourself, a television, a PlayStation, a gymnasium better than most outside… Easy life."

"That's bollocks, boss. You don't know what you're talking about."

"Oh?"

"No one gets it easy in prison. You have to come out of your cell sometime. Unless you're somebody or know somebody you ain't got a chance… The bullies and the predators know who you are before you do! You're not exactly good-looking, boss, so at least you got that in your favour… as for the perks you think you'd get? You always owe somebody something in prison. You owe somebody… because *they* let you live on *their* wing… half your workshop wages is *theirs*… your PlayStation is *theirs*… *they* might let you rent it for the week… for a small charge… *they* are not 'enhanced'… *they* ain't got no privileges… so in effect, your privileges are *their* privileges… And don't look at someone the wrong way… And God help you if you get lippy. Most prisoners have scars somewhere…"

"Yours?"

"Inside my head, boss, I'm lucky… I know people. Don't get me wrong, I'm expected to toe the line… the main man on the out is still the main man on the inside… he's still got blokes working on the inside… drug supply is a lucrative business… And I'm expected to do my bit… make sure people pay on time… keep a check of who owes who…"

"That has always bothered me, Smithy, and I won't pretend now… You're pissing me off when you talk about drugs… Between the two of us, how does the supply of drugs get into prison, like The Stretch?"

"I hear you, boss, and everyone knows what happened to your daughter… and I respect your anti-drug position."

"How'd they get in?"

"I hear you, boss, but I can't compromise the main man… I respect you, boss, always have, but some things I can't speak about… it wouldn't be just you and me… you're far too professional to not feed it back to your bosses… and because of your daughter you'd do all you can… It's been a bit of a crusade for you over the years?"

"Yes, it has."

"But… You'll never get drugs out of prison. Too much money involved… A lot of profit to be made… a captive audience… and the men inside, most of them have had drugs in their lives from their early teens… and the old saying, 'you can lock me up physically, but you can't control where my mind goes', and the drugs help them to escape."

"It won't stop me trying."

"I respect that, boss."

Chapter 23
18 MONTHS EARLIER
Mind Your Head

Fred knew the prison kitchen was an odd place; despite the knives and other dangerous equipment it was probably the safest place in any prison establishment; the prisoners that worked there were mostly hand-picked and from the moment they walked through the door they were kept so busy by the routine they often forgot they were in prison at all; the comradery, the sense of purpose and teamwork required to produce over five hundred meals at The Stretch, Fred knew, should not be overlooked. Prisoners saw the staff that worked in the kitchen in a different light, taking direction and orders without question; the *rules* were different, and gang affiliations were forgotten and left on the wings... The kitchen belonged to Fred and his rules applied.

Fred had flushed the toilet. Still waiting to see his doctor. He'd checked his hairpiece in the mirror, and looked at his watch, confirming everything was ahead of schedule, the pies were *finishing* and there were fifteen minutes before the wings had to be contacted... Time for some on-the-job training.

"Granger!"

"Coming, boss."

"Granger, what's rule number three?"

Granger had paused, six feet two, skinhead, tattoos on top of tattoos and about eighteen stone, "Is it, no worker will eat anything unless given permission by your good self, boss?"

"No, that's number five."

"Is it, I won't be expected to do anything that... that... you would not be willing to do yourself?"

161

"No, Granger!"

Granger looked puzzled and slowly shook his head.

"Rule number three is, 'every surface has to be clean enough to eat your dinner off!' Now I suggest you clean the toilet floor again or that's where you'll be testing rule number three."

"Got it, boss, on it straight away."

The new worker always got the worst jobs and Fred tested them daily for any signs of *backchat* or *bad attitude*, "And, Granger, have you eaten all the pies?"

"Very funny, boss, ha, ha, ha…"

Fred had surveyed his empire; everything was on schedule; even Walters had worked well, preparing the onions, and had passively listened to Fred's pearls of wisdom on efficient cutting methods, refusing to rise to any of Fred's jibes about 'how long do you think you'll last' and 'not even the onions can make this heartless criminal cry!'

Fred had dipped a spoon with exaggerated aplomb into the stew, checking the consistency before slowly raising a small amount to his lips, and he had moved the contents around with his tongue before eventually swallowing.

A skinny prisoner had sidled up, "Tasty, boss?"

"Taste, Benny, taste? Keep it plain. Keep it simple. Quantity, not quality. Do not be wasting my budget on making a tasty stew.

"Yeah, boss, but it's good, in it? Yeah?"

"Benny, this is the best stew I have had the pleasure to let pass my palate in the last fortnight… Well done!"

"See, I knew it was good!" Benny had smiled uncontrollably, rewarded for his efforts that morning.

Walters muttered, "We haven't had stew for a month."

*

Maddie had been on the telephone in the office. Fred made an exaggerated mime to ask if the call was for him; he was protective of her, she was a lot younger than he was, and he liked her but was often confused about his feelings for her. She was like a daughter to him, but this hadn't stopped him from groping her when he'd been drunk though he'd tried to laugh it off. When she'd come down the stairs holding one of the dresses, he'd laughed that off too, blaming his undying love for his wife, who'd walked out twenty years before, and stating 'there was always a chance she could come back, as long as I keep them.'

He'd gesticulated if she wanted him to have a word with the caller, but this caused her to half turn away. Fred approached the office anyway…

Maddie whispered, "Yes, okay, later. Yes, I promise…"

"Not for me, Maddie, did you say?"

Maddie had shaken her head and Fred noticed a flush in her cheeks, she whispered, "… talk later, yeah?"

"If it's personal you should have said. I can go," Fred had not moved.

"No… I've finished… What? You…" Maddie had lifted the handset to Fred who listened for a couple of seconds and hung up sharply.

"I've said it before, only bad things will happen if you get mixed up with the likes of him. He's not the right man for you. He'll use you like he has the others. You know that don't you? I can provide you with a list. Ask anybody."

"Harmless fun, Fred, that's all. I'm using him just as much as he's using me."

"You need someone you can rely on. Somebody who will treat you right."

163

"I'm thirty-five, Fred, divorced, single parent… Mr. Right does not exist. All men are shits… I've got the scars… and I know what I'm doing."

"But him? Governor Whitmore or *Witless* as I call him… he's after one thing, then he'll bin you like the rest…"

"Men do not *bin* me. And anyway, not all women want the same thing."

"But him?"

"Bit of fun that's all, some excitement…"

"But in the long term… some security… if *someone* was prepared to offer something more solid, more consistent… at least for your daughter… a future…"

"I'm not a charity case. I do not need a man in my life, or a *woman*, not in the way you mean, Robert and me get on just fine… use and abuse… I sometimes think life would be a lot better for *us women if* there were not any men around."

Price had tapped on the office door.

"Yes, young man? How can I be of guidance and a positive influence?"

"Mr Lambert, you promised to help me finish a letter to my mom."

"Yes, of course, to enrich, encourage and maintain family ties to promote a positive support network for a prisoner upon release."

Price had looked blankly at Maddie. She had ignored him as she did most of the prisoners.

"Everybody is worth a second chance, Pricey, your mother simply needs a little convincing, that's all…"

*

The Dedicated Search Team (DST) had entered the kitchen at eleven thirty in the morning. The DST specialised in searching prisoners and areas within prisons to find weapons, drugs, escape equipment, fermenting liquid (hooch) and anything deemed out of the ordinary that could disrupt the smooth running of the prison regime.

"Morning, boys," Fred checked the clock on the wall and calculated the food would still be on time, "Business or pleasure?"

When the officer in charge of the DST looked confused.

"In need of sustenance in your never-ending search, your quest, to maintain the safety of the establishment? What do you want? Bacon butty or egg baps, I can get Benny to rustle them up in no time. How about some water for the Cocker?" The drugs dog, excitable, was straining with anticipation, an overload of the senses from the kitchen.

"Not a social visit this time, Fred, I'm afraid. A random search... all right if I run Jasper around... he won't get in the way... just ask your lads to stand perfectly still if you will... be gone in five minutes," the DST officer was apologetic as he knew it was inconvenient.

Fred glanced at the clock again.

"Course you can boys... though I don't know what you expect to find... You know I run a *clean* kitchen, hand-picked everyone... nearly everyone... they can all be trusted..." Fred scowled at Walters, "I will not tolerate anything else. This kitchen is a sanctuary where we can respect each other..."

"And earn a top wage," a member of the DST quipped.

"Money is not everything... The satisfaction of hard work and commitment to good standards far out ways any pecuniary rewards... What do you say, Granger?"

"Whatever *you* say, boss."

Fred pointed to a slogan on the wall, 'Clean kitchen: a clean start'.

Fred watched as Jasper was sent into the vegetable refrigerator.

Jasper had *sat* at the back.

The dog handler hesitated; the DST stood rooted to the spot in disbelief – nobody had expected to find anything. The prisoners in the kitchen held their collective breath, nobody moved, nobody spoke, a game of statues where the first to move was the loser. The handler pulled himself together realising all eyes were on him. Fred leaned in to hear.

"Jasper, come here boy. Good boy," the handler whispered to his colleague, almost so the dog couldn't hear his next move, "I'll send him in again… just to double-check… don't want to rummage through the veg unless we must… it's nearly lunchtime… see if he *sits* again."

The colleague nodded. Non-committal – a needless search of the kitchen would leave them the butt of jokes for weeks.

Jasper had sat again.

Another colleague sidled up and whispered, "Has he ever found anything before?"

"Never."

"Does he sit regularly for no reason?"

"He's got a habit, just lately, of finding… Mars bars."

"That's helpful."

Fred coughed and resumed control of the situation, "Right, boys, what are you going to do? Decide… You have seven minutes before I get the food to the trolleys and ring the bell. Is the dog vegetarian?"

"Got to check it out, Fred," two DST members had put plastic gloves on and all eyes in the kitchen watched as they stretched the latex to make each finger and thumb comfortable.

"Just don't make too much mess. You won't find anything. Not in my kitchen… During all my years in charge… the white stuff in eighty-seven turned out to be talcum powder… a prankster… You've got five minutes."

The DST, on their knees. The walk-in fridge had mice. The scratching stopped.

"No mouldy carrots I hope… heads will roll if you've found anything passed its sell-by-date," Fred quipped.

The DST was not smiling. One opened his hand – on the palm a brown powder wrapped in cling film.

"Not a Mars Bar, Fred."

"Let me see, it can't be, not in my kitchen…" he read the prisoners' minds as they looked at each other, '*It's heroin*', "Not in my kitchen… The abomination."

"Careful, Fred, it's evidence… you can't touch it."

"Who has dared to bring this into my kitchen?"

Not a sound. Not a movement.

All eyes were on Fred. He was at the centre of the kitchen, and he searched the faces of the prisoners, the trusted workforce for an answer, before reverting his eyes to the DST, feeling humiliated he muttered, "Since my daughter's death, I promised… not in my kitchen… spot the signs… I should have been more vigilant… someone has taken advantage… thought they could stash their filth right under my nose!"

"Steady, Fred, don't work yourself up. It's everywhere, seriously, if you saw what we found on Alpha wing last week, it's to your credit you've escaped the stuff for so long," a DST member placed a hand on his shoulder, "I'll let the Governor know, it shouldn't hold the food up, we can't prove it belongs to anyone… Look at it as a small victory for us."

"You don't understand. This is *my* kitchen."

"Not your fault."

"More vigilant!" working himself up.

"Not your fault."

"How dare you!" glaring at Walters.

"Not your fault. You do our best," the DST officer tried to calm Fred.

Fred brushed the hand aside and made straight for Walters. Walters avoided eye contact.

"Come clean for once in your sorry life… Own up… I gave you a chance in here, against my better judgement, I didn't want you in here, I know how you live, what you get up to… your deals, your dirty money, the bullying… You are scum, Walters, the lowest of the low…"

Walters kept his composure. Eventually, he slowly shook his head.

"You're sacked… Get out of my kitchen!"

"You are making a mistake," Walters spoke evenly and with a dignity that exasperated Fred even more.

"A mistake! I don't think so… Last month no Walters and no heroin. This month, Walters, and heroin! You're sacked! Get out of my kitchen!"

Walters looked up and met Fred's eye,

"You're a fool, old man, you're ignorant and you're stupid. You're blind. No clue… No wonder your daughter's dead…"

Fred jabbed him in the chest with his finger, "Don't you dare…"

"You blame everything but yourself…"

Fred drew his fist back…

Fred staggered backwards, not everyone had seen the two-handed shove Walters had delivered to his chest, but everyone heard the snarl.

"Get out my face!"

Fred fell like the anchor man in a winning tug-of-war team, his legs couldn't catch up with the body, the body gaining momentum as gravity took over, but it wasn't a muddy field but a kitchen with obstacles. There was a loud 'DONG' as his head hit the side of a cast iron cooking vessel. (One of the DST members likened it to the sound when Jonesy had hit Bull with a chapatti pan in two thousand).

Someone sniggered nervously.

Somebody else muttered, "Oh, fuck!"

The dog barked and the chaos began. Maddie had pressed the alarm bell, which registered at eleven forty-five, and was the first alarm bell in the kitchen for fifteen years – and that had been a false one. The DST were now decisive, all had the training to deal with a violent prisoner, and they also knew the alarm bell meant staff from other areas would arrive within a couple of minutes.

"Stand still! Don't do anything stupid, Walters."

"Too late," he pointed at Fred's unconscious body and for a split second all eyes were averted. Walters sprang sideways and pushed another prisoner into two members of the DST, vats of stew were upended, splashing onto the floor with an eruption of aromatic steam. Benny began to sob. Two prisoners bent low and pulled Fred clear of the stew wave and Walters used their backs to vault clear of his pursuers, crashing into shelving where he flung empty metal trays at anyone too nearby. He managed to circumnavigate the kitchen spilling trays of pie, broccoli, mashed potato, and gravy in his wake. The air was filled with curry powder and flour as storage bins were toppled, only when reinforcements arrived, was he cornered in the meat freezer. Staff were prized at the freezer doorway but were held at bay by the threats Walters was making with a frozen leg of lamb.

"Steady, boys. Nobody gets hurt," Governor Whitmore had arrived and assumed control, he surveyed the damage done to the kitchen, calculating the disruption and which budget the repairs would most likely come out of, "You need to calm down, son."

"Call your officers off. Get them to back off."

"The fact is, son, you need to cool off," and with that, he slammed the freezer door, "give him ten minutes then get him to the seg. Where's Maddie, is she alright? What a mess!"

"It's Fred, Governor, been knocked clean out."

"What's the silly bugger been up to now? Got anyone from healthcare here yet? Over there, did you say?" Governor Whitmore picked his way using the clean bits of floor careful not to let anything touch his suit or his shoes, "Bloody hell, was anyone else involved? Never has so much mayhem, been created by one cretin, eh?"

Maddie was on her knees, an ear pressed against Fred's chest, and she was starting to panic. She suddenly screamed, "We need an ambulance!"

The mood turned sombre and when Maddie, who had stood up to allow Fred to get help, heard a member of the DST whisper to the nurse cradling Fred's head that *we've lost him* she began to sob uncontrollably.

Governor Whitmore pulled Maddie to her feet.

"Not Fred, you fool, *lost him* referring to Walters, but he's locked in the freezer, now pull yourself together and let the nurse do his job. *Look*, it was a carrot lodged in the throat, he's breathing again now… nasty bump though."

"Fred, can you hear me?" the nurse was crouching over him, "It's John, you've had a nasty bump to the head."

"To his hairpiece, more like."

Fred had opened his eyes. He was flat on his back, surrounded by officers, Maddie, and Governor Whitmore.

"Break it up, stop overreacting," Governor Whitmore elbowed everyone out of the way, "You lot, get some prisoners to tidy this place up, the others can go back to the wings. You've all got jobs to do."

While Governor Whitmore set wheels in motion Maddie furtively handed the sodden hairpiece to Fred. He wiped the excess stew from it but missed a pea as he replaced it on his head. Maddie was pressing his hand.

"You alright? It was a hell of a bump… I heard it from the office."

"Of course, he's all right, Mad," Governor Whitmore interrupted, "don't go soft on him, you'll have *me* crying in a minute…"

Fred stood up," Course I am," he glanced at the clock, trying to focus, "Lunch will be a few minutes late…" The look on Maddie's face suggested he was being optimistic. "Stop fussing…" Fred brushed the nurse's hand away who had retrieved the pea and surveyed the destruction, "What on earth?"

"The stews off, "Governor Whitmore quipped, "We could scoop it off the floor, give it a stir, none-the-wiser…"

Fred ignored the Governor, "Focus Maddie, grab Sid and Benny. Benny, stop crying, meet me at the veg. fridge. Tomorrow's salad is already prepped, it's in containers, lettuce, tomato, onion, cheese… plus two bread rolls per prisoner… Carton of orange juice… And a yoghurt… Right?"

"Oh, well done, Fred," Governor Whitmore acknowledged sarcastically, "You see, Mad, nothing fazes this man, nothing is more important than getting the lunch out… See, he's not so useless after all… Without people like him, important people like me would get side-tracked by petty considerations… Reminds me, I have the local MP at two and the press at three. Each to their own, Mad, and Fred's place is with the limp lettuce leaves…"

The nurse was still hovering. He was holding the remnants of the squashed pea.

"What do you mean, *what shall we do*? Do you mean with the pea?"

"Don't know if he should still be on duty… concussion, you know," the nurse was rubbing his chin.

"Go with him if you must, hold his hairpiece, help with the lettuce… He's not exactly playing rugby for England, is he? You can send him home after lunch. When you've finished lunch consider *yourself* on sick leave, Fred I don't want to see you for a month. Make it two! Young Maddie will take over. Go on holiday, take a trip abroad whilst you still can… You're always saying you've got plans so just get on with it. Go and play some golf and no cheating! Did you hear me?"

An incident on the eighteenth ten years ago had nearly come to blows and Fred knew who the cheat had been.

It was twenty minutes before Governor Whitmore remembered Walters. Two teams of officers were ready in full protective gear, but Walters had no fight left and only shivered about his human rights. Before he left the kitchen Governor Whitmore passed close to Maddie, paused for Fred to be within earshot and said, "See you tonight and wear the tarty outfit… And no knickers."

Fred slowly shook his head. He didn't feel right. He picked the bell up from the floor and began to wipe the gravy from its surface – he had closed his eyes but the ringing inside his head was persistent. Fred saw Maddie jab a finger in Governor Whitmore's chest.

"If you ever call me a fool again…"

"I was joking! Anyway, I'm glad the old fart's not dead… if it had been apple crumble today his death would have to have been logged as a death in *custardy*."

Chapter 24
17 MONTHS EARLIER
Sick of the Sick Leave

First impression of India? He hadn't liked it. Too hot, too busy and the place had made him look fat. In the airport he had knocked three people over, unable to navigate his way through the chaos and the noise, his head throbbing, and the sweat threatening to loosen his hairpiece. He had been supposed to be getting away from it all, instead, he was sitting in a typical tourist hotel surrounded by other white Europeans; sitting in a lounge trying to avoid conversation, thankful for the air conditioning, but knowing he was in the *wrong* hotel and suffering the looks of the staff suspecting he was not going to be a good tipper. He was alone again and regretting his decision to spend three weeks in India.

He was also regretting the abrupt message on Maddie's answer phone: '… and you can tell your boyfriend, wittering Witless, I have gone on an adventure to get my head together, so I am not *all talk* and don't expect me back anytime soon! You can cope if you can pull yourself away from the office telephone!'

Instead of an adventure he felt he had swapped one boring routine for another.

A firework had exploded in his head. He had held onto the table to steady himself before jumping to the window to check if the explosion had been inside his head or outside. Nothing but darkness. A waiter had moved smartly to his side and guided him back to his seat, tentatively asking if everything was to his satisfaction.

"It is not, I'm afraid. Is the city ever silent? I'm bored, hot when I leave the hotel and bloody lonely!" Fred held his chin in his hands.

"Sir, pardon me for intruding, I have a cousin who runs a very clean business. Make your stay most pleasurable."

"Young man, I am not a sex tourist! Clear the things away before I lose patience and tell your manager what you're trying to do."

"Please forgive, sir, we misunderstand each other. I can see you are an unhappy gentleman, and this makes me unhappy too. Why are you bored?"

Fred had motioned to the room, "This is not India, is it? This hotel could be anywhere in the world, the food caters for the western tourist and, to be honest, I feel uncomfortable with these pompous *twats* who love to complain about the service… and it's *my fault*, I didn't realise how bloody hot it was going to be."

"Sir, I don't know what *twat* is, though I like the sound of this word, let me clear your table and bring more tea… and I will think what to do."

"You're very kind. What's your name?"

"Sir, you may call me Ramesh. Better make it Ramesh One. *Ramesh* is a very common name, but please do not let the boss lady hear you calling me by name…" Ramesh scuttled to the kitchen.

Fred saw it all. Why had he not seen it before? Witless Whitmore had been too insistent that Maddie could run the kitchen in his absence. The head injury had allowed Whitmore to elbow Fred out of the way and put Maddie in charge. What if Whitmore had planted the bag of heroin in *his* fridge to discredit him?

"Sir, I have another cousin."

"Really!"

"Forgive me, sir, my other cousin is a most charming married lady, I see you need help, please let me explain…

Darjeeling Hills is the answer. A much better climate for you and some peace."

"Darjeeling?"

"Yes, like the tea, real Indian hospitality, good food… we take a little railway journey together. And not *so bloody hot*, as you would say!"

"I'm very tempted, Ramesh One."

"Please, sir, to go, you can leave the *twats* behind, yes?

Fred laughed and thought, why not?

*

Leaving Things Behind.

The crowded train, at last, started to leave the station at Kolkata. Fred's eyes had been focused on an old Indian man, squatting on the platform, appearing to be in the process of defecating.

"Mr Fred, what are you looking at?" Ramesh One scanned the platform but could not see anything out of the ordinary.

"Nothing, really… just thinking about what we all leave behind in this world. Did you say eighteen hours to Darjeeling?"

"Mr Fred, you are a funny man! It is a short journey in India."

*

Fat Man on a Donkey

"The hills are alive with the sound of tea leaves!" Fred had sung at the top of his voice.

"Mr Fred, I see you are happy but please stop singing… the tea leaves are sensitive to such violence… they need, what is the word… *tranquillity*?"

When Fred continued to sing, Manjit admonished him with laughter in her voice. "*Fat man*, please stop singing!"

"How very rude!" Fred had stopped and tried to appear angry but collapsed in a fit of giggles.

It had been the third day in the Darjeeling Hills, and it was the best Fred had felt in years. Ramesh One's cousin, Manjit, and her husband Zafar had taken to Fred instantly, and when Ramesh One had suggested Manjit should take Fred on expeditions into the hills to replenish his soul and to rediscover his zest for life, she had said in her best English accent, looking him up and down, '*That man* will need a donkey', and Fred had immediately rounded on her in Monty Pythonesque humour.

"Who are you calling, *fat man*?"

Manjit had led him into the hills. He was the father figure she sorely missed. Sometimes they walked, at other times she led him astride a donkey. Sometimes they talked. often, they enjoyed the silence, succumbing to the hypnotic effect of the landscape or the heavy anaesthetising scent of the wild hill flowers. When they returned to the modest dwelling both were somehow lighter and ready to greet Zafar and prepare the evening meal together.

*

The Fall

When he fell, it was fortunate he'd slipped off on the right side of the donkey, onto the bank of thick grass and not on the steep side where he would have been severely hurt. He wasn't physically hurt, he'd blacked out, a sharp pain at the back of his head and Manjit had said he'd been unconscious for a couple of minutes. He was bleeding from the mouth where he'd bitten his tongue but had insisted, he did not need a doctor. It had been the same day they had stumbled upon the plants... beautiful and dangerous.

There had been a couple of occasions after this when she'd caught him staring into the distance and she'd heard him muttering *I'm not the man I used to be.*

On the last night before Ramesh One was due to return to collect Fred, Manjit blew the candle out, and a dog barked in the distance, the first Fred had heard since he'd arrived in the hills.

"Manjit, do you believe in justice?"

"I believe in God's will."

"I struggle with that."

"I know you do, Fred."

"If you could do something. An action. To right the wrongs. To settle a score… to get justice?"

"Are you talking about your daughter, Fred?"

"How do you know it's not God's will, to use someone, to put someone in a position where they could get justice for the ordinary people… to punish the bad people in the world?"

"Fred, you need to rest."

"How many people, given the opportunity, would act to settle the score on behalf of the good people?"

"Fred, you are scaring me."

"A mother whose son has been murdered. I know she would understand what I'm saying."

Fred patted a package under his pillow and imagined the part of the garden where two new super-warmed greenhouses could be erected. His temples had started to ache as he drifted into sleep.

Chapter 25
16 MONTHS EARLIER
Back to Normal?

Fred had been early as usual. Immaculate. He stood at a work surface brandishing a knife with expert hands though his eyes seemed focused on something else in the distance.

Maddie had sidled up to him, "I hope I've managed to keep on top of things," she did not blush at the innuendo, but Fred continued to studiously slice the mushrooms, "I said I hope I haven't messed *your* kitchen up too much."

"Looks fine to me."

"Have you inspected it?"

"No, I don't need to."

Maddie had tried to catch Fred's eye, but he chopped the mushrooms even smaller.

"You've got a little colour and you've even lost some weight."

Fred remained silent and Maddie turned abruptly and sighed, "You've changed, Fred!" When she turned her back, he'd mouthed, 'If only you knew,' but she had stepped towards the office. On the way, Fred had seen her stop at one of the ovens, open it and retrieve a piece of paper. She'd crumpled it and dropped it in the rubbish bin.

Fred's eyes had glazed, and he had been thinking, 'It would surprise a few people... might even kill a few of them... What are *they* going to do? Send me to prison? I've spent the best part of thirty years in here already!'

"I really could, couldn't I?"

Maddie was on the telephone again and she hadn't heard. Fred imagined her cursing his fickleness to the Deputy Governor. He'd tiptoed close enough to overhear the last part.

"Look, Robert, you said *he* might not return. You said the job was as good as mine. Don't think you can mess me about, I've killed for less, you know? Only joking!"

Fred had gone to the toilet where he'd opened the crumpled piece of paper.

'I've missed you Fred, Maddie'.

*

'The Light…

With your index finger and your thumb, and with your eyes closed… press your eyeballs hard through the skin… not too hard… and you'll quickly see a speckled, kaleidoscopic pattern – there's red, white and yellow… and if you're patient you can discern all the colours that make white in the first place – and the flecks shoot about in regular patterns… it's mesmeric – beautiful… the eyes can start to hurt… but the beauty far out ways this. The pain is worth it. The beauty. And if you wait long enough the patterns evolve… to show even more clarity… until a moment of revelation – of pureness – of pure whiteness… of pure truth. The moment of madness or a fundamental truth?

The need to act in the way I did… for personal justice… revenge against the men… I think the plan was there all along, and the need, and now I had the opportunity. I saw what I could do, and I did it with relish.'

— Unattributed scribbled note found in the prison office kitchen

Chapter 26
16 MONTHS EARLIER
Was that a Bite?

"Haven't seen you for a while, Fred, been away?" the landlord pulled the usual, "Any food?"

"Did you miss me?"

"Not really. Felt it in my pocket, that's all, almost went bankrupt you were missing for so long."

"Charming."

"Your brother's already in," the landlord placed a pint in front of Fred and nodded toward his usual table.

"I haven't got a brother."

"Oh, I thought… no offence… well he looks like you… a lot… if you didn't have… if you didn't have hair, that is… he's early today."

"Better make it two then. Now I'm saving your business," Fred checked his hairpiece in the mirror behind the landlord, paid and carried the pints to the table, "and an apple crumble."

"All right, boss? Where've you been? Ain't seen you for weeks."

"I'm flattered everyone is concerned about me. I fancied a change… had a bit of leave left and I'd always fancied India. You're early today, Smithy, have you done a runner?"

"Got some news for you, that's all…"

"News?"

"Yes, about the idiot that attacked you. I told you before, I know people that know people…"

"It was hardly an attack. He shoved me over and I banged my head."

"Well, it can be sorted if you want…"

"Sorted? What does that mean?"

"Anyway, you like."

"You all right, boss?" Smithy nudged Fred.

"What do you mean?"

"Well, you have been staring into space a bit, letting me rabbit on… I thought you were listening, but I don't think you were, somehow… I even drank your pint and finished your pudding, and you didn't say anything."

"Did you?"

"Of course not, I wouldn't do that to a mate, boss."

"Can you yawn through your eyes, Smithy?"

"Eh?"

"Instead of yawning normally… mouth wide open…"

"Eh?"

"Scrunch your eyes tightly, so the yawn is dissipated… it feels like cotton wool being teased in your head… and you don't have to open your mouth at all."

"Are you all right, boss?"

"I'm beginning to wonder about that myself."

*

Chapter 27
12 MONTHS EARLIER
Setting the Hook and Playing the Fish

Fred finished a second helping of the sponge with custard and watched Smithy, at the bar, getting his lunchtime pint and as he pocketed the change he waited for the quirks and mentally ticked them off. He checked over his left shoulder for a potential threat, looked at the floor instead of the landlord and shuffled on the carpet on his way to the table.

"Fuck me, Fred, you can put it away, can't you? You're nearly as fat as me these days."

"I'm in training, aren't I?

"What for? The British Sumo Team?"

"Very funny."

"Got some more news for you, do you want to hear it?"

"Not particularly."

"Walters got stabbed the weekend…"

There was a pause. Fred gulped his lager… let out an exaggerated sigh and placed the glass on the beer mat.

"I suppose it was likely to happen. I mean with his type of lifestyle. Makes enemies all the time…"

"I've got an alibi for this one, Fred, I can safely say I was secure behind my door at the 'Grange… not me… but let's just say it was friends of ours."

"Friends of ours? Don't implicate me. I'm not your friend."

"I'm hurt, Fred, the weeks we've sat in here drinking together… if I'd known I would have sat somewhere else."

"What have you done, Smithy?"

"You said to *sort it* – so I did."

"I said no such thing, Smithy, I don't know where you got that idea."

"Fred, I said, *just say the word and I'll sort it out* – a few months ago… after you came back from India. The day you had apple crumble."

Fred said nothing. What had he done? He tried to remember. He'd had headaches, lost track of time on a couple of occasions, and turned up at work one day only to realise he'd been on a *rest day* and wasn't supposed to be at work at all.

"*Do what it takes*, Smithy, that's what you said, *about time someone wiped the smirk off his face*."

"I don't remember."

"It took a bit of time. He's been hiding in the seg. Well, he won't smirk again. It's the harsh reality: mess with one of my mates and you mess with me and my boss. There's always a price to pay, ain't there? There must be lines… we both know that. Walters crossed a line, that's all… and on your say so… the action was taken… and now we have a new line."

Fred didn't say anything. Smithy must be letting the idea sink in. Fred knew Smithy was cautious. He wouldn't pull too hard. It was always a delicate skill, Smithy must be thinking the hook was barely in the side of Fred's mouth, and if he pulled too hard now, too aggressively, Fred might still get off: confess all to his superiors, prepared to take the consequences for a moment of weakness. Fred realised Smithy must have landed *a few* over the years – it all helped Smithy's business. Fred watched Smithy as he got up and went to get him another pint.

"Fred, you've crossed the line. Now don't get all worked up about it, it's a small debt, in the great scheme of things and I'll help you sort it out. Before you know it, it'll be back to normal, debt paid off, retirement to look forward to… reputation intact… and we'll laugh about this."

"I couldn't possibly do anything… underhand."

"Such a quaint term, Fred, such an old-fashioned way of looking at things…" Smithy waited and retrieved some of the line, patience was the key…" But, Fred, you are *implicated*… but everything's all right… I'll get you through this… if *certain* Deputy Governor heard you'd put the word out to hurt Walters for what he did to you… it doesn't bear thinking about, does it?"

"I've only got a few years left… unblemished service…" Fred was enjoying this.

"That would work in your favour. It'll be easy for you… nobody would ever suspect you… you would be the last person anyone ever suspected… a bit like the Sally Army bringing Satanic literature in on a Sunday morning…" Smithy carefully waited, choosing his words, "Do you remember that female officer, the best-looking woman to have ever worked at The Stretch… late nineties… the year, not her age! I think… Barnet or Bernet? She could have had the pick of anyone: officer, governor, politician… just about anyone in the place… no one could work out *who* got her pregnant, she never said, and left under a cloud… Do you remember?"

"Tell me it wasn't you, Smithy?" he was really enjoying it.

"Not me, Fred, I'd have been so lucky! It was one of the South Americans, linked to a drug cartel, can't remember his name, but they got up to all sorts of physical exercise in the gymnasium storeroom. She made a deal. Nobody ever knew. His child for a very large pay-off… he was never getting out of prison… and she would never have to work again… his parents had a grandchild… she had a life of luxury in the south of France… and nobody ever knew,"

Smithy paused again, thinking he was letting an unexpected revelation sink in, "I know this will hurt, and I apologise before I say it, but nobody would ever suspect you of getting drugs into the prison because everyone knows about your daughter… you're whiter than white… you've challenged prisoners all of your career… and I admire you for it… the irony is, Fred, my old mate… If your daughter was sat next to us now, she'd want you to enjoy your retirement… and she'd laugh if you earned the money to do it by getting a small quantity of drugs into the prison… *She'd* see the funny side…"

Fred let his head sink to the table, his hands grasped so tightly Smithy must have thought he was about to fling his hairpiece across the pub in anguish. Fred let Smithy think he had miscalculated, pushed too far, and was about to lose the biggest fish he had ever played when he was poised over the landing net. Fred sneered but controlled his voice,

"Smithy, what do I have to do?"

"Just a small package," there was a tremble in Smithy's voice, he was trying to be calm, but Fred guessed Smithy this was at the most nerve-wracking point, he was about to land the *big* fish, and had to be careful, "… just a small package… inconsequential… insignificant…"

"Big words for you, Smithy… but the risks are all mine…"

"There would be a large wad of cash for you… and I'd get the Walters thing settled for good too."

"I don't know if I could do it, Smithy," Fred loved the pained look on Smithy's face.

"It's a one-off, Fred, you wouldn't need to know what's in the package if that's what's worrying you?"

"You seem to have me over a barrel, Smithy."

"To put it bluntly, my boss has… but it's only one package."

"Speaking of *barrels*, Smithy, can you get your hands on a shotgun?" no time like the present.

"Who are you going to shoot? Me?"

"Don't tempt me, Smithy, but I was thinking about my neighbour's bloody dog!"

"Have you ever shot anything before, boss?"

"It can't be that difficult."

"With your eyesight, a sawn-off would be best."

"All right. One package. And one package only?" Fred sighed in defeat.

"One package it is. I'll get it sorted, Fred, just think about the money."

Fred was thinking but not about the money. The plan was taking shape. As Smithy skipped to the toilet, Fred knew he was thinking he'd landed the fish of a lifetime.

Chapter 28
10 MONTHS EARLIER
Almost in the Net

A couple of minutes to six in the morning. Fred had been sick in the garden, in front of the greenhouses where the heat lamps burned brightly twenty-four hours a day, and it had nothing to do with his medical prognosis. Nausea still gripped, as he waited for the lock to click open at the prison entrance, and it was rooted in the cylindrical, cling-wrapped package sitting snugly in his underpants. On this damp morning, things had changed, the first fallen leaves had softened and were stuck to the floor; they were dead, trapped and slowly rotting.

The electronic lock clicked open. It was six o'clock on the dot, Fred confirmed by checking his watch for the fifth time – someone had reset the clock – he had counted on still having a few minutes to wrestle with his conscience – his hand was already on the handle and turning it before his brain had the chance to scream *you can still pull out, turn around and get* rid *of it!'* Too late – now he was inside, automatically pointing at his watch to mime the clock was wrong, though it no longer was – a puzzled look from the night officer and a shrug to suggest some people are never satisfied.

And the tray he picked up – number thirteen! His heart missed a beat. His finger didn't register – it never did – and he was about to turn round, make an excuse about feeling unwell when the night officer hit the override button. He was *in* now, he could no longer turn around, and he would have to go through the search process – it was too late.

"Mr Lambert, are you alright? You look very pale this morning," Miss Shudyamov ran her keen eyes over him.

"Coming down with something," he managed to mumble. It took all his self-control not to fumble with the package in his pants which was like an itch drawing his hands. He glanced through the window at the staff carpark and stumbled as he removed a shoe, dropping it to grab hold of the shelf.

"Mr Lambert, you don't look too hot!"

"Too *good*, I think you mean."

"Yes, you don't look too good."

"Felt a bit dizzy, that's all, be fine after a shot of coffee when I get in," his eyes followed one of the dog handlers as he crossed to the entrance. Just his luck! He did not have the usual Alsatian but a Cocker Spaniel, one of the special drugs' dogs – and these dogs entered the prison the same way the staff did!

"What is *dizzy*?"

"Lightheaded," he explained and mimed the act of fainting until she understood. He was caught! He knew how sensitive the dog's nose was, it wasn't just a trace of the stuff in his pants but a wedge – the dog would probably pass out in ecstasy. The more he tried to hurry to get through the search area before the dog entered the more his fingers refused to cooperate – now it was his belt he was having trouble with. He began to rehearse his defence. What defence? He was caught red-handed. Nobody else put his pants on. 'Did anyone else pack your pants for you?' He thought about collapsing to the floor. 'It was the bump to the head, Governor: concussion – irreparable brain damage – didn't know what I was thinking – well, I wasn't thinking – if I just resign, nobody has to know about this, do they?'

Miss Shudyamov's hands helped him with the belt, and she put his things in the tray, even recovering his shoe,

"You are so pale, Mr Lambert and your head feels, what is the word, *clammy*?"

The Cocker was in the prison. The handler shouted 'morning' in a confidant manner – the dog started to fidget, letting out a couple of high-pitched yaps.

"Calm down, boy, you haven't started work yet – he's always so keen."

"The dog is so cute," Miss Shudyamov's attention switched to the Cocker.

From such cuteness, life will come to a tragic end. Fred could already see the dog *sitting* in front of him and all the repercussions. The investigation, the media coverage and being ostracised by everyone he'd ever worked with – and the prison sentence to follow.

The handler crouched to one knee, clearly pleased with the attention of a young lady, and he spoke into the dog's ear, "What is it, Badger?"

The Cocker listened, paused, and replied in a series of half-yaps and full barks.

"Thank you, Badger, good boy, what would I do without you?" he looked at Fred and held his eye. Fred thought his knees were going to buckle.

"What is he saying, please? "Miss Shudyamov asked with fluttering eyelashes.

"He is saying, young lady, that Fred here has him all worked up!"

Fred's bottom lip started to drop – a full confession would be best.

"You've got me…"

"Badger says this old fart will not feed me! No matter how cute I am, so, please go and get the sandwiches you've left on the car seat!"

"You've got me…"

The dog handler left the entrance and trotted over to their car.

"What are you talking about, Mr Lambert? Of course, I've got you… you do not look well… I will help you…"

"I mean, you've got me there, I'm not allowed to feed the dogs… it would be a distraction… and I've got a tight budget…"

"Come on now, I'm sure he was *pulling your leg* – yes? – Sometimes you are too serious. I thought you English had a sense of humour?"

… And that's how it started… with the first package… he was told where to leave it… a safe place… not covered by the cameras on route to the kitchen… he didn't need to know who recovered the package… and the person who picked it up didn't know it was Fred who had brought it in. That's how it worked.

It got easier. Check the car park when you arrive. If there were too many cars for that time of day, assume there was an operation on – staff and dogs in position to search the staff entering the prison that morning – and if specific cars were in the car park in the same parking space, assume a drugs' dog was already on duty… Fred learned when not to bring stuff in.

Chapter 29
10 MONTHS EARLIER
In The Net

Smithy placed a bright pink envelope on the seat next to Fred.

"One thousand smackers! Sorry, mate, they must have run out of brown ones."

"I'm glad it's done. I nearly shit myself I can tell you. I have never been so scared in my life. I was this close to being caught."

"No, you weren't."

"You weren't there – I'm telling you… I'm glad it's done."

"Believe me, Fred, you will not get caught… Anyway, didn't you get a *buzz*… weren't you excited by what you did?"

"If you call a heart attack exciting!"

"We had someone watching you…"

"What are you saying?"

"What I am saying is, a person you do not need to know, made sure you got in safely… and will continue to make sure you are safe… Get my meaning?"

"You said, one package, Smithy."

"Triple H, my boss, is very grateful and wants to be *more grateful*… if you get my drift… There's the *easy way*… we all profit… there's nothing to it… you're in safe hands… There's a lot of money to be had by all… And there's the *hard way*…"

"Triple H?"

"Orrible Arry Enderson."

"What if I say no?"

"There is no *no*. You're implicated… Walters is in the hospital because of you… *He's* also got you on film accepting the first package… It would be a sorry way to bow out, Fred, do you know how many years it is for drug smuggling?"

"You're a bastard."

"You're right again, Fred, you have an uncanny way of knowing things. The contract is for ten drops. Just think of your pension bonus when you retire. You can have a holiday home in the Algarve… How about a hair transplant?"

Fred was thinking, 'Not too much longer to put up with this shit.'

Chapter 30
3 MONTHS EARLIER
Fish of a Lifetime

"Here's the deal, Fred, my old mate! It's a five-year plan. It's a sort of 'alias Smith and Lambert'… we're both old enough to remember…"

"Not funny."

"There's a *job* coming up… It's got your name on it… you will have access to every prison in England… that's three prisons every week… In your capacity as *Her Majesty's Food Commissioner to Prisons*…"

"You are joking… have you seen my CV… It hasn't been updated since ninety-five."

"You're not listening. The job has *your* name on it. Forget the Algarve, you can retire anywhere you like… Florida, Thailand… New Zealand?"

Fred sat calmly. He didn't do scared anymore.

"There's mega-dosh to be made. Triple H has already put the money forward, and invested in me… us… It's the perfect cover… Every prison kitchen in England… You visit, you impart your wisdom, and you *drop off* a package for our captive audience… we corner the market… and we watch the money roll in… It could not be easier… Most prisons don't have half the security as The Stretch… It'll be a cinch!"

"I just hope I'm up to it. Just seem to be getting a bit scatter-brained of late."

Chapter 31
Gutted?

Packages. Who's counting? One of theirs – one of Fred's. Fred's was Monkshood and plenty of it – he had perfected the drying of the root. Only one letter is different – Prison and poison. Prison is poison. Fred thought of the hundreds of twisted, poisonous minds together and despaired that anyone could escape without being tainted. The poison was pervasive – like the Monkshood if you brushed against the leaves... you'd carry a film of it on your person... Fred thought a person may survive but you could unwittingly poison others they touched.

And then the question: How many people... how many daughters could Fred save if he killed ten murderers? How many lives could he change if t*heir* poisonous existence was removed? They would not be able to taint the lives of others...

Chapter 32
1 MONTH EARLIER
And into the Frying Pan

Fred let Smithy work it all out, let him talk about his five-year plan and the Kitchen Tsar for Her Majesty's Prison Service... He ignored his greed as he spoke about the money, he said was invested in this scheme...

Fred's plants were almost ready.

Chapter 33
TWO WEEKS EARLIER
Practise Makes ...

Five-twenty. The alarm clock was stifled with a purposeful slap. Fred was already on the edge of the bed, slippers in place, and a resolute smile on his face. The dog started to bark but it seemed to have lost the power to hypnotise... even when the pitch increased Fred barely checked his stride to the bathroom. Today he was putting an end to it; perhaps the bump on the head had done it. Even his bowels cooperated this morning... 'Take that Tyson!'

Fred was a professional if something was worth doing... he didn't care for laziness or mediocrity. You only had to look at the restored furniture around the house to realise what a fine eye he had for detail, when someone bought a piece from him, they were getting a masterpiece. He couldn't remember the last time he'd sold anything. This morning he could have used the supermarket's brand of sausages, not even bothered to cook them, the outcome would have been the same, but the shoddiness would have grated on his conscience. The act itself would lose something; it would be cheapened by such cost-cutting... Tyson's last meal would be prepared with the finest ingredients.

"Sausages in the pan! Sausages in the pan!

"Sizzle, sizzle, sausages in the pan!"

Fred whispered the words he had sung to his daughter when she was a toddler. Every Sunday morning, they cooked sausage sandwiches for breakfast. She'd loved the machine Fred had picked up from a car boot sale, mixing exotic recipes, and feeding the meat mixture into real skins... and then she'd met Mike, or was it Steve... the first boyfriend... Trust him to be vegan.

Not too much oil. Turning frequently. Perfect texture. Nice and brown. High quantity of meat... not too fatty... no one could accuse Fred Lambert of preparing an unhealthy sausage. Fred's cooking never killed anyone. His smile returned. It replaced the stern concentration that had transfixed him for the last half an hour. Each sausage was lifted from the pan and placed on a piece of kitchen roll in a neat row. A second piece of kitchen roll was placed on top to help remove excess fat... he rolled the sausages for a few seconds, savouring the feeling beneath his fingers, eventually uncovering his work with satisfaction.

"Five for you and five for me."

Fred poured a cup of tea. He hardly noticed the yapping... Strangely, something usually so torturous hardly seemed to register this morning. He took two pieces of bread, lightly buttered them, added a couple of dollops of strong English mustard, and began to carefully load his share of the breakfast, pausing at two and debating whether he should eat five sausages at all as four would be healthier... They were particularly rich... Then he remembered *the plan* and smiled at the uselessness of the debate.

"Tyson, you get six, you are a lucky sod!"

Fred took his time with his sandwich, it was a solemn occasion after all, every drop of tea and a wet finger to remove every crumb from the plate before his gaze returned to the remaining six sausages. When the yapping stopped for a few seconds it acted as a signal for Fred to move, which he did almost robotically, but expertly, selecting the sharpest knife from the rack he made an incision in the six remaining sausages and removed a small quantity of meat, though his eyes never left the sausages, even when his left hand reached up to the cupboard, finding the knob with unerring accuracy, his eyes continued to trace every blemish, change in skin colour, every bead of oil remaining on his chosen weapon, his fingers found the small Tupperware box of the dried leaves of the plant he had been cultivating in the greenhouses. He looked over his shoulder.

"You were wrong, Mary, it took a while, but I got off my backside and I am *doing something,*" he blinked and added, "I must be going mad, Mary, I thought you were hovering on my shoulder, just how you used to do…"

Fred's fingers struggled with the Tupperware lid, it was a task Mary would have done, and he jigged around the kitchen, cursing *sod it,* until it opened with a *pop,* sending the contents across the work surface. *Master criminal,* he was not. He made sure he slipped some plastic gloves on before he swept the dried leaves back into the open box. Using a teaspoon, he sprinkled the poison into the gashes in four of the sausages and moved the other two to one side. Poisoning was hungry work and having changed his mind, he'd have them later. He smoothed the remnants of scooped sausage meat across the wound. If a job was worth doing.

"That's just fine. That will do the job, just fine…"

But would it?

Were four sausages enough? He'd read everything he could on Monkshood but there was no label he could turn to for the dosage required to kill an Alsatian dog.

"You're right, Mary," Fred felt her hand on his shoulder, the poison was concentrated in four sausages and not spread randomly like rat poison, "should do the job."

His heart stopped racing. Everything would be fine. The weapons were lined up on one of his best China plates and he took a deep breath ready for action. From his jacket pocket, sat on one of the kitchen chairs, he produced some sachets of tomato ketchup, he'd stopped buying the stuff, but the devil is in the detail, and he knew *she* did next door. *She* got through two bottles a week, the wind had blown her recycling bin over one week, and he'd made a note. Consequently, on a detour on the way home to a fast-food outlet, he'd kept his helmet on, simply walked up to a table of teenagers, pocketed five sachets, and walked out again, leaving them gobsmacked.

Changing his mind again Fred added the last two *normal* sausages and coated them liberally with tomato ketchup. They would be the *freebies* to get the dog *going*. He picked up the plate and made a half-turn to the back door. A dark silhouette against the frosted glass! A sharp rat-a-tat-tat!

Fred opened the door.

"Morning, Fred, parcel to sign for."

Fred's face must have asked a question.

"You really must remember to lock the gate… Then again you didn't hear the doorbell, you deaf bugger… The plants are coming along, what are they again?" the postman asked.

"None of your business."

"And why have you put a padlock on them greenhouses?"

"To stop nosey parkers, like you."

"Is your parcel something to do with them plants?"

"Mind your own business."

"… . Ooh, sausages! Don't mind if I do…"

Fred's face must have said *he did mind*.

"Don't be like that, Fred" the postman accused, "You can spare one for old greedy guts!"

"Not really, Bob…"

The postman withdrew his hand, "but I'd be doing you a favour…" he tapped Fred's midriff.

"No, you can't. Meats off… Can't you smell it? Throwing them out just now."

"Smell all right to me… Is this one of your tricks?"

"Suit yourself," Fred moved the plate toward the postman, "I hope you carry a *bog roll* with you, you'll need it."

The postman nudged the plate back, "Just sign for this, will you?"

"All right, Bob, now go and give somebody else a heart attack."

"… And a *good morning* to you too!"

Fred closed the door rudely in his face.

Bob knocked on the door loudly again.

"What now?"

"The postman always knocks twice!" Bob snatched a sausage and ducked out of range, scurrying round the corner of the house, calling back, "I'll take my chances… What doesn't kill you… Delicious!"

Fred examined the plate. The lucky beggar! Should have known. Bob was always lucky. Bob's wife had *run off* with a Moroccan she'd met on holiday, and two weeks later Bob had *shacked up* with the estate agent who'd come to value their house… and she was fifteen years younger than him. A week later Bob's works' syndicate had scooped a hundred thousand on the lottery… And to top that, Bob's son who'd gone travelling and was virtually missing for three years in South America had turned up married to some corn beef tycoon… sometimes life simply was not fair.

The dog was still quiet. A window of opportunity. A time for action. After another deep breath, he opened the back door and tiptoed onto the patio. He judged the sausages and muttered, "It's for your good."

It wasn't much of a life for a dog, chained up all day outside in all weathers, locked in the kitchen all night, he'd be doing him a favour… *cruel to be kind*… but what a way to go… The best sausages the bloody dog would ever taste. It would be a good way to go.

The dog had escaped on at least two occasions. He's had chances, Fred couldn't understand why he'd allowed himself to be recaptured. It must have been the shock to realise a world existed beyond the five-foot fence panels – or physically he just didn't have it in him.

Fred approached the fence. No life for a dog. Eat, sleep and shit. When the wind was in the wrong direction the smell seeped into Fred's house even though the windows were never opened. Fred remembered the time he'd seen the dog sniff its pelleted faeces and eat some of it. Was that *normal*?

It would be better after this. The dog could eat one last meal and enjoy one long sleep. Tyson was lying down, head resting on his forelegs, sad eyes looking alternatively at the back door of the house and the garden gate. Ears were poised for the faintest sound.

"I've got something for you."

Tyson lifted his head, glanced nonchalantly at Fred, and resumed his waiting posture.

"Sausages!" Fred hissed. He looked over his shoulder in case he'd spoken too loudly. He dangled a sausage over the fence but still no response. Tyson stretched, yawned, and barely made his chain rattle on the concrete slabs. Tyson resumed his vigil. Fred broke a small piece of *safe* sausage and threw it, dart-like, toward the dog. It clipped the dog's nose and dinked a couple of feet. Tyson barely blinked.

"What's the matter, you mutt? Not hungry? Too far away you lazy, four-legged shit producer… You can't be ill… Not today! These are the best sausages in the West Midlands!" Fred launched another piece, harder this time, and it slapped off the side of the dog's jaw – it rebounded a couple of feet. Tyson scornfully repositioned his head.

"Don't ignore me!" Fred hissed as the third piece of sausage left his hand.

Tyson's head moved so quickly; Fred was only conscious something had happened when he heard the jaws snap shut on the morsel.

"What do you think of that?" Fred flicked another piece and that too was plucked from the air. Tyson got to his feet. The change was startling – he hoovered the other freebies, his chain dancing into life as he strained for the furthest morsel. Tyson's *feeding* mode had been switched in his brain, and he shifted his weight onto his hind legs ready to launch at the next airborne present.

"That's the last two you get for free, you little shit machine," Fred spoke lovingly as to a puppy to get its trust and Tyson gobbled them down before they reached the floor, his front feet off the floor.

"Lovely, aren't they? Want the big one?" Fred showed a whole sausage, he moved it slowly across the top of the fence as if it was a finger puppet, and Tyson watched it hypnotised. Fred pretended to throw it. Tyson tensed and whimpered, whining when the sausage didn't leave his hand.

Fred froze. Tomato ketchup staining his fingers. He stared at the scar in the side of the sausage that concealed the poison – 'Do it, you fool, you bloody idiot. What are you waiting for? Coward!'

Tyson started to bark.

"No! No barking! The barking must stop…"

The barking rose in pitch. The sausage in the dog's eyeline.

But Fred could not do it. When it came down to it, he could not go through with his plan. He could not murder the dog.

"I am a coward," he whispered, replacing the sausage on the plate, "perhaps I am a limp lettuce leaf; a man of inaction after all. You lucky boy, you don't know how close you were..." he rested his forehead on top of the fence in absolution.

Something smacked against the fence, Fred staggered backwards still holding the plate, and one sausage rolled off and seemed to fall in slow motion to the ground, as the dog worked itself into a fervour... a fragmented thought, a moment of clarity, and Fred considered eating the sausages himself – *the dog wins again*!

Fred's head was scrambling, dazed by the noise, small detonations going off in his brain, and he was having trouble focussing. Blinking rapidly, he tried to wipe his eyes with his free hand.

And that's when it became ludicrous. Tyson launched himself at the fence again – he would have been clean over if it hadn't been for the chain – Fred had time to count the bristles and even to taste the dog's foul breath, and for a moment the dog's paws rested on Fred's shoulders. The chain had snapped tight. Tyson was in *no man's land, no dog's land*, his hind legs scratching precariously on top of the fence. Fred dropped the plate, and the dog's eyes followed the sausages but then, as if realising this was not the time to worry about food – their eyes met again – panic. Tyson tottered, mini steps, his weight was on Fred's side, but the hypotenuse chain continued to hold his head high and was beginning to cut into the throat. No barking now, just a crazy claw-paw shuffle. Fred was a statue.

"Steady, now…" Fred stepped forward, squashing a sausage, but the dog tried to snap at his hand – it was a fatal mistake. One of the hind legs slipped from the top of the fence… he seemed to lift momentarily on one leg, arching his back, but the other leg gave way and he fell sideways… eyes popping.

Eighty-five pounds of Alsatian thumped into the panel on Fred's side. The hind legs frantically searched for the ground and then for purchase anywhere they could. Fred closed in, trying to cradle the dog, trying to support the weight, but in his panic, with a twist of the neck, Tyson made another attempt to snap at Fred's hand, and this only allowed the chain to close more tightly on his windpipe. Fred collapsed backwards, avoiding the teeth, onto his backside, and watched helplessly, transfixed as the dog went into spasm – the hind leg twitched last.

Fred sat on a sausage, in the silence – Tyson was dead – hanged. It had been an accident. Surely, *she* would see that. Fred heard a low gaseous rumble before a stream of excrement burst from the dog, splattering his shoes and the bottom of his trousers.

Chapter 34
2nd OCTOBER, 12:00 p.m.
On The Eve

Fred was standing at the open back door. He looked at the empty kennel next door. Silence. Tyson was dead. An accident. WPC Bennett had seen it from his point of view. He'd called the police after getting rid of the *not-so-deadly* sausages; WPC Bennett had said it *was* an accident and had even spent two hours next door explaining what may have happened. Fred had even offered to dig a grave at the bottom of *her* garden if it would help. That's when it had threatened to kick off; she'd said she would be happy for him to dig a big hole, but it wouldn't be the dog she'd be throwing into it...

WPC Bennett had reminded him of his daughter and how she might have turned out; everything was because of his daughter.

The funny thing was, and he cast another look in the direction of the kennel, Fred was still hearing a dog barking at odd times in the day and night; he turned to pour another cup of tea from the kettle on the kitchen surface, it was as if Tyson had risen from the dead.

"Morning, Fred!" Smithy jumped at the backdoor, furtive as usual, looking over his shoulder and out of breath.

"What do you want?" Fred's heart hadn't even quickened, "You're early."

"Charming, Fred, a nice way to greet your business partner."

"Hope no one saw you."

Smithy shrugged as he entered the kitchen.

"The plan's changed and as well as the usual drop this afternoon, you've got to get *this* little beauty in," Smithy showed the smallest mobile phone Fred had ever seen, "don't look concerned, nearly one hundred per cent plastic – won't set the metal detector off."

"Fine."

"What? No argument? You don't want to discuss the ethics of such a move?"

Fred's face went blank, his left hand held the work surface for balance, Smithy's eyes never left him, ready to step forward if he toppled over.

"What's up, Fred?"

Fred regained his composure, he shook his head and appeared to regain his train of thought returned.

"What it is, Smithy, is I think I'm losing my marbles… The package for this afternoon… I can't for the life of me remember where I've put it. Don't get me wrong – it's in the house somewhere… I was looking for it when you showed up."

"Not in the usual place?"

"I don't have a usual place. I think my head's going a bit, you know."

"You senile old fart!"

They both chuckled.

"Help me look, won't you… I need it for this afternoon, and I'm under pressure to study for the Tsar interview next week… I know you said, I've only got to show up, but if a job's worth doing…"

"That's the attitude… you'll make me late, you will… I've got to be back at the warehouse in half an hour."

"It doesn't matter, they're not bothered, are they?"

"What do you mean?"

"Well, for one, you're always late and the warehouse never says anything, and for two, you've only got a few weeks left… they're hardly going to call out the search party even if you don't show."

"Suppose not."

"Smithy, I don't want to teach an old dog new tricks, but you'll find it quicker than me... you're the professional... just like when you were a kid... search my house methodically, quickly, don't leave any surface untouched... but don't ransack the place... it's not strictly an old person's house you're robbing..."

"I resemble that remark!"

"Start at the top and work yourself down... I've been known to hide it in the loo... I'll get a fresh pot of tea ready."

"Why don't you take it easy? You could always ring one of your buddies with a drugs' dog... he'll find it."

"That's not even funny..."

Ten minutes later Smithy had finished upstairs but reappeared in the kitchen wearing a set of Fred's uniform.

"What d'ya think? When we're both dressed in uniform, we could be twins."

"Not a bad fit, but why?"

"I've been thinking... we do look alike... and you don't seem to be... no offence, Fred... to be *there* of late... to be honest, mate, you're on the slide... I've got too much to lose and if you screw this Tsar job up, I stand to lose everything... So, I pretend to be you... I visit all the prisons... keep Orrible Arry happy... in fact, I don't have to let *him* know... secure my future... ironic, I'd be going back to lots of jails after I've been released on licence! What do you think?"

"With a bit of coaching... it could work... Saves me shitting myself."

"Hey, I knew you had problems but..."

They chuckled again.

Smithy resumed the search for the missing package, methodically going through the furniture projects in the lounge, checking the tops, the drawers, and the undersides. When he'd finished there, he was still empty-handed.

"Bloody hell, Fred, can't find it… all I've got is dirty fingers from the varnish stuff that's coated on all your bits of crap."

"Masterpieces, I'll have you know."

"I'll never get my hands clean."

"It'll turn up… head's been a bit of a shed recently… Oh, check the outside toilet… I spend a lot of time in there… coffee will be here when you return."

Smithy sneaked his way to the outside toilet, rummaged briefly, flushed the chain for good measure and returned to the kitchen.

"Nothing you senile old twat! You should keep that sawn-off somewhere safer, you know, I could take it back if you want. You're lucky the dog strangled itself. By the way, what happened to all the flowers? Looks like there's been a plague of locusts in the greenhouses."

"I'll be needing the gun, Smithy, sooner rather than later…" Fred stared into space again.

"Fair enough," Smithy grunted, "Just let me know when you've finished with it."

Fred laughed and shrugged, "Oh, you'll know!"

"Just get the phone *in*… the package will turn up."

"Okay, and it makes me think it would be wiser to increase the size of the packages… harder to lose… more profit too… Next time I see you I'll tell you where I found it! I've got to get back too; I'm preparing something special for the lads tonight."

"You'd better find it, I'm very late… See you Tuesday, Fred," Smithy smiled and edged out of the door.

"See you, Smithy… Aren't you forgetting something?"

"What?"

"You've still got my uniform on!"

"Oops! Hey, what's this in your jacket pocket?"

PART THREE

Chapter 35
OCTOBER 3rd 2019, 05:20
HMP The Grunge
Cell 121
Where Am I?

At twenty minutes past five Fred woke. He always did. Always twenty passed five – had to be awake before the dog started to bark. He reached for the bedside lamp and missed, or rather it wasn't there, and on his left-hand-side, he sensed a cold barrier where his wife's side of the bed should have been – he thought of a coffin in a vault – and realised this was not *his* bed. It was very dark, with almost no light coming through the barred window – his internal clock said twenty-past five, but he wasn't sure. He closed his eyes, ignoring the signs he needed the toilet, and tried to gather his thoughts – where was he? Who was he?

He'd walked toward the vehicle gate lock at eight o'clock in the evening. Smithy's battered wristwatch had said that. He'd knocked on the glass panel, catching a glimpse of a balding man in the reflection, almost startled at the makeover, pulling himself together as the gate officer turned round and saw him. Shuffling on the spot, acting like Smithy, not giving the gate officer his full profile, as the intercom was activated from inside.

"Smith A3264AG," he said, mimicking Smithy's annoying nasal grunt.

"Smith, you are three hours late! I know you're out soon, but this is ridiculous. What have you got to say for yourself?" The gate officer, a man in his mid-sixties squinted through the window into the semi-darkness afforded by the one dim floodlight above the vehicle lock.

"So, arrest me and put me in jail – or you could just do your job and let me in… I'm tired and bloody cold out here!"

"Do not take that tone with me, Mr Smith."

"Look, the bus broke down and I've walked the last seven miles… have I ever been late before?"

"Well, yes, too many times to mention… but not three hours! And the warehouse said you did not attend this afternoon. Where were you?"

Fred tried to keep his composure… trust Smithy to be late all the time… what had he been up to? At the back of his mind, he recalled something Smithy had told him about the old man who manned the gate at night, something about setting fire to his dinner.

"What are you going to do? Behead me? Look, I think I'm coming down with the flu, I'm cold, so unless you're about to try and burn the gate down again with your culinary skills to warm me up – please let me in!"

"Bit harsh, Mr Smith, but I'll contact the orderly officer, see what she thinks…"

"Who is it?"

"Mad Mimsey."

"You may as well shoot me now, eh?" Fred nodded and waited, scuffing his shoes on the kerb. When the gate officer turned his back to make the call, he couldn't help feeling the nakedness of his bald head with his fingers. He tapped the window and mimed, *I can go, you know if you don't want me*, but the gate officer lifted a finger before replacing the telephone receiver.

The vehicle lock started to slide open. It stopped, leaving just enough room for Fred's belly to pass through – he saluted the gate officer and mimed, *very funny* – this was it; he was inside the vehicle lock at the Grunge, slouched like Smithy, collar turned up as the gate closed behind him, pulling at Smithy's clothes because they made him itch.

"And what time do you call this, Mr Smith? I was just about to put you down as *breach of licence.* You'll still be up before the Governor in the morning."

"Give it a rest, Mimsey, he's just given me the third degree, I know I'm late…" Fred started spluttering, using a handkerchief to distract the orderly officer, "Bloody bus… and I'm dying here… Can I just have my bed?"

"It's CM Mimms to you, Mr Smith, and stop coughing in my direction."

"Sorry, Mimsey," spluttering even more.

"I give up, you'll get me shot, come on then… you're out in a month so I'll cover for you, just this once, so I don't have to put up with you for any longer…"

"Cheers me dears," Fred started to walk toward the inner gate to access the prison compound.

"Where do you think you're going? CM Mimms grabbed him by the sleeve. Fred froze. What had given him away? He coughed into the handkerchief to buy time and tried not to panic.

"Just want my bed…" his heart pounded; a pulse throbbed on the side of his head.

"Finger."

"What?"

"Index finger! I've still got your biometric to do – more than my job's worth."

So close, Fred thought, a finger's width from getting inside. He'd overlooked the possibility of a cat D prison having a biometric finger recognition system. Smithy would have been logged out in the morning, but Fred would not register on the computer on the way in. He smiled with the joke – he'd been *fingered*. But in for a penny… he placed his finger on the reader.

The reader turned red and beeped.

"You'll have to try again," CM Mimms directed.

Fred blew his finger for luck.

It turned red and bleeped again.

"Third time lucky, Mimsey."

Red and bleep.

"Ha, you'll have to let me go, that's the rule," coughing into the handkerchief and taking a step toward the outside gate.

CM Mimms was flustered, but managed to save the day, "The judge sentenced you, and the sentence is not up for another month or so – you do not have a get out of jail free card, Mr Smith, and stop calling me Mimsey!"

"Sorry, Mimsey – you're the boss. Spoilsport. You lot are sticklers for the rules."

Fred had followed the CM to Smithy's block where she opened an outer door to let him in.

"Good night."

"Good night, Mimsey."

"I told…"

Fred closed the door and remembering Smithy's description of where he lived, *an end cell befitting someone of my experience and years*, he quickly located Smithy's cell, turned the privy lock, and fell on the bed.

Chapter 36

OCTOBER 3rd, 06:30
HMP The Grunge
Cell 121
Who Am I?

Fred sat on the cell toilet; an aluminium toilet, cleaner than his own at home but to distance himself from Smithy he'd lined the seat with a layer of toilet paper before he sat down. There was a dull ache at the back of his head, and he rubbed it. Where was Smithy? He pulled the pale blue t-shirt away from his stomach and sniffed it. No mistaking Smithy's stale roll-up odour and he gagged, jolting his head and he slipped off the toilet seat to the floor.

He'd done it. The curry had been served. He remembered thinking he should have done it years ago; nobody could ever say that Fred Lambert was not a man of action. He'd left the moped running to annoy the neighbour. The backdoor had been unlocked and he cursed Smithy for not locking it and putting the key in the outside toilet. When his fingers gripped the cold metal, he'd stopped dead in his tracks.

"Turn that fucking moped off, you old bugger!"

That had got him moving. Fred had to stick to his timetable. It would not be long before the police knocked at his door, and it would not be to turn his moped off. *Note in the front porch. Note on the back door. Note fixed to the pink laptop.* One last look at the kitchen, where he and Mary had spent so much time together, where he and his daughter had made sausages on a Sunday morning, and where Smithy had stood. *Where Smithy had stood!*

"Oops!" Smithy had said, "Hey, what's this in your coat jacket pocket?"

Fred had winced.

Smithy had waved an extra-large pair of white frilly knickers in the air, his eyes lit up as he realised what they were, and Fred could see his mind working overtime to join the dots together.

Fred had edged closer.

"Now hold on a minute," Smithy had looked pleased with himself, "the dresses in the wardrobe... there was a lipstick in the bathroom... I couldn't find the shoes, though, is there something you haven't told me?"

Fred had smashed the smirk from Smithy's face with a right hook. He'd left Smithy dribbling on the floor.

"You can forget your five-year plan, Smithy! You can stick the phone up your *own* arse. I'm getting out. I'm a dead man walking and there's nothing you can do to stop me."

"If you don't turn that fucking moped off, I'm calling the police!"

The neighbour always had to have the last word. Fred smiled as he took a deep breath, closed the back door, and thought about the exclamation mark he was about to make. He let his eyes get used to the dark. He would be with his daughter soon. The dog had continued to bark and his moped mis-fired. The sum of his life of late. He had taken another deep breath and slowly walked toward the outside toilet. He'd smiled in the direction of the greenhouses and whispered *thanks* to Manjit, hoping she was happy and wished her many happy journeys in the Darjeeling hills.

He laughed, screamed, lost his breath, and tried to make sense of the image in the outside toilet. A dead prison officer sat on *his* toilet with most of his head blown away. *Smithy* sat on the toilet, trousers down, the sawn-off on his lap, most of his head splattered against the back wall.

"How dare *you* sit in my spot! The place *I* was going to blow my brains out!"

With a sharp pain in the back of his head, Smithy became blurry, and Fred had to clasp his neck. When he refocused, he was holding the sawn-off his finger caressing the trigger. What had he done? Had he chinned Smithy, picked him up and placed him on the toilet before blowing his head off? He couldn't remember.

"Well, that's it! What do I do now? I was working to a plan, it was simple, poison a few scumbags and turn the gun on myself but you've put your bloody foot in it, it's pathetic, what do I do? Sit on your bloody lap and pull the trigger? It's absurd... I need to think about this!"

Fred looked at the upstairs window, half expecting to see his daughter looking down on the farce, shaking her head at his incompetence. The dog continued to bark and the moped continued to misfire.

"What a mess!" Fred realised he still had the fourth note stuck on his wrist, "*I* won't be needing this after all," and he rested the sawn-off against the toilet wall, shrugged, and leaning Smithy to one side, fixed it to the buttock. He put Smithy's hands back on the gun and rested the barrel where his head had been. Fred pushed the door closed feeling it catch, as it always did, on an uneven paving stone.

"Think, Fred, did you kill Smithy? It's possible. If you didn't then who did? Can't see Smithy killing himself. It's obvious, it must be Orrible Arry or an associate, Smithy must have rung him and told him the plan's gone *tits up,* and Orrible Arry's lost it with him and redecorated my toilet with his head. Hold on Fred! You're going to be next.

Just a small point, you were just about to kill yourself so what does it matter if Orrible Arry does the deed for you, he'd be doing you a favour. There's a principle here. No scumbag is going to get the better of me. It's my choice when I die, and I've just decided I'm not quite ready…"

Fred closed the kitchen door and stopped talking. Where would be the best place to hide and try to get his head together? Whom was he trying to fool, he was hardly the type of man to be able to hide from a criminal gang, all he'd known was the inside of a prison for close to thirty years.

"If you don't turn that fucking machine off, I'm going to end up behind bars for what I'm going to do to you!"

Fred strode upstairs, took his uniform off, put it away, and put Smithy's clothes on that he had discarded on the bed earlier. He patted his wife's side of the bed, looked round the room one last time, his eyes resting on the newspaper clippings when he had been a *real* hero, and made his way back to the kitchen. He slipped into the garden, making sure the note was still on the back door and made toward a part of the privet fence used by Smithy to come and go unobserved.

"Oops," Fred imitated Smithy's irritating nasal tone as he retraced his steps to the toilet, lifted and pulled the door open again, exchanged wristwatches and with great ceremony removed his glasses and his hairpiece and put them on a shelf.

*

07:45
A Little Time
The stink would not go away. Fred lay on the bed looking at the ceiling, making out more patterns and discolouration as the morning light fought to get through the window that would not open; the cell reeked of stale roll-ups; it was in the pillow, the bedding, and the clothes he was wearing. Slowly the unit came to life. In-cell toilets flushing, taps running, and doors opening as some of the prisoners exited to take a morning shower.

"Ten minutes to labour. Outside workers to the gate in fifteen!"

"Smithy, are you going or what?" Someone tried the cell door handle and walked away. A few minutes later the unit went quiet, the cat D prisoners had left for work in the community, and the top privy lock in Fred's cell door was turned.

"Smithy, you going to work today, or what?"

"No miss," Fred turned to the wall, "I'm all flu'd up and I'm out soon anyway."

"You sound a bit off, no need to get lazy, and by the way, your cell stinks!" the officer closed the door and Fred heard her give *clear* to work.

Doing *time*. Looking at the walls, the ceiling, and the floor. Smithy had been right it wasn't easy, and Fred had only been killing time for half an hour. He felt a flutter in his chest and tried to breathe slowly until the palpitations subsided. Something he'd written in his diary in his bedroom flitted into his mind – 'the most dangerous soldier is the one that didn't care if they lived or died.'

His cell door burst open; he'd been dozing.

"Smithy, turn the television on, you must see the news! It's all about The Stretch and I know you were there back in the day."

Chapter 37
OCTOBER 10th 2019
HMP The Grunge
The Accidental Mass Killer

What sort of man am I?

I couldn't have done it. Never been that good at anything. Used to make a mean curry. They must have died from something else. Couldn't even find the volume button on the television. Something in the water? I didn't use that much. Did I? All those murderers inside The Stretch – it must have been one of them – doesn't that make more sense? Coincidence, I happen to put a bit of stuff in the curry. Food poisoning, yes, but not three hundred deaths. Need to look for the real cause of death if you ask me. I'm not capable of such a thing. As I said, I've never been good at anything. I can make a mean curry. Surely you must be *talented* to achieve such a result. It's not that I practised! I couldn't even poison the dog – that was an accident. It *was* an accident. That's what it was. It'll all come out in the end. 'Man accidentally kills over three hundred.' *The accidental mass killer*. No blame attached. Check my kitchen. Spotlessly clean. Exemplary record. Got to count for something. Always been fair. Can't attach blame surely. Never done anything wrong in my life – it's not like I'm one of them – I haven't got a criminal record – never had a speeding ticket. I didn't mean it. I mean the consequences. I meant a little *Delhi belly* but not this. Leniency. First offence. Let off surely. Conditional discharge? Over three hundred dead though! How about community service? I could cook for the homeless to pay my debt to society... Are you sure it was me?

*

Get Some Perspective

It's a matter of perspective. Most of them were going to die before their time anyway, and a fair proportion would have died in prison… poor lifestyle, and poor diet… in effect, I did society a favour. I saved the taxpayers millions by adding an extra ingredient to the curry. Millions will be saved over the years in one stroke. They were not contributors to society, they were the takers – murderers, rapists, and armed robbers. Technically… technically and factually, the world is a safer place. Technically and factually. I did what most of you have thought about doing – it was a death penalty if you like – it was heroic. It was courageous. It was outrageous. In a hundred years, it will be perceived differently, and I will be posthumously awarded a medal for services to Queen and country… you can keep my Long Service Medal… Technically and factually the world is a safer place.

*

Poor Old Smithy

What about Smithy? Was that me? Was it my fault? I don't know what came over me. I haven't felt well… haven't been the same – had a head injury, you know? That's what it was. Unconscious. Knocked off my moped too. Never blamed the prison… It's in the *accident book*… they're responsible… just as responsible as I am… don't you think? Yes, I was assaulted at work too… knocked unconscious… It's in the accident book. It's proof, isn't it? Not responsible. Diminished responsibility at the very least… Should not have been allowed back to work… they never checked me properly, did they, for any long-term damage? They are responsible at the end of the day. Smithy died because of negligence. Poor old Smithy… Old sod… Salt of the Earth. Not his fault he was an old lag… never had a chance… It was an accident of birth… An accident too! Could not be helped… it was always going to happen… Victim of society.

221

Wrong place at the wrong time. Worst case scenario – mental hospital for a couple of years... sort my head out... first offence... I think he was dead before the rest... Must be seen separately... Diminished responsibility. It was a one-off crime really... the three hundred are completely different... I've explained that... Accidental.

*

He Had It Coming

Get some perspective... He deserved it. He's been ruining people's lives all his life. He was a rat... doing the dirty work, running backwards and forward, delivering drugs, collecting debts, making sure some were punished... setting an example, he called it. People were hurt. Killed... by drug use or the reparations for not paying. He's probably killed hundreds... thousands... had a hand, or an arm, in many, many deaths... but was caught for one. He got off lightly, he was a dead man walking... if it wasn't me, it would have been someone else... eventually. His death has saved other lives... stopped others from getting caught up in drugs in the first place... You should be thanking me... I'm only guilty of not doing it sooner... but I saw the light... knew what I had to do... And sooner or later it was going to be him or me... It was somebody like him that supplied the drugs to my daughter!

*

My Fevered Brow

'My head aches so much... sometimes I can hardly lift it from the pillow... sometimes I'm fine... I have a surge... I have a purpose... I know what I must do... What is wrong with me? I hope I have enough time... I'm doing time... How many weeks have passed? What sort of man am I?'
— Ramblings recovered from a hidden compartment in the prison-issue pillow.

Chapter 38
You Screws, You Lose…

"Smithy looks pale, don't you think?"

"Says he's not well."

"Stopped smoking too."

"He's hardly been out his pad the last few weeks."

"Asked for cleaning materials. Been cleaning the cell, top to bottom, and even asked for some paint. He's out soon!"

"I've seen it all before. Getting toward the end of a long sentence… some of them don't want to be released… Scared."

"Institutionalised."

"Asked for new bedding, a new pillow and a new toothbrush!"

"The cheek… he's out soon… Does he think the Prison Service is made of money!"

"Did you give it to him?"

"He started to cry."

"Did you, though?"

"Yes, some of the things, I felt sorry for him."

"Gone soft you have!"

*

Pillow Talk

Smithy didn't have a lot to show for a life sentence. So much for a *criminal mastermind.* Empty shelves, an empty cupboard… the only thing he was good at collecting was dust. No books. No photographs. Fred had salvaged the best prison clothing from a scrunched-up pile under the bed and put them through washing and drying machines in the communal area, when everybody was at work, just so he had something clean to wear. He'd cleaned top to bottom to erase Smithy from the cell. Eventually, all that remained was the dark blue mattress cover and pillow and a stain in the toilet he disguised with blue toilet cleaner.

A few weeks must have passed. The news channel on the television said *they* were no longer looking for anyone in connection with the mass killing at The Stretch. On Friday he would be released with a resettlement grant in his pocket, all forty-five pounds of it, it was a fate worse than the life he had been living. In the hours of darkness... staring upward into the blackness... unable to discern the ceiling... he had wrestled with *the choice*... *the* choice all prisoners must wrestle with... in the lonely moments... an opponent calling from the *other side*... calling them to join them... explaining all the negatives, making *despair* an insurmountable wall... Fred knew where the ligature points were... he'd ticked them off as he cleaned the cell... He had had no intention of being arrested... perhaps this was always how it was going to end... the irony of a life given to the Prison Service... he would not waste the taxpayers' money for his incarceration... no matter how short it might be.

But when the stars behind his eyes took over... he'd quite liked the thrill of it all... turning the tables... hiding in a place no one would look, following his story on the news, knowing his name would be written in the history books.

When he used to play golf, he'd always had the notion he would take his own life before he became a burden to anyone, drinking his favourite whiskey and consuming the required number of tablets in the undergrowth overlooking the ninth hole. It was high above the course, and he imagined looking down on the golfers, putting on the green and maybe, being able to push the ball offline, just enough for another birdie to go begging, and to hear another player mumble under his breath – *this hole's cursed by Lambert.* Never wanted to be a burden.

"Mr Smith, I've got something for you… if you promise not to cry again," Fred opened his eyes, it was the *prairie dog* officer, "You all right, Mr Smith, you were staring into space?"

"What is it, boss?"

"I know you're out soon… and I really shouldn't… against the rules… but I have a new pillow for you…" She scanned the cell, chin held high, head moving from Fred to the toilet, to the window and the floor.

"It doesn't matter, anymore, boss."

The officer started to close the door then changed her mind.

"Look here, Mr Smith, I went to a lot of trouble to get this…"

"Give it to somebody else, boss."

"I insist."

"Jesus! Leave me alone!"

"Keep your hair on, Mr Smith."

It was probably the only thing she could have said to stop Fred in his tracks. They held each other's eyes – raised eyebrows, and when Fred picked up his pillow the officer thought he was going to throw it at her. They exchanged pillows in silence and the officer backed toward the cell door. She stopped…

"What's this?"

"A smelly prison-issue pillow?"

"Damaged."

"What do you mean?"

"This pillow is torn," she ran her finger into a slit and removed an envelope, "I may have to place you on report for damaging prison property."

Fred thought quickly.

"Come on, Miss, I'm out soon… the truth is… the truth is… I can explain… You can't trust anyone in prison… full of criminals… when I'm not here – out at work – you never know who can get in your pad… some things are personal… everyone has a *hidey hole*… understand, Miss?"

The officer juggled the pillow and the envelope, and glanced at the contents to confirm it was only paper and nothing more suspicious, before dropping it on the end of Fred's mattress.

"Your lucky day, Mr Smith."

"Thanks, Miss." The cell door closed.

The letter was addressed to Susan Naylor, an address in London, and was handwritten:

'Suse,

Don't forget! Friday 8th. November! 10 am sharp. Our life starts from then. Everything's sorted. Tickets etc. I can't say too much – you know what I mean. Told you I could do it, didn't I? Stay lucky. Don't forget the bag. I know you won't. But please remember the bag. Things come good, didn't they? I said they would. The chef business was the icing on the cake – one born every minute – I'm tempted to do the tour of the prisons myself, he's not up to it, but with the investments, I don't think I need to. Better to go now whilst my luck is running.

Friday!'

Smithy hadn't had the chance to post the letter. 'Suse' must know he would be out on Friday the eighth anyway, without the letter, and she would be waiting at the gate. *Interesting.* Who was she? Smithy had never mentioned anyone. Would she be waiting alone? She'd recognise straight away he wasn't Smithy – right? But what was in the bag? Money? Tickets to where? If she was alone, should he risk getting into the car – just for the hell of it – what did he have to lose? If she wasn't alone... carry on walking. Friday morning...

Fred was happier now. The cell was as clean as it was going to be, a bit of paint had managed to take Smithy's odour away as well as remove the stains and blemishes from the walls and ceiling. The news was still full of the awful atrocity at The Stretch but already there were indications *they were not looking for anyone in connection to the crime*. They'd started to run out of headlines too. 'The mad chef' and 'The cereal killer' and given way to 'The crazy curry killer'. They had interviewed everyone from ministers, who promised it would never happen again, to restaurant owners in Birmingham's *curry mile* who had already seen the marketing opportunity – 'Death by a curry! – All you can eat until you phall over!', 'What's your poison? – Madras or korma?' and 'Murder an Indian? Get yours before it gets you!'

Fred was dozing on the bed. He'd eaten the fish and chips from the servery... not as good as he used to make them, and he was now trying to calculate the number of seconds remaining until ten o'clock tomorrow morning... and was failing.

He opened his eyes when he heard a single tap on the outside of the cell door. He thought he saw the flap return to its place – someone had checked he was there and tapped the door to get his attention – and on the floor was a brown envelope. It could have been staff, they often slipped mail under the door without unlocking it, but mail was normally given out at lunchtime. Smithy had had no mail for weeks.

'Knob head' was scrawled on the outside. Fred thought, *must be for me then.*

'Smithy,
You always were a knobhead, and you will continue to be one until I Sellotape a stick of dynamite around yours and light the fuse. I will take great pleasure in personally doing this and I will do this as a favour, as you have been of service for thirty years, and out of respect to your dear mother, rest her soul, I will make your end a quick and painless affair. The boys think I'm mad for not wanting to inflict a more painful end, but I have made my decision.

I have had suspicions for a long time. The Dickie Bird says you've been cheating me since May 97 (please feel free to correct me if I'm wrong) – I let it go knowing I needed you on the inside to oversee the trade, to keep me abreast of the competition, but I calculate you have robbed me of two hundred grand from this side of the business alone. You are Allan Border! Small change for me it is true but there is nevertheless a principle involved. Nobody robs *me*.

When The Stretch hit the headlines, it made me right sit up, Smithy. The *Lambert* fellow was your geezer on the inside and the geezer earmarked to infiltrate every chokey in England, and I'd only just handed another two hundred grand to finance your Prison Food Tsar idea (Bribes included) – a touch of genius on your part, credit where credit is due – and that made me think long and hard. If you were capable of such audacity, what else have you been up to over the years? And you stopped your community work, the boys say you're lying low, you'll be twenty feet under the ground when I've finished with you.

In short, Smithy, this is how it plays out. We round it up to half a million. Nice round number and I teach you a bit of respect. It also compensates for the three hundred deaths! Most of them would have been my customers for years to come!
And then I attach a stick of dynamite to your dick or your Gregory Peck, you can choose, and light it.

The best plans are always the simplest.
Where's the milk and honey, Smithy?
See you Friday 8th morning – 10 am.'

Fred had the first stirrings of indigestion. He dismissed the notion the prison food had poisoned him – too poetic. Complicated. Orrible Arry Enderson was waiting for him as well as Suse.

"Orrible Arry Enderson," Fred enjoyed the sound the name made when he said it aloud.

Orrible Arry didn't know about Suse, or he'd probably have the money already. Half a million! Even if Orrible Arry had inflated the figure it must be a hefty amount. Nothing to lose. Death by ligature or death by dynamite is still death. Fred's bowel problems needed dynamite. If you're going to die you might as well live a little first. It was exciting. Fred's forehead was clammy, his pulse raced, he hadn't felt this good since...

Chapter 39
NOVEMBER 5th 2019
In Search of Dyer

"Dyer's been missing for days... Not answering the phone... I need someone to check he's still alive," the chief directed this at the room but meant DS Quirke.

DS Quirke was texting. She'd paused pondering why *enthusiasm* looked like an anagram for *euthanasia* this morning. She had endured another weekend with *Randy Andy*, against her better instincts, and had resolved to end the sorry romance by text this morning. 'Enthusiasm cannot replace imagination or experience. You have a toned and enviable body but without depravity, you do not have my attention. I do not want a puppy – pestering me with, *is that OK, is that good for you* or *do you want me to do what I was doing last night, again?* There are no rules. Everything is allowed. I should say it once and with no explanations. If you want to cuff me – do it. If you want to eat treacle from my tits – just do it. I'm a *Nike Girl*. And if I want to *peg you* – just bend over!'

"DS Quirke, I'm concerned about Dyer. Put your phone away... are you looking at porn again?" the chief gave her his sternest look.

"Caught me again, sir."

"I said Dyer's been missing for days. Someone needs to confirm he's dead... I mean alive,"

"If he's not, sir, can I choose whom I work with next time?"

"DS Quirke, that's not funny, but you can, and in the meantime, I need you to pop round, and make sure the arsehole is all right. He feels he's been well and truly shafted and, anyway, I have a duty of care, so make sure the arsehole hasn't pegged it…"

"Are you a mind reader, sir?"

"What do you mean, DS Quirke?"

"Just I was thinking the same thing!"

*

Even though DS Quirke had worked with Dyer for close to six months she'd never been to his place. She had never contacted him socially either, but she didn't know anyone who had. For all she knew he could have led a double life – but she doubted it. *All work had made him a dull boy.* DS Quirke confirmed the address from his file as he wasn't answering the phone and made her way to his home.

He was dead.

DS Quirke had suspected it for a long time – many hours in proximity inside cars and on trains had brought her to this conclusion. He looked dead from her vantage point. Looking through the basement window into a darkened room, she knew she should have knocked first but old habits die hard, and she hadn't noticed him at first, everything was still, he was silhouetted against a wall, a dark black outline, it was the moustache that gave him away, sitting in a chair, frozen, hands placed on his knobbly knees, a lesser person would have screamed, subconsciously she didn't want to let him know she was there, giving him the chance to bore her with the cinema history of *a scream* from 1927 to the present day, and part of DS Quirke hoped it was Riga Mortice, no, probably too strong, though the idea kept putting its foot through the door in her mind, his eyes were wide open, trance, not flickering – she thought *robot rebooting*, low battery or someone's flicked a switch to the off position. A lesser person would have been disturbed. DS Quirke already knew how disturbed she was.

There was a film of water molecules on the outside of the window on the small square above DS Quirke's vantage point. A couple of tears caught her attention, and she watched them, zigzagging until they reached the horizontal strip of wood encasing the pane of glass. She moved her head imperceptibly and licked Dyer's window.

DS Quirke didn't knock on the door or tap the window, instead, she retraced her steps up the stone staircase to street level, moving gently in case he saw her retreat and called her back. Avoiding the cracks in the pavement and any slab that was not completely intact she intended to return to her car – making two left turns, however, she suddenly arrived at the rear of Dyer's property. DS Quirke entered a shared garden through a green door, noting the rear of the property was no longer subterranean, there was a small excuse for a lawn, immaculate, and no doubt his responsibility, a couple of benches and a tree. She could not be more specific – she recognised grass, though Dyer would have lectured on the inexhaustible varieties.

The backdoor was locked – she tried the handle – and was solid wood. The rear window was masked by a net curtain DS Quirke's Nan would have been proud of but to the right was a smaller frosted window, evidently the bathroom. The net curtain tried to hide a study of some sort, though she was surprised at the disorder, stacks of books and shelves that were overflowing onto the floor. She thought about sitting on one of the benches, staking the place out, or waiting for a neighbour to appear, simply waiting for things to unfold – she genuinely did… she knead the rubber ball for luck before she picked up half a house brick and smashed the glass on the frosted panel and had managed to get her right leg and arm through before she realised the corpse was alive…

"Quirky, what are you doing?"

"Breaking and entering, sir."

"I can see that Quirky…" he was looking at the glass on the floor, and for a horrible moment she thought he was going to offer a large hand to assist her, but she wriggled quickly, both legs in and dropped to the floor…

"Mm… It's a right mess, isn't it?" DS Quirke made a nonchalant movement with a foot to move some of the glass to the side, noting the way his eyes followed the debris and only then did she realise he was armed with a rolled-up copy of *The Times*.

"Sir, before you do something that you may regret… I am going to make a cup of tea…" DS Quirke brushed herself down, swerved around him, and went in search of the kitchen. She had the kettle boiling, two cups ready on the side before she sensed Dyer behind her – holding a heavy teapot and an airtight container of tea leaves – he muttered something about if tea's worth drinking – no doubt he'd done a study on the best bloody tea leaves.

"You didn't answer the phone, sir."

"Mm…"

"The chief was… You didn't answer the phone, sir… The chief wants to know what's going on…"

"Mm…"

Dyer was back in the chair DS Quirke had observed him sitting in through the window. His hands made the teacup look doll-like and she could see he was returning to the place in his mind he'd been before she'd smashed the window. She wasn't used to Dyer being quiet. Withdrawn. Sullen. Depressed. She preferred it. (At least he wasn't drowning her with the scientifically accepted standard on the perfect length of time for brewing a pot of tea or the merits of stirring the pot with a spoon or not!)

233

DS Quirke wasn't used to talking with Dyer… until now, she had worked on and perfected a verbal and body language system aimed at trying not to get him to talk… it was a work in process… pretending to be asleep didn't always work. His eyes were now glazing, pupils dilated slightly… he was oblivious to her presence… she was a blur… lost to his vision… she should have been in Heaven, it was what DS Quirke had worked toward from the beginning… But she *needed* him.

If DS Quirke had a lighter, she may have set fire to his eyebrows or his moustache… in the name of science, of course, to see which was more flame retardant. She could have slapped him, but she did not want to touch him. A wet finger in the ear was ruled out for the same reason. She knew she wasn't good at this… the empathy… the ability to cajole, to support a colleague, this man, this 'Dyer'… back to life… to help him through this crisis. Did she even want to?

"Sir, did you know, in your right ear, behind the insanely long hairs you have growing there… It may surprise you to know, that I know they are called *tragi* hairs, and you have a visible piece of earwax. It's sort of a brown colour, like a blend of coffee, only the texture of honey… looks brittle… I guess… Where on earth does it come from?"

Dyer's eyes flickered.

"Is yours the same as mine? Can you get DNA from it? I assume you can… does the colour change, depending…"

Dyer's eyes blinked.

"What does it taste of? Will your earwax taste differently from mine?"

"Look it up yourself…" Dyer spoke in a monotone.

"I have a jar under my bed, it's an old Coleman's mustard jar… I washed it out thoroughly first… contamination… It contains dead fleas…"

"What's that you say?" Dyer with more animation.

"I use one of those combs you get when a child gets headlice... but I comb my cat with it... put a wet wipe next to me... and every time I remove a flea with the comb... simply pop it with my fingernails and wipe the body onto the wipe... flick the bodies into the jar at the end."

"I know what you're up to, Quirky!"

"I have another jar that contains the sleep from the corner of my eyes... some mornings I have loads... on others, nothing... Why is that?"

"Rheum."

"What about the room?"

"It's called rheum... R.H.E.U.M."

"Do you believe me, sir?"

"Not a word of it."

"Do you think you're the only one that's... With... What's the word I'm looking for?"

"Quirky, don't you think I know what people call me in the office? Don't you think I know the nicknames, the derogatory names, all the jokes at my expense... all the abuse?"

"So... Sir, you are an *arsehole*... and boring as hell too..."

"I was thinking eccentric idiot."

"No, sir, with respect, definitely an arsehole."

"I'm not good with people... generally... socially."

"Sir, well that makes two of us!"

Dyer stood up, DS Quirke shifted her body weight, prepared to parry any assault, but instead, he took her teacup and sprang to the kitchen, almost pulling her along in his slipstream. He made a *proper* fresh cup of tea in a precise and methodical manner, and showing he was recovering, explained the intricacies of what he was performing – DS

Quirke, of course, had started to switch off when the first miracle occurred. He handed the cup to her, and their eyes *almost* met.

"From one arsehole to another?"

"Sir."

The second miracle, "Right, Detective Sergeant Quirke, what do we do from here?"

"I suggest you fix the window... Start answering the telephone... The chief says the coroner has been *sorted*... And return to work."

"And you, DS Quirke?"

She remained quiet for a while, Dyer's eyes followed her as she paced the room, she finally decided to speak.

"Next to the jars under my bed, I have a series of boxes... In each box is a keepsake from every case I've worked on... And when the case is closed the lid is fastened on the box with a garish ribbon. The Lambert box does not have a lid on it yet... And I haven't even bought the ribbon."

"Why didn't you say something? I thought it was just me... something not feeling right."

"I have my reasons for not giving up on this case," her mind slipped to an image of the size 12 silver high-heeled shoes she had removed from the compartment on Fred Lambert's moped and were secreted in a box under her bed, "And I need you and your..."

"Powers of deduction and high intelligence?" Dyer asked.

"I was going to say your pedantic, annoying habit of wearing people down."

"And what are your *reasons*, Quirky," Dyer persisted.

"I'll tell you at the end."

Chapter 40
There are Ways…

The two ends of the rope were looped through a metal eye fixed into the brickwork just above the headboard. They were not tied too firmly, Elizabeth was more of an enthusiast than an expert, and she had discovered if you appear to be too practised or efficient at such things, *men* can become a little scared rather than excited. Anyway… he had initiated this… well, he could have said *stop*. His wrists were loosely looped by the 'u' of the rope, so he wasn't trapped… not until Elizabeth fixed them in position with some thick gaffa tape… anyway… he'd taken one of her sleep masks, taking it from one of her pink pillows without asking and he still hadn't panicked when she put tape over his mouth. After all, he said *he'd seen just about everything.*

He wasn't naked… Most men don't look great when they're naked… and this one was in the *fun* category rather than sexy. He was on his back with his arms above him and Elizabeth thought he expected the usual male fantasy… Unfortunately for him, she'd sneaked a *peek* as he was getting into the costume, he'd brought along with him, and she was going nowhere near *it*. There should be special barbers for those places… Some men need an expert to tidy those areas. Even Elizabeth drew the line at collecting pubic hair between her teeth… and she did not have a jar under the bed for that…

Elizabeth was dressed in the cliché rubber nurses uniform… His idea… Extremely tight in the areas that matter… Tight enough to stop the blood supply to *his* brain never mind to her breasts and thighs. The best stilettoes finished the effect and he'd almost dived for the bed before he fainted… And now he was restrained, his SOCO overall crinkled as Elizabeth straddled him, and she felt him strain beneath her… she dug her nails into the compressed rubber testicle before pushing it between her breasts to free her hands …

"So… Snotty… I have you… exactly where I want you… My name's Elizabeth."

He tried to murmur something pleasurable and bucked beneath her, Elizabeth was no cowgirl but the likes of Snotty could never throw her off. She rolled him expertly, the friction of the rubber helped, and he was suddenly on his front. He was a little confused and stopped moving, but when Elizabeth moved down onto his thighs and slapped his bottom, he regained some enthusiasm.

She looked at the white cocoon beneath her and giggled at the absurdity. Snotty, evidently put off by this became perfectly still… How had it gotten to this?

'Professionals Only' website. She had resolved to end her membership, amused at the lack of *members* available and annoyed at the lack of a more risqué clientele. Her finger hovered above *delete* when she noticed a profile – 'Strictly experienced only – I've seen things on the belt of Ryan…' DS Quirke recognised the line. Had *he* meant to type *Ryan*? Anyway, the post, reading between the lines, must mean Dick (Philip K). Sometimes you spot something, the stars align, you take a chance, and you get caught up in the idea this could be the one, not a meaningful relationship, but *the one from left field*, the exciting one, the one that's not put off by your outlandish ideas in the bedroom… And you arrange to meet, forgetting it's sometimes a very small world… And you walk into a pub and there's Snotty and he's spotted you before you have the chance to turn around. She could still have turned around and left him gawping, but she remembered how much he hated Dyer and she decided to stay at least for one drink.

Snotty could not back up his profile and DS Quirke was already calculating what trophy was available before escaping when she had an epiphany… one syllable more than orgasm and in this case more rewarding. He'd noticed her attention was wavering and had started talking about his favourite subject – Dyer. How much he detested him, how much he hated him, how he'd do anything to get one over on him. She didn't get it straight away, she thought he was talking about *having her*, how that would be the coup de grace in this war, being able to use it in the future. 'Dyer, keep your hands to yourself. Oh, by the way, she can't!' DS Quirke stayed longer matching him drink for drink until his tongue started to loosen, though he was still too guarded to admit outright he'd done anything *unprofessional*, she sensed the Lambert case was not as dead as it seemed.

"So… Snotty… What are you hiding? What are you not telling me? We both hate Dyer, don't we, but I feel you've *done him* this time… you've squeezed his…"

Snotty mumbled a three-syllable response and she cupped *his* to show she understood.

"You clever boy! Will you let me in on the secret if I ask you nicely?"

Snotty mumbled *err-err*, like the negative answer on television's Family Fortunes.

"Oh, you are naughty! Will I have to get rough with you?"

Snotty gave a consenting murmur but he stopped consenting when she started to cut the SOCO overall around his bum cheeks with a Stanley knife.

"I admire you, Snotty, anyone who can put Dyer in his place gets my unabashed admiration…" Elizabeth reached under the mattress and was flexing a riding crop at this point, a trophy from an earlier adventure, and using the end of this she pushed the sleep mask from Snotty's face just enough for him to see what she intended to do to him next, "But you see, I need to know your secret..." she was well practised at making a terrific swishing noise with the crop and though she hadn't struck him, she felt his cheeks clench beneath her..." Do you know the damage I can do with this... The marks it will leave on your bottom... you will, I assure you, never be able to drop your trousers again..."? she removed the tape from his mouth.

"You would not! Elizabeth!"

"Oh, Snotty, I will brand you so smartly, every time you sit down you will feel the ripples of healed skin through your trousers, and you will think of me, sat here, above you... And every year, on your birthday... I'll post a snapshot of your backside to your colleagues..."

"You would not. This is not funny anymore..."

She tapped his bottom, to get his attention, he squirmed but was trapped...

"Let's start with the Lambert case, shall we?" she thwacked the mattress to the side of his bottom. He must have felt the wind and the sound of the impact even made Elizabeth jump.

"What do you want?"

"The truth, Snotty... that's all."

"The Lambert case is finished with. Can't re-open it now... it's done with..."

"The truth, Snotty!" Another thwack of the mattress.

"All right... It probably wasn't Lambert in the outside toilet... There! Happy now?"

"Go on."

"Dyer has got a way of making me angry… we've been at loggerheads for years… it's not the first time we've crossed swords… And once I'd set up to prove he was wrong… You saw what he was like… Pompous prick! I wasn't going to feed his ego… He took a swing at me… You saw him… God knows who it was…"

"But the paperwork?"

"The powers that be needed a quick solution. They were prodding you two as well… You saw how it was… I had fingerprints all over the house that matched the hands in the outside toilet… And you had the confession… I didn't want to complicate matters… Or help Dyer… Okay! I could have tried harder with the dental records… but the powers above wanted an answer immediately… For God's sake, I got a promotion out of this!"

"So… Where's Lambert."

"Who knows… Who cares? If you look at his medical records, he didn't have long left anyway… Probably dead, lying somewhere in a mortuary as an unidentified body… Look the whole penal system was about to break down… riots were starting… We had to have a scapegoat… And *we* had a body… I mean, *I* had a body…"

"Talking about penal systems exploding… Have you wet yourself?"

"Oh, shit… I'm sorry… I was scared!"

"Close thing, Snotty, between scarred and scared, eh?"

Elizabeth wondered if she'd *demonstrated courage in doing the right thing, even in a challenging situation.* Bloody ethics.

Chapter 41
NOVEMBER 7th 2019, 16:00
HMP The Grunge
Cell 121
Memory Man

In a few seconds, it would be four in the afternoon…
Thursday… The day before he walked out of the prison… at
nine the next morning… Seventeen hours… a thousand and
twenty minutes… sixty-one thousand and two hundred
seconds… Had he just calculated that in his head? Can't be…
never been mentally agile. He started to recite every capital
city in Europe, alphabetically… he could do it as a child…
and he could do it now! He'd never felt so alive. Every Prime
Minister since Edward Heath… easy… he could remember
everything… All right, challenge yourself… nineteen-ninety-
four… every prisoner on your wing in cell order, all three
landings… Collins, short hair, Middleton, cock, Swindlehurst,
nice lad… he had them all!

 … Your daughter… The last time you saw her…
Alive… Everything she said… Everything she did… The
accusations… The recriminations… how she looked…
walking away… walking back to you… What she wore…
Not *whore*… the spittle in her hair… from you shouting…
what she wore! She slaps you… you slap her… on the floor…
Describe her eyes… never see them again… her eyes… the
number of rings and the number of eyelashes and the number
of hairs in her eyebrows… The colour of her eyes… the
tears… the shape of her teeth and lips that never smile
again… you slap her… she slaps you… Never saying her
name again.

Chapter 42
NOVEMBER 7th 2019, 17:00
HMP The Grunge
Duty of Care

Smithy hadn't collected his evening meal, commonly known as *the last supper* for a prisoner being released in the morning.

Officer Airnes declared, "Fuck him, he's been a right grouchy bastard the last few weeks. No work. No activities. Just on his own with his television and his endless bloody cleaning… Do you know he's blown most of my budget on his own this month… So, I say, fuck him," the officer was about to take the meal himself, saving it for later, when prairie dog piped up, "I'll just knock on his door in case he's asleep."

"Fuck me, are we running a room service?" Airnes was incredulous but followed her to Smithy's cell.

Prairie Dog knocked and pushed the cell door open.

"Smithy, what are you doing?" She was amazed a man of Smithy's size and with an aversion to any form of exercise was lying on the floor in the *press-up* position, "Aren't you too old…" She hadn't wanted to scream, she knew what to do, simply press the button on the radio attached to her belt and calmly state – 'Code Blue' – followed by the cell location. She pressed the button, but Smithy chose to convulse at the same time, almost leaving the floor in a paroxysm of taut muscle.

"Aaargh! Fucking 'Code Blue'! 'Code Blue'! Delta 118!"

Prairie Dog became *The Scream* from that moment – Officer Airnes explained that's how the system works. Prison staff live with it, embrace it, or get another job very quickly.

Smithy was strapped to the stretcher in the ambulance waiting in the vehicle lock for paperwork and the final clearance to go to an outside hospital. He'd regained consciousness a couple of times and snippets of conversation had registered in his brain...

"Unbelievable. This is not good at all. Not good at all."

"He's out tomorrow, poor sod."

"It'll be a *death in custody* if we're not careful and he doesn't make it."

"Shit, shit... shit!"

"We can't have another *death in custody*, can we, it'll look bad for the figures..."

"Not compared to The Stretch!"

"Not funny... We've had three already this year..."

"But this one's not our fault, is it? Natural death?"

"You've got a lot to learn! It's still a death in custody!"

"Oh, I suppose it is."

"If he can survive 'till tomorrow morning though... Technically he'll be off our roll... He will no longer count."

"Makes no difference to him. Who's on the escort with the body?"

"Well, he's not quite dead yet..."

"Yes, I know, it was a figure of speech... Who's with him?"

"Young Fletcher, I believe, she found him, so she's got to go with him... she'll learn."

"Only fair, I suppose, can she cope?"

"He's hardly going to run off! The medic says he's had some sort of seizure... Did you hear her 'Code Blue'?"

"Yes... quite extraordinary... Deserves to lose her evening off for that... Completely unprofessional... Ah,

Fletcher, there you are… I know it's your first escort, but I assure you it's a cinch. No cuffs are required. Simply accompany him to the hospital and stay with him to the end… Not that he's going to die…"

"No, sir."

"Don't look so worried. Between you and me, Fletcher, about eight o'clock tomorrow morning is the key time if you get my meaning?"

"Not quite, sir."

"Do I have to spell it out? Do not let him die before eight o'clock tomorrow morning! After eight it's a different matter… he's a free man… he can do anything he wants…"

"Like die?"

"Exactly! Have a quiet word with the nurse if you must… if the death is recorded as being after eight… right… we'll be in the clear."

"Isn't this a bit callous, sir?"

"Callous, Fletcher… Callous! Callous is you screaming 'Code Blue', alerting everybody to his collapse… If you hadn't panicked, if you hadn't done anything, we wouldn't be in this bloody mess, would we?"

"How do you mean, sir?"

"Look, Fletcher, you've got a lot to learn. We could have *found him* in the morning, sometime after eight o'clock… and not our problem… He would not have shown up on my bloody figures!"

"Oh, I get it. Well, can't we pretend… Put him back in his cell?"

"Are you mad, Fletcher? Other prisoners know because you screamed about it from the rooftops… and *they* can't be trusted to keep it quiet!"

"Sorry, sir, they didn't teach us this at college… I've got a lot to learn."

"Anyway, take on board what I've said… you'll be fine… pull this off and you may get a promotion out of this…"

As the ambulance door was secured and the vehicle lock gate was sliding open, Fred thought he heard one of the medics speaking to Fletcher before he lost consciousness –

"Don't look so worried, young lady, I do this all the time, we'll drive fast – it'll be a scream…"

He thought Fletcher had burst into tears.

Chapter 43
NOVEMBER 7th 2019, Late
HMP The Grunge
James 'The Flame' Roberts

The ambulance left HMP The Grunge, blue lights flashing, and OSG (Officer Service Grade) James 'The Flame' Roberts, who had just taken his place for the night shift, was lamenting on the thought you never knew what was just around the corner... and was smiling at the irony his colleagues often quipped they would have to carry him out of the place in a coffin. He resolved to do a little bit of work, and procedure, whilst he was still alive long enough to do it. The logbook entry gave the name and number of the prisoner in the ambulance, and he confirmed the prison roll-board was correct and had been amended accordingly. Only when he tapped laboriously on the computer keyboard did he realise it was Smith and that he had been due for release the next morning. 'The Flame' remembered Smith's quips about burning the gate down and smiled again.

"Poor sod," he stated phlegmatically, never mind *going straight*, more like straight to hospital... or straight to hell... Hope you make it, though... Not a bad sort..."

'The Flame' hit a few more keys with a heavy forefinger and scrolled to the 'next of kin' details. There was only one name listed and he dialled the number on file. He had *a game* he liked to play to pass the hours on a night shift.

"Susan Naylor?"

"Is this about Florida?"

'The Flame' had not expected this response, it did not fit in with *the* game and he almost hung up, but the female voice on the line continued, "I've packed the bag and I'm ready for Florida... A promise is a promise."

"Madam, we seem to be speaking at cross purposes here… This is HMP The Grunge, in the West Midlands… It's about your uncle…"

"Well, I'll be seeing *him* in the morning… Of course, I haven't forgotten…" and she hung up.

'The Flame' stared at the receiver for a few seconds before slowly replacing it on the cradle. The telephone began to ring.

"Good evening, HMP The Grunge…"

"I know that. You just rang. What about my uncle? Is everything all right? I'm supposed to be going to…"

"Florida. Yes, I know. The thing is it's your uncle, you see, been taken poorly, he's been rushed to hospital…"

"Rushed?"

"An emergency it was, a matter of life and death," he was warming to the game, "we don't think he's going to make it."

"Well, how far is the hospital?"

"Mrs Naylor, you're missing the point…"

"It's Miss."

"Miss… The point is it's serious."

"I'm picking him up tomorrow."

"In my professional opinion, I think this will be unlikely… Slim chance he'll make it through the night… If I were you, I'd expect the worse…"

"No Florida?"

'The Flame' was not used to being put off his stride and pulled the telephone from his head and stared at it again.

"Look, Miss Naylor, it was a medical emergency, blue lighted he was within the hour… very, very serious… I would be surprised if he made it."

"How far is the hospital?"

"*Made it*, as in survived the night, I'm trying to say he may die suddenly…"

"Oh, I see… because they can't find the hospital…"

"Not exactly… but I'm not supposed to tell you which hospital they're taking him to … there could be security implications if you know what I mean?" 'The Flame' smiled as he warmed to his game again – back on script.

"Okay." She hung up.

'The Flame' shook his head. Was she drunk, on drugs or just simple? She was spoiling his evening. He wasn't having this. He re-dialled her number.

"Miss Naylor, as I was saying, I'm not supposed to tell you, anything at all, but if I were you… Seeing how serious the situation is," he paused leaning back in his chair, savouring the dramatic pause, sipping tea from his cup, checking over his shoulder he hadn't left anything in the oven that could set the fire alarm off again, "If I were you…" he pressed a button on the console and a high pitched alarm suddenly sounded and with practised aplomb, he hung up. He cancelled the alarm, dialled out for a pizza… he hadn't ordered a curry for a while… not since… and stared at the clock counting the seconds until Miss Naylor called back. He'd played this game for years and never tired of it.

They normally rang back within five minutes. Normally. She wasn't playing by the rules. Twenty minutes later he rang her again.

"Look, Miss Naylor, we lost the connection there, don't be alarmed, a bit of an emergency…"

"Who is this?"

"The prison, Miss Naylor, the emergency, it happens all the time, you have no idea of some of the situations I have to deal with… Potential terrorist attack, nothing for you to worry about…"

"Oh, I see…"

"We're here to keep you safe… I've probably said too much already… The public has no idea what goes on every night in a prison such as this… life and death situations all the time… it takes a certain calibre of man to deal with it."

"Oh, I see…"

"Too soon for a full assessment, expect there'll be a full brief in the morning… for now we'll keep everything out of the public eye… unsung heroes…"

"Oh."

"When I met the Queen that was reward enough for me… I don't need medals for medal's sake…"

"The real Queen?"

"Yes, she takes a special interest in The Grunge, miss, I'm not supposed to let anyone know that… but," a moped turned the corner, his pizza was fast approaching, "She quite often uses some of us as undercover staff when she's on official duty… mingle with the crowd, you know, undercover, licence to kill… all highly trained… official secrets act and all that," the pizza delivery man tapped at the reinforced glass.

"What's happening now?"

"I think MI5 has just arrived."

"Who?"

"Your uncle will be at Redditch Hospital!" 'The Flame' accepted defeat and hung up.

Three hours later as 'The Flame' snoozed the phone rang persistently, and Miss Susan Naylor asked for confirmation of the address to *Raddish Hospital*.

Chapter 44
Euphoric x 2

And he could spell it! E-u-p-h-o-r-i-c. He knew he could spell anything. But he was in a hospital bed so something must be seriously wrong. Was he *Smithy* or *Fred* or morphing between the two of them? He had a surge of adrenalin, one that told him he was invincible… ignore the ageing body… the failing heart… the bowel problem… he was capable of anything.

A young female officer was asleep in the chair next to him. She'd curled her feet beneath her and had rested her head on the back of the chair against the wall. He recognised Miss Fletcher or Prairie Dog as her colleagues called her. She breathed steadily, through her nose, the easy, effortless sleep of the young. He watched his fat fingers reaching out to touch her hair and realised with shock they were making their way toward her throat. Well, *he was* Britain's most notorious mass murderer… A nurse looked through the glass panel in the door and his hands beckoned him, miming the actions of a pen and paper. He returned rather too quickly for his liking probably thinking he had something to get off his chest before he popped his clogs. He took the opportunity to check his pulse and blood pressure in the no-fuss method of someone used to working nights. The officer slept on.

'What's the use of a joke if nobody gets it? What's the point of a prank if nobody falls for it? What's the point of mass murder if nobody knows who did it? Worse still if nobody knows how clever they are?'

'I am different somehow, I've used the words *euphoric*, but it doesn't seem enough. I can see things now and I don't think anyone else can. I know they can't. Shall I lie here and wait for you to arrive? Not bloody likely! The plan has changed. The money would have been nice. A last hoorah. I had a few things on my bucket list, but they can wait. The plan has changed. I was confused before but now I know what I must do. I can see the light! There's a lot to be said for a near-death experience. I was in a daze, I couldn't see what I should do, what I was meant to do – *I can now*.

I've been touched. Chosen. I think it's my daughter. She told me what to do. I woke up charged with electricity – and God forbid anyone gets in my way. I look at the officer and I know if I clamp my hands over her mouth, or place my fingers on her neck, I can kill her. Odd from someone who has three hundred and sixteen already on their list? Please, let her sleep… I know what I must do. An *avenging angel*.'

It was safer to keep writing.

Chapter 45
Coincidence and Circumstance

Fred slipped from the bed.

"Mr Smith! You should not be on your feet. Get back into bed immediately," the young male nurse tried to step in his way.

"Desperate for the toilet, young man."

"You have a receptacle at the side of your bed."

"It's not anything a receptacle could handle…"

Tutting the nurse compromised, "Use the toilet on the left… press the buzzer if you need assistance."

Before Fred could close the door, a woman slipped in behind him, a large holdall clasped to her skinny body, closing the door firmly in the nurse's face.

"You are *not* my uncle!"

"Ah, you must be, Susan… Susie… Suse… I can explain," Fred had trouble seeing past the large, black-rimmed spectacles, the nose that was slightly too big for the face and the teeth that protruded from her top lip.

"How do you know my name?" she pressed the bag against him.

"As I've said… I can explain everything…" Fred wrestled with the idea of strangling her straight away, but he was also captivated by the absurdity of what she was saying.

"Is it terrorism? Are you MI5?" Susan's eyes were wide, waiting for confirmation, the pupils dilated, eager and searching Fred's face for an answer.

The toilet seat pressed against the back of Fred's legs. The cubicle was only just big enough for the two of them.

The pressure on his legs broke the spell and any thoughts of hurting her.

"Are you, though, MI5?"

"Listen, I do need the toilet… can you turn round while I?"

"Yes, no probs… Wow! MI5… Had to look it up…" She turned her back, hopping from one foot to the other, pressing the holdall against the door, Fred stared at the back of her neck, at the gap between the top of her blouse and the neat line of her bobbed hair. He flipped up the back of the hospital dressing gown and dropped onto the toilet.

"Oh, wow! God, have they got him… my uncle I mean… the terrorists?"

She paused as a stream of gas and excrement splattered the toilet. Fred flushed and she tried to turn around quickly but the strap of the holdall caught on a coat hook on the door.

"What do I have to do to help? Do I have to pledge allegiance or something?"

Fred reached across her to unsnag the holdall letting his nose take in the full fragrance of her hair, reminding him of decades ago, he placed his hands on her shoulders next to her neck, she didn't flinch, he could feel her pulse, a heart racing, full of life, so trusting, so completely trusting, *faster daddy, faster!*

"Susan, I can't tell you everything…"

"I know, I know…"

"It's strictly a need-to-know basis…"

"I know, I know… MI5, though, yeah?"

"Calm down, Susan, and listen… It is a matter of life and death… and your uncle is in *deep*. Real *deep*.

"He said he was…"

"He can't move at the moment… He's in a *dark* place… It's like everything's on top of him."

"He won't lose his head… He's not afraid of the dark…"

"It might be too late for that… He can't be contacted just now… but his part in all this now rests on your shoulders."

"Oh, wow!"

"Is the money in the holdall?"

"Yeah, and the tickets. Clothes are in the car boot."

"Tickets?"

"Florida!" Her face suddenly drained, and the tide went out, a bitter disappointment for a moment.

"Of course, it's still on, he'll join you later."

"There's a lot of money, you know, it just kept arriving… too much for me to count… I don't know where from…"

"You do now."

Susan frowned but shook her head with pursed lips.

"Susan, MI5 can't pay money into the bank for you, can they – it wouldn't be much of a secret, would it?"

"Oh, wow!"

"Yes, an MI5 operative working on the inside…"

"On the *inside*! Best place to find all the bad men!"

"Now you've got it."

The nurse banged on the door.

"Mr Smith, are you all right in there?"

"Shall we kill him?" Susan Naylor asked.

Chapter 46
NOVEMBER 8th 2019, 06:00
Redditch Hospital
Keep It Quiet...

Dyer was in his element. A hospital ward with soap dispensers everywhere. He gloried in the performance holding his large hands out in front of him as if he was on a West End stage. Members of staff swayed around him risking instant decapitation if they didn't.

A prison officer was perched on the edge of the chair in a side room, she kept looking under the bed in case someone was hiding there and was visibly startled when Dyer opened the door with a flourish. DS Quirke ducked under his arm into the room when he showed no signs of entering himself, as he was intent on exaggeratedly scanning the room for clues. The officer leaned forward to look in a mirror checking her neck for finger marks – she was a young woman on the verge of hysterics. She pointed at a handwritten note on the pillow before sobbing uncontrollably. DS Quirke realised the note was extremely important and they both grabbed it: Dyer because he was rubbish with young women in hysterics, and DS Quirke because she knew she might slap her. Dyer's large hands won and DS Quirke moved to the opposite side of the bed to keep out of temptations way.

The Chief of Police had told the Prime Minister the case was closed. They were going to have to tread carefully, not always easy with Dyer's size thirteens, but they had a tacit agreement they would not declare anything until Lambert was physically in their hands.

"Right, Miss... Miss?"

"Officer Fletcher," she took a couple of gulps of air and reached for a tumbler of water a nurse had left on the side for her.

"Officer Fletcher, pull yourself together…"

"He could have killed me! It's in black and white… what he was going to do to me… Smithy! Well, I thought it was Smithy… Says there he was somebody else! Going to kill me in my sleep… I mean whilst I was on duty…"

"Well, there you have it really," Dyer grasped the dilemma, "My report could suggest you were asleep, I have twenty-seven nurses that can confirm that."

"Twenty-seven?"

"There you have it! Exaggeration! Precisely. There were only two nurses on duty."

"You've lost me, sir."

"The note itself, my dear, complete fabrication. How well do you know this, *Smithy*? He's a bit of a joker I suspect. He's never going to see you again, so he plays one last joke on you… and you swallowed it hook line and sinker… I bet one of your colleagues put him up to it!"

This seemed to sway it for them.

"Now, Officer Fletcher, no harm done, if I understand it correctly, this prisoner, Mr Smith, who was due for release today has decided to put the fear of God in you by leaving a note pretending to be somebody else. This will probably be the making of you."

DS Quirke let Dyer carry on – sometimes it was best to.

"When you get back to the prison, act as if you simply took everything in your stride. No harm done. Nobody died, Officer Fletcher…"

At this she perked up considerably, checking her watch.

"Nobody died!" she repeated, "He's technically a free man… he walked out of here so he can't be dead, can he? He did not die in custody after all!"

"That's more like it, Officer Fletcher, why don't you ring the prison and inform them he survived the night and is no longer their responsibility… They will be pleased."

They left her to it and went in search of the nurse that had been on duty.

He'd had his ankles and wrists surgically taped together and had been fixed to the cubicle toilet. His name was Brett, but everybody called him Brettney. He was very excitable and referred to the events as something out of a 'Bonnie and Clyde' movie. If anything, he was disappointed he had not been *roughed* up a bit more and kept repeating it had been the best night shift he'd ever done. He hadn't read the note and for all he knew, it had just been one of those incidents with a pissed-off patient. When Dyer and DS Quirke left, he was re-enacting what had happened to any colleague within hearing distance and was looking forward to the local press coverage.

Chapter 47
NOVEMBER 9th 2019, Morning
Evebury Cemetery
A Meeting with the Dead

She was buried under a cherry tree in a corner of the cemetery. Every year when some of the fruit fell to the ground, some would drop to the stone leaving stains like tears. No amount of cleaning could remove them, and he stopped trying, realising it was impossible to preserve a spotless stone in the same way every life is tarnished by the bad things that happen. Fred still felt the rebuke – he'd stopped crying a long time ago, but the gravestone never did.

He brushed debris from the surface, broken twigs, and dirt from the general decay, paused to smile at a grey squirrel that mistook his actions for a free lunch, then felt his vision blurring as he was bent over, feeling he might pass out if he didn't make it back to the bench. The dizziness passed but the dullness on the side of his skull persisted. For a moment he pondered the *avenging angel* waiting at his daughter's graveside, in garish artwork, waiting for the next target to arrive. It was almost divine. Predictable. It was only a matter of time before *he* arrived at the cemetery, drawn irrevocably to his end, drawn by the certainty of this was how it was supposed to be. Fred had seen it himself – in the hospital – it was what he had to do, a task to accomplish before he could allow his body to fail, to let his life drain away.

He must have dosed. Shovels were digging. Two men were digging a hole next to his daughter's grave. He caught himself before he shouted at the violation; his next thought was for his wife, had she died too, of the shock, and only slowly did it dawn it was for *him*… Well, Smithy at any rate. He was put out by this and almost resolved to throw himself in the open grave to thwart him... This caused him to chuckle, and the gravediggers looked up with a look of accusation – *it was not a laughing matter!* Fred mouthed *sorry* and they started to dig again.

There was a figure crouched in the undergrowth partially obscured by the gravediggers. Without his spectacles, Fred couldn't be sure. In time the digging stopped, and the gravediggers paused in front of him – Fred felt obliged to comment.

"Oh, well done, fellas, good job."

They looked at him quizzically, "It's not a bloody spectator sport," before shouldering their shovels and moving off. Fred felt they were almost too *grave* in their behaviour, but it must be part of the job description.

Fred felt a presence behind him. The figure had skirted from the hiding position and was standing motionless at his shoulder. Fred listened to the wind moving some of the more delicate branches and waited. Fingers gingerly touched his shoulders, and then worked their way up to an ear, before pressing the top of his bald head.

"Mr Lambert? A ghost?"

Fred let the fingers confirm the evidence.

"Mr Lambert, say something. I'm shitting myself. You're dead! The graves there! You're supposed to be dead – it's been on the television and all the papers."

"Tom, I've been expecting you – I've been waiting for you."

"What? A sort of Grim Reaper'? Tom's fingers were now trembling, and Fred grabbed the hand, pulling it violently downward, uncovering the forearm.

"Still using I see."

Tom snatched his arm back replacing the sleeve.

"I thought it was you… No hair… but I still recognise you… a bit fatter… Not dead then?"

"Not quite… You're the same… except… paler… thinner… weaker… drug-using scumbag you always were… Murderer… my daughter."

"Hark who's talking!"

"Point taken."

"What do you mean? You've been expecting me? How did you know I still came here?"

"Let's just say, murderers always revisit the victim."

"Fuck you." Tom sidled around the arm of the bench, checked for observers, and sat next to Fred. He kept casting furtive looks at Fred, perhaps trying to convince himself he was real, and occasionally touched his coat sleeve, expecting the apparition to vanish.

"Who are you expecting, Tom?"

"Who says I'm expecting anybody?"

"The police? Or do you owe someone for your latest fix, or is it simply the paranoid, delusional twitchiness of a life-long abuser?"

"Fuck you!" Tom twitched uncomfortably, digging his trainers into the gravel path, the more he tried to keep still the more an invisible surge of electricity seemed to pulse through his body.

"… And I've read the pathetic poems… the love poems… you sometimes leave under pebbles on the grave."

"I loved her!"

"Loved her to death, more like."

Tom leapt to his feet, he couldn't find the words to express how he'd loved her, and Fred wouldn't have understood anyway, exasperated, he clasped his hands, trying to walk away but was locked by Fred's glare.

"Tom, watch you don't fall in the grave," Fred observed calmly.

"Mr Lambert, what do you want?"

Fred smiled at this. If he had explained what he was going to do to Tom, Tom would have started to run and not stop until a heart weakened by decades of drug abuse had given up – and that wouldn't do.

"Tom, I don't have a lot of time left, you could say I'm already dead, health problems... I won't bore you with it... I'm dying, and I deserve it... But I get to choose how I go."

"What are you talking about?"

"Shut up and listen! I've got a bag full of money... more money than you can imagine... and it's yours if you listen... A present from my daughter if you like... I want to go the same way she did... I want to feel exactly what she did before she died... I want to go to the same place where she is... I want to escape too..."

"How much money?"

"In your language, enough to pay any debts off, enough to get a stake in someone's business and set yourself up for the future... Get you off the streets at least."

"More than five grand?"

Fred laughed in answer.

"That much, eh?"

"Tom, see that grave there, I reckon you could fill it with pound coins to the brim and you still wouldn't be anywhere near the amount of cash coming your way."

"That's what dreams are made of."

"Yes, Tom," Fred murmured, "a grave full of dreams."

"What's that, Mr Lambert?"

"I said, start dreaming."

Fred told Tom where to meet him in a few days.

Chapter 48
NOVEMBER 12th 2019, Morning
Weymouth
Hello, Mary

Fred Lambert watched as Mary left the house. She checked the door was secure three times before limping to the bus stop. He knew her routine. He'd watched her at least once every three or four months since she'd walked out all those years ago. She didn't know. But then she wouldn't have recognised him dressed in his best frock.

Mrs Lambert left her house only two times a week. Once on a Sunday to walk to the local church for the morning service where, afterwards, she would wander through the headstones tracing the name of anybody buried with the same name as her daughter repeatedly until distracted by the vicar. The second occasion was a short bus ride to the local superstore on a Tuesday where she replenished the meagre supplies, she needed for herself and her cat and purchased the magazines that gave the stories behind the scenes for all her soaps. She needed the storylines before the programmes were aired as a shock was something she did not enjoy – if someone was going to be attacked on one of the soaps she needed to know before it happened so she could watch behind her hands.

She sat in her usual spot on the bus. Three seats back on the driver's side. Though she would only be on the bus for half a dozen stops, she glanced nervously out of the window, ticking off familiar landmarks, terrified she would miss her stop, terrified the hum of the engine would lull her into a stupor – conspire with the tranquilisers to prevent her from leaving the bus at all – and as the bus followed a circuitous route it would be several hours before it passed her house again. This had happened on numerous occasions. Having a bus pass meant drivers never kicked you off.

Fred stumbled down the aisle as the bus pulled away and sat next to her. He pulled the cap closer to his ears and noticed her discomfort because he was in *her space.*

"There, there, Mary love, no need to get jumpy."

She was slow to react. Slow to recognise his voice and to respond to her name.

"Mary, love, it's me, Fred. Just a brief *hello* really... put your mind at rest... help you out... you know... How have you been?"

"Dead?"

"Not quite... Close a couple of times... How's the cat?"

"The cat... she's fine... a great comfort... The best thing I ever did... after... you know..."

"Mary, love, don't upset yourself... I'm sorting everything... and I've managed to *right* a few wrongs... settled a few scores..."

"Fred, they said you killed hundreds of people?"

"Three hundred and sixteen, I think... Not people though... convicted criminals... drug dealers... organised gang members... the scum that killed our daughter... Don't cry, Mary... You'll miss your stop."

"How do you know?"

"Been watching you... Not stalking... Since you moved away... Occasionally on a day off, I didn't have a lot to do, so I'd come down here, make sure you were all right... But I'm leaving for good soon... I know I wasn't a good husband... Or a good father... But I've made a bit of a difference now, haven't I... Remember when you said, 'What are you going to do about it?' and 'How can you work in a place like that?'… Well, I bloody did something, Mary, didn't I?"

"The next ones, my stop."

"I know it is love… just wanted you to know I'm all right… I know you left me a long time ago, but I've always loved you and wanted to take care of you… I'm leaving this bag, here, with you… enjoy your life… Don't bring too much attention to yourself."

"What are you saying, Fred?"

"Just a little nest egg, that's all… give you some comfort… There are also a couple of tickets to a couple of your favourite locations… You need to get out more."

"Where?"

"You'll find out soon enough… Quickly now… Your stop… Bye, love, take care…"

Fred attempted an embrace, but Mary wasn't a hugger anymore and slipped from his arms, staggering down the aisle with a small rucksack. Fred watched from the bus, she wasn't comfortable, and it kept banging against her leg. Fred waved but she didn't see him as she almost tripped over the bag. He shook his head wondering how she was going to manage the rucksack with two carrier bags once she'd been to the shops. He imagined her leaving the rucksack on the bus. Hopefully, she would be all right. She would be when she saw the tickets for the tours of Emmerdale and Coronation Street film sets and the fifty thousand pounds in cash.

Chapter 49

NOVEMBER 20th 2019

Worcester Police Station

The More Things Change…

Things were changing. Things had changed.

Dyer was back at his desk, true, and he was still annoying, rearranging every item on it with meticulous care, clearing his throat regularly as if he was going to announce something of vital importance, still returning from the toilet with a paper towel in his hands, rubbing too vigorously, and dropping it from his full height into DS Quirke's bin. He was still fingering his moustache, either smoothing inward or smoothing outward, ten times in each direction, and raising an eyebrow when an idea occurred to him, and the unpredictable nature of this would have been hazardous to low-flying pigeons if they had been outside.

But things were changing. Things had changed.

He still walked in front, loping effortlessly with enormous feet, his hands shooting backwards, keeping DS Quirke at bay, threatening to swat people against the wall if you were unprepared.

But changing…

Dyer had his purpose back and he was going to *get* Fred Lambert.

DS Quirke was *Quirky* again; however, old habits die hard.

Dyer had wanted to wring Snotty's neck, he'd paced the office repeating over and over, 'Oh yes, oh yes', and DS Quirke had been tempted to arrange a meeting but had discovered Snotty was conveniently in South Africa following a sudden family bereavement. The evidence was there but it wasn't simple. The chief, his superiors and the Prime Minister had cut corners to close the case, and the fact that Dyer was on a final, final, written (*this is bloody it*) warning meant nothing short of dragging Fred Lambert into the office by the scruff of his neck would have done.

But they were a *team*.

Since the episode in the hospital, they were looking at Fred Lambert's life, re-checking what they thought they knew about him and accessing CCTV footage from cameras across Worcestershire and specifically Evebury under the guise of a county lines drug supply investigation. Fred Lambert had gone to ground. He also had a young woman called Susan Naylor with him (The Grunge had confirmed this) though they had no idea what her role in the case was. They had the *avenging angel* note and other pieces of evidence quickly followed.

A transcript from a telephone conversation received in the early hours of the morning confirmed what they already suspected –

"Hello? Can I speak with Sid Dyer… No, wait a minute, I mean CID Dyer… Please?"

"Madam, this is DI Dyer speaking."

"CDI Dyer, is it?"

"Yes, madam, close enough. Are you drunk? Who is this?"

"D.I.C Dyer… Dick Dyer… ha ha ha."

"Madam?"

"He's alive, you know?"

"Is that you, Mrs Lambert?"

DS Quirke was listening on the other extension, thankfully nobody else was there. Mrs Lambert was drunk, giggly and none too coherent.

"I'm ringing about my cat, mainly, and my husband… He's dead you know, my husband, I mean… not the cat… Well, he might be too… Probably missing his mommy… You said if there was anything you could do to help… Can you check on the cat for me? My husband can't, you see because he's dead… Yes, very dead indeed… blew his bloody arse off… I mean his head, I think…" more giggling and samba music in the background, a band playing, people dancing, "Just thought you might like to know… how dead he is… very, very dead… And you were so kind to me once… Got your card here… Tried to buy a round of drinks with it…" an extended giggle and they presumed she had fallen off the chair, "Are you there, Dicky? Just thought you should know how dead he is… And if you could check on the cat… I really can't remember what I've done with him… My cat… Not my husband… Very dead he is… or is it the cat that's dead?" At that point, the line had gone dead.

*

Where are you, Fred Lambert?
DS Quirke was relieved Fred Lambert was still alive. Glad he had not lost his head in his outside toilet. Whether he had *lost his head* in another way would be up to the psychiatrists once he was in custody. They needed to confirm he'd switched places with a man known as Smithy, a man who'd recently come to the end of a lengthy prison sentence. Snotty had put it on record that the man in the toilet had been Lambert and the body was now under the ground next to the daughter in an Evebury cemetery. At the crime scene, Snotty had taken fingerprints from the house and matched them with the body and they had all assumed they'd belonged to Lambert. Prison staff had since confirmed Lambert's fingers never operated the biometric recognition system due to years of varnish and glue abuse. Snotty wouldn't have been pulled up by such an inconvenience, DS Quirke thought he would have sworn to match a DNA sample from a hair in Lambert's hairpiece if he'd had to – anything to get one over on Dyer. If Dyer had asked the Chief of Police to exhume Lambert's body, DS Quirke was certain Dyer would have ended up buried to his neck in the same grave. They were on their own for now.

Fred Lambert was on the run. It should have been simple; confirm the body in the grave was Smithy without digging him up. Surely, they had a set of Smithy's fingerprints on the database. But Snotty had been under just as much pressure as Dyer... get the perpetrator... identify... and close the whole thing off. Snotty, the deviant, had not only been negligent in his work but also covered his tracks... Once he'd set out to thwart Dyer he could not turn back. Hard copies of fingerprints were *mislaid*. DNA samples had been purposely contaminated, if fingerprints had been downloaded on the computer they were not in the proper file or they had been filed under a different name. He was not expecting a re-examination or an enquiry. Case closed! Snotty had got DNA evidence of Lambert, no doubt taken from his bed and upstairs bathroom, and it matched DNA on fragments of the uniform found in the outside toilet. In effect, Snotty had DNA evidence matching Lambert but not the body in the toilet that was now six feet under.

DS Quirke at her desk was scanning a report she'd written up after a return visit to Fred Lambert's house. Everything had been wiped clean, there wasn't even a trace of any oily substance that had coated all the furniture. Snotty had either done it himself or supervised a team to wipe every surface contaminated by the body in the toilet. Top to bottom she had not found a trace. Through the back window, her eyes had been drawn to the toilet, incongruous with a missing door and exposed to prying eyes. The greenhouses were empty now and the lawn still showed signs of trampling from a few weeks ago.

She'd approached the toilet along the path realising Snotty had not overlooked a thing. On the night of the grisly discovery, DS Quirke had noticed the contrast between the bright white masonry paint on the back wall and the livid fragments of skull splattered like a piece of Hockney artwork. Now everything looked seared. Her fingers had traced blistered paintwork and some areas that had caught fire were smudged or blackened with traces of carbon.

"Liz! Liz! He done that with a blowtorch!" Mrs Tyler stood at her fence.

"A blowtorch?"

"Yeah, bloody nerve... asked me to mind my own business... said it was the *procedure* at a crime scene because of health and safety or was it, health and hygiene?"

"The nerve," DS Quirke replied, "that's men for you."

"Ain't it just."

"Who was it, not that you were being nosey or anything?"

"The little fella... the one who was shoving the arsehole with the big nose... Not that I was watching or anything... Told me to mind my own business, thought he was going to burn the whole thing down... Might have done if I hadn't been here... he nearly caught me..."

"Boys and their toys..."

"If you play with fire, you get burned."

"Always..."

"Liz, got time for a cuppa?"

"Mrs Tyler, I would but I have to be somewhere else," she was in the process of locking the backdoor and exiting via the side of the house when she realised Mrs Tyler had said something important, "Mrs Tyler, he nearly *caught you* doing what?"

"Did I say *caught*?"

"Mrs Tyler, it will go no further... you have my word."

She wrestled with the dilemma. She never *helped* the police on principle... what sort of example would she be

271

setting her daughter? Thankfully today her daughter was at school.

"Don't tell anyone, but I was going to nick the toilet seat... I had the lid off when I heard the car... I don't want the rest of the seat now he's blistered it to fuck... look at the state of it."

"The lid?"

"Yeah, sell it at a car boot sale but then I thought I could sell it on eBay... once everything's died down... last resting place of Britain's most notorious killer."

"Do you mind if I see it?"

"It's in the kennel."

"Don't touch it... I'm coming round."

"Better watch the dog."

"Funny."

The toilet lid had one perfect handprint, four fingers on the outside and a thumb on the inner, neatly preserved in an oily substance. Mrs Tyler was not happy when DS Quirke took the lid for evidence but perked up when she suggested a better idea. DS Quirke hinted at the potential market on the internet for bricks, supported by photographic evidence, coming from the toilet of 'Britain's most notorious killer'.

She slipped the report into the file and looked at the next one. Dyer had ushered her into the gent's toilet, and he'd put a finger to his lips.

"Listen to this," he'd rasped.

"Are you dealing with the Lambert case?" A male's voice.

"The case is officially closed," Dyer's voice and DS Quirke could tell he was on the alert for the Chief of Police checking what *he* was up to.

"Funny, isn't it? I've spoken to him. Sat next to him the other day. His daughter's grave. Didn't seem very dead to me."

"Who is this? Chief, if this is some sort of joke?"

"Will there be a reward?"

"Sir, your name?"

"I'll be in touch... I know you'll be tracing my call and will be speeding to my location as we speak..."

Dyer's eyebrows had twitched as he rubbed his hands together. DS Quirke had mimicked him and rubbed her hands together too.

"Why does everybody think we can trace a call 'just like that'? This is Worcestershire... not a set for bloody Mission Impossible!" he'd almost chuckled.

She closed the file on her desk. It wasn't quite ready for the chief. A colleague threw a report in front of her.

"Liz, it's a stolen red tricycle in Evebury, and we know you and the arsehole are keen for any information in the town. And because it's *red* it should be right up his street."

When she'd frowned.

"He reads Russian shite, you know."

Chapter 50
NOVEMBER 22nd 2019, 03:00
The New Bridge, Evebury
Avenging Angel

It was the biggest tricycle he could find. Fred had stolen it from a garden in the middle of the night, he'd walked for hours on a mission, and he knew he would find it, it was pre-ordained, pre-determined... simply a matter of time, and, of course, it had been the same colour as the one... years ago. It was still a child's tricycle and that was important. He'd left an envelope containing a hundred pounds for the tricycle. Susan had wanted to go with him, but he'd been glad to leave her behind for a few hours – a chance to get his head together.

He'd waited for Tom to show up. Almost three in the morning in a playground next to the road leaving Evebury town centre; he'd been lurking under the road bridge since midnight, waiting for any stragglers to make their way home, standing perfectly still with his back against the concrete, hidden by one of the rectangular supports, invisible in the shadow, at one with the rust and the dripping moisture, invisible like he'd felt he'd become over the years. He no longer felt the cold though it was below zero. Some of the puddles out of the shadow of the bridge had begun to freeze, a couple of the streetlamps on the road above went out (a council money-saving measure) making the night even darker and when he was sure there were no more people about, he edged to the playground and sat on a swing. He was barely able to fit between the chains of the swing and contemplated moving to the seesaw but found the image of a fat man on a child's seesaw too absurd in the context of what he had in his mind.

He was in the park again. She was a toddler. Playing one of *her* games – she was always an organiser – she was *safe* as long as her feet didn't touch the green of the park floor, she could claim sanctuary on the play frame, the slide, the swings, the seesaw or the roundabout, but the clock was ticking, and *the monster* would suddenly start to count down from ten when the sanctuary would no longer count, but *the monster* always made a mistake… turned his back, distracted or found himself on the wrong side of the equipment… and she could make her escape to a different piece of equipment to claim a new sanctuary. She would scream and scream… and both would laugh until the tears rolled down their faces.

"Monster can't catch me!"

Sometimes they did.

Tom sidled up from the darkness and sat on the swing next to Fred.

"Have you got the money, Mr Lambert?"

Fred tried to recapture his daughter in his head, but she was gone.

"Mr Lambert! Hello! The money?"

"Do you think I'm crazy? Do I look mad to you?" Fred spoke evenly, his words pushed to Tom on a breath of wind that made Tom shiver.

Tom considered this, giving the question due consideration. Fred didn't blame him having read the reports in the newspapers himself. He could see Tom was trying to play it cool, Fred had promised him a lot of money, and he didn't want to blow his chances by saying or acting in the wrong way. A single vehicle passed above them heading for the bridge and in a strange piece of choreography they turned their heads at the same time to hide their identity from the occupants – though the distance and darkness made this impossible.

"Play it your way, Mr Lambert, you asked me here, on the bloody coldest night of the year so far, so you tell me how it's going to be."

The silence again. Not even a sound from the deep, slow-moving river, merely yards away. The only sounds were in Fred's head – the sounds made when the traffic lights changed from red to green on the bridge. He shook his head.

"Why did she die, Tom?"

"… And I didn't, you mean?"

The lights in his head again.

"It wasn't my fault!"

"Of course, it was, Tom! It had to be!"

"… You knew how she was…"

"What's that supposed to mean?"

"Come on, Mr Lambert, she was your daughter…"

"If that's an accusation I will strike you dead where you sit!"

"Of course, it isn't! What I mean is… always outdoing herself… you know… wanting a higher high… a longer high…"

Fred let this sink in – *'Faster, Daddy, faster…'*

"Mr Lambert, I was the one trying to get her to take it easy… you know, to play it safe… But she was always chasing it… I was always the coward… The sensible one… It's God's truth!"

Fred knew it was the truth, but it wasn't going to make any difference.

"Anyway, Mr Lambert, you can't kill me in a playground… too many bad vibes for the kids that come here every day! Even killers must have standards!" Tom tried to make a joke.

"Tom, I was out of order, you're right, sorry."

"… And you're old and fat…"

Fred allowed himself a smile though all he could hear was the colour red. He eased himself from the swing, the chain caught on his jacket and Tom had to release him complaining of numb fingers. Fred walked toward the park exit and gestured with his head for Tom to follow. The tarmac path was wide enough for the two of them to walk together. On their right, the Avon flowed powerfully but quietly in the opposite direction to what Fred had taken. On the left were the sports field, a wide expanse of green that flooded regularly when the Avon burst its banks, and the path itself was shrouded by an avenue of mature lime trees, leafless but large branches affording them cover as they trudged along.

"Where are we going, Fred?"

Every few strides Fred slowed to savour the journey, the *quiet*, examining the tree trunks and watching the river when they passed an access point where anglers had smoothed a path. He smiled at a couple of life-buoy stations, bright red plastic guardians, thinking to himself they would not be needed tonight.

"I said, where are we going?"

"We used to walk up here all the time. I think her name is still etched in one of the trees somewhere... Happier times. She loved being here... had no fear of the water... Many a picnic we've had on one of those benches," he pointed at a fixed picnic table, tutted as he noticed a discarded wine bottle, and excused himself to pick it up, "I'll just get that," and he dropped it in the nearest bin.

"Are you all right, Fred?" Tom had flinched when Fred brushed passed him with the bottle.

"Never better. I just want to sit at one of these tables, take some of the stuff you idiots take, and float away to where she is... That's all I want."

"Money first."

277

Fred stood at the riverside, staring at the water, hypnotised by the patterns of the flow and eddies, only moving when Tom pulled at his sleeve.

"The money!"

"All in time, have a little patience… You know, come the Spring I reckon I'll have saved the town… People will flock here to walk where 'the mass killer' walked, where he used to push his daughter on the swings… the public is a gruesome lot… There are tours following 'Jack the Ripper's crime scenes, you know… There'll be people taking photographs of my house and the prison…"

"Best sign an autograph for me now then."

They continued to walk upstream toward the rowing club. On a slipway that gave access to people's boats, Fred paused again to impart another bit of wisdom.

"The English language is odd… The verb 'to row'… the act of arguing verbally… always makes me smile… or 'to row'… to propel your boat using oars… spelt the same but different… always found these things funny…"

"Yeah, hilarious."

"Tom, the bags in the undergrowth, to the left of the rowing club lockup…" and he pointed to an area where the single lamp from the rowing club couldn't penetrate the bushes.

"Where exactly?"

"In there, are you scared of the dark, a little bit further…"

"All I've got is a kid's bike…"

"That's it, it's just behind it."

"Oh, I see…"

Fred swung the nine iron… the first blow glanced off his shoulder and there was a moment when their eyes met… one had a purpose, the other panic… the second blow struck true before Tom could get his arm in the way… he must have heard a hissed *fore* as it struck… Fred was worried he'd killed him outright and was relieved when he felt a pulse in his neck.

Fred crouched by the river at the bottom of the slipway and slowly let both hands submerse, delighting in the coldness, setting his fingers tingling, and a swan appeared, gliding effortlessly toward him, hoping for a snack – even though it was close to three thirty. Fred smiled and remembered the countless times they had thrown bread to the swans and ducks, remembering her delight, her squeals as they were overwhelmed by their numbers, giggling when he said, 'We'd better make a run for it, before the birds picked you up and fly off with you, dropping you at the North Pole'.

He walked back up the slipway and flung cold droplets of the river into Tom's face. The tricycle was sideways to the slope. Tom's hands were taped to the handlebars and his trainers were taped to the pedals – for good measure more tape had been wound around his waist to fix him to the saddle. His knees and elbows stuck out ludicrously. Tom had just enough time to gasp, "What the fuck!" before Fred fixed more tape across his mouth and threw the leftover roll into the undergrowth. Fred then tutted, retrieved the roll, and found the nearest bin. Tom's eyes were wide. Fearful. Helpless. Embarrassed at being taped to a child's tricycle.

"Do you think, if I push you fast enough, you can make the other side of the river?"

Fred turned the tricycle and began to push it toward the river, Tom braced his legs to prevent the front wheels from turning and it dragged on the floor, scratching a mark in the concrete. Fred stopped at the edge. The swan bowed its head.

"You're not going to get enough speed if you don't pedal!"

Fred pulled the tricycle back to the top of the slipway, and massaged Tom's shoulders, before moving around so his eyes were close to Tom's.

"It's not that deep really... twenty feet if that... if you can get enough speed, you can make it... you really can... Don't worry about the cold... A young man like you... probably got all sorts in your system... won't even feel the cold... You will make the other side..."

They rolled and skidded to the edge again, the front wheel touching the water, the swan impassive, waiting, expectant... and again Fred pulled the red tricycle back to the top of the slipway. This time when Fred looked into Tom's eyes the fear had lessened... the tears had stopped... he was breathing more evenly... Perhaps he could see Fred was only trying to scare him... he hadn't even wet himself... there was a smugness that suggested 'you have to be better than that', or 'I'm bored with this.'

"We can make it, Daddy, we can!" Fred hissed, "Faster, Daddy faster!"

Fred tilted the tricycle backwards, only the back wheels were on the slipway, and he ran as fast as he could, picking up speed, the swan moved aside, and the tricycle ploughed into the river. Fred had intended to let go but he slipped at the edge and followed Tom into the river. They were both on the shelf, in the shallows just off the slipway, the tricycle bobbed supported by the air in Tom's clothing and turned slowly in the current as the flow gathered to take the sacrifice... Fred's hands were still clasped to the frame... Fred caught his breath... he couldn't do it... he didn't want to kill Tom and he tried to scramble toward the platform, but the current was taking him too. He let go of the bike and his fingertips caught the wooden structure of the platform… he turned back to Tom to grab some part of him, but he was too late, and his eyes stayed with Tom as the river swept him away and he sank below the surface.

*

When Fred opened his eyes, he was clinging to a body next to a riverside apartment near the park's exit. He was shivering holding onto his daughter. Only when he'd started to control his breathing did his daughter disappear and he realised he was clasped to a wooden sculpture as if his life depended upon it. He looked at the river as the swan turned and swam into the gloom. He let go of the 'The Penny Whistle' sculpture and stumbled into the darkness.

Chapter 51
NOVEMBER 25th 2019
Interview Room, Worcester Station
Orrible Arry Enderson

DS Quirke spoke for the benefit of the tape, "Present are Mr Harry Henderson, his brief, Geoffrey Ramsbotham, Detective Inspector Dyer and me, Detective Sergeant Elizabeth Quirke." She looked at one of Britain's most infamous crime lords, he was relaxed in the chair, sipping from a bottle of water; he'd winked at her when she'd entered the room but was now staring at Dyer who was having trouble getting comfortable in his chair and had decided to stand up instead. Mr Henderson had a warm smile that matched the patter that poured from his mouth. DS Quirke had been worried he would refuse to speak. In effect, he wouldn't shut up.

'What's the apple? Don't you know anything? Apple core... score. What's the score? What's happening here?

'Like a kipper. That's what it was. He done me up like a kipper. Just like he has with you two. Not that I'm admitting anything, you understand, you seem to have me on a technicality... When you crashed into my haddock... Haddock? Haddock and bloater. Motor... the boot flying open, as it did... a crash you caused, by the way... Didn't know you were the Sweeney Todd, did I... Yeah, sorry about the eye. No geezer saw me put the bag in there... Point of fact... A set-up for all I know... Funny how you were there so fast... My brief will put you straight on a few things... A couple of right-handers in a battle cruiser on a normal Saturday night ain't the crime of the century... You going to tell me you had an invite to their Otis next? Otis Redding... wedding!

'I've only got your word for it… a bag of wonga. That's your version… and some *Jackanory* from a mass murderer… trying to blackmail me… I told you; I never saw the bag in my boot… You did? I was too busy rubbing my neck… Whiplash I shouldn't wonder… Whiplash that you caused… Bloody mayhem! What a *fracarse*… I will be suing for injuries sustained. Hope you're insured. And if I understand you correctly, not only did you lose the bag… alleged bag… but you lost the geezer responsible for the murder of three hundred innocent lives… I'll concede that point… not exactly innocent… but murder is murder at the end of the day… Can't have one rule for one… How did all this happen? I'm on the straight and narrow… that's your opinion… And you seem to be the common denominator in this farce…

'Look, I got a call… Mickey Mac… I knew him by that name… used to work for me years and years ago… that's your assertion and an accusation… No contact at all… no proof… I'm doing you a favour… helping you with your enquiries… So, he says he's got something for me, making all sorts of threats… didn't Adam an' Eve him for a second, but a geezer in my position can't be too careful… He's a proper character, giving it the large and I can't be letting a no mark drag my name into the gutter… I've got a reputation… Steady… I told you I was on the straight and narrow… It's all interpretation at the end of the day… So, yes, I agreed to meet him.

'Ten o'clock on a Friday night on a bloody bridge in Evebury… as if I haven't got better things to be doing … No, it's alright, Geoffrey… I've got nothing to hide… I appreciate you giving up your time to sit here with these bottle and stoppers… I use the term loosely… I'm the innocent party here, Geoffrey.

'You ever been to Evebury? It ain't even got an airport... or a bloody motorway running straight to it... and it's mostly shut... Evebury... We settled in a battle cruiser near the shake and shiver... It was quiet... We didn't know there was going to be an Otis next door... more about that later... Anyway, the geezer told me to meet him alone on the bridge... I say bridge... It's not a proper bridge like in London... It's got a stream called the Evion... Avalon... no, the Avon, that's it... nothing like the Thames... Told me to wait in the middle under the bloody coat of arms... a crown and two odd yellow things... Yeah, now you mention it, they could be bales of wheat... built in AD1856... Got a head for figures, always have... and the shock, obviously of what happened to me has left the date embedded in my brain... AD1856... probably been abandoned since then...

'This bald, fat geezer approaches... I give him a butchers and sort of recognise him... years ago... boat race was familiar... since I allegedly knew him... and it was dark... he started to talk all kinds of bollocks... I can't remember any of it... Disingenuous? I'm in shock don't forget... I'm not withholding evidence... It can't be, what's the word? Corroborated? Yeah, that's the word. He was clearly half a pound of butter and up close I didn't even think it was Mickey Mac at all... Whom I'm alleged to know... To have known... Whatever. I was the one in danger. Half a pound of butter on the loose... you had him in the shovel, correct me if I'm wrong, and you let him go... I should be suing you for that as well! The crux of the matter is... The half-pound of butter grabbed me and tried to push me over the edge into the shake and shiver... over the edge... built of rock, like a castle effing rampart... I've already said it don't matter what was said... Inadmissible... and I may incriminate myself... Incoherent... Rambling... when I said push, it was going to be both of us... His intention was for both of us to fall... clearly mad... Had me in a bear hug... Had his arm through the arm of his holdall... Bag? Perhaps it was his dirty washing... It was his bag... I never looked inside... What's so important about the effing bag? Full of bees and honey? If you say so. It was attempted murder... add it to the charges for him... I would have been brown bread. The bag caught on the rampart... stopped us toppling... I admit he had me on the hop... wasn't expecting a bit of barney rubble... got my balance... Do you know how cold the water is at this time of year... Enough to say my blue swimming badge would not have saved me. Geoffrey here would still have sued you... Anyways a couple of passers-by came to my aid... Not thugs... Alright, I'll concede this point... they were associates of mine... I wasn't going to a strange town on my own... Call the bottle and stoppers? Are you having a bubble bath?

'I was doing my civic duty... He was a danger to the public... And to the convicted criminal as it turned out... You should be thanking me... an award would be nice... it would have been a citizen's arrest if you hadn't let him go... again. I didn't know who the geezer was at the time... as it was, I had Britain's most dangerous man in my grasp and, of course, I would have handed him over... We were most definitely not dragging him with us, we were *accompanying* him to a safe area... There were no witnesses... it's an effing ghost town... By the whale bones? In the gardens? What, they were real whale bones? We've got effing bigger toothpicks in London. You won't find a mark on him... Oh, I forgot, you let him slip through your fingers... Again.

'I bought him a drink... Jackson's Bar. If you say so... I thought, it might settle his nerves... and mine... a very traumatic episode... he was still talking bollocks... have no recollection of any conversation… You're supposed to slap somebody if you think they're in shock… Dog and bone? I tried calling the old bill… I didn't have a signal… It's in the middle of effing nowhere… I was about to get rid of him… Yes, Geoffrey, I'll rephrase that, for the record, I was about to leave the Godforsaken town, find the nearest city, and drop him off (no pun intended) at the cop shop… But… this redheaded dustbin lid approached the table… hadn't realised an Otis had spilt over from the hotel next door… and this redheaded dustbin lid started… well she started barking, like an effing Cherry! Cherry Hogg… effing dog!'

*

NOVEMBER 25th 2019
Interview Room, Worcester Station
Mrs Tyler
A Dog Barks and a Big Dog Barks A lot
DS Quirke spoke for the benefit of the tape, "Present are Ms Julie Tyler, who has declined the presence of a brief, Detective Inspector Dyer, WPC Bennett and me, Detective Sergeant Elizabeth Quirke."

"Look, I never speak to you lot, do I… my kind never do… and I don't see why I should now… Will you watch your nose, you nearly took my eye out then! I'll give you rude! You called her a Tasmanian Devil! So, what if she kicked you in the shin… and bit your hand… she was being suffocated… have you seen his hands… like a bleeding duvet coming at you. She was protecting herself…"

"For the benefit of the recording, DI Dyer has left the room," interjected.

'I've got nothing to say… except *he's* an arsehole… I ain't going to say nothing that drops anyone in the shit… The way I see it… it was the perfect wedding until you lot turned up… a great laugh, lots of booze, plenty of arguments and a good punch-up at the end… Who could want more than that?

'Yes, they have started to sell… It was your idea! Plenty of idiots… customers, out there wanting to buy genuine bricks from his outside toilet… Do you know, by the time I knocked it down I had three hundred and seven bricks… and as of yesterday I'd sold five hundred and two… and counting… The toilet itself? Sold it too… fifteen times already… Rather flush?

'Look, Liz, off the record… between you and me, yeah? I was at my cousin's wedding with little Frank… he's a lovely fella… he's dying… he's not even that old… he's got very yellow fingers… that's all you need to know… I was told he's got a nest egg hidden away… anyway, he's a nice fella… stinks a bit… I told him to get some fresh air… I took him a drink outside… and realised I'd lost Taz… I hadn't seen her for a while… I checked the hotel and was told she was heading for Jackson's… There's a climbing frame in the garden and she's been known to tie some of her cousins to it… in fun, you know… Jackson's was filling up, it was after eleven… sort of an overspill from the hotel… we have a sort of agreement with the hotel, you see, if there was going to be any trouble… to let it happen in Jackson's and the carpark… It's an unwritten rule…

'Anyways, I clock her hair through the window… She's got her back to me… Can't hear me and I have to go in… Jostle some of my boys… feel their bums as is the way of things… And she's sort of stood there like a statue… staring into the corner… staring at a group of heavies… not from round here… completely out of place… a couple of them were mean looking… I think they were supping up… a few of our boys had already clocked them as the possible fireworks for the end of the evening… the truth about my boys is they'll always fight the biggest fellas... always fight fair... I didn't notice the fella in the middle... he had his head down... he was sitting next to the fella who was in charge of them... All I know is I'd never seen them before...

'Taz started barking... high pitched barking... and the place went dead quiet... And he looked up... they sort of pinned him then, as if he might make a run for it and Taz said at the top of her voice... *Old bugger killed my dog!*

'I took it in straight away. Our boys crowded around. You can't kill one of our dogs without there being a reckoning... Only thing worse is if you kill a horse. I looks at Fred... our eyes held each other... enough said... it *was* the old bugger that killed my dog... But he was *my* old bugger... if anyone was going to give him a slap it was me and not some dickheads from out of town... and there was no mistaking him... lost his hairpiece and his glasses had a strange look about him... It was him, but it wasn't! Can't explain it. Something different... couldn't put my finger on it... No, I wasn't thinking about what he'd done at the prison, to be honest... he killed my dog... Nuff said!

'They stood up, like... One of my fellas said, see, told you they was big fellas, and somebody else said, it don't mean they can scrap... The one in charge of them tried to... what's the word... smooth over... placate... yes, there was a holdall... and a red book on the table... Anyways one of my fellas said... it's not important which one... he'd fight either one of the heavies or one after the other in the carpark... all civilised like... The one in charge didn't want any of it... But you know what it's like at a wedding... a fella from the groom's side... a cousin of a cousin... said it wasn't fair and that he should have first choice in deciding who fought who... That's when somebody got shoved... I didn't see... but the table was knocked... a beer glass went over... his expensive trousers got the brunt of it… he wasn't happy and the next thing the table went flying…

'I don't even think the heavies were roughed up that much… you know, typical wedding… a chance to settle a few in-house scores… they might have been the spark and I'm not saying they weren't hurt but if you check the injuries on our side… friendly fire if you like… cousin on cousin… far worse… complete uproar… chairs flying… No place for the old bugger… he could have got hurt… I kicked the fire door open and shoved him through… Had to save Taz, didn't I? Can't have her biting strangers, you never know what she might catch… That was the last time I saw him. Honest.

'The CCTV says what? That I looked in the bag? And I pocketed the red book? A conversation with him? Not likely… we were the best of enemies… I may have said, if I see you again, I'll kill ya! There were a few notes in the bag… lay on the top… the rest was mostly newspaper… I don't know what happened to the money… The red book? Search me…

Liz, I'm not saying anything else.

Chapter 52
NOVEMBER 30th 2019
Worcester Police Station
Escaped

DS Quirke watched as Dyer searched the office. He was looking for his shoe. He'd made the mistake of showing his bruised toe to a colleague, Orrible Arry had stamped on it *by accident* on the night Fred Lambert had slipped through our fingers, and the shoe had *disappeared*. DS Quirke hoped it turned up soon as Dyer's bright green socks were threatening to trigger a migraine.

The trail had gone cold... when Ms Tyler had pushed Fred Lambert through the fire escape and hugged him that last time, he'd turned and casually slipped into the darkness; and as he'd picked his way through the undergrowth, probably to emerge on Cooper's Lane, Dyer and DS Quirke had passed him, only feet away, arriving in their car in response to a call from the hotel. If DS Quirke had glanced to her right, she may have seen him... if she'd managed to see passed Dyer's nose. Ten seconds later Dyer had hit the back of Orrible Arry's car. The boot had flown open revealing an empty holdall and in the mayhem that followed Dyer had received an elbow to the eye and a bruised toe.

DS Quirke flicked open a file on her desk. She reread two notes left by Fred Lambert in the room where he and Susan Naylor had been hiding.

'I'll leave this for you. You need all the help you can get; the Press are never kind. And whilst I've got this pen in my hand it'll stop me from strangling her!

Bless.

She spends hours stacking the money in towers in the centre of the room. Fifty's, twenty's, tens, and fives. I painstakingly count it, and carefully put it back in the holdall, in neat bundles, but as soon as I leave the room, she empties the bag again, on the floor, mixes it all up and starts to build the towers again.

I was in a fever yesterday, she said I didn't return to the room until half past four in the morning. I knocked the towers over and she was upset because my shoes squelched on the carpet, and I'd left boot prints on some of the notes. I was moaning about Tom. She put me to bed with a hot chocolate.

Bless.

The wellies were yellow. She'd lost the red ones. She never looked after her stuff. That bloody overflow in the carpark at the bottom of the lane, behind the garages, she always wanted to go there after a good downpour. It would have taken the council ten minutes to sort it! It didn't matter if Dad wanted a lie in! It was Autumn, conker collecting is another pointless activity, buckets full of useless things, to the park and back all bloody morning: a growing mound in the back garden.

The *lake* that morning was deeper than usual. I tried to distract her, but she was always headstrong… she didn't get it from her mother… I insisted she was not to try and pedal through it… I'd even grabbed the back of the tricycle… the back wheels were scraping and skidding on leaf debris, but I was winning until she made a run for it. She was crying, getting into a right state, the cry when she wasn't getting her way… I had one hand on the tricycle and the other buried in the hood of her anorak and she kicked me, hard in the shin… she slipped from my grasp and rushed into the puddle. It was deeper than she expected and before she got anywhere near the middle, she toppled over… face first into the dirty, cold, water, struggling to right herself... water in her yellow wellies and air trapped in her anorak.

Of course, I was the one who had to get her out. Cursing. Swearing. She stormed off, stomping up the road so I pushed the tricycle into the puddle and left it there, following my daughter at a distance.

Suse would write a list of items on the back of her hand to remind her when she got to the supermarket. She'd put her gloves on halfway there because it was cold and forget about the list. She'd come back empty-handed or with stuff we didn't need.

Bless.

I'm watching her sleep. Eyes dancing behind lids. She's not my daughter. She mumbles *Florida* at irregular intervals.

I don't like myself. If I'm honest I haven't for some time, but I think I've overstayed my welcome. Three hundred and sixteen, plus Smithy, plus Tom, that was an accident, plus the dog. Suse can have some of the money and her life in Florida. There's a red book in the bag and even I can see its value. Orrible Arry will want to get his hands on it... if it fell into the *right hands,* he would be looking at a long stretch behind bars. It will be enough to tempt him... and the river has always been my friend. The last act of justice. He's been responsible for more deaths than me!

I don't like the man I've become... it's time to put an end to this. Orrible Arry will answer for my daughter.

Suse cried when I told her the plan was changing. When she cries there is not one part of her face that does not join in.

Bless.'

DS Quirke flicked a second file open.

'I wasn't *man enough*. Again! I couldn't even fall off the bridge. Lucky to get away. I could have jumped… it would have been easy… sorry end to a sorry life… only, I hesitated, and the opportunity was lost. Story of my life. Got roughed up for my weakness. Suse is making a fuss of me… she's not bad with the cotton wool and a couple of plasters. Saved by the dog! Who'd have thought it? Turns out the neighbour wasn't a bad sort, after all. Heads throbbing again, I suppose it's the excitement…

It's dark… I'm writing this, the streetlamp comes through the window, Port Street is quiet… I've seen one cat in the last hour and a half. Suse is snoring on the sofa… her hands are in prayer beneath her cheek… I know what she's praying for… and I will make it happen.

I don't want to be me anymore. I'm a coward. I've spent my life hiding. I thought I could fix it; I spent close to thirty years working with offenders, fooling myself that the path to redemption was rehabilitation, turning lives around. What's the adage? If I can save one life it would have been worth it? I was lying to myself. I was worthless and I hid amongst the worthless.

Something snapped and I decided to do something. Revenge? Retribution? Justice? The accidental mass murderer! What a joke! Hiding behind the self-righteous hatred of a father that's lost a daughter? Hiding again, you see, hiding from myself. Blaming everyone but myself. What a man I have become.

We'll be gone soon. The avenging angel has had his day. I'll leave this note for you. I am a coward and one day I'll give myself up. This sorry excuse for a man has found the answer to his suffering.

I'm not around the bend! It might be the beginning of the bend or is it part of the bend at the beginning, no, it's the part at the beginning of the bend, leading to the place around the bend. I've still got my sense of humour…'

DS Quirke looked up as Mrs Quibble marched into the office. Everyone stopped what they were doing in respect of the elderly cleaning lady. She held a shoe in her hand, letting it drip on the floor before she cut into the silence.

"If you lot spent more time catching murderers than playing me up with your shenanigans, to be sure the world would be a safer place, so it would. Now who put this shoe in my mop bucket?"

The lid was to be kept on the case. The British Government did not want the public to panic, but it was more likely to hide the incompetence of several high-flying Ministers, having made previous announcements to placate an uneasy public at the height of the crisis. DS Quirke knew it would suit them if Fred Lambert died quietly of one of his many reported ailments and it could be swept under the carpet. She dreamed Fred Lambert was hiding in plain sight, working at a fast-food outlet, looking at the public over a deep-fat fryer.

It was two in the morning, DS Quirke was trying not to give Dyer any attention, he was cleaning his keyboard... taking each square key from the board and rubbing it vigorously with a yellow duster... he'd dropped three so far during this process and had to scramble on his knees under his desk... he has to do this regularly... at least three times a week... whenever he leaves the office someone takes the keys off and replaces them in a random order. He'd dismantled his chair last week, one of those adjustable ones, and cleaned all the parts... the chair no longer went up or down but is jammed at a height where he can't get his knees under the desk. And now he's whistling, through his moustache, some inane melody, over and over...

DS Quirke's computer bleeped... she has an email... she put the stapler back on the desk, she'd been about to hurl it at Dyer...

'I wasn't as ill as I thought... I knew my doctor was an idiot... I've got months left, I'm sure. I wanted to let you know how I am... It can get boring ... few people speak

English. The red book it turns out not only listed everything Smithy knew, but it had a list of important contacts if you needed a false passport or a bit of plastic surgery... always fancied a hair transplant... Can't believe *she* thought she could pocket the book... I let her have the bag... hardly anything in it... I'm almost glad my plan to kill the boss failed... not completely... but you have to make the most of things. As she said when she shoved me through the fire door on the night I failed: 'You might be an old bugger, Fred, but you're my old bugger. I know you never meant to kill my dog, but you must admit our feud was great while it lasted. You don't belong here anymore'.

She hugged me. All the time I thought we hated each other. That's when I got the book back.

'Now off with you... If I ever see you again... I'll kill you myself!'

She slapped me round the face... just for luck.

'That's for the dog!'

Perhaps something rattled in my brain. From that moment I started to pull myself together.

Susan's in Florida. I got her a job working in the laundry servicing the Disney parks. Had to grease a few palms. She knows nothing about anything of this and I'd appreciate it if you left her alone... I had to get her away before I killed her... She's waiting for the FBI to contact her – dressed as Donald Duck.

I know what I did... I am fully responsible... I wrestle with my conscience every day and when you trace the origins of the email you'll know where I am... So, I look forward to doing this in person, Fred.

Chapter 54
JANUARY 2020
British Airways Flight
And Now What?

Dyer had the window seat… it made it easier for DS Quirke to escape when she had the need, and she knew she would have the *need* a lot: it was going to be a long flight.

The British Government had listened incredulously to the plan for Dyer and DS Quirke to fly halfway around the world to get their man. The Home Secretary eventually agreed. He wanted everything kept quiet and insisted on secrecy. The Home Office had pulled a few strings and though no extradition treaty existed with Britain it was hoped Fred Lambert could be persuaded to accompany Dyer and DS Quirke back to Britain. The context of his messages led them to believe this was the case. It was also an opportunity to improve diplomatic relations.

The chief had been very pleased – 'take as long as you need, Dyer, but come back with your man'. DS Quirke saw it as an opportunity to tick Japan off her list. She was excited by the prospect of an *adventure* in the Far East and duly cancelled an upcoming meeting with her therapist, and she wondered if the code of ethics applied once she'd left Britain.

Dyer's tray had rhythmically gone up and down twenty times before she snapped, placing her hand firmly on the surface to stop it moving – the slap made other passengers nearby fall silent. She removed her hand and watched as Dyer struggled to free a small bottle of sanitiser from his trouser pocket, squirt some on the tray and begin wiping to expunge traces of her microscopic cells with a handkerchief.

Against her better judgement, DS Quirke said, "You won't need that in Japan, sir, they're a very efficient and hygienic race by all accounts."

"Yes, you are probably correct. Are you ready to tell me why you're so interested in Fred Lambert?" Dyer continued to wipe.

"Not until the end," DS Quirke reminded Dyer. She waited for him to comment on hygienic practices. She was not usually correct about anything, not completely correct, you never were with Dyer, he always had an addendum, an extra fact to put a person in their place, or a thirty-minute lecture on the flaws of a hypothesis.

He took a deep breath; she felt the cabin pressure alter.

"Wuhan is, of course, in China... Not Japan. Now I can tell you something about China... Got these food markets... live food markets... a complete anathema to the in-flight meal we're about to be served with..."

How many times could DS Quirke say *arsehole* before the plane arrived?

PART FOUR
Chapter 55
Wuhan

FEBRUARY 2020

Acceptance

The plastic surgeon held the blade up to the light, suddenly making rapid slices through the air at an imagined enemy, and though he was Chinese, he spoke in an accent that would have fitted in at Oxford or Cambridge.

"As you can see, I am an expert, see how deftly I handle my knife?"

Fred stared at the space where the blade had swished.

"I am the foremost plastic surgeon in the whole of China and because China is so vast, I am, by default, the foremost plastic surgeon in the world."

"And most expensive?"

"No questions asked, Mr Snow, means the price is very high. This is not the National Health Service, after all, and I am the plastic surgeon, the man so expert in his field, when you regain consciousness, you may look like Bruce Lee or in your case Brenda Lee, if you wish…"

"You have a list of my requirements, Mr Yo."

"I am the plastic surgeon, Mr Snow, and I will follow your directives… just once it would be nice to hear, *go for it*, Mr Yo, something completely random… freestyle your way on this one!"

"I hope you are joking, Mr Yo."

"I am the plastic surgeon and I've never been more serious, see how the light glints on the sharp edge of my knife. Mr Snow, you have paid well, and as your plastic surgeon, you must expect a lot of pain, it will be months before you are completely healed, but if you keep taking the painkillers there is no reason why you should not make a complete recovery."

"Mr Yo, is there much to do in Wuhan?"

"Believe me, it is the best city in China to *lie low*. It is very large, there are lots to do, and do you know the best thing? Nobody has ever heard of it! If you let me make you look like Bruce Lee, nobody will ever recognise you again… anaesthetic please!"

"More like, Brenda Lee, please, and do you know Dr Blidasabat by any chance?"

The anaesthetic began to bite, and Fred thought of his daughter and the chemicals she had put into her body, but the last thing he heard was Mr Yo's words of wisdom, 'If you can't live with yourself, Mr Snow… it is better to become someone else!'

*

Time to Face Up

'I tried to put on a brave face… I tried to put on a brave *new face*, but the pain was as excruciating as Mr Yo had warned. Operation followed operation. Painkiller followed painkiller. The rehabilitation lasted for months but as things turned out there was nothing else to do anyway. I never did get to see much of Wuhan; I was hiding in the one place in the world where everyone was watching at the start of the pandemic, but I was still hiding from myself, sitting in a darkened room trying to come to terms with my demons… until I was no longer myself, I was now someone else, and finally able to face the truth. This is what happened.

It was the day Ronaldo got Rooney sent off at the World Cup. The infamous wink to the camera.

"Freddie boy, to what do we owe the pleasure?"

Two officers took a step back as I entered the small space from where they were in the process of serving the lunchtime meal to the prisoners on Alpha wing.

"Well, you can put a white hat on for starters, you should know better… you attended the last food and hygiene course!"

"Sorry, Fred."

A chorus of boos from the line of prisoners, pleased to see an officer in discomfort.

"And you lot can shut up or I'll put rhubarb on again instead of rice pudding on Sunday!"

"Sorry, boss."

I checked the Food Complaints Book and the temperature of the food with a metal probe I produced with a flourish, causing a couple of the prisoners to *whoop* as if they were watching a magic act. Satisfied everything was running smoothly I signed the book and had just left the servery area when an alarm bell was pressed on the three's landing. I was the first up the stairs and at the entrance to the landing with one glance summed up what was happening: there was a scuffle going on in one of the cells, shouting and grunting… a number of the prisoners were watching from a safe distance, not getting involved… several cell doors had already closed as the more sensible prisoners decided to keep well out of the way… I made eye contact with one particular prisoner on the landing, someone from the kitchen, who with nothing more than a lifting of an eyebrow and a slight movement of the head, suggested I should *get in there straight away*. Other discipline staff were appearing behind me at the top of the stairs as I got to the cell door.

Two prisoners were locked in a grotesque dance, not sure which one of them was supposed to lead, up against the back wall of the cell, half a step toward me, too focused on their drama than on me shouting for them to *break it up!* The wrong place, no room for a threesome and we all fell to the ground in a violent game of twister. By the time the other staff could untangle the limbs, I was on the bottom of the scrum, having trouble breathing and feeling uncomfortable because something was pinned beneath my groin.

"Fred, will you roll over, you're lying on my arm, and I can't get to his wrist!"

"Happy to oblige, if you could take your head out of my arse!"

I moved to reveal the prisoner's clenched fist which was still holding a shank. To his credit the prisoner's initial response of *how the devil did that get there?* would long be remembered in adjudication folklore, especially when the prisoner suggested I'd disarmed him with the weapon I kept down my trousers! For weeks afterwards, I had to assure colleagues I had not been castrated.

I'd regained my feet and was the last person about to leave the cell, but as I dusted myself down, I nudged something under the bed with my foot, and stooping down I retrieved a brown substance wrapped in clingfilm, shaped like a mini hotdog... pocketed it on the blindside of any watching eyes, and as I exited the cell stated, "I thought I'd dropped my pen."'

*

Saving Her
'The alley on the side of the chip shop smelled of urine, and a couple of black bin bags that had been discarded and forgotten about had been attacked by rats at the corners. I slid the key into the lock and had to play with it, the way you do when a copy is not quite perfect... but it turned eventually... and I slipped into Tom's flat. No carpet on the stairs. A single living room and a dirty mattress on the floor in the corner. A

dirty mattress where my daughter allowed her life to be corrupted. I was there to save her.

A single white ankle sock screwed up in the duvet.

I retreated to the sofa, retching, fighting for breath, and calming myself by counting the bits of debris on the floor. A piece of pizza crust. A chocolate digestive biscuit. A single cotton bud. I should have left then, I did get to the top of the stairs but turning to check I hadn't left anything behind, my eye was drawn to a shiny sliver of foil, and retracing my steps discovered a flat box, carelessly nudged under the sofa by Tom's boot… and I had to open it, didn't I? Needle spoon, lighter and wraps of brown I knew was heroin.

… And to teach them a lesson… To teach *her* a lesson… You must get to rock bottom before you can recover… a couple of nights in the hospital would do it. I added the contents of the wrap I'd got on Alpha wing to Tom's stash… Any father would have done the same… I wanted to save her from this life.'

— Two extracts from a journal recovered after Fred's arrest.

Chapter 56
APRIL 1st 2020, 09:00
HMP Long Stretch
And Here We Are Again

"Acting Detective Inspector Quirke and you are expecting me."

It sounded good, but not, evidently, to the woman sitting behind the reinforced glass at the entrance to HMP The Stretch, who reached for a cup of tea, taking a slow and lengthy gulp, before taking DI Quirke's ID offered through a sliding security panel on the desk in front of them.

DI Quirke had not expected to be at The Stretch again so soon and she'd been extra careful when parking her car and sure enough, the old jobsworth appeared, scuttling out of nowhere to check she had the right to park in the visitor's carpark. They exchanged pleasantries through the window and when he recognised her from their previous meeting, he rechecked the passenger seat before stooping to look under the car. DI Quirke took the opportunity to open the car door and she caught him a glancing blow to his shoulder, but he didn't give her the satisfaction. Inscrutable.

"I am on my own, Covid didn't get you then... and I assume I'm parked correctly?"

"Yes. Yes. On your own. Good. Over three hundred deaths the last time you were here... and now this bloody pandemic... but I don't think I could face <u>him </u>again!"

"I'm pleased to see you too," DI Quirke muttered.

"Oh, Oh, Miss, you can't wear that in there," he cheered up when he noticed the pink face mask, she had taken pains to embroider LQ in bold black cotton, *rules are rules...*"

Dyer would have liked the new-look search area with its multiple hand gel sanitisers though the standard masks would have been inadequate for his nose. Governor Young met her on the other side of the search area. DI Quirke noticed he was allowed to wear a black mask with the digit three embroidered in gold and was at pains to point out his recent promotion, with a larger desk, a new improved coffee machine, and most importantly a proviso he was *strictly* not allowed into the main body of the prison. 'You can't have the decision makers mixing with the general prison population at a time like this, simply can't take the risk of becoming infected and making a mistake through ill health.' In answer to her question as to how many prisoners were infected at this time, he evaded the question with 'the benefit of his new office meant he had a view, not only of the prison blocks in the distance but of the carpark and staff mess too.' When she showed no interest in following him to his office, he collared Officer Overhill and told him to escort her to the Care and Separation Unit. It was the same Officer Overhill who had shown the crime scenes on the wing and in the kitchen on that fateful night.

"It's a bit different to the last time I was here. Didn't they change the name to Middle Lartin, or something?"

"The minister resigned, and I think they forgot. In all my years, it's the best it's ever been…" Officer Overhill was leading DI Quirke through deserted corridors, heels echoing madly despite her best efforts to step carefully.

"Pardon the observation, Officer Overhill, but it seems a bit, a bit…"

"Dead?" He chuckled.

"For a prison with hundreds of men, and compared to *that night*, is it normally so quiet?"

Officer Overhill stopped abruptly and became stony-faced.

"Have to stop you there, Miss, in the Prison Service we never use the 'Q' word."

DI Quirke was puzzled for a moment until she realised, he meant the word *quiet*. He started walking again or shuffling to be more exact, a hip operation would be needed soon.

"You'd be surprised how many times things have gone *tits up*, no offence Miss, by someone carelessly using the 'Q' word."

"None taken. A superstitious lot, are you? A bit like the Shakespeare play you can't speak of?"

"I'm not good at trivia, though I once read Romeo and Juliet… well, I started it…"

"You were saying, it's the best it's ever been?"

"Oh, yes, after the murders we had almost an empty prison for weeks… much better without prisoners… we had a lot of empty cells, but prisoners were refusing to transfer here… I can see their point of view… Anyway, just as we were recovering, and starting to fill up again, the pandemic started… a bit of a Godsend really, put a limit on the number of prisoners allowed out of their cells at the same time. Too risky to run a normal regime… we've been lucky so far though; we've had no positive cases…" he paused as we passed the entrance to the kitchen and pointed at a new plaque which read 'Whitmore's Kitchen.'

"Officer Overhill, what's the food like now?"

"That was in bad taste, Miss! Let's say the curry's not very popular."

"Nice touch, though, after the first victim."

"Leaves a bad taste again, Miss, this was and will always be known as 'Fred's kitchen' to anyone who has done any service here." Officer Overhill shook his head and shuffled on.

At the Care and Control Unit, Officer Overhill shook his head again.

"This sums up what's wrong with the Prison Service today," pointing at the shiny new sign, "used to be called the Segregation Unit but it seems that sounded too intimidating for *the men!*"

He left DI Quirke there, having pressed an intercom button, and she heard him tutting and muttering to himself as he retraced his steps down a connecting corridor. She must have been the first outside visitor to the Care and Control Unit since the start of the pandemic, and she sensed the discipline staff, who were sitting in their stand-down room, arm's length apart, were suspicious of her visit. Ten men of various ages, held her stare, giving her the once over, some women would have felt intimidated, but DI Quirke stated in a very business-like manner.

"Clothes... Off... Now. All in an evidence bag, please, including your pants! You can keep your face masks on."

A couple of officers gulped. Someone sniggered. She may have been joking.

"No? In that case, one cup of coffee, milk, no sugar, and there'd better be biscuits."

The ice was broken, and she was soon sat in the interview room with a jam doughnut and a large coffee in a mug with the words, 'Collective noun for prison officers – a turn of screws' printed neatly on its ceramic surface. It was a dark room, a wooden desk separated by a reinforced glass partition, and she kept an eye on the metal door waiting for the prisoner to arrive. When it opened, the prisoner was pushed into the room, the conversation with prison officers ended mid-sentence as the door snapped into place, and he stood there for a moment irritated at the perceived slight. The plastic chair was too small for him... his knees stuck up above the desk... he put his large hands on them for want of a better place... and focused on the wall behind my head.

"Aargh, Quirky, I wondered when you'd get here. Is that jam on your chin?"

The prisoner messed with the face mask, covering his nose which had escaped as soon as he had spoken.

Oh, Dyer, how had things got to this?

Chapter 57
FEBRUARY 2020
Wuhan, China
Table Tennis anyone?

DS Quirke's favourite spot in a hotel room in Wuhan. A window on the tenth floor overlooking the river and the green park area out of place in the centre of all the concrete; a window opening outwards allowing DS Quirke to dangle her legs outside; a window that would allow her to fall, to be dashed to pieces on the pavement below – if she wanted to. The temptation! Due to the rapidly changing situation in Wuhan, within days they had been under *house arrest* or restricted for their safety from leaving their hotel rooms and the pursuit of Fred Lambert had been thwarted by something that would be known as a world pandemic. Covid 19. A pandemic DS Quirke could cope with but as day leeched into day, leeched into Dyer, leeched into more Dyer, her only English-speaking human contact, her mind began to play tricks. Perched in her favourite place, arguing with her inner voice, *if he knocks on the door in the next five minutes I'll jump, if he knocks to the tune of the William Tell Overture, or he knocks in Morse code I will jump* – it was only day five of this torture but already DS Quirke could see no option. All flights were suspended and there was no knowing how long how they would be guests of the Chinese Government. Unprecedented times.

To the Chinese officials, *their safety* meant no electronic devices and limited landline telephone access. They were *their* guests and they aimed to make the stay as *comfortable as possible*; exceedingly polite until either of them attempted to leave the corridor on their floor where they were met with *the corridor only for exercise: please return to your room*. Even Dyer had met his match; he could hypnotise a few at a time with his large hands and even confuse some with his sabre-like nose, but through the sheer weight of numbers, DS Quirke was reminded of a film where a black scorpion was overrun by stinging ants, his protests were rebuffed with ease. It did not matter that he was a British citizen. His frustrations turned to DS Quirke. After the tenth lecture on how to wash her hands thoroughly, she was nearing breaking point.

It was Beethoven's Fifth this morning and he marched in with his over-long stride.

"Aargh, Quirky, what do you find so fascinating with the view from that window? Don't forget to put your mask on. I'd be careful if I were you… one slip and you'll be an amoeba-stain on a Wuhan pavement. Do you know how many atoms make up the typical human body?"

DS Quirke prepared to jump.

"I do not have time to educate you this morning, Quirky, as a matter of fact simply popped in to let you know you will not see me for a few days…"

Popping in usually meant at least five hours. She wasn't going to let her guard down.

"… The little people have provided me with the paper I requested and I'm going to make a start on my memoirs… seeing we've got so much time on our hands…"

Exceedingly large hands.

"I suggest you stop wasting your time staring out the window and find something constructive to do… you'll catch your death sitting there in that wind… and put your mask on."

The door snapped shut. DS Quirke should have been elated but as her feet regained the carpet she was already looking ahead, perhaps sensing a trap, and realised she would be the one that would have to read Dyer's memoirs! How long does it take for a person to go insane? Her hands were back on the window ledge when there was another knock on the door. It was a polite tap, and the person did not barge into the room uninvited. It saved her life.

"Enter."

When the instruction was ignored, she repeated the word but to no avail. A further polite tap, which she ignored on principle for thirty seconds, scanning the city, the bridge in the distance, no traffic, the bridge like the backbone of an unearthed dinosaur, and a third tap which began to upset her composure. DS Quirke stomped to the door and pulled it open like a wrestler about to grapple with it. A fourth tap was already in motion and the knuckles came to rest on her chest.

Their eyes met. In DS Quirke's head, imaginary fingers plucked random words from parts of her brain, all in a microsecond, words like *lust*, *frustration,* and *fuck*, and rolled them neatly into a ball which she smashed with a table tennis bat straight at him. Not only did he control her best shot, but he returned it with interest. This man was going to control the rally, put DS Quirke in positions she'd never thought of, move her around the table with ease, make her the table and she knew the table was in for a right battering… was she up for it?

"Miss Quirke, may I have the pleasure…" removing his knuckles, "of introducing myself? I am Mr…" with his left hand he conjured an ID badge, "I am Mr Hwow, direct from the esteemed Chinese Government. I am here to make your stay as… bearable as possible. Forgive me if we do not shake hands."

He said bearable, DS Quirke heard *pleasurable*.

"May I come in?"

She stepped aside. She didn't say anything… couldn't trust herself… as he glided past, she felt static in her nylon top. He walked to the window as she closed the door. He produced sanitising gel from a pocket and carefully attended to every finger before caressing the window ledge where she had been sitting. DS Quirke sat on the only decent chair in the room, managed to fumble her mask over her ears and mouth, and crossed her legs tightly.

"Miss Quirke, we are trapped here, but I will not allow such circumstances to prevent me from entertaining an esteemed guest of the Chinese nation. Miss Quirke, I love China. Please allow me to impart some of my love, to make your stay most rewarding. If there is anything you want to know, to try, to experience, please to let me know... and I will do my best to satisfy your every whim..."

His fingers stopped moving and he turned to fix her with his dark eyes.

"Surprise me," was the best she could do.

"Tonight, Miss Quirke, you will be... how to phrase it? You will be undone by the humble chopstick. I will bring dinner at seven... be prepared."

Something in the way he said, 'be prepared', and the way his left eyebrow challenged her, forced her to say, "Mr Hwow, I am not scared."

She managed to lock eyes with him. After a few seconds had passed he pulled his face mask down, smiled to acknowledge the challenge, and as he left, he said, "Miss Quirke, you have nothing to fear but your limitations."

DS Quirke lay on the bed and stared at the ceiling. What had just happened? She removed the Police (Conduct) Regulations Handbook from beneath her pillow, her only reading material, and fingered the pages. She really should try to make more of an effort when it came to controlling her *urges. Standards of Professional Behaviour...*

*

Blurred Edges

Elizabeth would not normally *get naked* on a first date. (Not strictly true – a downright lie – but not like this!)

She'd made the effort. She was wearing the one decent dress she'd brought, a short black number, showing podgy thighs, the one that pushed her breasts together in, what she knew, was a provocative manner: it was a dress that never failed. Her hair was in a high bun accentuating a round face, and beneath the mask, she had full red lips, and she was wearing her *special*, black-rimmed glasses, the ones that made her look a little vulnerable, almost helpless. She needn't have worried.

A polite tap on the door at seven. She ignored the notion it could be Dyer. Mr Hwow was in an immaculate tuxedo. Bow tie. A Chinese James Bond. His left eyebrow trembled as he sized her up, a table tennis ball being juggled on a bat before he deemed the best way to serve to his opponent. An imperceptible gesture with a finger, moving away from the door to allow a waiter to wheel a trolley into the room. Several covered dishes and a bottle of champagne in an iced bucket. The waiter left immediately, and Elizabeth watched as Mr Hwow slowly closed the door, transfixed by fingers as they turned the lock. She sensed trouble.

"No shoes, Miss Quirke?"

She looked at her stocking feet.

"… you believe all Chinese men are short and you hope to make me feel better?"

Off balance. A good service and it was one nil to Mr Hwow. Not sure what to say and mentally fumbling for the loose ball at her feet thinking about the section on *equality and diversity.*

"A joke, Miss Quirke!"

When she frowned, he quickly served for two-nil.

"You think Chinese have no sense of humour!"

She was going to need a bigger bat.

"Miss Quirke, I think you should drink something, you are looking a little pale."

"Mr Hwow, just because I am British does not mean I want to drink all the time, and as for being pale… that is almost racist!"

"Forgive me, I do not want an international incident."

"I was joking too, Mr Hwow," one point to her, "and as for the shoes, I have not been out for so long I've simply got out of the habit." Two-two, surely?

"In my country, a woman that greets a man with no shoes on," their fingers touched as a glass of champagne passed between them, "wants to make love to that man…"

Three-two. Slightly flummoxed but warming up. Still in the game.

"Forgive my ignorance, but I hope you can control yourself."

"I can, Miss Quirke… I will leave it up to you entirely if we are to make love before or after we have eaten…"

She almost dropped her bat, removed her mask letting it fall to the floor, gulped the champagne in one and indicated a refill.

"British girls are not that easy!" She'd lost her self-belief and missed the ball completely so much for *honesty and integrity*.

"Easy? Not easy, I hope, Miss Quirke, as I like a challenge."

The second glass disappeared.

"Tonight, Miss Quirke, I intend to undress you using only chopsticks…"

Surely not! More bubbly, please.

"… and I will be blindfolded!"

314

She no longer knew the score. A heat was spreading… the table tennis ball had probably melted. When she did not reply, letting her bottom lip drop with confusion, though he must have seen this as a provocative pout, he removed his tuxedo, placing it on the back of the chair.

And still, Elizabeth did not speak.

Glass and bottles were now on the floor.

He approached, produced a blindfold from his sleeve which he positioned on his head but above his eyes, and with a flourish four chopsticks magically appeared in his hands.

And still, Elizabeth did not move.

A waft from the trolley? Egg Foo-Yung? Her head was scrambled. Closer. The dangerous Mr Hwow narrowed his eyes, and with two chopsticks in each hand rehearsed at a distance what he was about to do, memorising the route they would take, playing the rally in his mind.

"Miss Quirke, stay perfectly still… and no harm will come to you…" he slipped the blindfold over his eyes.

First contact; a strange embrace on the outside of her hands at the side of my body. Tracing circles, and then to the tips of her fingers, and gently back to the wrists, the sticks parting as if feeling for a pulse.

"Now I have you…"

Running up naked arms to the shoulders. Goosebumps – increased resistance. The change in texture from flesh to material and arriving at her neck – the sense he could somehow slice through the windpipe if he had wanted. Holding both earlobes – teasing them gently, vulnerable to a lover's teeth. DS Quirke's glasses were the first to fall. Expertly clasped, slipped from her face with a lover's caress, and dropped into the champagne bucket.

Unerringly back to her ears and scalp, pressing on points to make her toes curl, thighs warm and nipples tingle;

315

hairclip removed and discarded to the carpet and hair falling to her shoulders. The impossible! Painting her face, drawing symbols with the tips of the chopsticks on her cheeks, she knew he could count the number of hairs in her eyelashes if he had inclined. The hands of a master.

He moved behind her, teasing the skin above the zip of the dress, spelling a word, before the zip was slowly clicking southwards, easily, not complaining, to the base of her back. The straps lifted from her shoulders and the dress fell, catching on nipples, solid enough at this time to have rested a couple of table tennis bats on them. The chopsticks gently lashed the naked skin, confirming no bra, before moving to the material of her knickers. They confirmed the existence of stockings.

He moved silently to the front. Elizabeth normally shameless was glad of his blindfold. Helpless. Undone by chopsticks. Nipples free, and pulses of electricity, caused her little toes to spasm. He stopped tormenting and dropped to his knees. The fastenings to her stockings were unpicked.

"Are you ready, Miss Quirke?" as he pulled her knickers to the ground where they rested on her feet like a pair of white plimsolls. Her mind wandered to *fitness for duty*.

Chapter 58
Care And Control Unit, HMP Long Stretch
A Prisoner of Convenience

"Ooh, Mr Hwow, I don't think I've ever been more ready!"

"Quirky! Did you hear me? Is that jam on your chin?"

She wiped the jam, examined her finger and was about to lick it clean when she realised Dyer's eyes were examining it like it was under a microscope, and before he could expound on the relative molecular structure of a good strawberry jam, she clasped her hands under the desk and gave them a good rub.

"So, Quirky, what does the chief say? How much longer do I have to sit in here?"

"Not long, sir, the chief's working incredibly hard behind the scenes…"

He wasn't. If the chief had his way Dyer would never get out. 'Serves the silly sod right!'

"He's asking questions, sir… pulling a few strings… he knows people, as you are aware."

The chief was asking questions but not the ones Dyer might have expected. His main question had been, *can't he be kept there indefinitely? Throw away the key?* The prisons' minister had agreed to a short-term solution. To placate the Chinese, he'd accepted the need to make Dyer a *special* case and lock him up in a Maximum Security prison. The fact Dyer was an innocent man was irrelevant. There was no doubt Dyer had been framed at the airport and held by the Chinese in a tit-for-tat argument in the blame game regarding Covid 19 (The Prime Minister had called it a *twit for a twat* when told Dyer was involved) and diplomatic relations were at a low point. At the outset, the Chinese had asked for five

Chinese dissidents to be returned for Dyer, but once they had realised whom they were holding the Chinese had agreed on a one-for-one swap, settling for an ageing fast-food catering assistant who was no longer sure of his own identity thanks to early onset dementia. To save face the Chinese had asked that Dyer be held in a British prison for a short time *to see how you like it!* Ultimately, the prison's minister had explained, 'simply because the man's an idiot is not reason enough in the twenty-first century to keep someone behind bars indefinitely.'

"… I'm sure high-level meetings are going on as we speak."

Chapter 59
FEBRUARY 2020
Wuhan Airport
Discretion is the Better Part of...

"Please cover your mouth and your nose with the mask," the Chinese official, probably a distant relation to the carpark attendant at the Stretch was confronting Dyer, "it is to prevent the possible spread of infection."

"Bit late for that, wouldn't you say?" Dyer said under his breath, but DS Quirke could tell it wouldn't end well.

"Please, I did not understand..." the official placed a hand on Dyer's arm. She was plucky... DS Quirke tried never to touch him.

"I was saying, it's too late, it's already spread, hasn't it?"

"Please, I do not want you to spread the virus."

"You started it," he said, under his breath.

"Pardon, sir?"

"I said, the mask is too small. In the west most of us have larger proboscis'... larger hooters... massive noses... this cannot do the job."

Their eyes locked. Dyer tried to swat her away with a raised eyebrow. Inscrutable, she dodged and took hold of his sleeve.

Six weeks in the hotel had come to a sudden end. Given an hour to pack they were rushed to the airport, the last flight for the British to leave Wuhan, and they were on it. Fred Lambert would have to wait, though she scanned the queue just in case the dice had rolled in their favour for once.

"What you say? You say all Chinese have small faces with flat noses?"

"Not at all… but now you come to mention it," he was barely audible, but she heard it alright.

DS Quirke was tempted to say Dyer should have read the Police Handbook instead of writing his memoirs.

"Please, to stand over there… we do baggage check…"

"Oh? And why me, may I ask?"

"We do ten per cent. You are ten per cent."

Dyer tried to shake her hand free, "There are twenty-five in the queue. Ten per cent is two point five…"

"Your point is?"

"You've searched three people thus far… I will be the fourth… which will take it to sixteen per cent by my quick calculation."

"You refuse my request?"

"You said ten per cent, not me."

She snapped her fingers and a couple of armed guards approached. Dyer snorted, causing everyone to take a step backwards, picked up his suitcase, and the petulant Detective Inspector trudged to the search counter. Though the rest of the queue had wanted to stay and watch the confrontation they were ushered through the portal and could only observe at a distance.

Bright red plastic gloves were being stretched as she put them on. Expert fingers doing their job. Folding back the top layer of Dyer's case and removing the top layer of clothes: the bright yellow underpants. She had a smug look on her face. She paused, savouring the moment as her hands rested on something in the case hidden from our view. The practised moment when she had found something.

Dyer looked in DS Quirke's direction. He'd picked up the folder containing his memoirs, perhaps it was in his mind to cover the damning evidence, and as the Chinese official placed her hands on the kilo of heroin, he smacked her on top of the head.

He was not on the flight home. DS Quirke enjoyed the extra legroom this afforded her. She was woken by a stewardess when the meal was being served and had asked for *vibrating chopsticks* before she had known what she was saying.

*

APRIL 1ˢᵗ 2020

A Plot

"Quirky, are you listening or thinking about your next doughnut?"

"Vibrating chopsticks."

"Utter nonsense, as I was saying, someone put that package in my suitcase... I've got my suspicions..."

"The package was sorted, sir. What's the saying? Smoothed over. The reason you are still here is that you assaulted a government official with your memoirs!"

"Is that all?"

"Turns out she's the daughter of some high-ranking party member in the Chinese Government... we have to be seen to be doing the right thing... we have a lot of trade with China... well, we will if we ever get back to normal."

"There were only fifty sheets of paper in that folder... you should see it now... knock her unconscious with it!"

DI Quirke tried not to think of his memoirs. She knew they would be a burden in her life in the future.

"Quirky, listen... are you listening, Quirky?"

"Sir?"

"I've heard things, Quirky, sat in here..."

She perked up.

"I've heard voices, Quirky, and I've made notes..."

"Don't worry, sir, it could happen to the best of us… sat in here on your own… the four walls… most prisoners hear voices in their heads after a while." Cruel, but for a moment she was no longer 'acting Detective Inspector', in fact, no more Dyer at all… sectioned.

"Quirky, what are you talking about? Listen! There's something afoot. In here there are some high-profile prisoners and I've heard some damning stuff."

"Go on."

"Extremists," he whispered, holding up a finger that disappeared in his moustache, he leaned forward, repelling her, but beckoning her closer, "There is a plot… as soon as the lockdown is over, *they* are going to spring into action. I've got names and a couple of leads."

When DI Quirke didn't say anything, he became more frantic.

"Quirky, this is big, don't you see?"

There was a knock on his door, signalling his time for the interview was over.

"Quirky, it's urgent!"

"Lives at risk, sir?"

"Well, yes, obviously, but a chance to make a name for myself… I mean, a chance to make a name for ourselves, to put the Lambert fiasco behind us… but you need to get me out of here before they can put their plans into action."

He was gone. Returned to his cell. DI Quirke looked through the small slit in the door as he was ushered away, haranguing the prison officers, using his fingers to count the number of complaints they had not dealt with. He was up to nine before the cell door was secured in his face.

Chapter 60
MAY 2020
Chief's Office
Dostoevsky and Floaters

Acting DI Quirke was about to knock on the chief's door, it was partly open already, but she paused when she heard voices.

"Crime and Punishment, you see, don't you?" the chief had made a decisive point.

"What are you blabbering on about? Stick to the point, I haven't sat on an Inter-City 125, on my own, to not have you stick to the point. The Home Office has better things to do than to put a special train on just to get me here, believe me!"

"It wouldn't have been a 125… when was the last time you caught a train *up north*, as you put it?"

"Stick to the point, if you can?"

"He's read it twelve times, you see?"

"Read what, for God's sake!"

"Crime and Punishment. Dostoevsky. That is what we are up against!"

DI Quirke heard air being expelled. The man from the Home Office was either impressed or had sat heavily in one of the chief's chairs and the filling had surrendered.

"I see."

"Yes, anyone who can read Dostoevsky once, let alone thirteen times, is a force to be reckoned with."

"I thought you said twelve?"

"He's got a copy from the prison library so I'm assuming it's thirteen by now."

"Look, I think I can be candid with you, Dyer's an embarrassment, he's got to be sacked, far more trouble than he's worth, I mean even the Chinese didn't want to keep him, and my contacts in the Home Office told me, only the other day, that the discipline staff at The Stretch were threatening strike action if he wasn't moved on within the week!"

DI Quirke had heard the chief threaten the same thing on numerous occasions and now with full Home Office approval, she expected the worse.

"Listen to me, Horace, any large organisation like the Police Force, and I'm sure it's the same in the Home Office, needs people like Dyer. I know I detest him as much as the next man but let me explain. There is an adage that the cream rises to the top in our professions. Let me tell you it is a fallacy. If it was true the cream would be skimmed from the top every couple of years, are you following?"

"Not quite, old chap."

"Look, Horace, we are the cream! I do not want to be skimmed, and surely you don't either, to be replaced by some career professional… let's face it, neither of us is brilliant, who is these days, but I quite like my job, the salary and the perks that come with it, the odd weekend by the coast, and I'm sure you do too, so how do we maintain the status quo?"

"Enlighten me."

"Horace, every so often a turd rises to the surface, a *floater* if I can be crude, the bit that refuses to be flushed away, and it sits there with the cream. That's DI Dyer. At every level of organisation, there's a floater. If you sack these people willy-nilly the likes of you and I risk being exposed! I might berate the idiot, and threaten him with dire consequences, but heavens above, I don't mean it!"

"Very good. I like what you did there."

"What? I know there will come a time, and it happens every few years when the sword will have to strike, another restructuring, or a cost-cutting exercise to balance the books, it is the time I am always preparing for, a time when the floaters can be fished out by someone with a strong stomach, to be sacrificed so the likes of you and I can remain sitting pretty."

"Dirty business. There must be a massive pile of…"

"Must be, Horace! Things are always rocky for a few months until I can promote another idiot into the position of floater… Who's that? Quirke, what the devil are you doing?"

"Sanitising, Chief."

"Quirke?"

"Covid-19, Chief, sanitising all the door handles."

"All right, all right, come in, this is Horace Walpole from the Home Office."

They did the new Covid-19 *rock, paper, scissors* greeting, the one where you offer a hand, an elbow, and a fist with limited success.

"Quirke, Home Office Horace, and I have been trying to finalise DI Dyer's return to the fold. Unfortunately, it's imminent…"

"Yes," Horace smirked, "it would appear the Prison Service has had enough. Do you know he's generated more Complaint Forms than the entire population of the Stretch in the short time he's been there?

"He can be hard work, sir."

"Hard work? He's a stickler! And there's nothing worse than a stickler."

"Quirke, you saw him this morning, what's your opinion?"

"Opinion, sir?"

"What can we do with him? He will be released in the next few days and we're in *lockdown*… there's barely enough crime for the humble bobby on the streets, let alone an annoying DI like Dyer."

"He mentioned something *big* concerning extremism."

The chief and Horace slowly shook their heads.

"That's quite enough of that! As I was saying, there's barely enough… the irony of this lockdown is that even the criminals are paying heed… I wonder when things return to normal if we shouldn't have a *national lockdown month* once a year. Good for the figures and time to catch up on paperwork."

"Got it," Home Office Horace, "if I might suggest *furlough*?"

"Furlough?"

"Yes, send him home for the duration. Work from home directive… he'd hate that, wouldn't he?"

"Yes, he would. Perfect!"

"Chief, what about me?" DI Quirke had quite enjoyed the temporary pay rise.

"Mm, Quirke, I've got you in mind for something down the line, but in the meantime, door handles, was it? You are promoted to C.S.I as of now."

Her eyes widened in expectation of a much-vaunted secondment, but the chief poked her between the eyes.

"Chief Sanitising Inspector! I want every surface in this place wiped down three times a day!"

DI Quirke retreated from the inner sanctum but not before she heard Horace ask in all seriousness, "How do I recognise a floater when I see one? Wouldn't want to get my hands dirty."

Chapter 61
JUNE 2020
Chief's Office
Sanitised

Acting DI Quirke hovered at the back of the office.

The chief looked up but couldn't hide the dismay he was feeling, fiddling with his spectacles on the bridge of his nose before returning to the document on his desk. Dyer, all knees, and elbows, fiddling with the blue latex gloves they were all supposed to wear; the extra-large wasn't quite big enough and Dyer was carefully trying to pinch and pull the rubber onto the fingers to force 'the damn things on'. Occasionally, he would adjust his face covering, exposing his nose and then his moustache, muffling a tut of exasperation at the impossible task. He was silent… perhaps the hours in prison isolation had had some benefit. The latex tore on Dyer's left hand and he ripped the entire glove off and dropped it in the chief's bin. He reached for a replacement from the box on the chief's desk but as he removed the top one, he was bemused to find every glove in the box had been knotted together by the longest finger.

The chief reacted to this by marching to the door, opening it with authority and shouting, "Very funny!" He slammed the door, had taken a step toward his desk before he opened the door again. "And if I find out who's been adding mayonnaise to the bottles of sanitiser there will be trouble…"

At his desk, he remained standing with his back to us, staring out of the window.

"Quirke, you are responsible for this… the gloves… the sanitiser… what on earth?"

"Sorry, sir, they get bored… especially at night… since the lockdown… there's only so much paperwork…"

"All right, all right! Now as I was saying (*or not saying*) it's good to have you back, DI Dyer."

"Thank you, sir."

"But… I'm sending you home."

"Yes, sir."

"What do you mean, 'yes, sir?', don't you want to question it?" the chief sensed a trap.

"No, sir."

"You're up to something, Dyer, and I don't like it! Let me be clear, you will be working from home for the duration, and it could be months…"

"Yes, sir."

"It could be months, Dyer, nothing is bigger than Covid, it could be years (*hopefully*) so don't think you can simply return to the office before we're given the go-ahead!"

"No, sir. I've got something I'm working on of national importance."

"I'm not interested, Dyer, do not telephone, do not email, do not do anything until I contact you. Is that clear?"

"Yes, sir." Dyer slowly got up from the chair, I could tell he wanted to say something but perhaps the back of a prison cell door had been a salutary experience.

"Quirke, on the way out, can you find out which idiot has covered my car in those bloody plastic aprons… it must have taken them hours to tie them together like that… no wonder there's a shortage!"

"Will do, sir."

"Why, Quirke, why?"

"Boredom, sir, and"—she closed the door—"I'm sorry to have to inform you, sir, that it's not mayo in the sanitiser. Boys will be boys! If you know what I mean?"

The chief screwed his face up and tried not to think of the alternative.

Quirke's Car
Raskolnikov

"Any sign the chief might allow you to have a car again?"

Dyer glanced to his right, acting DI Quirke swerved to the middle of the deserted road, but Dyer decided to treat the question with contempt. Silence. Driving Dyer home. Normally she'd be happy not to give him an opening but any silence these days allowed odd thoughts to enter her head; on a couple of occasions lately, she'd blurted odd phrases and was beginning to suspect she'd been brainwashed during her time with Mr Hwow, and it was to avoid saying *vibrating chopsticks* that she asked, "National importance? Is this the stuff you were trying to tell me in The Stretch?"

That didn't work either. He exhaled deeply, causing the front windscreen to mist, and because he knew the blowers were faulty in her car, he snapped at the button to lower the window on his side; too much snap and the button jammed in the *down* position letting in the thunderstorm, lifting the numerous discarded sweet rappers from there hiding places, lifting them in a vortex to Dyer's eye of the storm. He sat there, unflinching, with a Worthington's Original attached to his moustache until a gust of wind threw half a bucket of water through the window as DI Quirke turned a corner and dislodged it.

The big drip was saturated. Raindrops trickled along his eyebrows, moustache, and the tip of his nose, but he sat there with greater things going on in his head. Only when DI Quirke stifled a giggle, thinking about the possibility Dyer had undergone Chinese water torture, did he say anything.

"Raskolnikov."

"Sir?"

"*Crime and Punishment*."

"Sir?"

"Dostoevsky? Second only to William Shakespeare in understanding the dark side of man's nature and the heinous crimes we are all capable of committing. You should read it."

"How do you know I haven't? I think you're assuming a lot."

"Have you read it?"

"No."

"Raskolnikov. Fred Lambert. The anti-villain. Anti-hero. On the surface a man with a decent side to his nature. Caring: a bit of an idealist, but not strictly a bad sort. The crime: some might sympathise with his motives and if you're going to kill anyone let it be the dregs of society. A miserly moneylender in the book and men convicted of serious crimes at The Stretch. Throw into the mix some sort of psychosis, to explain the actions of a man who appears to have lost his mind, Raskolnikov was in a prolonged fever and Fred Lambert was clearly *on the edge*, and we have an odd similarity. You never did say why you were so keen to pursue him."

At this point, Dyer leant forward and cleared the remaining water from his face, a small pool formed on the mat at his feet before it was absorbed and before she had time to reply.

"Do you know who eventually got the better of Raskolnikov, leading to his conviction and sentence?"

"Let me guess. A very intelligent, super vigilant, hardworking, underpaid detective?"

"Not strictly true. Povetkin had a part to play but ultimately it was Raskolnikov who confesses. Conscience. He can't live with himself. He submits to the law."

DI Quirke pulled to the kerb and Dyer got out. He ignored the storm, leaning in through the broken window, eyes fixed on some of the debris on the floor.

"Fred Lambert will come to us, Quirky, mark my words, sooner or later he will return, and I will be able to put an end to the case."

DI Quirke was about to pull away when his nose jabbed back into the car.

"And in the meantime, keep your ears and eyes open. There is a plot afoot. Extremists! I'll be putting it together during this, so-called, furlough, and I'll let you know when I've got more… and I'd get this window fixed if I were you."

Chapter 62
MAY 10th 2022
Worcester Police Station
Many Happy Returns

"Here, *Dyerbolical,* there's a… well I'm not quite sure really… let's just say there's someone… *something*… asking for you downstairs."

DS Quirke shook her head at her colleague's lack of political correctness. Perhaps she was finally getting there.

"Very funny but I'm busy on a matter of national importance."

"You would be! Suit yourself. I've missed your witty ripostes and… *Dyertribes* over the last… how long exactly has it been? Thought you'd taken early retirement!"

Dyer tried to reposition his chair, turning his back to the antagonist, and getting as close to the desk as his legs would allow. In the background, a couple of high-fives were exchanged and *Dyertribe* was scribbled into a file that was put back on the shelf.

"Look, Quirky, during my incarceration on two separate occasions I heard specific details of a plot. The first was on the exercise yard, 'as soon as the lockdown is over and they release me, we're going to move in, carefully, like stepping to avoid IEDs, and we'll have plans of the town by then, bro!'. I wrote it down verbatim as soon as I returned to my cell. The next was a conversation I heard through the window, 'How you recruiting, bro? You got to be careful. Use people they won't recognise. For the surprise element, yeah? We using backpacks, right? Obvious, bro, but the lightweight ones, adjustable, we got to be prepared to move fast. Maximum impact, bro!' It all adds up, Quirky, there are dangerous people in prison."

When DS Quirke did not reply Dyer reached under the desk and produced a folder which he smacked onto the surface causing the office to pause.

"This is what we are dealing with!"

When she did not reach for the folder, he added, "You can read this in your own time, it contains an analysis of every terrorist group active in the world today, concentrating on the Islamic extremists, linking threads to some of the prisoners at The Stretch… I've spent the furlough working on this."

She was still coming to terms with the fact she was no longer acting detective inspector.

Dyer raised the index finger of his right hand, someone shouted '*howzat*', but undeterred he produced a sheet of paper from his inside pocket to a chorus of '*piece in our time*' and leaning forward he whispered, "I have contacts in the censor's department in the prison, I have copies of incoming and outgoing mail, as well as transcripts from several important telephone calls, and I now know the name of the ringleader! Asif Iqbal. He is about to be released from The Stretch… I don't know where the attack is going to occur, but I'm convinced I'm right!"

Ms Brenda had been waiting twenty minutes to hand herself in. She'd asked the desk Sergeant for Detective Inspector Dyer but was still sitting uncomfortably on the hard wooden bench when a small man walked through the main door.

"Chief?"

"What is it, Sergeant?"

Ms Brenda sensed the new arrival, the chief, belonged to a different era of policing, she suspected he was *inspecting the frontline* and had not quite embraced the notion that *the public is our friend and not the enemy*.

"Chief, sorry, sir, I'm not quite sure…"

"Spit it out, man!"

"This *person* has been waiting for DI Dyer for some time."

"What? DI Dyer? I've been trying to forget him."

"It has been over a year, Chief and Covid didn't get everyone."

"Bad taste, Sergeant."

"Sorry, Chief."

The chief turned and Ms Brenda climbed to her feet.

"For DI Dyer, did you say?" the chief was transfixed by the large bosom, the sheer height of the woman balancing on high heels, with a mop of dark, curly hair.

"Yes, a matter of urgency… I'm here to present myself…"

The chief's jaw dropped, "Now you come to mention it, I did ask DI Dyer to get someone to give me a hand immediately, young Fleming's got long Covid, and I've been waiting for the agency to send someone for weeks." The chief stared for a moment peculiarly, causing the Sergeant to scratch his ear very slowly, "Are you up for the job, Miss… Mrs?"

"Security cleared for thirty years and call me Ms Brenda."

"You don't look old enough, my dear. Sergeant, leave Ms Brenda to me, follow me… or better still… better take the stairs… you go first, my dear."

The chief, shamelessly staring at Brenda's bottom, as they started up the stairs, had a twinkle in his eye, thinking the day could not get any better. Ms Brenda glanced over her shoulder at the Sergeant who was shaking his head, probably thinking it takes all kinds to make a world but at least it would look good on the diversity figures! She looked at the chief and thought, there was no accounting for a public school education.

Chapter 64
MAY 10th 2022
Worcester Police Station
A Plot is Afoot

Dyer continued to refer to highlighted snippets from the volume of research and DS Quirke was forced to read them. 'How are the training camps going?' 'Plenty of foreigners in the town, bro, Americans, Japanese, Chinese…' 'Some are flying in from Pakistan two months before the big day.' 'We'll be like martyrs, yeah, going down in history, be remembered as the first and the best.' 'Recruited some from the college to do the dirty work in the days before the attack.' 'Supply chains are covered. People have got our backs. Investment, bro, we're only as strong as our weakest link.' 'Survival of the fittest… and not everyone can survive.' 'Nothing comes in, nothing goes out that we don't know about. Let's make it hot!' 'We can't afford to fail.'

"You see, Quirky, classic tactics, the Art of War… Sun Tzu… what do you think?"

DS Quirke was saved from committing herself by the sudden appearance of the Chief and a transvestite.

"Good work, Dyer, it's about time you did something worthwhile…"

"Thank you, sir, have you got time to take a closer look now… did you get my email… it's of national importance."

"What's that, Dyer? Why would I want to look at some bizarre plot you've been working on? I'm talking about Ms Brenda; she's going to be an asset to *my* office."

Before Dyer could say anything else, the telephone in the chief's office started to ring and he ushered Ms Brenda through the door, with a protective arm across the shoulder.

DS Quirke was reminded of the grappling before a scrum begins to set. Everyone in the office was stupefied, mouths had fallen open, and eyes were asking for an explanation.

"She's rather tall, don't you think?" Dyer was always on a different wavelength.

The chief's door wasn't closed, and she heard the following.

"What's that? MI5, did you say? Code word? What's that? Oh, bloody hell, yes, of course…" At this point, the chief lowered his voice, as instructed, and must have gesticulated for Ms Brenda to close the door; she did this with a wink aimed at Dyer whose eyebrows nearly dislodged two of the square ceiling tiles and he had to spend the next five minutes ignoring colleagues who were convinced he was *in there*.

When the chief opened the door, he was deathly pale; he cleared his throat to make sure he had the attention of the room.

"That was Reginald. Forget I said that name. That was MI5. What I am meaning to say is that, is that everything I'm about to say is strictly… err…"

"Top secret," Ms Brenda placed manicured fingers on his shoulder.

"Indeed. Exactly. Top secret. DI Dyer has uncovered a terrorist plot… it is of the utmost urgency… MI5 think that DI Dyer is correct and that the threat is imminent. Their intelligence states an Asif Iqbal will be released from The Stretch tomorrow and we are to expect an attack in Stratford-upon-Avon immediately. MI5 states there will never be a better opportunity to round the whole terrorist cell up in one go. Thanks to DI Dyer, they have asked us to act as their backup in the operation this weekend. All leave is cancelled. Any questions?"

"Chief?" Dyer obviously, "The last piece of the jigsaw, how do they know it's going to be Stratford?"

"Appears Mr Iqbal asked for this destination on his train ticket on the travel warrant!"

Another hand from the back of the room, one of Dyer's main tormentors.

"Correct me if I'm wrong, but Stratford is South Warwickshire's beat and not ours! They're not going to be happy about this."

"It will be a joint operation but thanks to DI Dyer we'll be taking the lead... acting with MI5. Now, I'll leave DI Dyer to get you all up to speed... Now Ms Brenda, where were we?"

"You were just about to show me..."

The door slammed shut.

"I had bloody tickets for the Villa game! Bloody typical."

"I know what it is! It's *Dyerbolical*!"

Chapter 65
MAY 12th 2022, 10:00
HMP Long Stretch
As If

Two prison officers opened the cell door in the Care and Control Unit. Asif Iqbal stepped forward a scowl on his face befitting a dangerous man. He refused to acknowledge the officers as they politely asked him to get his possessions together for the short walk to the reception block where he was to be released from prison custody. He strutted in the officer's wake, at his own pace, a Richard Prior *walk* from the film *Stir Crazy*, his five-feet-two build suggesting he would take *no shit!* When a couple of prisoners shouted through their cell doors when they realised, he was leaving, 'No surrender, bruv!', 'Keep fighting!' and 'Alu Aqbar!' he screamed, "Don't touch me, Officer!"

This caused the officers to jump and turn around in surprise, their faces asked how they could possibly have touched him from three feet away.

"I will not be intimidated!" he continued to scream.

*

Stood in reception signing for valuables from the safe and taking his travel warrant Asif Iqbal smiled at the escorting staff.

"Sorry you had to put up with that little charade over there, please accept my humble apologies, as I appreciate what you have to put up with in your job, but you know how it is…"

The officers looked at each other, slightly confused, and the one in charge made a point of rechecking the paperwork on the desk to make sure he had the correct prisoner in front of him.

"... mostly mindless idiots, violent thugs, and you need to find a role that gets some respect to survive... once again, my most sincere apologies if I have upset anyone or caused a single moment of distress..."

By the time Asif Iqbal walked out of The Stretch, the prisoners left behind in the Care and Control Unit would not have recognised him, and they would have pinned him against the fence in the exercise yard to steal his trainers or touched him up, depending on their mood. Asif was now clean-shaven, with hair slicked back with gel, dressed in tight Amani jeans and a subdued pink sweater. He was shaking the hands of any member of prison staff in his vicinity.

Chapter 66
MAY 12th 2022, 11:30
HMP Long Stretch, Deputy Governor's Office
Red Dragon

Acting Deputy Governor Young was visibly perturbed. He was pulling at his shirt cuffs, something he reverted to when he was nervous, a remnant of bullying at Eton, and was about to ask the shady figure looking through the blinds into the carpark if he fancied another coffee from his latest *super-duper* machine when the telephone rang. The shady figure had not been impressed by the 'I'm the youngest Deputy Governor ever, Young by name too!', nor had he shown any interest in his collection of origami figures dotted around the office, and it was for these reasons Governor Young made a point of getting to the handset first.

It was the reception staff.

"Oh, I see, he said that to you, did he? Anything else? And he has a Porsche waiting? Oh, I see…"

The MI5 officer waited to be briefed. When Governor Young hesitated, trying to reinstate his self-importance, the MI5 officer picked up a large red paper dragon and held it by the wings threatening to pull the thing apart. Governor Young caved in immediately, disclosing what Asif Iqbal had told staff in reception, 'it was all going to change in Stratford-upon-Avon', something about a canal barge next to the Theatre the hub of the operation, and that the next time they were there, they would not recognise the place. The travel warrants? Simply played up to his bad boy image to be an extra drain on prison service resources.

The MI5 officer returned to the window to see Asif Iqbal get into a bright green Porsche Cabriolet and winced when it reversed over the foot of an Officer Service Grade, causing the MI5 officer to put a little more stress on the dragon's wings. He was amused as several officers left the prison to go for lunch and a cigarette break, ignoring the man on the floor, and if the MI5 officer had not asked for an ambulance himself there's no telling how long he would have remained there. When the dragon was placed on the desk unharmed and the MI5 officer had left in pursuit of the Porsche, acting Deputy Governor Young locked the office door and sat down on his comfortable chair, letting out a heavy sigh as he closed his eyes.

Chapter 67

MAY 12th 2022, 12:15

Stratford-upon-Avon

The Good, The Bard and the Ugly

The chief and Ms Brenda were hunched over one of the raised tables in the Shakespeare Theatre café on the ground floor; it looked like they were about to engage in an arm wrestling competition; the chief was propped on a raised stool, staring at the figure-hugging red Lycra across Ms Brenda's chest, having taken a bite from a falafel wrap but pushing it away in disgust, suggesting it was the reason he had 'not been to the theatre for years.' Ms Brenda was half perched on her stool, unable to lift herself with dignity to a comfortable position due to the tightness of a black skirt that wanted to clamp her thighs together; she was stirring sugar into a flat white coffee and keeping a running total of the number of people in the café itself, clocking their faces, making snap judgements, assessing their demeanour… it was a habit from thirty years prison service and it would never stop.

Ms Brenda looked out across the river. Stratford-upon-Avon. It was a beautiful Spring Day with early season warmth, the crowds had returned to the Warwickshire tourist hotspot, and it promised to be the first *normal* year since the pandemic. Everything was open and Chinese and American tourists were contesting the best seats in the cafes in the town square. There were queues of people waiting to be photographed at The Bard's statue next to the showman dressed as a statue of Richard the Lionheart who came to life when someone stopped in front of him. Ms Brenda had marvelled at the hours the character must have spent to get ready. There had been a nod of respect between them.

On the river, only the most perfect swans had passed this year's audition and were parading to a violinist who had set up near the canal and river junction. On the grassed area next to the Royal Shakespeare Theatre at least three amateur performers were vying for the attention of mingling tourists, and snatches of Macbeth become Juliet become Richard the Third whenever someone took a breath – it was exciting, there was a hum about the place, and it was accompanied by the pervading battle of fast-food aroma as hotdogs, beef burgers and fish and chips competed to satiate the discerning palate. It is Shakespeare's birthplace and ominously his resting place: the good, the Bard and the ugly.

"Never thought I'd see the day when we would all be dancing to Dyer's tune, eh, Ms Brenda? Seems I may have misjudged him, hard to believe as I pride myself on recognising an arsehole when I see one. Can't believe it! I'm usually a good judge of character and it takes a lot to pull the wool over my eyes… Ms Brenda, when this is all over, why don't we spend a weekend away from it all, and discuss your career prospects, I know a splendid hotel in Brighton."

Ms Brenda picked up the flat white to prevent the chief from becoming intimate and was saved from having to reply when the chief's mobile rang… 'I Want to Break Free.'

"Chief here… go on. He's on his way, but he's in a car… go on… Heard to say nothing is to happen until he gets here… Got it, thank you."

The chief slipped the phone into an inside pocket and was made aware of an approaching MI5 operative by a flick of Ms Brenda's curly fringe. The operative was dressed as Macbeth, the costume last worn by Christopher Ecclestone, and he seemed very pleased with himself.

"Chief, our man at The Stretch has been in contact, Asif Iqbal had a conversation with a screw in reception…"

"Think you'll find that's an officer, to you," Ms Brenda corrected, "And I think you could have made more of an effort…"

"… At least I'm in costume, madam, and they say I can keep it when we're done!"

"Boys will be boys."

"… As You Like It, madam. Anyway, it's the barge moored opposite we need to keep an eye on… I'd better get back to the balcony… the best vantage point… perk of the job… Don't worry about the barge, a contingency plan is in place, and it will be taken care of…"

The chief ordered his fourth expresso and updated the team on the change in the plan through a mike attached to his collar, allowing Ms Brenda to slide from the table and approach the café window overlooking the river. She stared at the barge but also clocked the faces of every tourist that passed as she was working on an agenda the Chief knew nothing about.

She knew the people in the café were staring at her calf muscles, the sheer power they must possess, and she knew the chief was probably smiling at an image of Ms Brenda wrestling him into submission in a hotel room in Brighton. One helluva lady!

Chapter 68

MAY 10th, 12:30
Stratford-Upon-Avon
And Never the Twain Shall Meet?

Orrible Arry Enderson slowly shook his head, sitting in the back of his Jaguar, which slowly turned left onto Waterside, inching along, trying to avoid a collision with a tourist more intent on a bag of fish and chips.

"If you ask me, don't see why that Shakespeare fella decided to write his plays here in the first place… Full of fast-food crap, no place to park and who builds a fire station with a tower next to the river in the busiest part of town?"

"That's the theatre, boss."

"You're having a giraffe! Find a place to park, I need to stretch my bloody legs… This is our fifth lap by my reckoning…"

Orrible Arry Enderson chuckled, he would have shown that Shakespeare fella a thing or two… It would have been a fitting legacy to have your own life remembered in verse. Would his be a comedy or a tragedy? He suspected 'Old William' hadn't written much on the life and deeds of a drugs baron and his empire. He tried to remember Macbeth, he'd been forced to study it back in the day, perhaps he should commission a modern interpretation based on his rise in London's drug world instead of in some bleak and barren part of Scotland.

Amused. He was at the height of his power, had amassed a fortune and had managed to stay out of prison… If you had the right people on the payroll and the best lawyers, you were untouchable… almost untouchable. He'd been considering retirement when Smithy had come up with the Prison Tsar idea… genius really, and he'd been unable to say no. It was to be a final act to his glittering career, instead of the haphazard supply of drugs into any given prison, this had been an opportunity to organise and monopolise the whole business of supply right under the nose of the prisons minister. It had gone wrong. Smithy had miscalculated. *He* had miscalculated and it irked him that they'd been thwarted by a prison chef. Not only that but the Lambert fella had had the effrontery to try to kill him! Since the farce of that evening, his run-in with Dyer and Quirke, the Lambert fella had started to torment him; Lambert had sent messages bragging about the amount of money in the bag, but he'd also threatened to put the red book into the hands of the law. The red book was very incriminating, it linked him to murders, and blackmail and spelt out his operation in embarrassing detail, and even level-headed Geoffrey was worried. He'd traced Lambert to China but had been forced to call off the pursuit due to the pandemic; it had not been a complete waste of time as the opportunity to get one over on DI Dyer had presented itself. 'Nobody crashes into the back of one of my motors without payback.' It hadn't cost too much to get heroin into Dyer's suitcase.

Geoffrey had insisted on insurance: a muffled thud from the direction of the Jaguar car's boot confirmed insurance should never be overlooked. It was a fair trade, the *odd* woman in the boot for the remnants of the half a million and the red book; it had been easy to find Suse in Florida and the only surprising thing about the whole business had been Lambert's readiness to agree to a trade, but as the Orrible Arry reflected, Lambert wasn't a proper criminal, more an accidental mass murderer, who probably still had a conscience. Get the exchange done, deal with Lambert later and then retire… he checked his watch… half an hour to go.

Chapter 69
MAY 12th 2022, 13:00
Stratford-upon-Avon
Much Ado That Ends Well?

DS Quirke stood on the rowing club bridge conscious she was too conspicuous, she was the only one not moving, as tourists filed past on the one-way system, either going to the park or returning to the town; Stratford was as excited as the swans and mallards on the river flapping at the merest hint that someone was about to throw bread for them; it added to a feeling of unrest and unpredictability. The green barge had flowerpots on the roof. Nobody had gone anywhere near it since she'd been watching; Trojan horse or innocent tourist barge?

Below, a rowing boat passed with a couple of giggling Chinese tourists, the girl screaming and holding on to the sides as the man struggled with the oars because they'd turned into giant chopsticks. The orchestra in the bandstand warmed up and someone was playing *chopsticks* on the keyboard. DS Quirke pinched herself.

She watched the Avon, staring at the eddies and patterns, as it flowed beneath her. Her mind wandered back to the man who had saved her as it always did when she was near a river. It had been two years since the trail had gone cold when she had flown out of Wuhan, two years when the world had been disrupted by the pandemic. A part of her had wanted to let him go. He'd saved her life! It would have been easy to let him slip through their investigation, especially when Dyer had taken it so badly and become depressed. It would have been the ideal opportunity. And her motivation was nothing to do with her being a *good cop*. If she'd bothered to attend the therapy sessions, she may have had an inkling, but she knew something for certain and she mouthed the words, 'I'm not finished with you, Fred Lambert.'

Her mind was brought back by the sound of someone retching on her earpiece. It must be operative five. He'd been stuck on the tourist wheel for the last hour; he had the best view of the tennis club, cricket ground, picnic areas and car parks, as well as the bandstand and the front of the theatre, well he did when he was at the top of the wheel, but now she could imagine him on his knees, inadvertently pressing the transmit button, as he was sick in front of the kiosk.

Part of her wanted Dyer to be right about the plot, he would be distraught if he was wrong and she would have to pick up the pieces, but an attack in the heart of this town didn't bear thinking about. She'd left Dyer stood at the Queen Victoria Clock shaking his head because the time did not agree with his wristwatch. He'd been involved in an international incident; groups of American and Chinese tourists were disputing who had arrived first at the monument and both were refusing to allow the other to have the first photograph. Dyer flashed his ID, confiscated a camera from each group, and insisted they line up altogether, alternately for a group snap, there had been smiles and handshakes, but Dyer's diplomatic triumph was tempered when he stated with authority to confused faces, 'Now there's a tale of two cities!'

"Operative five! Stay off the net!" the chief's had had enough of the vomit broadcast.

An MI5 officer cut in, "I say again… am close to the barge… say again… something's cooking all right… (*crackle*)… heat rising… coming from the barge… (*crackle*) … getting closer… smells… like… bomb… (*crackle*)… a crack in the curtain… something's cooking… say again… smells like a bomb… (*crackle*)… chemical… quite pungent…"

DS Quirke saw the Porsche Cabriolet stop by the entrance to Butterfly World and cause a mini-traffic jam as Asif Iqbal got out and the driver insisted on a three-point turn before getting out of the car and hugging him farewell. Asif savoured the fresh air and stated to a couple with a broad smile, "It's good to be alive and free!"

Her eyes followed his path to the tourist wheel where he shook his head at a man being sick on the grass. His attention is drawn to the bandstand where the brass section has just begun to play the opening bars from the *Dambusters* theme. He beams at a family tucking into sausage rolls.

"Makes you proud to be British, doesn't it?"

Asif Iqbal picked up speed, jumped aboard the barge and disappeared through the hatch door at the rear, the MI5 officer is close enough to report *whooping and backslapping* from within its bowels.

Operatives four and three approached her from the Tramway above the park, where they had been watching from a bench. They looked worried. Their faces said, *looks like the arsehole's right*, perhaps they were genuinely concerned about the plot, but DS Quirke thought they were more concerned about having to live in the afterglow of Dyer's success. The three of them watched the barge.

The directive in her earpiece was *to wait*.

*

Ms Brenda watched the chief arguing with Macbeth. The chief did not want *to wait* and buoyed by his seventh expresso was wired for action. A group of tourists were crowding in thinking it was part of some staged entertainment. Ms Brenda slipped through the glass door onto the terrace. She stood behind Orrible Arry Enderson as he looked at his watch, looking over the green barge to the bandstand, deciding which was the quickest way to cross the river to the other side. He chose the small ferry to his right having noticed the landing jetty and calculating he had enough time before his rendezvous at the bandstand with Fred Lambert. Orrible Arry's patent leather shoes scuffed on the metal walkway. Ms Brenda's heels sparked and Orrible Arry turned sharply but he only saw a *fat bird* messing with her handbag.

She didn't have a plan. She was making it up as she went along. Suse was a hostage, and it was her fault. She'd poked Orrible Arry too hard and now he had the upper hand. She followed Orrible Arry to the ferry, a quaint one-man operation, a shallow wooden boat, and joined him in the queue.

*

DS Quirke saw Ms Brenda slip out of the café. She couldn't miss her bright red top.

Operative four has seen her too and says, "Who the fuck *is* she?"

DS Quirke mumbles something about *authority, respect, and courtesy* but she's spotted someone else too. She leaves operatives four and five on the bridge and starts to run through the crowds toward the terrace in front of the theatre.

"Why is Orrible Arry Enderson in Stratford and why is Ms Brenda following him?" she says this out loud but mutters under her breath, 'Who the fuck *is* she?' Cutting a corner, she bumps into a woman playing the violin, almost knocking her into the river, thinking she would have had to jump in to save her, and then she knows! Could Dyer be right twice in one day? Raskolnikov has returned right under their noses! To be honest you could get the complete cast of the novel under his nose. Ms Brenda is Fred Lambert.

In her earpiece she hears, "… get ready, all operatives be prepared… on my call…" and moments later, "… smells like… Bomb… Bombay mix…"

She passes the theatre terrace, glancing through the open window, and sees the chief grabbing Macbeth by the lapels, shouting 'We have to move in', waving his fist in the air, and she pauses long enough to hear an American couple start to clap.

"Isn't this great? It's so British!"

*

The ferryman pushes his boat from the jetty. Ms Brenda ignores the commotion of a woman jumping aboard at the last second as her attention is on the bandstand until a funny little man dressed in black from head to toe appears on the roof of the barge in front of it. The band is playing 'All Things Bright and Beautiful' but nobody is listening, all eyes are on the barge, the little man has his arms in the air, and only the swans move thinking he's going to throw something for them. He drops his arms and seven figures swarm from the bowels of the barge, all in black too, full beards and black bandanas with a rehearsed precision – and each has a rucksack! They scatter, running across the picnic area, shouting something that's lost in the panic and screams, and the bum notes the orchestra is suddenly hitting. Ms Brenda saw people freeze, mid-sandwich bite, others throwing themselves to the ground and others running in a crazy game of British Bulldog.

Orrible Arry is on his feet now trying to get a better look and Ms Brenda sees an opportunity and sidles up to him. They watch as one of the figures in black, heads straight for Dyer. Two men with him dive for cover, but Dyer sticks his arm out, as if to signal right, and takes the young man clean off his feet. Dyer throws himself on top of him pinning him face down on the ground.

Ms Brenda had time to read a sign on the side of the barge that had been unfurled, 'Hell's Kitchen: Spicy Hot Food' before an explosion ripped the bottom of the barge away. The little man on the roof was thrown clear, landing on a blanket laid out for a picnic, springing to his feet to gesture, 'What on earth?!'

Orrible Arry staggered as the ferry pitched on the upset river and toppled headfirst into the river. Ms Brenda tried to grab his hand, but the current had him already. She heard an American voice, "Wow, honey, do they put this show on every week?" and a round of applause before she belly-flopped in after him, 'What was it with this bloody river?'

She was struggling against the current. Orrible Arry had laughed, 'My blue badge ain't going to save me now,' but his bravado was giving way to panic, and the coldness of the Avon was winning. The ferryman had thrown a buoy but missed and it joined Ms Brenda's wig that had made a bid for freedom. Her heart was pounding and for a moment she thought both were not going to make it. That had once been the plan but as the Avon closed over her head, she swallowed water and repeated in her head, *'Faster, Daddy, faster.'*

*

DS Quirke heard the words *stand down* in her earpiece, seconds before the limpet mind ripped the barge apart and watched helplessly as Orrible Arry and Ms Brenda went for a swim. She berated the ferryman to get to the bank as quickly as possible, listening to operative two trying to report 'a frogman had been hooked by an angler down by the lock.' By the time DS Quirke had jumped from the ferry the two rhythmic swimmers were close to the bank and she was able to grab Orrible Arry by the collar. She pulled him to safety, and he clung to the side. When she turned to Ms Brenda, she'd slipped back into deeper water and had a look of resignation on her face.

"Oh no you don't!" DS Quirke jumped in, the cold water took her breath away, but she had her under her arms, "That was a very brave thing you did," she gasped in his ear.

"Thank you. He might be a nasty piece of work, but I couldn't let the river take him."

"No! Not *him*. You pulled *me* out of the river in Evebury when I was a little girl." She showed him the rubber ball.

Ms Brenda sighed and slowly nodded, "You kept it all these years? It used to be my lucky charm. It *was* you? I'm glad I did."

Nearby on the riverbank, an upset angler was making his point.

"That's just typical! Quiet day, my arse! I hook an effing frogman... there's an effing explosion... and now an effing crossdresser has completely ruined my swim... I'd just baited that area!" He'd had enough and was packing up for the day, evidently in a right strop, and now Dyer had arrived treading on a part of his fishing pole in his haste to join DS Quirke.

Orrible Arry, shivering, perked up when he saw Dyer.

"Have you shit yourself again?"

"It's vindaloo," Dyer stated in a way that was obvious to anyone with half a brain.

When everyone looked confused.

"Appears it was a publicity stunt. Very bad taste! An attempt to take over the fast-food market in Stratford-upon-Avon. Copped a load of Vindaloo from a backpack I squashed."

"How *very interesting*. Anyway, now the excitement is over, I'll be on my way... good to see you, Dyer, thought you were still in China? Need to get back to 'the Other Place' before you crash into the back of my Jag, again!" Orrible Arry made his excuses.

The angler had fallen to the ground, holding his head, DS Quirke thought he was going to cry. Worse, he started to wail, "Do you know how much a fishing pole is?"

Orrible Arry seemed to notice Ms Brenda for the first time and took a double take as if to say, *you don't see that every day* but due to the circumstances politely said, "Well, thank you for that, saving me I mean, now what's the quickest way to 'the Other Place?'

When nobody replied because DS Quirke, Dyer and Ms Brenda didn't know what he was referring to, he almost shouted with exasperation, "The Other Place, for God's sake!"

The angler stopped wailing long enough to suggest one suicide attempt per day was quite enough, before explaining the 'Other Place' was a café/venue on the lane just up from the Theatre, and you had to get to it by walking around the pathway as the ferry was not safe anymore! He'd got back to his feet and was now waving a shard of the broken pole above his head, daring anyone to disagree.

That's when DS Quirke saw the armed-response vehicle ploughing a furrow across the picnic area, quickly followed by a 'fast-response park warden' waving a notebook above her head.

"Nobody moves! Put the pole on the ground, now!"

"I have a fishing licence and a permit to be here."

"You can't drive across my grass like that, even if you are the police."

"Officer, I'm soaking wet and need to dry off… unless there's a law prohibiting me from taking a dip in the river, I'll be off… if it's all the same to you?"

"DS Quirke, West Mercia, this woman has just saved *his* life, but I'd be grateful if nobody goes anywhere until I can check why *he* is here in the first place. He has been a person of interest in the past and, strangely, he's in town during an anti-terrorist operation."

"All I know is my Jag's double-parked over there somewhere."

"DI Dyer, in charge of this operation…"

"Broke my pole!"

"In charge of this fiasco, more like!" Orrible Arry laughed.

"DI Dyer, as I said, in charge, seems it wasn't a terrorist plot after all… the explosion? Nothing to do with me…"

At the word's terrorist plot, Asif Iqbal, who was being escorted to a waiting police vehicle shouted, "I'm suing the lot of you! Wrongful arrest. Assault! Criminal damage. You've killed two swans and a mallard. You've blown my boat up too. Terrorists!" he accused.

"What about my grass? It's taken five years to get it looking this good."

"Quiet!!"

The armed officer had taken the safety off, and DS Quirke could see by the glazed look in his eye, he was prepared to shoot the next person to speak. The silence was stark compared to the bedlam that had preceded it. DS Quirke looked at Dyer and thought he was putting a brave face on things, considering his career was on the line. The silence was broken by a madman shrieking from the other side of the river, "Brenda!!"

The armed officer turned his weapon and fired before he knew what had happened. (If you look closely at the theatre when a particular light is falling mid-afternoon, you can still see the bullet hole in the wall which missed the chief by centimetres.)

"Brenda, darling, are you alright? My God, what's happened to your hair? Was it the explosion?" the chief was frantic.

Everyone in the farce looked at the chief; he was sobbing, and DS Quirke thought he was going to jump in and attempt to swim across, and he only started to pull himself together when Macbeth grabbed him by the shoulder and dragged him to one side.

Cue the supporting cast that appeared on the ferry's jetty on the chief's side of the river. Two police officers, a parking warden, and a small woman with strikingly short peroxide blond hair, dressed in bright green trousers and a garishly pink jumper; DS Quirke could see she had wet herself and pushing the hands away that were supporting her, she screamed across the river, "It was him! Locked me in the boot of his car! Him! Castigated me! I mean kidnapped me… Yes, that's right, *him*! Why's he soaking wet?"

Three of the response team trained their weapons on Orrible Arry and the other three on Ms Brenda. A couple changed their mind and retrained their weapon, confused by the term *him*, moving from Ms Brenda to Orrible Arry, but then remembering the recent mandatory training package which had explained 'the right to identify as the gender you wanted to be known as', retrained their weapon on Ms Brenda, in case the screaming woman had not undergone the necessary training and was confusing *him* when she meant *her* or vice versa. And another one retrained their weapon on Orrible Arry in case she had. Simple.

Dyer suggested they cuff both to be on the safe side. A round of applause from the audience, behind the chief, who had been following events since the impromptu balcony performance. Further confusion as nobody was quite sure who was allowed to search Ms Brenda. DS Quirke stepped forward to save the embarrassment, and whispered in her ear, "Sorry about this."

Ms Brenda cleared her throat, before announcing, "DI Dyer, my name is, at any rate, it was, and still is legally I think, Fred Lambert. I believe you have been looking for me?"

Dyer raised an eyebrow, and we all flinched in case another round was accidentally discharged.

"Raskolnikov, I knew it!"

"He said, *Fred Lambert*, you arsehole," Orrible Arry lost a little composure when his handgun was removed from his belt, "I've got a licence for that," but was visibly unsettled when a tightly bound red book was removed from the inner pocket of his jacket, "how the devil?"

Fred Lambert whispered in DS Quirke's ear, "I'd take a good look at the red book if you know what I mean…"

"This *arsehole* has finally got his man… and woman… I mean men… I mean, you know what I mean. Both of you are under arrest!"

Chapter 70
JUNE 2nd 2022
Chief's Office
The Wrong Man

DS Quirke had edged her seat to one side, away from Dyer, whose gangly legs always threatened to touch anyone in the vicinity. From her vantage point, under the desk, she saw the chief press a drawing pin into his thumb.

He continued to smile as he asked, "The *wrong man*, you say, after everything that has happened? Case closed. Case not closed – behind my back. Case open, again. Case closed again, now, or so I thought! I almost lost my head with that stray bullet. What exactly do you mean, the *wrong man*?"

Dyer tapped the end of his nose, "I have my suspicions, sir."

The chief pushed the pin deeper and a droplet of blood fell onto the cream carpet.

"This had better be good."

Dyer was about to elaborate in his usual flamboyant manner but stopped himself. He took a couple of breaths before coming to a decision.

"I don't have suspicions, sir."

"Dyer! So, help me, God, I'll hang, draw, and quarter you…"

"I didn't have suspicions, sir, but Detective Sergeant Quirke does, and I'm inclined to agree with her. Liz, if you would like to explain?"

DS Quirke pulled her chair closer.

"The wrong man. Or the wrong woman, sir, Fred, or Ms Brenda, how do you want me to refer?"

"Get on with it before I bleed to death."

"Under interview, Fred Lambert states he did not kill Smithy or Tom. In the case of Smithy, Fred returned from The Stretch intending to commit suicide. I believe him when he says he was going to blow his head off with the sawn-off shotgun until he found Smithy already dead in exactly the place, he was going to end his own life. At the time Fred thought he may have done it and had visions of holding the weapon and looking down on Smithy, but I think he was in the middle of a nervous breakdown. Now he's on medication and stable he's sure he didn't kill him. He thinks Orrible Arry Enderson is responsible, but Arry's got a cast-iron alibi and there are no CCTV images of any of his known associates in or around Evebury at the time of the murder. Arry did seem surprised when it was put to him, sir."

The chief placed his head on the desk, but DS Quirke would not be deterred.

"In the case of Tom, Fred admits to 'accidental death'. Yes, he had planned to kill him, but when push came to shove, he was adamant it was an accident. Changed his mind but lost his grip on the tricycle once they'd fallen into the river. Very remorseful now, sir."

The chief started to bang his right fist on the desk, not violently, like he was running out of energy.

"What about the other three hundred and fifteen or is it sixteen, I'm losing the will to live... have you spent too much time with this buffoon," pointing at Dyer.

"That's just it, sir, our experts, having tested the samples remaining in the greenhouses, and in consultation with the curators at the Poison Garden in Northumberland, believe the variety Fred smuggled back from Darjeeling was not as deadly as *he* thought. Remember he stated they were seven times more deadly than most Aconites? He was wrong."

"Can I charge him with having the wrong variety of Aconite seeds…" The said, chief flippantly.

"Bear with me, sir, from Fred's notes, his calculations of the amount required to add to his curry, even if he was heavy-handed, our experts think only a small number might have died and that's not certain even for those in poor health to begin with – most should have recovered."

"How did they die, damn you!"

"I believe another person added a further significant quantity of the plant to the curry."

"Perhaps Fred Lambert miscalculated, put twice as much in the curry than he intended to, you said yourself he was having some kind of breakdown."

"Sir, he's a chef, he knows about ingredients, and there's one more thing… he's confessed to being responsible for the death of his daughter. Why would he confess to that but not to Smithy and Tom? He added brown powder he found in the prison to her stash. He wanted to scare her, put her in the hospital, and give her the jolt she needed to turn her life around. Turned out the powder was lethal. A few prisoners nearly died at the time… it was on the news, sir."

"Do what you have to do, DS Quirke, let me die in peace."

DS Quirke led the way. Dyer closed the door with a bang, the chief's head shot up and he looked over his shoulder for a bullet hole. DS Quirke opened the door again.

"And there's one more thing, sir… Fred Lambert is adamant he did not poison Deputy Governor Whitmore either, though he admits to loathing the man, I'm getting the CCTV footage again from the night of the mass poisoning," as she pulled the door closed, she had time to see the chief make the sign of the cross on his forehead in blood from his thumb.

Chapter 71
JUNE 7th 2022
HMP Long Stretch
The Number One Governing Governor's Office

"Mister Dyer, Detective Inspector Dyer again, I presume, it's good to have you on our side of the fence after your last stay with us," the Number One Governing Governor, Governor Hugh Young, newly promoted, could not hide the coolness in his voice.

"Yes, a strange turn of events," Dyer stared out the window toward the main body of The Stretch.

"You generated more complaints than any prisoner we've ever had the pleasure to incarcerate, if *they* hadn't released you when they did, my staff would have walked out in protest."

"I had a lot to complain about."

The Number One Governing Governor, Governor Young, unconsciously did a head count of the origami figures in his office, something he did when he was lost for something to say. When the ten were present and accounted for, he brightened and spoke.

"Right, anyone for coffee, I'm sure you will be impressed by this little beauty, top of the range, befitting the Number One Governing Governors position. Cappuccino, Latte, expresso, decaf?"

"Ooh, yes please, Cappuccino…" WPC Bennett from the door where she was guarding the corridor. Dyer's look of disgust poked her between the eyes, and she stepped outside again. Dyer had requested *muscle*, but the chief had said WPC Bennett would suffice as the prison was full of *roughtie-toughtie* officers that could assist if required.

"Do you know why we're here, Governor Young?"

"It's Number One Governing Governor, Governor Young if you don't mind."

"Murder, Governor Young, specifically the murder of Deputy Governor (at the time) Whitmore, who, correct me if I'm mistaken, would have been the Number One Governing Governor in front of you?"

"Are you suggesting I had anything to do with his murder?" Governor Young shrank into his chair. DS Quirke drove him further into it when she asked what had happened to the previous Number One Governing Governor.

"Number One Governing Governor Vanessa Eggington, lovely person, terrific Number One Governing Governor… a terrible loss… a road traffic accident. A hit and run. Killed her outright and the horse she was riding… still haven't caught the driver…"

"Seems to be a pattern emerging, Governor Young," DS Quirke couldn't help herself, "or should that be temporary acting Number One Governing Governor, Governor Hugh Young?"

Governor Young gulped his Cappuccino, it was too hot, and he started to splutter.

"Who did kill Deputy Governor Whitmore?" Dyer above the splutter.

"No, I did not!" Governor Young jumped to his feet.

"Did not what?" Dyer took a step forward, knocking a red dragon off the desk with his elbow and trampling it before Governor Young could leap to the rescue.

"Kill him!" Governor Young picked the dragon up and tried to flatten the wings.

"Nobody said you did, but as Shakespeare said, perhaps 'you doth protest too much'."

"You said, *Hugh did kill Deputy Governor Whitmore,* when I took a sip of Cappuccino!"

"*Who* not *Hugh*. How did you get to be a Governor? I'm expecting the killer to arrive shortly, I've sent for them," Dyer swatted Governor Young back into his chair with his nose.

Seconds later an officer tapped on the door and entered.

"You sent for me?"

"Bloody hell, Officer… Officer Underhill, isn't it?" Governor Young sprang to his feet, "Did you kill Deputy Governor Whitmore?"

"It's Officer Overhill, sir, and not to my knowledge, in all my days, sir, I've not exactly been exemplary, but I have drawn the line at murdering anyone, though there have been occasions, specifically in ninety-seven when Governor Hardnose scratched my car in the carpark and refused to pay for the repair…"

"Well, what are you doing here, this is a murder investigation?" Governor Young sat down again.

"Sent up to give them a hand, sir," indicating Dyer and DS Quirke, "in case it turns ugly."

"I asked for a couple of *heavies,* how old are you, Officer Overhill."

"Sixty-four in September, sir."

"Sign of the times, DI Dyer, I'm afraid," Governor Young explained, "nobody wants to be a prison officer these days."

"He's right, sir, it's not fun anymore, too many rules, once upon a time if somebody stepped out of line you could give them a good…"

"That's quite enough, Officer Overhill…"

"… and they respected it, sir, expected it, sir, only now they get away with murder…" The officer tailed off as Maddie barged into the office, a blur of black and white chequered trousers, a white kitchen jacket and a blue plastic cover on her hair.

"This had better be important, little man..." she stopped when she saw Dyer and DS Quirke, "I was just about to ring the bell, I had to leave that incompetent fool of an assistant to get the food out so if the food is not up to scratch, you'll be responsible."

DS Quirke closed the door, nodding at WPC Bennett to remain vigilant in the corridor.

"Maddie, we have a problem," Dyer began, "would you like a chair?"

"I've got a kitchen to run." She slowly sank into a black leather chair offered by Dyer, directly opposite Governor Young.

"Having watched the CCTV, Maddie, this is what I think happened to Deputy Governor Whitmore."

Maddie crossed her arms and waited.

"Coffee, anyone?"

Chapter 72
JUNE 7th 2022
HMP Long Stretch
The Importance of Being the First

DS Quirke explained.

Deputy Governor Whitmore had watched Fred leave the kitchen tracking his movements until he left the establishment ten minutes later. The Deputy had been in the Control Room, officially to *show his face*, making sure everyone was doing their jobs, signing documents to be collated and stored at the end of the shift, but really to check the bank of CCTV cameras, and to ensure he had a clear path to the kitchen.

The Dep. entered the deserted kitchen a few minutes later, managing to avoid anyone on the route that could have delayed his mission with an inopportune question. Only one camera operator noted mentally where he was, 'after a free meal again', and did not pass this on when their shift finished. This was why he could not be located when events began to spiral out of control less than a couple of hours later.

The Deputy Governor made himself comfortable at the kitchen office desk. Fred's desk. He was aware he was rubbing Fred's nose in it as he helped himself to Fred's coffee, the expensive one, an extra-large cup, and after he took a swig.

"Thanks, Fred, you old bastard."

He put the cup down... he found it a little bitter tonight and added some sugar before he turned his attention to the container of chicken curry he'd retrieved from the shelf under the bain-marie. On the lid it was written, 'For Maddie, do not touch, Fred'.

"Clever, Maddie, nobody would touch it with his name on it, but you are such a tease, you know I hate the prick…" He served a large portion onto a grey plastic plate, forgoing any rice and savoured the aroma… He took another swig of coffee, exhaling deeply.

"Fred, you're a prick, but you make a mean curry."

Stifling a yawn he spooned a large mouthful, yawned again, and was wondering if there was a naan bread lying about somewhere when the tingling of his tongue was mistaken for the effects of a chilli.

"Wow, Fred, you fucker, that's got a kick to it!"

The Dep. resolved not to be beaten by any curry Fred could make, no matter how hot it was and washed it down with more coffee. He was probably asleep before the first pains could stir inside him, the tranquilisers in the coffee, but must have been semi-conscious when the convulsions hit, as he fell sweeping the container to the floor, some of the sauce must have collected in a slight depression in the floor, and as the Dep. attempted to crawl he collapsed, unconscious, rubbing his nose in Fred's handiwork – he must have been dead before the prisoner in the segregation unit.

*

"He was always a greedy bastard. One rule for him and another rule for the officers. He told them they were not allowed to eat off the servery on the wings. Serves himself right. He did me a favour, it was meant for me, and it was my name on the lid, Fred tried to kill me… you'd better add that to the list of charges. Now, if that's all, I've got a meal to serve, "Maddie placed her hands on the arms of the chair and shifted her weight, "I've got a bell to ring!"

"For whom the bell tolls, Maddie, and we're not quite finished," Dyer stepped forward, Governor Young stopped recounting the origami figures, Officer Overhill glanced at his watch knowing he was on a lunchbreak in twelve minutes, and DS Quirke cleared her throat, produced a memory stick from her pocket and said, "This is the CCTV of the kitchen on the day of the mass killing. Fred Lambert oversees the three vats of curry, nobody else is allowed to stir them… prisoners are preparing the ingredients and bringing them to him and adding to the contents… at this point, he tastes the curry regularly… he adds a powdery substance from a tub he keeps close to him and from that point no longer tastes it. He guards his work until it is time to ladle the contents into portion-controlled silver foil containers… except for a five-minute toilet break, he has problems in that department, you, Maddie, take over… produce a bag from your pocket and empty the contents into the vats before Fred returns… you help put the cardboard lids onto the portions… we can guess what Fred added but what did you add?"

"Flour, I think, it needed thickening, and you can't prove otherwise."

"We probably can't, but there was something else on the recording."

Chapter 73
JUNE 7th 2022
HMP Long Stretch
Doors

Ten silver foil cartons of curry on each tray. Chicken curry, Halal curry and veg curry are ready for the trolleys. Fred rang the bell for the last time, allowing prison officers to push their trolleys to the wings. He locked the gate as the last one left and then checked the Bain Marie to ensure there were a few extra portions in case the wings needed anymore (a miscount of numbers or an accident during serving).

"Maddie, luv, you may as well get off, I'll sort the lads out," he always lets her go early and sorts the last six prisoners himself. She left through the prisoners' exit, letting the prisoners into a changing area, where they could discard 'soiled whites', and swap work boots for their trainers, and she secured the outer gate behind her before Fred had the chance to catch up. When the prisoners were ready, he asked for permission to send them back to their wings using his radio, and he rubbed them down taking his time to thank them for their hard work.

Maddie re-entered the kitchen through the side gate, walked across the now deserted kitchen to the wash-up area, retrieved an orange polystyrene fast-food box, and used a marker pen to write on the lid, before putting it in a specific place on a shelf under the Bain Marie. She entered Fred's office, dropped several tablets into the coffee pot, retraced her steps to the side gate and slipped out just as Fred walked back in from the prisoners' exit.

Fred Lambert stood still, surveying his kingdom, before he walked around, checking gas and electric appliances were off, and that the knife cupboards were secure, finally, he bowed, lowering an arm across his chest, like an actor leaving the stage for the final time, and turned the lights off.

*

The Point

"And your point is?" Maddie settled back into the chair.

"The point is, Maddie," DS Quirke tapped Governor Young's desk telephone, there is also a record on the system of you calling Deputy Governor Whitmore to tell him there was supper in the kitchen waiting for him in the usual place."

"Not only do we think you added something extra to the curry that helped to kill over three hundred prisoners, but you killed deputy Governor Whitmore with a meal you knew he would eat once you'd told him it had been put aside for him. The only question that remains, Maddie, is why?"

Maddie sprang from the chair, it toppled backwards onto Officer Overhill's foot, and she was across the desk and behind Governor Young before anyone could react. She had a handful of hair and was pulling his head backwards and pressed against his throat was a large, red-handled, knife.

"Madelaine Butchart, I'm arresting you for the murder…"

"Shut up! You pompous man. The more *you* talk the deeper the blade goes, got it?"

Dyer stopped talking. Governor started to whimper, and blood started seeping onto the blade's edge. DS Quirke, who had been *tiny stepping* toward the office door, froze as Maddie's eyes caught her.

"If you move again without my say-so, you'll be picking his head up off the floor."

Officer Overhill picked the chair up.

"Now, unless you want another death on your hands, I'm going to walk out of here and out of the prison, and none of you stupid men are going to lift a hand to stop me. I think I'll take this snivelling excuse for a man with me, but if you keep crying, I will be forced to remove your testicles, one at a time, and leave them behind."

"In all my days, I've never seen anything like it…"

"Shut up, old man!"

"… a red-handled knife! You can't be gutting the Governor with a red-handled knife…"

Dyer's eyebrows lifted and the backdraft caused a white origami swan to topple on the windowsill.

"… the red handled knife is strictly for Halal meat and the number one Governor is not Halal," Officer Overhill shuffled toward Maddie oblivious of her threat, "now if you'll excuse me, in all my days, I'm on my lunch break in two minutes, and nothing is going to stop me from taking my regulation break, it's in my union handbook…"

"Stay where you are, old man, or I swear, I'll slice his neck clean through!"

"… in all my days, I'm sure you've got the culinary skills to fillet this chicken, and you've got to do what you've got to do, no offence Governor, but you've already had a hand, by the sound of it, in the deaths of three hundred and sixteen deaths…"

"Three hundred and seventeen," Dyer couldn't help himself, "and I think you'll find she killed someone by the name of Smithy too when he surprised her when she was collecting the last supply of Aconite from Fred Lambert's greenhouses."

"… and one more won't matter, here nor there, no offence Governor, in the great scheme of things, what's one more body, one more victim, to the total? The Home Office will replace the Governor in a couple of weeks, in all my days, here one day gone the next…" Officer Overhill closed the distance.

"I swear, if you don't shut up, you'll be next, old man!"

Officer Overhill stepped right next to Maddie, "… plenty of more Governors in their ivory towers, and in all my days, I've been kicked, punched and spat at, but I've never been stabbed, and you'll be putting me out of my misery, as well as completing a *full house*, which would be funny, if it wasn't so sad, in an odd sort of way…" Officer Overhill clamped onto Maddie's hand and the knife seemed to take on a life of its own, vibrating against the Governor's neck before it jumped toward Officer Overhill and embedded itself up to the hilt in the crease between his left shoulder and his chest, "… in all my days, this is going to hurt in the morning, better in than out, never thought I'd save the Governor's life…" he still had Maddie's wrist clamped and she could not pull the knife out.

Governor Young had fainted. Maddie let go of the knife and for a moment an unnatural calm descended and only the faint sound of the coffee maker could be heard. DS Quirke took the opportunity to open the office door to let WPC Bennett into the office. She had not heard a thing and had to put the coffee and large piece of black forest gateau, the admin girls had provided her with, on the floor before getting her cuffs ready. Only when Dyer opened his mouth again.

"Madelaine Butchart, you are under arrest…" and placed a large hand on her arm did she screamed, "Get your hand off me! You dirty man, you're all the same!" and she lunged for the Governor again and began throttling him. WPC Bennett secured one wrist with the cuffs and with DS Quirke's help, levered first one hand and then the other from the Governor's throat.

"… in all my days, this is the highlight of my career, my time in the service, they might even let me retire early after this, or I might bleed to death, but at least I won't have to come to work again, how did she get the knife out of the kitchen, supposed to be tallied and accounted for, I wonder if I can keep it as a memento, but she was in charge, I suppose if there is a God, who checks him to see if he's doing the job properly…"

"Fucking men, I'll kill the lot of you! You think you rule the world, well I showed you, didn't I, I made a start, and I won't be the last!" Maddie was escorted to the waiting police van, turning her vitriol from Dyer to any man on the route. She trod in the cake. A dam had burst, and she was unable to stop or calm down until she was sedated by the psychiatrists in a secure hospital.

As Governor Young regained consciousness and before Officer Overhill was attended to by paramedics, the former was heard to say, "You'd better report to my office, first thing Monday morning, I'm going to suspend you, Officer Underhill, you can't speak to a Number One Governing Governor like that!"

"It's Overhill, sir."

*

"So, Quirky, DS Quirke… Liz, now we're at *the end*, you've explained Fred Lambert pulled you from the river when you were a toddler. He saved your life. He was the hero you never knew. The man you were always looking for subconsciously, though you may have gone off the rails a bit over the years, one too many encounters, as you say, but it did give you the extra motivation to get to the bottom of this. But there's one thing I need to ask," Dyer slowed and was walking at the side of DS Quirke.

"As long as it doesn't concern the car you *mislaid* the first time we were here."

"Very humorous. I was wondering if you've put in for a transfer?"

"Is it *the end* for us, you mean?"

Dyer stopped walking and called after her, "Yes, that is it precisely, Liz."

"If you call me Liz again, it *will* be the end. The name's Quirky, to you."

Chapter 74
JUNE 2023
HMP Sull Futton
Changing Lives

Ms Brenda sat in the prison library. Atonement. Surrounded by young offenders, discussing their lives and the bad choices they had made. Most of their lives had been interrupted by drugs. She had their full attention. She was the most infamous prisoner in the system but most importantly, and most remarkably, she was an example to everyone that you could change your life completely. She was training to become a qualified therapist, and she planned to spend her life trying to change the lives of young prisoners for the better. If she could save one life it would be worth it! She was, after all, the complete embodiment of change! She was happy with who she was. She no longer had to hide.

The prison officer in the corner glanced at his watch and casually approached the circle, he waited for an opportune moment to interrupt.

"All right, gentlemen, and ladies, finish off for today, please, dinner will be on the wings in twenty minutes. Ms Brenda, I think it's your favourite today!"

THE END

Acknowledgements

It's been a long journey and without certain individuals kicking me up the backside I would not have reached my destination.

Thank you to my wife whose unwavering encouragement and love have kept the light on when I've wanted to sit in the dark.

Thank you to my daughter who has read the manuscript through its numerous drafts and given positive feedback and many helpful suggestions. I love you very much. She has now set out on her own journey at university to study Creative Writing.

A special thank you to Kay and Lynn, the first to read the manuscript, I'm sorry I made you laugh and cry! And thank you to Hayley, a complete stranger who works in M & S in Stratford upon Avon, who saw me writing and asked to read the manuscript. Your enthusiasm was a massive encouragement!

I would also like to thank Bill, currently incarcerated at Her Majesty's pleasure, for his help with Orrible Arry Enderson and for his knowledge of cockney rhyming slang.

Lastly, a massive thank you to Laura Joyce, a professional editor, whose services were invaluable. Her insight and expertise helped pull the whole thing together.

About the Author

Mark Phillips worked in a High Security prison for close to thirty years. He had daily contact with serial killers, psychopaths and sociopaths, and the experiences have shaped the dark humour seeping from his written work.

He is an English graduate and qualified English teacher who swapped the classroom for a prison landing on the assumption inmates are easier to deal with than children!

He currently lives in Evesham, Worcestershire, and hopes DI Dyer and DS Quirke will put the spotlight on the town.

Afterword

DI Dyer and DS Quirke will return shortly in a new case in the Summer of 2024. And I'm sure it will be *Dyer*bolical.

Printed in Great Britain
by Amazon

39964982R00215